11-2016

D1074546

THE RULES OF LOVE & GRAMMAR

Center Point
Large Print

**This Large Print Book carries the
Seal of Approval of N.A.V.H.**

THE RULES OF LOVE & GRAMMAR

Mary Simses

CENTER POINT LARGE PRINT
THORNDIKE, MAINE

This Center Point Large Print edition
is published in the year 2016 by arrangement with
Little, Brown and Company,
a division of Hachette Book Group, Inc.

The text of this Large Print edition is unabridged.
In other aspects, this book may vary
from the original edition.
Printed in the United States of America
on permanent paper.
Set in 16-point Times New Roman type.

ISBN: 978-1-68324-175-1

Library of Congress Cataloging-in-Publication Data

Names: Simses, Mary, author.
Title: The rules of love and grammar / Mary Simses.
Description: Center Point Large Print edition. | Thorndike, Maine :
Center Point Large Print, 2016.
Identifiers: LCCN 2016034843 | ISBN 9781683241751
    (hardcover : alk. paper)
Classification: LCC PS3619.I5667 R85 2016 | DDC 813/.6—dc23
LC record available at https://lccn.loc.gov/2016034843

To Rebecca Tucker Holliman,
my childhood friend and fellow detective
(or were we spies?)

and

John Frederick Sutton,
my ninth-grade English teacher,
who encouraged my love of words

I mean, don't forget the Earth's
about five thousand million years old, at least.
Who can afford to live in the past?

—Harold Pinter

THE RULES OF
LOVE & GRAMMAR

CHAPTER 1

A noun is a person, place, or thing.
Bad <u>luck</u> comes in threes.

The sound of hammering on the roof wakes me, and for a moment I don't remember where I am. I glance at the white coverlet, the pink rosebuds on the wallpaper, the jar of sea glass on the dresser, and I remember I'm not in my apartment in Manhattan. I'm in my old room, in Dorset, Connecticut, in the house where I grew up, in a bed with a mattress that feels much too hard.

It's Thursday, and if it were a normal Thursday, I'd be getting up and going to work. But my job of four years is gone, eliminated in last Friday's corporate reorganization. If it were a normal Thursday, I'd be looking forward to spending the weekend with Scott, maybe in the Hamptons. But Scott's gone, too. He's fallen out of love with me and in love with a paralegal in his office—another reorganization. I should be back in my apartment, grieving over my losses, licking my wounds, but I can't even do that. Yesterday, a chunk of my ceiling collapsed from a water leak and I had to evacuate, probably for three weeks. So, here I am—jobless, homeless, and single.

All I want to do is sleep through the rest of my life. And somebody is banging on the roof.

I head down the back stairs and into the kitchen, where the copper pots hang over the island like a constellation and my mother's collection of blue and white Staffordshire china gleams in the corner cabinet. Through the bank of windows, I see the long stretch of lawn that slopes gently toward the rocks and sedges. The waters of Long Island Sound flash and sparkle in the sun, and a salty breeze sings through the window screens. A lone kayaker skims by, his oar dipping in and out of the water.

"Anybody home?"

The house is empty.

I look at the wooden countertop, at the usual clutter of papers and magazines and unopened mail. Leaning against the toaster is a note from Mom, written in her wide, slanted architect's lettering. *GRACE, GONE TO DEAL WITH THE FLOWERS AND THE CAKE. SEE YOU AFTER WORK.* The flowers and cake are for my father's sixty-fifth birthday party, which takes place here in two weeks and to which my mother has invited a hundred and thirty people.

The hammering continues, driving me down the hall, toward the front door, the old pine floorboards creaking under my feet. A small pile of books rests on the bottom of the staircase banister, where the mahogany ends in a swirl.

Wallace Stevens, W. H. Auden, e. e. cummings, Anne Sexton. Dad must be teaching his modern poetry master class this summer.

Each year he swears it's going to be his last year teaching, but then he lets the university talk him into doing it *one more time.* I don't think they'll ever really let him go. It was even a huge deal five years ago when he said he wanted to step down as head of the English Department, give up his administrative responsibilities, and return to just being a professor. From their shocked reactions, you'd think he'd told them he was going to open a strip club.

Outside, the June morning is warm. The dew on the grass dampens the soles of my feet as I step onto the lawn. The air smells dank, like seaweed and oysters and mussels, a very New England smell.

Two men are on the roof, tool belts slung low on their hips. "Excuse me!" I yell. They peer down at me, and I realize I haven't even brushed my hair. I give a little wave.

"Hey," the shorter man says, waving back and then scratching his beard.

I tighten the belt on my robe. "What are you doing? Putting on a new roof?"

The shorter man drops his pile of shingles. "Yeah, you got it. I'm surprised this one lasted as long as it did."

I glance at my watch. "Do you know it's only eight twenty-five? Isn't that a little early?"

The men look at each other. "Uh, well, we always start at eight," the taller man says, tucking in his green Down's Auto Body T-shirt where it's popped out in the back.

Maybe in a perfect world, one in which I still had my job and my boyfriend, not to mention my ceiling, this wouldn't seem so outrageous. But today it does. Today I just want to sleep.

"Sorry if we woke you up," Auto Body says. He stares at the legs of my pajamas and grins. "What are those, anyway? Dogs?"

I look down. "No, actually, they're reindeer. And Santas." I stuff my hands in the pockets of my robe. "I like to keep the Christmas spirit going all year." I'm not about to explain how I ran out of my apartment with barely the clothes on my back and how I'm lucky I had these here.

"Ah," he says. "Good idea."

"So, is this going to take long?" I ask, wondering how many mornings my sleep will be curtailed.

The bearded man glances at the roof. "A couple of weeks, maybe longer, depending on the weather."

I make a mental note to pick up a pair of earplugs. "I'd better leave you to your work, then."

Back in the kitchen, I furiously sort through the mail, throwing out the junk and making piles of what's left—invitations, bills, magazines, and catalogs. There's something so comforting about order. The counter already looks neater, giving me a small sense of accomplishment and relief. I gather up the scraps of paper—receipts from the dry cleaner's, stickies with phone numbers on them, and an envelope on which my father has scrawled a line, probably part of a poem. *She leaves them in her wake.*

I turn to a little stack of photographs. The picture on top is of an old barn, its wood weathered to a soft chestnut. Another photo shows the interior, where a ladder leads to a second-floor loft. There's a drawing of the barn next to the photos—a little rendering Mom has done. Someone must have hired her to refurbish the space into an artist's studio. She's added a number of windows, allowing light to stream in and illuminate a whimsical figure she's drawn by an easel. This little touch, so typical of Mom, makes me smile.

Most of the second floor of the barn is gone in Mom's sketch. What remains looks just the right size for a sleeping loft or a reading nook. My mother has added a window up there and has replaced the ladder with a staircase. I can't help but wonder if this little loft is really a shrine for my sister, Renny, who always loved to curl up in a cozy space with a book.

The doorbell rings, and I set my mother's drawing aside. I can see Cluny's red Jeep through the front-door side lights as I head down the hall.

My best friend since our first day of school at Smithridge Elementary, she still lives in Dorset, with her husband, their two young daughters, and five adopted animals—two dogs, two cats, and a canary.

"Grace!" She greets me with a big smile. A breeze ruffles the hem of her long skirt and lifts her hair, and her auburn curls float behind her willowy frame as if they have a life of their own.

I pull her into the front hall and give her a hug. "It's great to see you. I wasn't expecting you until later."

"I know, but my meeting at the printer's got switched to this afternoon. We're running proofs on some new cards."

Cluny has her own line of greeting cards, featuring drawings she creates with pen and ink and watercolors. She places dogs and cats and other animals in human situations, doing things like blowing out candles on a birthday cake, sailing a sloop in a race, drinking cocktails at a party, and relaxing in beach chairs by the ocean. I'm so proud of how successful she's been, with her cards in gift shops all over the country now.

"I figured while I had the time this morning, I'd see if you were up," she says.

I lean against the Chippendale chest. "Oh, I'm up, all right. The roofers woke me. They've got nail guns that sound like AK-47s. And they'll be here for at least two weeks."

"Don't worry," she says, casually flicking her hand. "We've got plenty of things to do. You'll be out of the house every day."

"But I don't want to be out of the house. I don't want to see anybody. I want to stay in and sleep."

"What? Not when you're finally going to be here for more than a day! How many years has it been since you've had a real visit, Grace? I can't even remember." She brushes a strand of hair away from my face and softens her voice. "The point is, you're here now, and you can't lock yourself away like some kind of depressed person."

"But I *am* some kind of depressed person."

"No, you're not. You're just going through a rough patch."

"This is a lot more than a rough patch. I lose my job, and then Scott dumps me. And then my ceiling comes crashing down." I can feel my eyes getting prickly. "I just want to hibernate." I walk down the hall, toward the kitchen.

"Grace, you'll find another proofreading job. And you'll—"

"It wasn't proofreading," I say as I stop. "I was reviewing translations done by computers and correcting the mistakes. It's much more complicated than proofreading."

She puts her hand on my arm and gives me an apologetic look. "I'm sorry. I know I always get that wrong."

"It's okay. Everybody does."

"Anyway, I know you'll find another job."

I wish I could be that optimistic. I don't even know where to start. "It's hard thinking about a job when I'm so upset about Scott. How could he do this to me? We were about to celebrate our one-year anniversary. We had plans to go to Italy this fall. *Italy.* And then he tells me about Elena, the paralegal from Structured Finance."

Cluny gives me her concerned-mother look as we walk into the kitchen. "It just means he wasn't the right guy for you, Grace."

"I guess not." I look away and dab my eyes. "Oh God, I just want to go back to bed."

She sits down at the table. "No. You can't go back to bed. You can't spend your whole time here in your . . ." She waves her hand, and her eyes go to my legs. "Your Christmas pajamas."

"I can find some other pajamas."

She gives me an exasperated look. "That's not the point."

I pick up the coffee carafe. A cup or two is still left. "Do you want some of this?"

"That much," she tells me, making a narrow gap between her thumb and index finger.

I fill a mug halfway for her and another for me, and then I open the freezer and inspect the ice cream containers lined up like silos. Chocolate chip, mint chocolate chip, cookie crunch, banana swirl, strawberry cheesecake.

"Got enough ice cream in there?" Cluny begins to count the containers.

"Excuse me, but did you know that *desserts* is *stressed* spelled backward?"

"Is it really?" She moves her finger as if she's writing the letters in the air. Then she smiles. "You're right."

I grab the cookie crunch and take a seat across from her at the table. *"All natural,"* I say, reading the words on the label and savoring the first spoonful. "You would like this." When I turn the container around, however, I notice that some-one has left out the comma between *Madison* and *Wisconsin* in the company's address. Sometimes I hate myself.

"I have something that will cheer you up," Cluny says as I put another spoonful of ice cream in my mouth. "Are you listening to me?" Her green eyes dance.

"Yeah, I'm listening."

"You're not going to believe whose picture is on the front page of the *Review.*" She pulls a piece of folded newspaper from her handbag. "Guess," she says, keeping the paper concealed with her hand.

"I'm thinking." I scoop up another spoonful of ice cream. "Teddy McRandell?" Teddy went to Smithridge Elementary with us and was always getting into trouble. I heard he recently moved back to town. Apparently he's in real estate development and he bought the old Lawrence estate.

Cluny laughs. "No, it's not him. Try again."

I put my spoon on the table and sit up straight. "Just tell me. I hate how you always do this."

"Do what?" She guards the newspaper.

"Make me guess."

"No, I don't."

"You've done it ever since we were kids, back in our Nancy Drew days, when we wanted to be detectives. Whenever you found a clue, you'd make me guess what it was."

"Spies."

"What?"

"We wanted to be spies, not detectives."

"No, I wanted to be a detective, you wanted to be a spy. Now show me what you have to show me."

She opens the folded paper, revealing the front page of the *Dorset Review*. "Read this." She points to a caption underneath a photo: FORMER RESIDENT RETURNS TO DIRECT MOVIE.

Peter Brooks, 33, director of three hit romantic comedies, including *Paris Love Letter*, has returned to Dorset after seventeen years to film scenes for a new movie. Brooks will be in town for the next two weeks.

I stare at the man in the photo, with his wavy, brown hair, blue eyes, and smile that almost jumps off the page, and my heart stops. It's Peter, all right. I pick up the paper for a closer look, and instantly I'm back in my emerald-green dress. I'm at the Dorset Yacht Club, and it's May of our sophomore year of high school, seventeen years ago. As the band plays a cover of the Shania Twain–Bryan White song "From This Moment On," Peter and I are slow dancing. His arm is around my back, his breath warm on my neck. I close my eyes and lean against his chest, and it doesn't seem real. This isn't the same Peter who has thought of me only as a friend for the past three years, while I've imagined so much more. This is a different Peter, who finally, today, has begun to look at me with new eyes. And here we are. And it's magical.

I glance up.

Cluny is smiling. "Your old high school sweetheart, a big-time Hollywood director, back in town. What do you think?"

"I think we had one incredible night, Cluny. One dance, one kiss. But it was a short romance."

"Maybe, but you had a long friendship before that. And they always say a romance that grows out of friendship is the best kind."

I study the photo, Peter's eyes, warm and friendly, gazing back at me. "Hmm. Is that what they say?"

"You know the romance part would have lasted a lot longer if things hadn't happened . . . the way they did." She swallows the last few words, her voice becoming quiet, and I know what she's thinking. *If things hadn't happened the way they did the next day. With Renny.*

"Hey," she says, steering the conversation in a lighter direction. "You've seen all of his movies, right?"

"Yeah, I've seen all three."

"Me too," she says. "I liked *Paris Love Letter* the best." She grabs my mug of coffee. "I'll heat these up." She walks to the microwave, and I watch the cups revolve on the platter. "He was always such a movie nut. Like you. Remember how he used to sneak us into the Dorset Playhouse? He'd buy a ticket and go in, and then we'd knock on the side door and he'd open it?" She hands me my coffee and sits down. "God, he was cute."

The memory makes me laugh. "I can't believe we never got caught." When the playhouse closed a few years ago, I couldn't help but wonder if they'd gone broke from kids like us sneaking in over the years, but I know that's absurd.

Cluny leans back in the chair, crosses her arms, and gives me a self-satisfied glance. "It's more than a coincidence, you know."

"What's more than a coincidence?"

She gestures at the newspaper. "Peter, back in town. You back in town. At the same time."

"So we're both in town at the same time. Don't give me any cosmic mumbo jumbo, Cluny. There's nothing so strange about that."

She sits up straight. "Are you kidding? The odds against it must be a billion to one. It's happened for a reason. You were crazy about him. He was crazy about you. You need to see him. It beats sitting around here by yourself, eating pints of ice cream." She looks at the ice cream container as though she might try to confiscate it.

I grab the container and pull it to my side of the table. "That's ridiculous. I wouldn't even know what to say. Too much water under the bridge. That was a long time ago." I pick up the spoon.

"Oh, come on," she says. "Time has no meaning when it comes to love." She puts her hand over her heart.

"Where did you get that? From one of your Louise Hay books?"

"No, you always used to say it. Back in high school. Remember?"

I point my spoon at her. "Well, you shouldn't listen to everything I say. Besides, I don't think it would be a good idea to see Peter. It might be uncomfortable. You know, because of the way things ended."

Cluny is about to protest, but I cut her off. "Look, my apartment won't be fixed for three weeks. So while I'm stuck here, my plan is to sleep, eat junk food, read trashy novels, go to my dad's party, and try to forget for just a little while that right now my life is a total mess."

"Grace, come on, this is *Peter* we're talking about. We used to bribe Renny to drive us around town looking for him. That's how crazy you were about him, remember?"

I remember. Of course I remember.

"By the way," she adds, "today that would be considered stalking. And we'd probably be arrested."

"Yeah, they've ruined everything fun."

I gaze out the kitchen window, onto the swath of grass that pushes the land toward the sound. A small sailboat whizzes by in a puff of wind. I look at the wooden table, at the scratches and cracks that have collected over the years. They look like the lines a fortune-teller might read to predict the future. I wonder what they would say about mine.

Cluny leans closer. "And this will be a good distraction. Something to help take your mind off Scott and your job and your apartment. Plus, I'd love to see Peter again. Get the details on what he's been doing all this time. It's so exciting that he's back in town." I can feel her staring at me. "Don't tell me you haven't thought about him." She sounds a bit smug.

She's smug because she's right. Of course I've thought about Peter. Long before I began to see his name appear in magazines and entertainment blogs, there were things that reminded me of him, things that made me wonder where he was and what he was doing. *Twister* would come on TV, and I'd think about the night we went to the Dorset Playhouse and watched it from our favorite seats in the balcony. Or I'd be in a luncheonette and hear someone order a coffee milk shake, and I'd remember the afternoon at the Sugar Bowl when we drank so many coffee milk shakes we were both awake all night, jittery, talking to each other on the phone. Or I'd hear "Claire de Lune" on the radio, and I'd think about the day I heard Peter playing it on the piano in the empty high school auditorium.

Cluny looks at me. "Yeah. I thought so."

I shake my head. "No, it's not like that. Of course I've thought about him, Cluny. But I got over him a long time ago. I had to. You know that."

"We should go see him," she says. "We'll find out where he's staying. It'll be like solving a mystery. Just like when we were kids."

"Are you going to dig out your detective handbag?"

She sighs. "I wish I still had it. Remember all the great stuff we put in those things? Tweezers? Handkerchiefs?"

"Those big magnifying glasses we got at the stationery store?"

"From that salesman who always had the horrible dandruff."

"Remember how we bought those little black notebooks?" I say. "For jotting down clues?"

"God, everything was a clue. What about that time in fifth grade when you thought the man and woman who lived at the end of your street were bank robbers hiding from the police?"

"Well, they looked suspicious," I say, feeling the need even now to defend myself. "Come on, the wife, with all those weird hats and the sunglasses. She was *always* wearing sunglasses."

"She had an ocular disease."

"Even so." I give a dismissive wave. "And what about the husband? He always seemed so wary of everyone."

"Grace, they were retired schoolteachers in their eighties."

"Oh, so retired schoolteachers in their eighties can't also be criminals?"

She gives me a skeptical look. "Besides, the husband was in a wheelchair."

"Yeah, but he was fast in that thing."

She taps a few crystals of sugar into her coffee. "I'll tell you what I also remember." A sly smile crosses her face. "How you rang their doorbell and told them you were collecting for the Red Cross."

I'd forgotten that. "Oh my God, yes. So I could peek inside for stolen money. I thought they might have a safe."

"And they believed you. They actually gave you

ten dollars." Her voice is full of awe, even now.

I raise my hand as though I'm taking an oath. "Which, I might add, I immediately turned over to the real Red Cross."

"Yes, you did . . . after you dusted it for prints."

"Well," I say, "a detective's gotta do what she's gotta do."

Outside, the wind chimes jingle, and a breeze sends a branch of hydrangea tapping against the screens. I feel a little wistful for the old days, a little sad to have lost that time in my life when the tiniest burst of imagination could power an entire summer day.

"I think we were great detectives," Cluny says. She's silent for a moment. Then she adds, "We could resurrect our skills and find Peter."

I try to think of a way to convince her, once and for all, that I'm not interested, because I can sense what she's going to say next. "Cluny, he's married. I read that a long time ago. And he probably has two gorgeous children." Everybody else does. Why not Peter?

"He *was* married," she says. "But he isn't anymore. He's divorced."

"He's divorced?"

Cluny's eyes light up as she perceives a spark of interest. "Yesssss," she whispers.

"Oh, forget it!" I catch myself. "I'm not doing it. Besides, I just want to stay home."

She sighs. "I know. In your pajamas."

"Yes." I hitch up my Santa bottoms.

"Eating ice cream."

"And why not?"

"Whatever you say, Grace. But, just so you know, cookie crunch is like a gateway drug. It leads to coffee toffee and chocolate-chunk chip and all those varieties that are much more dangerous. It's a slippery slope."

"Okay, just tell me this." I pick up the newspaper article and point to the photo. "How do you know for sure he's divorced?"

She winks. "Google, baby. How else?" She moves her fingers as though she's typing. "And, yes, I cross-checked the information on several different sites. All very reliable." She raises an eyebrow. "By the way, do you have any idea how many results come up when you Google *Peter Brooks movie director*?"

I take a sip of coffee. "Five hundred and twelve thousand, something like that."

Cluny tilts her head and gives me a long, hard stare. "Oh, so you *do* know."

Damn it, she should *have been a spy.*

She narrows her eyes. "Good guess, Einstein. I'll pick you up tomorrow at ten. Dust off your detective handbag."

CHAPTER 2

Prepositions often indicate where
one noun is in relation to another.
*It is never a good idea to store a bicycle
<u>inside</u> a damp garage.*

The next morning, I wake up bright and early again, to the tune of nail guns on the roof. Mom has already gone to work, but she's left another note in the kitchen. Although it's still two weeks before the party, she's got me tackling her to-do list. First task: find the plastic coolers she says are in the garage. That's easier said than done. My parents are genetically incapable of throwing away anything.

I head out the kitchen door and across the lawn to the garage, where I take inventory. Dad's blue Chrysler and my old yellow Volkswagen Beetle sit in two of the three bays. In front of the cars is a large space filled with things my parents can't part with. It looks as though a tidal wave came to shore and swept out again, leaving its debris—a rusted hot-water heater; a motorbike without an engine; two pink porcelain lamps with frayed wires; a mahogany table missing a leg, with the splintered half of a Louisville Slugger baseball bat as a prosthesis; old car tires; tennis rackets; gardening equipment; a microwave oven with no door; cans of paint labeled Versailles Blue; and two stacks of plastic coolers with hinged lids are just a part of what's there. The garage is our own Sargasso Sea.

I manage to clear a path to the coolers, and when I lift off the one on the top of the pile, what I see behind it makes my breath catch in my throat. It's Renny's racing bicycle. Although I can still see bits of the names Schwinn and Paramount, the frame, once a bright cherry red, is covered with dust and grime. The tires are flat and cracked, and the material on the sidewalls is flaking off. The wheel spokes, once shiny silver, are dark gray and speckled, and the chain is encased in rust. The bell Renny loved, with the blue enamel flower, is still on the handlebar. But when I pull the ringer, all I hear is a grinding sound.

I remember the summer Renny and I bought our bikes; she was twelve and I was ten. After weeks of stopping by the Bike Peddler, the cycling shop in town, and studying the different models, I decided on a new Raleigh Mercury, white with orange and gray trim. Renny had been eyeing the Schwinn for a while, even though it was second-hand. We trotted into the store, our pockets bulging with cash we'd saved from chores like dog walking, weed pulling, and window cleaning, supplemented with money from Mom and Dad, and we walked out with the bikes. I'll never forget how proud and grown-up we felt, having made our first big purchases on our own.

I look at the Schwinn now, and I can see Renny, the way she used to bend over the handlebars in her Peace Corps T-shirt, her long legs pedaling defiantly, probably to the tune of some teenage-angsty Tori Amos song playing in her head. Her tawny hair would fly behind her as she breezed down a hill, turning a corner ahead of me.

Often, on sunny summer mornings, she'd say, *Come on, we're going for a ride.* We'd fill our water bottles, stash sandwiches and fruit in our baskets, and we wouldn't come back until evening. Usually we'd ride with a particular destination in mind—a friend's house, the beach, or the Hickory Bluff Store and the dock. But sometimes the destination would find us.

One Saturday when I was thirteen, we rode to Miller's Orchards, a farm in Dorset where apples have been grown for more than a century. We bought cheese and crackers and juice in the market, and then we walked into the orchards, where the trees grow in rows on a hundred and fifty acres of green land and the branches stretch their arms toward the sun. As we picnicked, the sky began to rumble and turn purple, and before we could reach the parking lot, it started to pour.

We ran inside the market, and the woman at the cash register gave us each a black plastic trash bag to wear. She cut holes in them for our necks and arms. The ride home was crazy, with rain pelting our heads and water running down our hair, into our eyes. The trash bags flapped in the wind, and the puddles splashed up and soaked us, but we laughed and screamed the whole way. I often think of that day when I think about Renny. I look at it as a kind of high-water mark in our relationship, because it was after that when things started to change.

I move the rest of the coolers out of the way and stare at the bike. I still can't believe it's here. I thought my mother had donated it to the thrift shop years ago, when I told her she could take my Raleigh there. I pick up the Paramount as though I'm moving a patient in critical condition, and I carry it outside.

"Are you really planning to ride this?" Cluny asks as we lift the Schwinn into the back of her Jeep and close the tailgate.

I'm not sure what I'm going to do with the bike. It's been years since I've ridden one, unless you count the stationary bikes at the gym, and I don't even get on those very often.

I slide into the passenger seat. "I don't know. Right now I just want someone to clean it and get it running again." It almost hurts to look at it the way it is.

Cluny turns on the radio—some station comes on with wind chimes and flutes and the sound of breaking waves, the kind of thing you'd hear if you were getting a massage. Gravel rumbles under the tires, and the dream catcher hanging from the rearview mirror sways as we head down the driveway to the green mailbox at the end, followed by the faded sign bearing the words Private, No Trespass, the *ing* having fallen off years ago.

Cluny turns onto the road, and we leave behind the little peninsula people often refer to as Hammond's Point because the property has been in Dad's family for three generations. The road meanders along the water, a brackish breeze sweeping in through the windows. I look for glimpses of blue where the sound peeks in from between the houses and trees. Most of the homes in the neighborhood are old colonials or farm-houses—many, like ours, from the eighteen hundreds. The lawns are sprawling, adorned with sturdy oaks and maples that have seen generations of children swing from their branches or scuttle up their trunks for a better view of the water.

Turning away from the sound, we travel the next few miles up and down hills flocked with the dense growth of summer and the faint smell of honeysuckle. I remember how Mom used to clip honeysuckle sprigs and put them in jelly jars for Renny and me when we were kids, the yellow and white blossoms dangling like little bells, the scent perfuming our bedrooms.

We round the bend where the white-shingled Presbyterian church sits proudly at the end of a large, green rectangle of lawn.

"They finally put up the new steeple," I say. The old one caught on fire a few years ago, and the church had to raise the money for a replacement.

"I think it looks good," Cluny says.

I liked the old one better, but I don't say anything. The new steeple seems a little too modern, and I wonder if it's even made of wood or if it's been molded from some synthetic fire-resistant product.

On Wallach's Road we pass an antique red clapboard house, once a dance studio and now the home of Bellagio, an Italian restaurant. I think about all the *pliés* and *relevés* I did in that little studio, when I was seven and eight, trying to learn ballet. People are eating pizza and chicken Marsala in there now, ordering ravioli and eggplant parmigiana.

We drive by the trio of Victorian houses that are home to Elephant's Trunk Antiques, Nutmeg Market, and Sage Hardware. The structures, with their porches festooned in gingerbread trim, sit back from the road, nestled together like girls in white party dresses waiting to be asked to dance.

Cluny glances at me and grins. "Has your dad bought anything new at Sage lately?"

"No, thank God. At least, I don't think so. Mom keeps a pretty good eye on that."

Sage Hardware is one of my father's favorite stores, although he's always had a complicated relationship with tools. Years ago, Mom finally decreed that he could only go in there and look—that he couldn't buy anything because he might hurt himself again. One summer, when I was nine, he decided he wanted to build birdhouses, and not from kits but from scratch. He went to Sage and bought a bunch of tools, went to the lumberyard for the wood, and then he came home and promptly cut himself with a saw, resulting in twenty-one stitches in his finger and a lecture from the emergency room doctor about tool safety.

Now he only goes in to browse. He likes to pick up hammers, drills, and soldering irons; to open sets of wrenches and admire their sleek, silvery designs; to check out stud finders, flashlights, and fasteners; and to chat with the sales guys about sockets and ratchets. I've caught him in there a few times, pining over storage boxes and workbenches. He's even written poems about the store. "Zeal," inspired by the saw incident, was about the fine line between knowing when to be careful and when to let yourself go.

We make a quick stop at the harbor, where Cluny and Greg keep their Boston Whaler. A half-dozen boats glide by, heading down the river toward the deeper waters of the sound, their engines gurgling in low, throaty voices. Across the river, stately old homes with dormers and gables and filigree porch railings sit on wide, green lawns that wander down to seawalls.

I follow Cluny into the Hickory Bluff Store, where the collection of boating equipment and beach-related odds and ends hasn't changed. While she buys an oyster knife, I peer into a mahogany case with a dusty glass top, heartened to see there's still candy inside and recalling how Renny and I would buy M&M's and Snickers bars here and eat them on the dock out back while we dipped our feet in the water. Without even looking, I know there's an old refrigerator full of bottled drinks on the far wall and a room off to the side where they sell bait. It's comforting that these things are still the same.

When we drive into town, however, it's a different story. I immediately notice a new awning over the Sugar Bowl, the luncheonette where all the kids hung out when we were in high school.

"When did they put that awning up?" I ask, pointing to the yellow building with the pink geraniums in the window boxes.

"I don't remember," Cluny says, taking a quick glance. "In the spring, maybe. I think the blue and white looks pretty."

I'm not so sure, and I wonder what was wrong with the old yellow and white one.

We pass a children's clothing store called Twenty-One Balloons. It must have sprung up since the last time I was in town, back in the fall. I try to remember what business used to be there, but I can't.

Cluny parks, and we lift Renny's bike from the Jeep, pushing it slowly down the sidewalk to the Bike Peddler. Bells jingle when I open the door. Bicycles of various styles and colors and sizes, from tricycles to tandems, sit in racks on the floor and hang from the ceiling. Cycling clothes, helmets, water bottles, baskets, bells, and other accessories are wedged into every square inch of space, and the air is heavy with the smell of rubber.

"This place looks so different," I whisper. It seems a lot smaller. Or maybe it's just because I've grown up. It's probably been twenty years since I've set foot inside here.

"I think the old guy who owned the business when we were kids sold it," Cluny says. "What was his name? Scooter something?"

"Dees," I say. "Scooter Dees."

I walk the bike toward the checkout counter in the back, past a man in a navy T-shirt. He's talking to a woman and her daughter, but he looks up and glances at me with soft, brown eyes.

"I'll be with you in a minute," he says, and then he smiles.

One side of his mouth edges up a little more than the other. A lock of dark-brown hair falls onto his forehead. Around six feet tall, he's got the build of a tennis player, lean and muscular. There's something vaguely familiar about him, but I can't place his face. I'm guessing he's around my age, but he doesn't look like anyone I remember from school.

I lean the Paramount against the side of the counter and follow Cluny around the shop as she browses.

"Greg was in here last year," she says. "Buying bikes for the girls." She picks up a yellow reflector from a basket of accessories, looks at it, and puts it back. Then she leans toward me, lowering her voice. "I was just thinking. I know you've got rent to pay and bills, and I know your parents will always help you out, Grace. But if you ever need money or anything, Greg and I are here to lend a hand."

This catches me off guard. I feel grateful, but I also feel a little uncomfortable, especially because my parents made the same offer. Does everybody else know something I don't? Am I never going to find another job?

"That's really nice of you, Cluny. But I'll be fine. I got some severance pay when I lost my job." I leave out the fact that I've already spent a lot of it on bills. "And I have a fair amount of money saved up." That's also a lie, but I could never borrow money from a friend, especially from Cluny. It's the kind of thing that can destroy a relationship.

"Oh, I'm sure you've put away money for a

rainy day," she says, a little too quickly, as though she's not totally convinced. "But if you run into any problems, you know we'll help. I mean, what are friends for?"

I thank her, unable to meet her eyes.

As we step closer to the counter, I notice a stack of flyers on the top and I lift one off the pile.

Fourth of July
Dorset Challenge Fund-Raiser

The Bike Peddler and the Dorset Land Conservancy have teamed up for a great fund-raising event to be held Wednesday, July Fourth. Start the morning with a complementary continental breakfast and then ride through beautiful eastern Connecticut on a five-mile, twenty-five mile, or fifty-mile adventure.

"Hmm." I dig into my handbag for my black Sharpies and pull out the one with the fine point. I remove the cap, releasing the pungent odor of whatever it is they put into Sharpies to make the ink last forever. Then I change the first *e* in the word *complementary* to an *i*.

"What's that?" Cluny looks over my shoulder. "Uh-oh, what are you doing?"

"It's a flyer for a bike trip. There's a typo." I take the stack from the counter.

Cluny grabs the Sharpie. "Hey, come on," she whispers. "You're not at your old job anymore. They might not like you fixing their stuff." She glances toward the door, where the bike-store guy is standing now, still in conversation with the mother.

"But if I've noticed it, so will everybody else. And it's wrong." I pull the marker from her hand. "Do you know what came across my desk the day before they cut our whole department?" I ask, continuing my corrections. "A bag of *chivda*. It's this Indian snack with rice flakes and things in it. The bag said, *Bombay Garden Chivda, The Taste of People.* Can you imagine? As if there were ground-up people in there."

"Yuck," Cluny says, making a face.

"Exactly. So much for computer translations. It reminded me of that old movie *Soylent Green*, where everybody's living in the future and they've run out of food, so they're eating ground-up people."

"Stop." She raises her hand.

"Anyway, my point is, being correct does matter. It can mean the difference between *The Taste of People* and *The Taste People Love.*" Just as I'm about to aim my Sharpie at the next flyer, I hear a voice.

"Excuse me. What are you doing?"

I look up. The bike-store guy is staring at me with those brown eyes.

"Bye, Mitch," the mother calls as she and her daughter leave.

"I'm just fixing these," I tell him. "You've got a typo here. A typographical error." I smile.

"I know what a typo is," he says. "And I don't need our flyers fixed." That lock of hair is still in the middle of his forehead. I wonder if he realizes it. He grabs the flyers, but I clutch them tighter.

"I can fix these in sixty seconds," I say. "Even less—I mean fewer. I'm just trying to be helpful."

Mitch tugs harder. "Stop messing with them."

"Come on, Grace," Cluny says. "Let's get out of here."

"But they're *wrong,*" I say, holding on tighter.

Maybe it's the sugar from the cookie crunch I ate last night, but for some reason I just can't let go of those flyers. Mitch and I keep tugging until he pulls so hard, I lose my balance and stumble backward, crashing into a bike, which crashes into another and causes a domino effect. In a few seconds a dozen bikes have fallen, and I'm tangled up in several of them, one of my sneakers caught in the spokes of a wheel.

"Ow, my back."

Cluny rushes to pull the bikes off me. "Are you all right?"

"I don't know. I think so." I start to get up.

"Here." Mitch extends his hand. "Let me help."

"No, no, I'm fine," I say, too embarrassed to accept his offer. I pick myself up and survey the mess. Most of the flyers have scattered across the floor, but several are blowing through the air, propelled by two large, elevated fans.

"I'll clean this up," I say as I begin to gather the papers.

Cluny joins me. "Yes," she says. "We'll have this picked up in just a minute."

"No, you should sit down so you don't break anything," Mitch says. At first I think he's talking about my legs, but then I'm not so sure. He snatches a flyer from the air.

"I'm fine," I say. "And we want to help." I grab a flyer that's stuck to the back of a fan, the paper fluttering at the suction from the blades. I place the rest of them in a pile on the counter. "I'm really sorry."

He gives me an exasperated look. "Do you always go around fixing what other people write? Even when they haven't asked you to do it?"

"She gets a little carried away sometimes," Cluny says. "She has three copies of *The Elements of Style*." She looks at Mitch, who doesn't seem to be registering this. "Strunk and White?"

He doesn't say anything. I wonder if he's even heard of the book. Probably not. He begins to pick up the bikes I knocked over.

"I didn't mean to mess up everything," I tell him, although when I glance around the room, I can't help but think the place looked pretty disorganized already. Cluny and I move to help, but Mitch puts his hand up, halting us.

"No, I've got this," he says. "You've done enough already."

I don't think he means that in a good way. I'm about to tell Cluny we should leave and find another bike shop when Mitch notices the Schwinn leaning against the side of the counter. He walks toward the bike. "What's this? Is it yours?"

"Yes," I tell him. "It's a Schwinn."

"I know," he says. "A Paramount." He runs his hand gently over the seat. "These were great bikes," he says, his voice quiet, studied. "Top-of-the-line for their time. This one here—she's got to be over thirty years old."

"I'd like to get it fixed," I say.

He bends down to take a closer look. He examines the frame, his eyes wandering over the grime on the tubes, the rust spots on the chrome, the bits and pieces of the Paramount name still visible under the mess. He looks at the wheels and runs his fingers along a few of the spokes. He nods at the rusted chain and derailleur. He picks up the cracked cables, noting the wires under-neath, and lets them fall back into place.

"It could use some work," he says. "Looks as if it's been stored in a damp place and just forgotten." He brushes a piece of flaking leather off the seat. "Everything needs to be replaced or repaired." He looks up at me. "But we can do it."

"That's what I was hoping to hear," I say as a young guy with a beard and a little hoop earring steps from a doorway to the left of the checkout counter and wheels a gray bike across the floor.

Mitch straightens up. "So you didn't just come here to correct our flyers, then." He glances at me from the corner of his eye, a sliver of a smile on his face.

"No," I whisper. "I didn't."

"Well, you've got two options here," he says. "We can fix her up using new parts." He runs his hand over the front brake. "Or we can do a restoration and use original parts—Weinmann Carrera side brakes, Shimano gears, Brooks saddle, that kind of thing." He begins to pick at the dried black tape around the right handlebar, pieces of it falling to the floor. "Then the bike would look like it did when you bought it."

I don't tell him I didn't buy it, that it was Renny's. I just nod. All I wanted to do was get the bike cleaned and working again. I wasn't planning to do anything special with it. But the vision of a restored bike with vintage parts begins to blossom in my heart.

Mitch continues to pick away at the tape until it's gone and what remains is a section of shiny silver, a vision of the way the bike looked when Renny had it. And now I have my answer.

"I'd like to restore it," I say.

"I think you'll be happy with the result," he says. "Why don't you give me your name and number, and I'll call you after we price it out?"

He passes an index card to me, and I jot down my info.

Picking up the card, he holds it close to his face. "Grace Hammond."

"Yes," I say, ready for the usual question. "I'm related to the poet D. H. Hammond. He's my dad. And, no, I don't write poetry."

"Poetry?" he asks, looking a little confused. "I was just going to ask what these last two numbers are. I can't read them."

"Oh." I grab the card and rewrite the digits.

The bells above the door ring, and a very tall, stick-thin woman in skinny jeans and platform sandals walks into the store. She has a big head of wavy, blond hair that she flips off her shoulder as she struts to the counter.

"Mitchell," she says, in a low Southern drawl. "How ya doin' today, darlin'?"

Her voice sounds familiar, and I'm trying to place it when she turns to Cluny and says, "Hey there."

"Hello, Regan," Cluny answers.

And I know exactly who it is: Regan Moxley. Her family moved to Dorset from Texas when we were in middle school. She was always a troublemaker. In seventh grade she told Cluny and me that we were supposed to get on bus eight for a field trip to the natural history museum when it was really bus two, and we ended up at a *Sesame Street Live* show with all the little kids. But that was nothing compared with twelfth grade, when she stole my boyfriend, Grover Holland, from me. I heard she'd moved back to town.

"Regan, you remember Grace?" Cluny says, never one to forget her manners. "From high school?"

Regan steps back, looks me up and down, and smiles. "Grace? Oh, hi there. I didn't recognize you." I can just tell what she's thinking. *You look like you gained a little weight.* Trust Regan to notice the five pounds I'm constantly trying to lose.

She turns to Mitch, who is behind the counter, removing an inner tube from a box. "Mitchell, did my mountain bike come in yet?" she asks, batting her eyes at him.

"Not yet, Regan. The beginning of next week, remember?"

She purses her lips. "Hmm, okay. Just thought I'd check." She looks at me with a puzzled expression. "Didn't your hair used to be a couple of shades lighter, Grace? Almost blond? Maybe that's why I didn't recognize you. You know, some highlights would really brighten it up." She runs her hand through her own hair. "You might want to consider that."

"Yeah, I'll keep it in mind, Regan."

She stares at my hair for another moment and then says, "So, what brings you to town, Grace? Visiting family?" She snaps her fingers. "Oh, wait, I heard there's some big party coming up for your dad."

"Yes, that's right."

"Seems like a lot of people are going, although I never got my invitation." She laughs as though she's joking, but I detect a serious undertone. Regan has never liked being excluded from anything.

"It's mostly family," I tell her. "And some close friends of my parents."

"Ah," she says. "And do you have a date coming out from New York to join you? I heard you live in the city." She steps toward a blue mountain bike on a stand.

"No, I'm not bringing anyone from New York," I say, wondering why Regan Moxley still has the ability to put me on the defensive. I sneak a peek at her left hand to see if she's wearing a wedding band. She married Roger Webber, the captain of the football team, but I heard they divorced ages ago. I don't see a ring.

Regan glances up from the blue bike as she runs her hand lightly over its seat. "A single girl in the big city." She looks at Mitch, who is holding a hand brake lever and writing something on a pad, and she gives him a little smile.

"Actually," I say, stepping closer to the counter,

"I'm not single. This is my date right here." I plant my hand firmly on Mitch's toned arm. It's rock solid.

He looks at me, a brief shimmer of surprise in his eyes.

I grin. "We've been going out now for . . . oh, four or five weeks, I guess. Right, Mitch?"

"I think it's more like six," he says, catching on. "Maybe even seven. I've lost track, it's been such a whirlwind romance. Even in that short time, though, I feel as if I've gotten to know you so well—all of your interests, your endearing little habits . . ." He glances at the stack of flyers and then looks back at me, as though he's stifling a grin.

Cluny bites her lip, and I hope she doesn't laugh.

"I feel the same way, sweetie." I give Mitch's arm a playful squeeze.

"Well, that's so nice," Regan says. "I didn't realize you were involved with anyone, Mitch."

"He likes to keep that stuff kind of private," I say, giving him a wink.

He winks back.

Regan slips her hands into the back pockets of her jeans. "I saw your cards in Nutmeg Market," she tells Cluny. "They've got such a big display of them now. Business must be good."

"Yes, it is," Cluny says. "Thanks."

Business is really good, but Cluny's too modest

to tell Regan her cards are now in more than two hundred gift, gourmet, and specialty stores across the country.

"Well, I've got a few ideas for you," Regan says as she picks up a pair of sunglasses from a display on the counter. "For your cards—if you're interested."

Cluny shoots me a glance. I know my mouth is half-open. I can't believe the nerve. "Oh, sure, yeah," Cluny says. "Thanks, Regan. I'll let you know."

Regan puts the sunglasses on, appraises herself in a bicycle mirror, and then returns the glasses to the counter display. "And what about you, Grace? What kind of work are you doin' these days?"

Oh God, the dreaded question. I'm not about to admit to Regan that I'm out of work.

"She's a proofreader," Mitch says before I can come up with a reply. "Get out your *Elements of Style.*"

"You're a proofreader? I thought you'd be some big-time writer by now. I mean, the way Mr. Palmieri used to talk about you in English class."

"I'm not a proofreader."

"It's a private joke," Cluny says.

"Actually, I review computer translations and fix the mistakes," I say, standing up a little straighter.

Regan just stares at me.

"Here's an example. Have you ever heard of *chivda*?"

"Chiv what?" She squints.

"*Soylent Green*," Mitch says as he picks up a stack of mail. I see him grin.

"What kind of soy?" Regan asks.

"Never mind," I say.

"What are you doing with yourself, Regan?" Cluny asks, and I silently thank her for changing the subject. I can't wait to hear the answer. The only thing I ever remember Regan doing well was flirting.

"Oh, me? I own the bookstore," she says, flicking back her hair.

Regan owns a bookstore. That can't be right. "You own *what*?"

"The bookstore down the street. It used to be the Open Book."

"You own the Open Book?" I can't believe it. In school, she never read anything but SparkNotes.

She straightens the green jewel on her necklace. "As of three weeks ago. I changed the name to Between the Covers."

"That's an interesting name," I say. "So many connotations."

I'm sure Regan's father bought the bookstore for her. He made a killing years ago when he sold his publishing company. He was the creator of *Tell All* and the *Source*, two gossip rags that are stocked in the checkout aisles of every grocery store in the

50

country. He made six hundred million dollars on the sale, and he can afford to buy Regan whatever business she wants, and keep it afloat as well.

"Well, I've got to run to boot camp—my exercise class," she says, glancing our way for a second. "Did you sign me up for the bike trip, Mitch?"

He looks up as he tears open an envelope. "The one with the complimentary breakfast?" He gives me a little glance. "Yeah, all done."

"Oh, I don't care about the free breakfast," Regan says. "But did you sign me up for the *long* ride? The fifty-mile ride? The others are way too easy."

Mitch nods. "Yeah, I've got you down. Fifty miles. You're all set."

"Okay, good." She looks at me. "I try to get all the exercise I can. I like to stay in shape." She brushes some invisible piece of lint off her skinny jeans. "You should do the bike ride, too, Grace. You could do the baby ride. It's only five miles. I mean, in case you can't handle anything more intense." She takes out her lipstick and touches up her lips.

Baby ride?

I lift my chin. "Oh, I *am* doing the bike ride," I say, ignoring the fact that I haven't been on a bike in years. "That's why I'm here. I'm getting my bike fixed so I can take it on the *long* ride."

Cluny's looking at me as though I've lost my

mind. But how hard can a fifty-mile ride be? I've driven fifty miles plenty of times.

"You're doing the ride?" Mitch asks as he points to me with a catalog that has training wheels on the cover. "The long one?"

"Of course, honey." I walk to the counter and reach for one of the flyers, my own correction staring me in the face. I scrawl my name and information on the bottom and hastily write a check for seventy-five dollars. Seventy-five dollars I shouldn't be spending.

"Well, that's great," Regan says. "I didn't know you were a cyclist."

I try to look surprised. "Me? Oh, sure. Huge cyclist. I ride in Manhattan all the time. I love dodging the buses and the cabs. It adds an element of danger you don't get out here."

Cluny pushes me toward the door. "Come on, I've got a proposal to work on. I need to get back."

She's about to turn the knob when Regan says, "Sooo, Mitchell, guess who came into my store the other day?" Without waiting for a reply, she adds, "Peter Brooks, the movie director."

"Hold on," I whisper to Cluny as we both turn around.

Mitch barely looks up. "The director who's in town?"

"That's the one," Regan says as she leans over the counter, her chest grazing the edge. "I went to high school with him." She winds a lock of hair around her finger.

"Really," Mitch says, crumpling up a piece of paper.

"Sure thing." Regan glances at her fingernails. "He walked into my store and remembered me right off the bat. Oh, he was always the biggest flirt. Had every girl thinking he was in love with her."

"Seems as though everybody's going crazy about that movie being filmed here," Mitch says. "Personally, I don't think it's such a big deal."

"Well, it sure is to me, because I know Peter. And he looks good, by the way. That man is *hot*." She shakes her hand as if it's on fire. "They've been filming over at Rance Marina. I went there yesterday and got to see some of the action." She raises her chin just a little, as though her entire persona might be elevated by the gesture. "Peter said I should stop by again and watch another shoot."

Mitch nods. "Well, I hope you have fun then."

I stand there by the door, dumbstruck at how Regan still manages to get under my skin. So what if Peter told her to stop by his shoot? I'm sure he'd make the same offer to me if I saw him. He's a friendly guy.

"Oh, I sure will have fun," Regan says. She waves to Mitch. "Well, tootle-loo." Then she saunters toward Cluny and me. "Are you girls going to watch the filming while the crew's in town? I'm not sure Peter would remember you, Grace. But you might enjoy it anyway."

Something twists inside me. "No, we're not going," I say. "We're not interested in any of that."

Regan leans in close. "Well, if you change your mind, I can probably find out where they're going to be. Peter and I are like this." She holds up two fingers, pressed together. "Oh, and you should come into the store sometime. Come look around. See what I've done with the place." She flicks her hair a final time and walks out the door.

I heave a deep sigh. "She hasn't changed much."

"No, not too much," Cluny says.

"All right," I say. "Let's go. I know you've got work to do, and I guess I have to face the rest of my mother's to-do list. She's going to run me ragged helping her get ready for the party."

Mitch clears his throat. "Uh, about that party . . ." He flips through the rest of the mail. "I don't see my invitation here, so don't forget to send one." He points to me. "After all, I *am* supposed to be your date."

I laugh. "Right," I say playfully. "I'll put you on the list."

CHAPTER 3

An adjective provides more information
about a noun.
*Engaging in conversation during a meal can
prevent an <u>awkward</u> silence.*

At dinner that night, Mom, Dad, and I sit at our usual places at the dining room table, just like we always did. Twilight is settling, the color is receding from the sky, and the evening air is cool. I stir my corn chowder and glance across the table at the empty seat.

I imagine Renny there, the way she looked when she was young, in one of her spaghetti-strap tops, her long hair tied back in a scrunchie. Mom tells her to take off her Walkman headphones while she's at the table, and Renny obeys but she starts singing some New Kids on the Block song, just to drive Mom and Dad crazy, and then I join in, and we're laughing, and then Mom and Dad are laughing, too. I want to remember those days, the days before anything bad happened.

"Sorry to hear about the problem with your apartment," Dad says as he reaches for the salt. "And your job, of course." He pauses and then adds, tentatively, "And Scott." His silvery-white hair is combed carefully behind his ears, and his glasses, which look too big on his face, are out of style by at least a few years.

"Yeah, I guess I got the trifecta," I tell him as the faint sound of a foghorn slips through the open windows. "Bad luck coming in threes." I lift my spoon from the bowl and study the white kernels of corn, the little bits of bacon, the sprigs of thyme floating on the surface of the chowder.

"I guess you did, Gracie. But I'm glad we're getting to spend a little time with you. We thought you'd only be here for the party."

"That's right," Mom says. "We don't get to see you enough." Her lavender blouse is soft against her fair skin; her ash-gray hair caresses her cheeks. She's still as trim and petite as ever, and I think about the times I've seen men, even a few younger ones, give her a second glance.

"What do you mean?" I ask. "You came into the city last month and we had dinner."

"No, I mean we don't get to see you *here* enough," she says.

"But I was here . . . in the fall, wasn't it? I remember the leaves turning."

Dad dips his spoon into his chowder. "That was months ago."

"And you were only here for the day," Mom says. "You raced back to Manhattan, the way you always have."

"I probably had a business trip coming up or something."

Mom dabs the side of her mouth with her napkin and smiles. "Well, now you don't."

I want to say, *You're right. Now I'm really stuck here,* but I don't say anything.

Dad looks at me. "So, Grace, what are your plans while you're here?"

"I don't really have any plans," I say. "See some friends. Maybe read a few books. Wait for my apartment to be fixed."

"And how about your job?" he asks. "Are you going to work on that? Do a little research? You'll have plenty of time."

I drag the spoon through my soup. I wish he wouldn't ask me about this. "I'm supposed to meet with someone from Owens and Fish when I get back to New York."

"What kind of work would they have for you?" Mom asks, sipping her wine.

"Oh, it wouldn't be to work there," I say. "It's an outplacement firm. You know, where they give you advice on writing your résumé and using your contacts, and you're supposed to go in every day and sit in a little cubicle and make phone calls."

"Sounds awful," Dad says, removing his glasses and rubbing the red spot where they always pinch his nose.

"Doyle." Mom gives him a stern look. "Don't be negative. The idea is to stay motivated, keep working on finding the next job."

He twirls his glasses between his fingers. "How much motivation can you find sitting in a cubicle?"

When I look at it that way, I have to wonder myself. Going in day after day, making cold calls to people, conjuring up everyone I've ever known who might know somebody who might know somebody who might be willing to talk to me. Still, I have to do it. How else am I going to find a job?

A bird lands on the windowsill outside, takes a couple of hops, and flutters off. "At least it's a place to start," I say, trying to convince myself.

"Well, what are you looking for?" Dad asks, and I know we're off and running into the land of You Should Be Doing Something Better with Your Life.

I stare at the landscape painting above the fireplace mantel and wish I could walk into those yellow hills and cool myself in the green river rather than sit here and tread the same ground again. "I'm going to keep doing technical writing."

"More vacuum cleaner manuals?"

"That's not all I did," I remind him. "I was fixing computer translations, and I also wrote promotional material and product brochures. You know that. And, anyway, there's nothing wrong with writing manuals." I try another spoonful of the soup, but it's starting to taste a little too spicy. "Don't you think it's important for people to know how things work? So they don't make mistakes? Use something the wrong way? Maybe get hurt?"

"You hated working there," Dad says.

"I liked it."

He sits back in his chair and studies me, his eyes tired, the skin under his chin sagging. "You've got a gift, Grace. Those poems and stories you used to write in school, and that play you wrote in college. Not everyone can do that, you know."

"It was a screenplay. And nobody is advertising for story writers and poets these days, as far as I can see. At least technical writing pays the bills. Well, it *did*."

He puts his glasses back on. "I'll bet there are lots of creative things you could do besides technical writing that would pay the bills. I'm not saying you have to be a poet."

This is where I need to take a deep breath and count to ten. I need to remember he's probably just doing what he thinks is best for me. But I don't do either of those things. "Can we please not get into this again?" I ask. "I'm not Renny. I don't want to be prodded and pushed." My spoon clatters into the bowl, sending drops of chowder onto the plate and the table.

My mother rubs her forehead, suddenly looking older than her sixty-two years, and lets out an exasperated sigh. "Your father's just trying to help." She glances at Dad, some unspoken language flowing between them.

Maybe it's always going to be this way. Maybe it will never change. Like that saying *Nature abhors a vacuum.* My parents want to fill the space that Renny used to take up, and who else is left to do the filling?

Mom stands and collects the soup bowls. I follow her into the kitchen and spoon the chicken curry and rice into serving bowls while she puts the green beans on a platter. The only sounds are the *clink* and *clank* of utensils against metal and porcelain.

We sit down at the table and pass around the food. "Your dad's been busy this summer," Mom says, and I'm relieved she's changing the subject. "He's been writing a lot."

I think about the envelope I saw in the kitchen. Small, blue spiral-bound notebooks of plain, white paper are what my father usually writes in, but he'll use whatever is handy in order not to lose his train of thought. The word *lightbulb,* scrawled on the back of an electrician's business card, might not be a reminder to have the electrician do something with the lightbulbs in the house. It might be the genesis of a poem about a man who, in changing a lightbulb, begins to think about his father, who was struck by lightning. In fact, that actually happened, and the poem my father wrote was called "Standing on a Ladder in the Kitchen."

"Is it going well?" I ask him. "The writing?" I think about the envelope. *She leaves them in her wake.* Was he writing about Renny?

He takes the rice from my mother. "Yes," he says. "It seems to be going well."

"Dad's also teaching," Mom says. "Modern poetry again. The master class."

"I figured that," I say. "I saw some of the books."

My father takes the serving spoon and drops a large scoop of rice onto his plate. "I've been tinkering with the course. Switching out a few of the poets. Adding a little more Millay, some Elizabeth Bishop."

I've always liked Elizabeth Bishop, but I don't say anything. No sense encouraging him.

"I'm teaching the postmoderns in the fall," he says, placing the bowl on the table. "Aren't you a fan of Margaret Atwood? I thought I'd include her." He keeps his gaze on me, his eyes encouraging me to respond.

"I like some of her poetry."

"How about " 'The Moment'? Do you remember that one?"

I pretend to think for a second. "Not really."

"That's funny. I thought you once wrote a paper about it."

Freshman English. Mrs. Townsend. "Maybe," I say. "I don't know."

I take a few of the string beans from the platter and arrange them on my plate in neat lines. I can still feel his eyes on me.

"So many implications," he says as he helps himself to the curry. "Of course, the environmentalists like to take it literally. But there's so much more—the idea that meaning in life comes only from striving. That as long as you're striving, you're part of the world, but once you stop . . . well, that's when everything crumbles, isn't it?"

I wonder if he's referring to me, specifically, and then he starts to recite the poem. His voice is slow and even, his poetry-reading voice, as he describes the narrator standing in the center of a room, which quickly becomes a house, then a half acre of land, a mile, and, finally, an entire country, all of which the narrator believes he can own, can lay claim to.

My father stops, one side of his mouth rising expectantly as he waits for me to pick up the next line, the way we did when Renny and I were young and he would fill our heads with Shakespeare, Dylan Thomas, Emily Dickinson, e. e. cummings. When we'd talk over dinner about imagery, metaphor, and rhyming schemes, discuss assonance and consonance, repetition and rhythm. We'd ponder Robert Frost's "Birches," and Coleridge's *Rime of the Ancient Mariner*, and Robert Burns's "To a Mouse," all in the course of one meal. But that was a long time ago, and I'm

62

not looking to earn points from him anymore, to try to stake out my little corner of his universe. I'm sure he misses having Renny here to play this game with him. She was always more eager than I was, smarter than I was, and he was always happy to lavish her with attention.

"I don't remember it," I tell him, scooping the curry from the bowl.

"Oh, don't push her, Doyle," Mom says. "She's tired."

He repeats the lines and then, with a defeated look, gives up and turns back to his plate.

Mom starts talking about a meeting she went to this morning about a house she's designing. "The property is complicated," she says. "The permitting is killing us, especially the wetlands."

Dad nods.

"And the owners keep changing their minds about what they want. They're adding a lap pool, which is going to be an environmental nightmare." She starts indicating the location of things on the dining room table. "The house is here, and the lap pool would have to be over there somewhere, but the estuary is there . . ." I'm lost in the invisible landmarks, seeing only the smooth grain of the cherrywood. Then she says, "And now they want a spiral staircase." She pauses. "In a tower."

There's a minute change in her expression at the words *in a tower,* a little stiffness around the

63

edges of her mouth, although no one but my father or I would notice—at least, not unless they knew the story. About a year after Renny's accident, Mom began what Dad and I call her shrine period. She started adding extra features into some of the houses she designed, things that hadn't been requested by her clients, things that reminded her of Renny and her love of books, nature, and sports—a cozy little reading area above an almost hidden back staircase, a grotto-like indoor pool, or a turret room on the top of a house where someone could sit and stare at the treetops. Mom became obsessed with getting these elements into the final plans and into the houses. Maybe she felt she had to do it in order to keep Renny's memory alive. I don't know. She stopped after a few years, but not before she almost lost her partnership with the firm because of it.

There were only a few complaints ever made about the shrines, but one of them bubbled up to the senior partner before any of Mom's allies could run interference for her. The whole thing came to a head on the evening of the high school production of *Hamlet*, in which I played Ophelia. Mom never made it to the play because she was in the senior partner's office, fighting to keep her partnership with the firm. In the end, she retained her position, but it was touch-and-go for a while, and she had to agree to go to counseling. The complaint was about a tower with a spiral staircase leading up to it. The tower, with its small window at the top, was reminiscent of the one in the fairy tale "Rapunzel," a favorite of Renny's when she was little.

Now that I'm older, I can understand how hard it must have been for Mom back then. I'm sure I saw only a sliver of what she was going through, but I remember the dark circles under her eyes and the clothes she wore that hung on her like hand-me-downs from some absent, larger relative.

"So, how's the party coming?" I ask, hoping to loosen the tightness around my mother's jaw.

Dad shakes his head. "I told your mom to keep it simple, but you know how she is. She doesn't know when to quit. Everything she does, it's full steam ahead."

He's right about that. I glance around the room, admiring her touches—the area rug with its blue and white floral pattern, the powder-blue drapes, the gleaming white fireplace mantel, the painted mural of fields and trees above it, and the antique table where we're seated.

"I guess you've seen her handiwork outside," he says, winking at Mom. "She whipped those gardens into shape. I don't think Martha Stewart could have done a better job." He looks at my mother with pride. "She's tamed those geraniums and trimmed the echinaceas, and I think the hydrangeas are bluer than your eyes, Gracie."

He smiles at her, and my heart melts a little.

"The party is coming along fine," Mom says. "We're up to ninety-five people." She reaches for the dish of chutney. "But I'm guessing we'll end up with over a hundred." Her face brightens. "Oh, and I heard from Roberta Carson today. They won't be able to come, but she told me Julie's getting married. Little Julie. Do you believe it?" She spoons more curry onto her plate.

Julie Carson, getting married? I used to babysit Julie, before the Carsons moved to Milwaukee or Minneapolis or some other place that starts with an *M*. "No, I don't believe it. I remember her as a scruffy tomboy."

"I do, too," Mom says with a laugh. "But time marches on. And you'll be next, honey." She looks at me with the tiniest bit of pity, and then she adds, "I never really thought Scott was a good match for you."

"I'm beginning to feel as though nobody did except me."

"He just seemed so . . ." She glances at me as if I'm supposed to supply the word.

"Self-absorbed?" Dad says as he swirls the wine in his glass.

"Afraid so," Mom says. "Sweetie, I can't believe you don't have a line of eligible men at your door." She reaches out and pats my hand. "You're so smart and so pretty. In a city of eight million—"

"Mom." I pull back my hand. If I hear about the eight million people one more time, I'm going to throw myself off the roof. "It's hard to meet nice guys, even in Manhattan. In fact, it's probably harder there than most places."

"Maybe it's something you're doing that you don't even realize," she says. "Like . . . I don't know, giving off negative signals."

"Why would I be giving off negative signals?" I look at my father for some help, but he just shrugs, as though this isn't his territory. "You make it sound as though I'm wearing a red circle on my back with a diagonal line over the figure of a man."

"I'm just saying you might not know it, honey. Otherwise, I can't understand why nothing has worked out for you. After all, you have had some nice boyfriends."

"I've had losers."

"No, you haven't."

"Yes, I have."

"What about that fellow you were seeing before Scott? I think he was in banking. David somebody-or-other. With the two first names."

"David Martin? The guy with the old, green MG?"

"Yes. He had that cute little sports car."

"Mom, David Martin was a total cad, and that cute little sports car broke down more often than it ran."

"Oh, MGs are notorious for that," Dad chimes in, as if he could possibly be an expert on anything mechanical.

"On our third date," I say, "we stopped at a light around Eighty-Sixth and Second, and the car conked out. Just wouldn't go. David told me to get out and push while he jump-started it. So I did. Crazy, I know. Why couldn't he have done the pushing? He knew I could drive a stick. Then, a couple of weeks later, it happened again, and we had a repeat performance. When it happened the third time and he suggested I get out and push, I got out and left. That was it for David."

Mom's shoulders slump. "I didn't know about any of that."

"I try to spare you the harrowing details."

She sighs, and I push around my food while my other ex-boyfriends march through my mind in a little parade. Bill Stoddard, who was far more interested in my father than in me, and Ted Ecklund, who had to plan his whole schedule around when the football games were on TV, and Gordon Hackley, who wanted to open a chain of restaurants for dogs and was trying to get on *Shark Tank* the last time I saw him.

"Look, if Julie Carson can land a husband, you certainly can," Mom says. "Roberta emailed me her picture. She still looks like a tomboy, if you ask me."

I really don't want to hear anything more about Julie Carson. I grab a roll from the basket. "I found the coolers you were looking for."

"The coolers?" she says. "Oh, right. Well, that's good. I'm never sure what's in that garage."

"What coolers?" Dad asks.

"The ones in the garage," I say. "You know, in the *storage area?* Once in a while you guys really ought to take a look at what's out there. You might find something interesting."

Dad tilts back his wineglass. "Like what?"

"Like Renny's bike." There's a moment of silence running between my parents. "The Schwinn," I add.

"The Schwinn?" Mom mumbles as she holds a forkful of rice in midair.

"Don't you remember? Red road bike? She got it when I got my Raleigh?"

"You girls had quite a few bikes over the years," Dad says.

"Yes, but this was her last one. It was called a Paramount."

Mom shakes her head. "I don't know. Maybe I'd remember it if I saw it." She looks away.

"I didn't know we still had Renny's old bike," I say. "I thought you gave it to the thrift shop ages ago when you took mine there."

"Well, I guess I didn't," she says, with that little edge in her voice that sometimes comes out when she talks about Renny. She glances at my father. "Doyle, would you please pass the butter?"

"The bike's a mess," I tell them. "Really dirty and rusty. The salt air's gotten to it. I couldn't believe it was out there all this time. I took it to the Bike Peddler to see what they can do."

"Are they going to fix it?" Dad asks.

"I think so. I'm waiting for them to get back to me."

"What are you planning to do with the bike?" he says. "If they can fix it, I mean. Are you going to take it back to New York? Is it safe to ride a bike there?"

"I'm trying to figure that out. I don't have a lot of room in my apartment, but I'm not going to put it back in the garage. It shouldn't have been out there in the first place." I look at Mom.

She frowns at me. "So what are you saying? That the bike was my responsibility?"

"I'm just saying, once in a while you should take a look at what's in the garage. If you did, you would have seen that it was getting ruined."

She drops her fork, and it hits the plate with a *clank*. "I didn't let it get ruined on purpose, if that's what you're implying, Grace. Why would I do that?"

"I'm not saying you did. I'm just saying it was out there and nobody bothered to notice, and now it's ruined." I reach for the butter and knock over my wineglass, one of a set Mom found tucked away in some shop, antique crystal from Prague.

The glass shatters, and red wine spreads across the table, toward Renny's empty seat. Mom throws a napkin over the wine, and I run to the kitchen and grab a roll of paper towels.

"Sorry about the glass," I say as I finish mopping up the spill.

"It's all right," Mom says, a resigned expression on her face.

My father's sitting in his seat, but he's not looking at me. And he's not looking at my mother. He's studying the mural over the fireplace, those yellow hills, that green river. Maybe he wishes he could walk into it as well.

It's only ten o'clock when I go upstairs to my bedroom. I turn on the bedside table lamp, and the light hums through the shade, a quiet amber glow. I fold down the white coverlet, climb into bed, and lie between the crisp sheets, my head half-buried in the soft pillow.

The wallpaper, with its pink rosebuds, wraps me in a gentle embrace, and I remember the day Mom took me to Accents, a home decor shop that used to be in town, and I picked out that paper. I was in ninth grade, trying to decide between rosebuds and daisies. I chose the rosebuds because they reminded me of the roses that grow on the trellis behind the house.

I gaze at the bookcase across the room, the bottom shelf lined with poetry anthologies. The book with the gray cover summons me, and I cross the floor and pull it off the shelf. Back in bed I find the poem, but as I read the lines I realize I don't need the book because I already know every word. Dad is right, of course. I did once write a paper on this poem. I always thought it was only about nature and its dominion over mankind. How we believe we can possess something—that house, that acre of land—but how nature reclaims everything in the end. I guess my father thinks the poem is about striving and struggling and needing that to stay alive and to stay connected with the universe. What I think now is that the poem is really about the overall transience of life. You're here one moment, and the next you're gone. Lifetimes are short, in the general scheme of things, and some, like Renny's, are shorter than others.

CHAPTER 4

A verb describes an action or a state of being.
A good detective knows how to spy on people.

I pull into Cluny's driveway and beep the horn. She comes running out a minute later, dressed in a gauzy top and flowing skirt, carrying a pair of flip-flops, making me wish I'd worn something better than my tattered jeans.

"Just like old times," she says as she climbs into the passenger seat of the Beetle. "Saturday-morning breakfast at the Sugar Bowl."

I pull out of her driveway. "Old habits die hard."

She reaches into her handbag, a big drawstring affair made of floral fabric. "Check this out," she says, removing something she's torn from the newspaper. "Your horoscope for today."

"Oh, here we go again."

"No, come on, listen to this:

A social event could bring you into contact with fascinating people in interesting fields, some from far away. Discussions may inspire your involvement in new pursuits. You could find yourself in an exotic place. This will be an evening to remember."

"All that's supposed to happen today? Seems like a lot."

"Grace, this is real. I read it and immediately thought, *This means Grace is going to get a job.* Besides, there's going to be a new moon tonight, which means it's a good time to embark on something. So that would be a job. Don't you see?"

"No, I don't."

Sometimes I can't believe how a brilliant artist and otherwise smart woman can be so gullible about certain things, like these horoscopes. Once, when we were young, Cluny insisted that if she could just get on a TV talk show and tell everyone to join hands and love one another, it would happen. It wasn't from an overinflated opinion of herself; she just believed that if someone, anyone, could remind people of their inner goodness, then goodness would follow.

I'm way too skeptical. "That horoscope could be about anything," I tell her. "They're written by people sitting around drinking coffee with their feet up on their desks. Or worse, by computers. They're not divine providence."

"That's not true, Grace. They're written by astrologists, who study these things—the planets, how they're aligned, the angles, all of that. It's complicated, but they know how to interpret the data and figure out what's going to happen."

"Keep dreaming," I mumble as I make a right

onto Baxter Field Road. There's a big addition going up on the house where the Holbrooks used to live. And the widow's walk is gone. "Look at that." I point to the house. "Remember the parties Ben Holbrook used to throw there? How we'd go up to the widow's walk and fling water balloons off the roof?"

"Ah, those were good times," Cluny says, her voice sounding a little dreamy.

"The addition ruins the house, though."

"You know," she says, "you can be kind of critical, Grace."

I press on the gas. "You're just upset because I don't believe in horoscopes."

When we reach Main Street, traffic is crawling, and I notice little tents and tables of merchandise set up in front of the stores. The street is crowded with shoppers, mostly women dressed in shorts and T-shirts, exercise clothes, tank tops, and sundresses. The few men I see look bored or dazed, some of them holding the hands of small children, most of whom also look bored or dazed.

"Wow, I forgot it's the weekend of the sidewalk sale," I say.

"It's even more packed than last year," Cluny says. "I hope we can get a seat at the Sugar Bowl."

"Me too. I'm dying for their apple pancakes."

As we wait for the traffic light to change, I gaze at the shoppers and remember how Mom used to drag Renny and me to the sidewalk sale when we were kids. "My mother always loved this," I say. "She used to turn it into a kind of mystical experience, as though she was hunting for some special thing she didn't even know she needed until she found it."

I can see her on the sidewalk, picking up candlesticks, place mats, sandals, a skirt here, a lamp shade there, giving each item a thorough examination, as though it might be telling her something about itself that wasn't readily apparent.

"She's always had a way of spotting cool things," Cluny says.

"Yeah. If I hadn't learned her skills in weeding out the junk to discover the gems, I never would have found my purple jelly shoes."

"Oh my God, I *loved* jelly shoes," Cluny says. "I had that pair in hot pink."

"I remember. Oh, and I got my cassette player–boom box at the sidewalk sale one year."

"Another great find."

"And that denim shirt I thought looked exactly like the one Jason Priestley wore in *Beverly Hills, 90210.*"

"Yes, you wore it all summer," Cluny says. "And I had that blue dress that looked like one of Tori Spelling's."

"I wish I still had that shirt. Wait, what am I saying? It's probably in the attic."

"Knowing your parents, I'm sure it is."

The light finally turns green, and we pass the Sugar Bowl's blue and white awning and the sign with a cup of coffee on one side and a bowl of sugar on the other. I pull into the parking lot in the back, trying my best to avoid the potholes left from last winter's storms. There's one empty space, and I take it.

The second we walk inside, I'm hit by another wave of memories—sodas and French fries with Cluny after school, and grilled-cheese sandwiches with Renny after her Saturday sports practices.

I look around. "You were right. It's really crowded."

We walk along the U-shaped counter, where every stool is taken, and past the sign boasting *World's Best Apple Pie*. There's been heated competition for years among the eating establishments in Dorset over which one has the best apple pie. The sign in the lobby of the Dorset Inn says *Best Apple Pie in the Universe*, but that assumes there is life on other planets and that those lifeforms, whatever they are, have apples and ovens and the desire to make pies.

Having Miller's Orchards in town is what started the competition decades ago and what keeps it alive today. For years I've heard about the street fight that erupted back in the fifties between the owners of Chester's and the Sea Grape, two restaurants that faded into oblivion long before I was born. Apparently the two men got into it over their apple pies. Some say it's just a country legend, but, judging from how seriously people around here take their pies, I wouldn't be so sure.

I glance at the framed photos on the walls as we follow the hostess to a booth—an orange sea star; a striped chambered nautilus; a spiky, purple sea urchin; and the silvery inside of an oyster shell. "New decorations," I whisper to Cluny.

"I'm so glad they finally got rid of those paintings of doughnuts and muffins," she says.

I kind of liked them, but I don't say anything.

Fortunately, everything else is the same—the high-backed booths running along the walls, and the tables in the middle, the glass salt and pepper shakers and frosted sugar dispensers, the blue and white checked curtains tied back with tassels.

Cluny and I slide into our booth and order coffee from a waitress with a haphazard bun, broad shoulders, and *Luann* on her name tag. I study the menu, relieved to find that it offers many of the old standards, like apple-cornmeal fritters, apple pancakes, and baked apple French toast, along with steak and eggs and a lobster omelet. Luann returns with a carafe, pours our coffee, and takes out her pad and pen.

I order the apple pancakes and take a sip of coffee, which tastes metallic, as if someone dropped a few pennies into the pot while it was brewing. That hasn't changed, either. Cluny orders the artichoke-and-mushroom quiche. I'm about to ask Luann for more milk when another waitress walks over. Her name tag reads *Dee*.

"You're right," Dee says to Luann, her voice quiet but excited. "I wouldn't have recognized Brittany Wells in a million years. She looks so different in person."

"I thought she'd be a lot taller," Luann says. "She's a tiny little thing."

"Brittany Wells is here?" Cluny asks. "The actress?"

"Sure is," Luann says, looking pleased that he's the one to provide this information. "Over there, with some other people from the movie. I heard one of the guys is the director."

"The director?" I straighten up.

Cluny looks at me and mouths, *Peter!* "Where are they sitting?" she asks.

Luann points to someplace behind my side of the booth, a place I can't see from where I'm sitting because the back of the booth is too high. "At the middle table," she adds. "There's a skinny girl with long, dark hair. That's Brittany Wells. She's just drinking lemon water. Probably why she's so skinny. And some guy with hoop earrings. He looks like he needs a shave. I think he's an actor, too." Luann puts her pad in her apron pocket. "He ate two orders of apple pancakes." She raises two fingers. "And look how skinny *he* is." She pats her stomach. "Maybe I need to move to California," she jokes as she walks away.

Cluny slides toward the end of her bench to take a look, and I grab her wrist. "No, don't!"

"Why not?"

"He might see you."

"That's the point, Grace. We should say hello."

I wish I hadn't worn my old jeans. And why didn't I put on more makeup this morning? "I'm not ready. I can't see him looking like this. Besides, he's with other people. We need to come up with a plan first."

"I thought you didn't care."

I pull my hairbrush, my compact, and my Rose Glow lipstick from my handbag. "Cluny, he's a former boyfriend. I don't want him to think I've gone to seed." I apply the Rose Glow to my lips. "Or that I walk around in ratty clothes like this all the time."

"But you do."

I sigh. "Let's just figure out the plan." Figuring out the plan was always my job when Cluny and I were in our detective phase. "All right, we need to do some reconnaissance," I begin. "Make your way to the edge of the bench, just until you can see his table. But don't let him see you."

"How am I going to do that?"

"I don't know. What do you have in your hand-bag? Anything you can use to make a disguise? A scarf or a hat, maybe?"

Cluny puts her handbag on the table. "Sure, I'll

just pull a sombrero right out of here." She makes a face. "Why can't you do this, Grace?"

"Because I'm in the wrong position and you're in the right position. I'd have to go to the edge of the bench and turn around, and then he'd recognize me right away."

"All right," Cluny says as she digs through her bag. A moment later she holds up a pair of large, black sunglasses.

"Perfect."

She puts them on and arranges her hair so it covers the sides of her face.

"You haven't lost your touch. Now take a look."

She inches her way to the edge of the bench and peers around. Suddenly, she straightens up. "It's him!"

"Are you sure?"

She leans forward and adjusts her sunglasses. "Yep. He's talking to another guy. He doesn't have any hair."

"Peter's *bald?*"

"Not Peter," she says. "The other guy. And he looks really good. Peter, I mean. Oh, wow, yeah." She goes silent for a moment, her fingers gripping the edge of the table. Then her hands fly to her chest. "Oh my God, somebody else just joined them. I think it's . . ." All the color has left her face. "It's *Sean Leeds.*"

"What? You're kidding!" I start to stand, to get a glimpse of the actor *People* magazine recently named Sexiest Man Alive. Then I catch myself and quickly sit down. "Are you sure?"

Cluny looks again. "Yes, it's definitely him. He just sat down two seats from Peter." She bangs her fist on the table. "Oh God, he's so handsome. I'm going to faint."

I'm dying to look. Peter's back in town, *and* he's with Sean Leeds. "All right, tell me exactly what they're doing." My hand trembles as I dump a packet of sweetener into my coffee.

"Okay, let's see," Cluny says. "Besides Sean and Peter, there are two other guys—one is the bald guy, and the other is the one who needs a shave. And there's Brittany Wells. Wow, she really is tiny."

"Okay. So what are they doing?"

"They're just talking. Oh, wait. Peter's on his cell phone now. And Brittany's drinking her lemon water. One guy is eating something. Looks like seeds. No, that can't be right. I don't know what it is."

"Who cares what *he's* eating? What's *Peter* eating?" I ask. He can't be eating seeds. He always had the apple pancakes.

Cluny leans out a little farther. "I can't tell."

"What about the other people?"

"I just told you what they're eating." She lowers her sunglasses and glares at me.

"I mean, can you tell who they are?"

"No. Which is why we should just go over there and say hello." She starts to rise again.

I grab her by the forearm and yank her down. "Not yet. We're still in the reconnaissance phase of our mission."

"Well, what else do you want to know?"

"Are the other guys actors?"

Cluny focuses again on the table. "I don't know. I recognize Sean Leeds and Brittany Wells, but I don't know who those other two are."

"They always say when you see actors in person, they never look the way they do in the movies," I remind her. "Just like the waitress told us."

A coy smile emerges on her lips. "I don't know about that. Sean Leeds sure looks like Sean Leeds to me."

"Then who are they?"

She grabs my compact and opens it, displaying the mirror. "Here, Nancy Drew, remember how to use this? You look and tell me if they're actors."

I slide to the end of the bench and pick up my lipstick. Then I lean my head out of the booth, hold up the compact, and apply my Rose Glow once again.

Tilting the mirror to the left and right, up and down, I sweep the room, taking in a woman with snow-white hair, a mother and a small girl, three men in business suits, a young guy with wire-rimmed glasses. Then I see a table of five, and there's Sean Leeds, and, oh God, Cluny is right. He's so handsome, his dark hair flecked with bits of gray, his eyes so soulful they could melt butter in a freezer, his teeth like miniature sculptures. I linger there for a moment, watching him as he eats something from a bowl. Cereal? Oatmeal? Seeds? I can't tell. I move the compact just a touch. And there he is. Peter.

I stare into the mirror, unable to take my eyes off him. He's talking on his cell phone, and he looks tan. Very tan. He's wearing a black T-shirt with a design on the front, but I can't see what it is. A pair of sunglasses hangs from his T-shirt pocket. His hair is still thick and wavy. No gray. Old memories begin to stir. Peter and I in middle school, working on an English project in the library (was that the year we acted out scenes from *The Great Gatsby*?). Peter and I in a blue-hulled Boston Whaler with Tom Hartney and Caroline Kent, Tom piloting the boat to Bluff Island, where we swam until our lungs ached and the skin on our fingers turned to prunes. Peter and I in a booth here in the Sugar Bowl, sharing a piece of apple pie with a scoop of homemade vanilla ice cream on the side. At the Dorset Playhouse, sharing a package of red licorice. At the Cinderella Ball, sharing a kiss. That kiss.

Why am I starting to feel like a goofy teenager again? I might as well be back at Baxter Middle School, waiting at the end of the hall for a glimpse of him.

Cluny is looking at me, eyes wide, a big smile

on her face. "So? Did you see him? He looks good, doesn't he?" I don't answer for a moment, and she laughs. "What's going on?"

I close the compact and meet her gaze, my pulse thundering. "He looks really good, Cluny. He looks great. I can't believe he's here. I feel so—I don't know . . ."

I run my hand over the smooth surface of the compact and think about something I once heard on the radio, about how people never forget their first love, how first loves are actually imprinted on our brains—hardwired. And how first-love couples who get back together later in life have a greater than 70 percent chance of staying together for good.

"Let me take another look," I say.

I open the compact again and adjust the mirror so Peter is in view. No cell phone now. He's got his head back and he's laughing and I could swear we're back in high school because the gesture is so *Peter.* I tilt the mirror toward the other people at the table. They're all laughing as well, and I feel a little jealous. I look back at Peter. God, he's handsome. And it's not just the way he looks. It's the way he seems to command the table. I feel that old tug. I can't take my eyes off him.

Now he's talking to Brittany Wells, and as I watch he looks up and stares right at me, straight at me, into the mirror. He doesn't take his eyes off the mirror for a second. Can he see me in the mirror? Oh my God, he must see me. I put the compact down, turn around, and look at him.

And now he's waving. He's *waving* to me! And he's gesturing for me to come over. I think I've stopped breathing. He waves again, and a glint of light flickers off the sunglasses that hang from his T-shirt. I feel the last seventeen years begin to dissolve.

"Cluny, we're going over there," I say as I rise from the bench.

This time, she clutches my arm. "What?"

"He saw me. He knows I'm here. He waved to me, to come over. Let's go."

"No, wait. You go first. This is your chance to talk to him alone. I'll come over in a minute. Oh, and fix your hair on the side there." She points, and I reach up and smooth my hair.

I stare at Peter as I walk toward the table. He looks like the old Peter, but a more mature version. A Peter who has done a lot with his life. His face has lost that soft, boyish appearance, but there's still something so sweet about it. I think it's his eyes, sparkling blue, like sea glass.

Gliding right up, I tap him on the shoulder. He's listening to something the bald guy next to him is saying about skiing in Switzerland. Peter turns and looks at me, and when he does I feel as though I've been punched in the stomach. He shows no sign of recognition. In fact, he looks surprised at having had his conversation interrupted. Now I want the floor to open and swallow me in an act of mercy.

He's about to say something when a tall brunette, dressed in white jeans and a blue tank top, sidles up to the table. "What took you so long, Melissa?" he says. "We saved a seat for you."

That's when I realize he wasn't signaling to me. He was waving at her, at this *Melissa* person. And now I'm here, and he doesn't even know it's me, Grace Hammond, who's just discovered she's still wild about Peter Brooks after all these years.

I must be turning crimson, because every part of me feels scorched and prickly, as though I've been caught in a brush fire. I want to run, but my feet refuse to move; it's as if static has disrupted the signals between my brain and the rest of my body.

Peter turns back to me. "Is there, uh, something I can help you with?"

"Peter, it's me. Grace. Hammond. From Dorset High." I look around at the other people at the table. The conversation has quickly tapered off. "I didn't mean to interrupt. It's just that I saw you were here and—"

"Grace?" He stands up. "Grace Hammond? Oh jeez." His face breaks into a huge smile, his eyes brighten, and he grabs me and pulls me in for a hug. He smells like cedarwood and rosemary and something else—like Peter. It's all wonderful.

"What are you doing in town?" he asks when he finally lets me go. "Do you live here?"

I keep it simple, telling him I've come from Manhattan for my father's party. "We're celebrating his sixty-fifth."

"That's great," he says. "And how are your parents? Still in the same house? Out on the point?"

He remembers the house. I feel a warmth go through me. "Yeah, they're still there. And they're fine, thanks."

He looks me up and down. "God, Grace, you look wonderful. Really. I can't believe you're here." He reaches out and touches my arm, and I could swear we're the only two people in the room.

"Brooks made that decision, not me," one of the men at the table says a moment later, and Peter looks around with a start, as if he, too, thought we were alone.

"Hey, let me introduce you to the group," he says. "We're working on a project. These guys are part of my team." He lowers his voice and leans a little closer. "I live in L.A. now. I'm here doing a movie."

"Yeah, I think I might have heard that," I tell him, trying to act nonchalant as drops of perspiration trickle down the back of my shirt.

He turns toward the table. "This is Grace Hammond. Grace and I go back to the days of

middle school. We have a lot of history together."
He smiles at me. "Don't we, Grace?"

"Yes, we do." I can feel myself blush.

"This is my assistant director," he says, introducing me to the bald man, whose name is Art. The man who looks as though he needs a shave is Jerry Ash, Peter's director of photography. "And this is Brittany Wells," Peter says. "One of the finest actors around."

Brittany gives me a tepid wave, and I recall that just a few weeks ago, I saw her in *Liberty Revival*, a film about a group of college kids who attempt to build a life-sized replica of the Statue of Liberty out of Styrofoam in order to win a huge cash prize and save their school from bankruptcy.

I feel hit by a surge of embarrassment as I say hello to Melissa, Peter's production designer, the woman he was really signaling. But I forget that within seconds, as soon as I come face-to-face with Sean Leeds. I try to say hello, but the word won't form properly and comes out as a seagull-like squawk.

Sean Leeds takes my hand between his, stares straight into my eyes, and says, "Hello, Grace. I'm Sean."

Even though I've heard his voice in more than a dozen movies, as well as on *Stat!*, the TV show where he played Steve Franklin, an orthopedic surgeon, none of that has prepared me for hearing him speak in person. His voice is deep and smooth, and his smile is disarming—even better in person than on-screen. He seems so honest and genuine that I'm caught completely off guard. I can barely think. I just stand there, holding his hand, until he pulls it away gently and says, "It's nice to meet an old friend of Peter's. He's lucky to have come from such a great town."

I manage to tell him I love his work or something equally fawning, and then my mind flashes to Sydney Parker, the actress Sean was dating until recently, when she broke off their two-year relationship. I'd always thought she was crazy, even before their breakup, because I'd heard she demands a hot tub in her dressing room and tons of Skittles candies—but only the yellow ones. Somebody has to pick out all the yellows! I glance at Cluny to summon her over, but she looks as if she's secretly snapping pictures on her cell phone while pretending to be reading text messages.

"How long has it been?" Peter asks me.

"Seventeen years," I tell him. I think about how fast those years seem to be falling away now, and I wonder if it feels that way for him.

"No. Really?" He frowns a little, as though this can't be true. And there's something in his eyes—a mist of sadness, maybe a hint of regret. "I haven't seen you since just before you left town. We were sixteen, remember?"

He glances across the room and rubs the back

of his neck. "You know, you're right. It *has* been that long." He studies me again, from head to toe, and I stand there, mentally squirming, hoping he can see beyond my old jeans and wrinkled tee. Then he says, "Gracie girl, you look fantastic. You don't look a day older than you did in high school."

I smile. He thinks I look good. And he's using his pet name for me. "Nobody's called me Gracie girl in a long time."

He laughs, and then he shakes his head, slowly, as though he still can't believe we're really here together. "I remember the day you won the tenth-grade essay competition as if it was yesterday. And all those spelling bees in middle school . . . you were invincible." He glances across the room for a moment as though he's picturing this. Then he says, "So tell me, what are you doing with yourself these days?"

What am I doing? I start to panic. I don't want to tell him I just lost my job. Or that I'm a technical writer. Or that I haven't won any competitions in years. I'll sound like such a loser compared with him. "I left a friend back at the booth," I say as I give a frantic wave to Cluny. This time she notices and dashes over.

"Peter, do you remember Cluny Barrow?" I ask. "I mean Hart. She was Cluny Hart in high school."

He hands a waitress his black American Express

card. "Sure. How could I forget Cluny? You guys always hung out together." Peter gives her a big squeeze and then introduces her to the group. She can barely speak by the time she gets to Sean, who is in the midst of autographing take-out menus for a couple of elderly ladies.

"Okay, people," Peter says. "I'd better get going. I've got work to do." He smiles at me. "I'm so glad I came here today. I was feeling a little nostalgic for the apple pancakes, and then who do I run into but you?"

So he did have the apple pancakes. "It was great to see you again," I tell him, my eyes lingering on a little wavy section of hair above his left ear.

"Hey, ladies," Sean Leeds says, his gaze going from Cluny to me. "You two should stop by the set sometime."

"Ooh, that would be fun," I say. "I've never been to a movie set."

I'm about to ask where they're filming when Peter says, "We can make that happen, but I also have another idea. Why don't you come to the party tonight?"

I look at Cluny, who has turned so pale, I worry she's gone into shock. "Party?" I ask. "What party?"

"At my house," Peter says. "I'm having a few people over. Around eight. It's kind of a thank-you to the folks in town who have helped us. The production company set it up."

"Sure, that sounds nice."

"Believe me, it's not the kind of thing we'd normally do in the middle of a shoot, but there were scheduling issues with a few of the key guests, so we're having it early. And, anyway, I'm happy to do what I can to give a little something back to Dorset."

"It's at your house?" I ask.

"Yeah, the house I'm renting. On Mill Pond. Two Forty-Four."

"Okay, great," I say. "We'll be there."

Peter looks at Cluny. "Oh, and bring your husband." Then he says to me, "And, of course, if you have a boyfriend, Grace . . ."

A boyfriend? He thinks I'm dating someone? All of a sudden Scott Denby feels like three lifetimes ago. But I'm not sure what to say. I wish there were a better expression for not having a boyfriend. *Between relationships?* Sounds too presumptuous. *Single?* Sounds too, well, single. "I'm not seeing anyone at the moment," I finally say.

I catch a flicker in Peter's eyes. "Really?" he says. "Then that makes two of us."

CHAPTER 5

An adverb tells us more about a verb
and answers *how, when,* or *where.*
Preparing <u>carefully</u> for an event can mean the
difference between success and failure.

"Oh my God, Cluny. How can I go to this party? I have nothing to wear." We sit in the front seat of my car, in the parking lot behind the Sugar Bowl. The engine is off, the windows are down. I'm mentally reviewing my closet.

"You must have something," she says.

"Yeah, pink and green preppy dresses I bought at Snapdragon the summer I worked there during college. I can't wear those."

"Don't you have any other cocktail dresses here?"

"I do, but they're too . . . *Connecticut.* I need something edgier. More Hollywood." I run my hand over the steering wheel. "I really want to look good for this party. Peter was so sweet. And did you hear the way he asked if I had a boyfriend?"

Cluny grins. "He couldn't take his eyes off you."

"Really?" I'm getting chills just thinking about it. "I need something fantastic to wear."

"I don't have any Hollywood clothes, either," she says.

"But you've got tons of nice things," I tell her as a car pulls in next to us. And she does. I've seen photos of Cluny with Greg at local charity events for animal causes and children's relief organizations she's involved in, and she always looks great. I wish I were five foot eight and not five foot six. Then I could borrow something from her.

"What do you think people wear to Hollywood parties, anyway?" she asks.

"I'm not sure," I tell her. "Maybe the same kind of clothes they wear to movie openings."

She looks out the window, contemplating this. "I don't know. You might have to buy something new, then."

"I'm coming to the same conclusion." It's an expense I don't need right now, but, with the sidewalk sale taking place, maybe I can find something at a good price.

Cluny laces her fingers together. "If you want something a little funky, we should go to Bagatelle."

Bagatelle. Nice but expensive. I think about my bank account, which is shrinking by the minute. I can't keep up with Cluny at Bagatelle, but I don't want to give her any more reason to think she needs to loan me money. "Yeah, okay."

"I bet they'll have some good deals," she

adds, reading my mind. "Sidewalk sale and all."

We walk out of the parking lot, onto Main Street, and make our way through the crowds. I stop to say hello to Mrs. Meisner, who's been a friend of Mom's for years. Dressed in peach golf shorts and a matching peach top, she smells like Calvin Klein Eternity, the only perfume I've ever known her to wear.

"Come over for a drink," she says, touching a tanned hand to my arm. "We're always around at cocktail time." She winks and walks away.

We pass racks of sweatshirts, sweaters, dresses, and beach cover-ups and weave through piles of jeans, from the darkest inky blue to the palest shade of iceberg. One store has a table overflowing with handbags. I stop to pick up a plastic tote and, almost without thinking, check the inner pocket. There's only a price tag in there. I put the bag back and keep moving.

Mom once bought a handbag at the sidewalk sale, and after she got it home, she found a little note in the inside pocket, written in Hindi by someone in India. Translated, it meant *Good luck to you.* She carried that note in her wallet for years. It's probably still there.

Cluny waves to Poppy Norwich, who's across the street, loaded down with shopping bags. Poppy went to middle school with us before going away to prep school. Now she's married and lives in town and writes personal growth books. Her latest, *What You've Been Doing Wrong All Along*, was a *New York Times* bestseller. I've been tempted on more than one occasion to buy a copy, thinking maybe I could pick up a few tips. But then this jealous feeling about Poppy having done so well starts to nag at me, and I opt for a beach read instead.

We make our way to Bagatelle, where women huddle around the racks out front, elbowing one another as they try to lay claim to the best items. Cluny and I approach the racks, vying for space. A young woman, probably a college student, sits at a card table, looking bored and drumming her fingers on a cash box. With her long, tan legs and blond hair flecked with even lighter streaks, she looks like the poster child for summer. The words from an old Don Henley tune, "The Boys of Summer," pop into my head. I can almost hear the electric guitar notes that sound like the cries of seagulls.

Cluny nudges me. "Hey, check this out." She holds up a lavender dress with a jeweled top. "Do you think it would look good on me?"

"Yes, it's gorgeous! You could wear it tonight. Try it on."

I cull through the racks, but nothing jumps out at me. I want to look perfect for Peter. I want to look pretty and sexy. Years from now I might reflect back on this moment—how I bought the dress for this party and how this night changed my life. I feel as though something magical is going to happen. Maybe Peter will fall in love with me and ask me to move to California. We'll get married and have a house in the canyon. I'm not sure which canyon, but I'll be happy with any canyon as long as it's not the kind that's always catching on fire or having mudslides.

"There's more sale stuff inside," the girl at the table says, giving us a sleepy-eyed look.

Cluny and I walk into the store. While she heads toward the dressing rooms in the back, I scan the dresses in the sale section, quickly eliminating each one in my size—too short, too much spandex, too bright, a neckline that would plunge to my navel. There's nothing for me.

A saleswoman walks toward me, her hair swept up in a big twist, her face a billboard of makeup. She's wearing huge false lashes and thick streaks of black eyeliner. Perfume oozes from her—something Oriental, heavy on the sandalwood. She looks around fifty, maybe a little older. "You look like you need some help, honey," she says, one hand in the air as though something's about to float down into her palm.

"Oh, no, I'm fine," I say with a tepid smile. "Just browsing."

I glance at the women in line at the checkout counter, arms laden with clothes, and I'm about to give up. And then I see it—a rose-colored silk dress, cinched at the waist, with straps that crisscross in the back. Perfect! I grab the hanger just as another arm reaches for it.

"Sorry," I say as I clutch the dress to my chest and watch as the other woman disappears into the mob. With newfound hope I head toward the back of the store.

"Cluny," I whisper as I approach the four dressing rooms. "Where are you?"

The wooden doorway of the dressing room on the far right opens a crack, and a waving hand emerges. "In here."

I slip inside to find her zipping up the lavender dress. "Wow. You look beautiful," I say as she turns to view herself from the side and back.

I hold up the rose-colored dress. "What do you think about this?"

"Oh, that's pretty," she says. "Try it on."

I'm about to undress when I hear a voice outside the room.

"Let's see, we'll put you right in here, honey." It's the saleswoman with the big hair. I can smell her perfume even through the wall. "That's going to look so cute on you," she says.

A second later there's another voice. "This is just a li'l ole last-minute thought. There's a party tonight, and I have something all picked out, but, you know, I'm not dead set on it."

"Regan Moxley!" I whisper to Cluny.

"Would y'all come in here so you can zip me up when I get this on?" Regan says.

"Sure, honey. Tell me when you're ready."

The door to Regan's dressing room closes, and Cluny and I rush to the adjoining wall to hear what she says.

"This is just like the old days," Cluny whispers as she steps out of the lavender dress. "When we wanted to be spies."

"You wanted to be a spy," I remind her again. I pull off my jeans and T-shirt. God, I wish I had Cluny's shape. Two kids, and her stomach is as flat as Kansas.

"So, you're going to a party?" the saleswoman asks.

"Yes," Regan says. "With the actors in town. You know, Sean and Brittany and . . . well, all of them."

"She's going?" I whisper. "How did she find out about it?"

Cluny shakes her head and steps back into her skirt.

"And listen to how she's talking about them," I say as I pull the dress over my head. "*Sean* and *Brittany.* As though she knows them." I can almost feel my veins clog with indignation.

"Oh, honey, you're so lucky," the saleswoman croons.

"The director invited me," Regan says.

Peter invited *her?*

"We went to high school together," Regan adds. "I think he was secretly in love with me."

I gasp. "That's a—"

I'm about to say *lie,* but Cluny clamps her hand over my mouth. "Shh!"

"I know we would have gotten together," Regan says, "if his family hadn't moved away. Luckily, I had a lot of other boys after me."

Cluny looks at me as she puts on her blouse. "She's crazy."

"She barely knew him." I feel a knot in my stomach.

"Well," the saleswoman says, "no wonder why he invited you. Maybe he's still interested, honey."

"Oh, I think he is," Regan says. "I can always tell."

"What a liar," I say as Cluny zips up the back of my dress.

"Don't worry," Cluny says. "She's not even his type."

I look at my reflection in the mirror, at the straps that cross in the back, the little gathers at the waist that make the silk fall in a soft way. Cluny nods approvingly. The dress is on sale for a hundred and fifty dollars, a steal in this place. I study the smattering of freckles across my nose, the green flecks in my blue eyes. I pull back my hair to see what it would look like in an updo. Then I let it fall to my shoulders, the loose waves settling back into place. I spin around and watch the dress move with me.

I'm about to tell Cluny I'll take it when Regan says, "Could y'all come in now?"

"Oh, sure," the saleswoman says, and I hear the door to Regan's dressing room open and close. "Oh, my, look at you. You're going to turn every head at that party. That dress is perfect. Sure wish I had your cute little figure."

"Hmm," Regan says. "I think it's too long. I'm going to have trouble walking in it. And see over here . . . this kind of puckers out. It's way too loose."

"I wonder what she's trying on," I say. "Sounds as though it's something full length. And we're wearing short dresses. I can't go in the wrong thing." I don't want to make a clothing faux pas at Peter's party and start things off on a bad note. I'd never forgive myself.

"I'm sure other people will be wearing short dresses," Cluny says.

Will they? I wonder. I analyze my reflection again. What if Regan is dressed in something so mesmerizing that *she's* the one who gets Peter's attention instead of me? What if he ends up taking *her* to L.A.? I have this horrible vision—Regan dressed in a long Gucci gown with a neckline down to her navel and Peter, in an Armani tux, seated next to her. They're in one of the front rows of a huge auditorium. Someone calls Peter's name, and he stands and makes his way to the stage, where a woman is holding a gleaming

Oscar statuette. I'm watching the whole thing on TV, of course, at my parents' house, because I still haven't found a job and I've lost my apartment for good, due to nonpayment of rent, and the only clothes I have left are my pj's with the Santas and reindeer on them.

"Oh, we can fix that, honey," the saleswoman says. "We'll take it up there, nip it in here. Go on out to the three-way mirror, and I'll get the seamstress to pin it."

"Come on." I grab Cluny's arm. "Let's get out there so we can see what Regan's wearing. She knows what to wear to a Hollywood party."

Across from the dressing rooms is an area with a small platform, like a stage, surrounded by a three-way mirror, and, standing on the platform, preening and looking at her reflection, is Regan. She is not wearing a full-length dress or a full-length skirt or a full-length anything. And she is not wearing something that needs to be taken in. Regan Moxley is wearing the shortest, skimpiest, tightest dress I have ever seen, made entirely of silver sequins. And she looks terrific.

I swallow, and it feels as though a marble is going down my throat.

Regan sees us in the mirror. "Oh, hey, girls. Y'all doin' a little shopping?"

"Just looking around," Cluny says.

"They've got a lot of things on sale," Regan says, although I can't imagine the dress she's wearing was marked down. She twirls, admiring her reflection, and I can't turn away, as much as I want to. Those legs. That body. Then she gives me a long, appraising stare, and, although she doesn't say a word, I can tell what she's thinking—that the dress I'm wearing is a dud.

Regan flicks back her hair. "Are you wearing that to the party tonight, Grace?" Then she covers her mouth. "Oh, wait. You're invited, right?"

"Yes," I say. "Cluny and Greg and I are all going."

"Oh, the three of you. That's nice. What about Mitch?"

"Mitch?" I'm about to ask what Mitch has to do with it, and then I remember he's supposed to be my boyfriend. "Oh, he can't make it. He has a . . ." My mind unplugs for a second, and I can't think of what to say.

"A bike thing," Cluny says.

"Yes, a bike thing. A race."

"At night?" Regan says, giving me an incredulous look. "In the dark?"

I swallow. "Well, yes. It's, uh, a charity thing. To raise money . . . for the visually impaired."

"Oh," she says with a shrug. "Well, too bad. It should be a fun evening."

She runs her hands down her sides and hips and continues to view her reflection. I can't believe how tall and skinny she is. I wonder why such a great body has to be wasted on her. Life is so unfair.

"I'll just take the dress the way it is," she tells the saleswoman, who looks delighted. She's probably calculating her commission.

"Well, I'll see you there, girls." Regan throws back her shoulders and moves like a lynx down the platform's little steps and into the dressing room.

I look at myself in the three-way mirror, and the rose-colored dress looks dull and archaic, like something that would be in the final-sale rack in the back of a thrift shop.

"I'm not taking this," I tell Cluny. "I'm going back for one more look."

The crowd at the front of the store has doubled. There must be twenty women hovering around the sale racks, like coyotes feasting on a carcass. They're pushing and shoving and emitting strange guttural sounds I've never heard humans make. There's so much grabbing and jostling, I'm afraid to get too close. Now I'm in the middle of the store, where nothing is on sale. I look around aimlessly. I don't know what I'm doing here. I'm just about to give up. And then I see it. Regan's sequined dress. It's here. Maybe I'm in the right place after all.

Every piece of clothing in this area of the store has something a little different, a little trendy, about it. I pick up a black one-shoulder dress with two big, rectangular cutouts that would expose part of my stomach and back. Forget it. I keep looking, combing through the racks, and then I spot a dark-green dress. Green was Peter's favorite color when we were in high school. He had a dark-green baseball cap he practically wore out one year.

The dress is sleeveless, and most of the body is made of a stretchy fabric, except for the accents, which are lace. It looks like a great combination of sophistication and sex appeal. I check the price. Three hundred and ninety-nine dollars. There's no way I can afford that. I start to put the dress back, but then I see Regan saunter out the door with a little flick of her hair and a bounce in her step, and I can't let go. It's as though the hanger has grafted itself to my hand, and I know I have to do this. It's like an investment in my future. Mine and Peter's. What could be more worthwhile than that?

"I'm trying this on," I tell Cluny when she walks up to me.

She throws back her head. "Va-va-voom! Wow. You'd really wear that?"

"Sure," I say. But now she's got me worried. "Why? Do you think it's a little too young?"

"No, no, if that's what you want to wear, go for it. It's just different from your usual style. Just because Regan's wearing that sequined—"

I wave her off. "Regan who?"

She puts up her hand for a high five, and I slap it.

I step inside the dressing room and pull the green dress over my head. It's tight, but I know it's supposed to be tight. It's short, but I know it's supposed to be short. I suck in my stomach and evaluate my reflection. I put my arms over my head. The dress inches up a little, but not too much. So far, so good. But the lacy parts are another matter. There's no lining under them, so you can see right through to my skin. That's okay for the shoulders and the V-neck. And I can pull in my stomach so it doesn't pop through the lace diamonds on the sides. But I'm not so sure about the big triangles that go down the outsides of my legs. They start as points, at my hips, and then get wider as they race to the bottom of the dress.

Yikes. That's a lot of bare leg. And I don't have the legs of the college girl out front, or of Regan Moxley. I wonder if I can pull this off. And if I'm going to spend four hundred dollars to do it. I draw in my stomach again and take another look. And then, without considering it a second longer, I wriggle my way out of the dress and march to the checkout counter, my Visa card firmly in hand.

Yes, I can pull this off.

CHAPTER 6

A pronoun takes the place of a noun.
For a moment, <u>she</u> felt certain <u>she</u> was
channeling Marilyn Monroe.

I'll never pull this off.

I stand in front of the mirror in my bedroom, minutes before Cluny and Greg are due to pick me up, and I feel as if I'm dressed in a sausage casing. It might be green and lacy, but it's still a sausage casing. What was I thinking? The mirror in the store must have been the kind that makes you look taller and thinner than you really are. The mirror in my bedroom is more like the one in *Snow White.* It doesn't lie.

I should never have bought this dress. Peter doesn't expect me to look like some Hollywood starlet wannabe. He expects me to look like the grown-up version of the girl he knew in high school. And this isn't it.

The doorbell rings, and my heart jumps. It's Cluny. She's here. I walk down the stairs, slowly, carefully, in the black strappy sandals she loaned me. When I step outside, she's standing there in her new dress, the light from the lanterns falling softly upon her. "Wow, you look great," I say.

"Thanks," she says. "So do you."

I glance at the lace panels running brazenly down my legs. "No, I look awful. I'm going back into the house to change."

"Change into what?"

"I don't know. Sweats?"

"You can't go to the party in sweats."

"Exactly."

"What? You're not going?"

"You'll have to make my excuses and—"

"No," Cluny says. "I'm not letting you spend the night with Ben and Jerry. Come on, Peter invited us to this party. He wants to see you. And you look great."

I don't move.

Greg steps out of his Tahoe and whistles. "Whoo-ee, look at you, Miss Grace." He's got the kind of effervescent smile that artists doing character sketches love to exaggerate, and a big, six-foot-four frame to carry it off.

"Greg, stop it right now," I tell him.

"What are you talking about?" he says. "You look great! You look sexy!"

"Sexy good or sexy bad?"

"Grace, you're overthinking this," Cluny says. "Come on." She points to the Tahoe.

"I'm not going."

"Sexy good!" she says.

"Really?"

"Yes. I promise."

"All right." I follow her across the gravel driveway, teetering in the heels.

Greg opens the back door and motions toward the seat like a limo driver inviting his passenger to enter. I slide into the car, the dress shinnying up my legs like a snake. I tug it back down.

"So," Greg says as we pull onto Salt Meadow Lane, "sounds as if this Peter Brooks is really interested in you, Grace."

"He was in high school, but it's been a long time since then." I pop a breath mint into my mouth as we round the curve.

"Well, he sure seemed interested this morning," Cluny says. "I could tell by the way he was looking at you. It reminded me of when Greg and I first met." She glances at her husband. "You sat down next to me in the lecture hall. I think it was a psych class."

"It was," he says. "And I pretended I needed a pen."

Cluny smiles. "As if I didn't know. You just had that vibe. I could tell you were interested."

"Really? And I thought I was being so clever with that pen excuse."

"I just want a little time to talk to him alone," I say, imagining a walk under the stars, a chance to catch up.

"If anyone can figure out a plan," Cluny says, "it's you."

Greg glances at me in the rearview mirror. "I'm

going to check him out, you know. I'm not letting some guy from Hollywood waltz into town and think he can just run off with our Grace."

I shake my head and laugh. They're so good to me, Cluny and Greg, and I feel a little pang of guilt when I think about the jealousy I felt when Cluny first met him. Seniors in college at the time, Cluny and I spent hours burning up the phone lines between her apartment, in Antioch, Ohio, and mine, in Middlebury, Vermont. She would explain, in excruciating detail, their every encounter, every conversation, every *everything*. I thought he was going to take away my best friend, but all he wanted to do was make her happy and become part of her world. When Greg and I finally met and he told me how nervous he was that *I* wouldn't approve of *him,* I couldn't help but fall for him as well.

The night glides by through the car window, and a few minutes later we're on Mill Pond Lane, where the houses sit on two-acre parcels and old, leafy trees line the long driveways. As we go around a bend, I see lights from a line of cars, and a valet, with glowing orange sticks, directing them into a driveway. This can't be it. Peter said *a few* people were coming. This looks like a hundred. How am I ever going to get him to break away for a romantic walk if he's surrounded by an entourage? I have a sudden, sour taste in my mouth.

"This must be the place," Cluny says. "Wow."

"No kidding. This is huge. This isn't *a few people*." Maybe I should have stayed home, curled up in bed eating Chunky Monkey and watching *Sleepless in Seattle* on Turner Classic Movies.

We crawl toward the valet in a tedious conga line of cars and then turn into a long gravel driveway bordered by hundreds of flickering luminarias. At the end is a circle and, behind it, a large, stone English country–style house with gabled roofs and three chimneys. The house looks vaguely familiar, and I wonder if I ever came here for a high school party or a babysitting job. Honeyed yellow light pours from the downstairs windows as clusters of people move around inside. The sounds of conversation, laughter, and music carry from the house to the car.

"It's showtime," Greg says as valets open the doors for us.

I pop another mint into my mouth, step out, and give my dress one final tug. Greg steps between Cluny and me and links his arms in ours, walking us up the path to the open front door and into a large foyer that's scented with something sweet.

"What's that smell?" Greg whispers.

"I think it's jasmine," I whisper back. "Probably because Sean Leeds is here."

"Jasmine?" Greg asks, looking confused.

"I'll explain later," Cluny tells him.

He obviously doesn't know that in Sean's last movie, *The Only One for Me*, he played a perfume-company executive who travels to South America to win back his ex-girlfriend. In the final scene he presents her with a bottle of Catch Me!, a perfume he created just for her. A perfume company recently produced a jasmine scent called Catch Me!, and now women everywhere are following Sean with their bottles, spraying the air around him.

A server stands in the foyer, a tray of glasses in his hand. "May I offer you white wine or champagne?" he asks. I'm not sure, but I think he's staring at the diamond cutouts in my dress. "Or, if you'd like a mixed drink, the bar is straight ahead, in the living—"

I grab a flute of champagne before he can finish his sentence. Cluny takes one as well, and we follow Greg into the living room, where he heads to the bar. There are at least a hundred and fifty people here, standing in groups, seated on the white sofas and chairs, and perched on the oversized white ottomans. The room is packed. I don't see Peter anywhere.

I also don't see anyone dressed like me. No one is wearing anything even close to this. The women are all in chiffons and silks in pastel shades; dresses with flowing ballerina skirts, dresses with layers of ruffles, dresses with jeweled necklines. I glance at my right leg and the green lace that travels down it like a wide highway. People are staring at me. I lift the flute of champagne and empty it in one motion.

"Nice house," Cluny says, looking around.

I scan the room, noticing French doors in the back that open onto a patio, and a doorway on the side that leads to a library with ebony floor-to-ceiling bookcases. I can't help but feel I've been here before.

"Does this place look familiar?" I ask Cluny. "Did someone we went to school with live here?"

She waves to Greg, who is still in line at the bar. "No, I don't think so."

I look for Peter, but I'm suddenly hemmed in by a crowd of people, and they're talking about vacations in St. Bart's, their favorite farm-to-table restaurants, the advantages of Guatemalan over Colombian coffee, the shooting schedule for tomorrow, the rewrites and the dailies, and problems with the air-conditioning in some of the trailers. I feel out of place.

I spot Brittany Wells, chatting with someone who looks a lot like Christian Taft, the actor who recently did a film about a man and his clairvoyant dog. I see Kip McDonald and Nancy Grohl, members of the board of selectmen, the town's governing body, and Wade Fisher, head of the chamber of commerce. Bibi Anderson, the cheerleading-team captain when we were in high school, is in line at the bar, talking to a man who I think is the chief of police. Bibi's gone blond, and she looks great. Dressed in a pair of flowing white, silky pants and a fitted jacket, she looks as though she should be in a movie herself. Or running a movie company.

"Let's find Peter," I tell Cluny.

We skirt a tufted, blue leather coffee table and weave through groups of people and in between couples. I hear a woman say she was *talking to Halsey the other day,* and I wonder if she means Halsey Sherman, the producer. In another group, a man in a black shirt with rhinestone buttons and a skinny black tie says, "I'm trying to get them interested in the project, but I don't think they'll invest. She only likes to do movies about divorced women over forty who come from dysfunctional families." The man next to him sips his drink and says, "I heard he only likes to do movies about married men who have affairs with divorced women over forty who come from dysfunctional families." They nod, mulling this over.

There must be a DJ, although I don't see him. Adele's "Rolling in the Deep" is playing from speakers hidden somewhere. A man walks by with a tray of wasabi shrimp and avocado canapés, and my stomach rumbles, but I look away, pretending not to notice. I'm afraid if I eat one bite, I'll burst right out of this dress.

I spot Buddy Rance pop an hors d'oeuvre into his mouth. He sees us and waves. Six feet tall and two hundred fifty pounds, Buddy still has the same round face and dimples he had in high school, making him look perennially young.

"Oh my God, there she is," he says, walking toward us. "Grace Hammond." He clutches me in a bear hug. "Great to see you."

"How are you, Buddy?"

"Pretty good. You know, same ole, same ole." He gives Cluny a kiss on the cheek.

"You look great," I say.

Buddy pats his stomach. "Aw, no. Too much pasta. I gotta do something about that." He sighs. "But you . . ." His eyes zero in on the lace snaking down my legs, and he gives me a mischievous grin. "Nice dress."

I shake my head. "Stop it, Buddy." I want to tell him, *It's all Regan's fault,* but he'd never understand.

"No, I like it, I like it." He motions for me to turn around. I oblige. Nobody but Buddy could get me to humiliate myself even further than I already have.

"Okay," I tell him. "Show's over."

He leans closer to me. "Your ears must have been burning the other day. Dave Lewendowski and I were talking about the time in middle school when we took your sneakers outside and threw them on the roof of the gym."

"I remember that," Cluny says.

"Me too," I say. "I could have killed you guys.

Mrs. Jenks got so mad when I tried to play basketball in my bare feet. And then I borrowed Sandy Farley's sneakers out of her locker and ended up with a foot fungus."

Greg walks toward us, holding a tumbler filled with ice and a clear liquid I'm guessing is vodka. "That took forever," he says. "Long line at the bar."

"Jeff Bromley's here," Buddy says. "Have you seen him?"

I shake my head. "No, not yet."

"And Marylou Felk—or, uh, Watson, I mean. And Krista Baroni, or whatever her last name is now."

"Oh, Krista's here?" I ask. I'm surprised at this. The last time I ran into her was in Manhattan, and she told me she'd been living there for two years. We made small talk about getting together, but we never did it.

"Krista's married again," Buddy says. "Living back here."

I try to wrap my brain around the fact that Krista's on marriage number two when I haven't even had marriage number one.

Cluny sips her champagne. "We heard Peter did some filming at the marina."

Buddy's face glows. "Oh man, that was fun. I got to talk to Brittany Wells. She's here tonight, you know. She asked me where the organic juice bar was in town. I told her I'd take her there, but she said she could find it herself."

"Buddy, you're happily married." I give him a playful slap on the arm.

"Just window shopping," he says. "I never touch the merchandise."

"Speaking of marriage, where's Jan?" I ask.

"Home with the kids. Sitter got sick and canceled at the last minute."

"Well, tell her we missed her."

A server walks by with a tray of olive crostini, and Buddy takes three. "You know, my Rance Marina sign's going to be in the movie," he says. "Peter told me."

"A little product placement?" Greg asks.

"Gotta get it where you can." Buddy looks at the crostini for a second before slipping them all into his mouth at once.

Oh God, I'm so hungry. I think about grabbing three of them myself, but this dress is so tight, there's just no room for error. And, with my luck, somebody would see me, and by tomorrow it would be all over town. *Did you see Grace Hammond at the party last night, wolfing down the canapés? No wonder she couldn't fit into that dress.* I look at my empty glass. I shouldn't be drinking anything either, but I've got to get my protein somewhere.

"Have you seen Peter?" I ask Buddy. "We can't find him anywhere."

"Last time I saw him, he was outside." Buddy

points toward the open French doors at the back of the room. "Talking to Regan."

Regan.

I grab another flute from a passing tray and remind myself that Regan is not Peter's type. And that she's the one person here whose dress is shorter and tighter than mine.

I drink half the glass, and we head out of the air-conditioning, onto a stone patio lit by sconces and hurricane lamps. A brick walkway leads to a pool, about thirty feet away, where the turquoise water shimmers like the ocean around an exotic tropical island, the kind of place where I imagine Peter goes for vacations or maybe even has a spare home. This would be the perfect spot for the two of us to sit, look up at the stars, listen to the trill of the crickets, and talk about old times. But not tonight, because at least thirty other people are out here, chattering and laughing, and you couldn't hear a cricket if it were sitting on your shoulder.

I scan the crowd and finally spot him. He's standing in a small group, with two men and three women, and he's dressed in faded jeans and a light-blue oxford shirt with the sleeves rolled up. He looks so handsome. In fact, he looks so much like he did in high school. He may be older, but he's really still the same boy. He hasn't changed a bit.

I don't see Regan's silver dress in the group,

and I let out a sigh of relief. "At least Regan's not there," I tell Cluny.

But I'm wrong. An instant later one of the women turns her head, and it's Regan. She's standing right next to Peter, and there's not a sliver of a sequin or a breath of spandex on her. She's wearing a one-shoulder, coral-colored silk dress with a flowing skirt that almost goes to her knees. Her *knees.* I glance at my half-naked legs, and I want to kill her.

"I take that back," I say. "She's over there, right next to Peter." I nod in the direction of the group. "In that very conservative coral dress." I drain the rest of my drink.

"What?" Cluny searches the crowd. "Oh my God. What happened to the silver thing?"

"I don't know," I say as Regan throws back her head and laughs at something.

I can't believe she did this to me again. It's just like the time I wanted to get on the cheerleading squad and Regan told me tryouts were on Wednesday when they were really on Tuesday. I walked into the gym in a little pleated skirt and T-shirt, ready to shake some pom-poms, only to find the school band in the middle of practice, marching around in lines and doing turns. I almost got mowed down by a tuba player. And then the band director, Mr. Elkhorn, stuck a baton in my hand, thinking I was there to try out for baton twirler. The whole thing was a nightmare.

"Ladies," Greg says. "What's going on? Are you going to introduce me to Peter or what?"

"Uh, yeah," Cluny says. She takes my arm and gives me an encouraging smile. "Come on. Let's do it."

It's when we walk across the patio that I feel the alcohol kick in. There's a disconnect between my head and the rest of my body, as though my head is a balloon that was tethered to the ground and has now been set loose. And my legs—they're getting out in front of me, leaving the rest of me to catch up.

As we approach Peter's group, I notice how close he and Regan are standing. You couldn't slide a credit card between them. And she's so naturally tall that when she looks at him, their eyes are almost on a level playing field. She makes a comment and brushes something off his shoulder. Now she's touching the back of his neck, bringing him closer so she can tell him something. What is she saying that's so interesting? Why is he listening? Doesn't he see who she really is? *What* she really is?

I glance at them again. Regan is leaning in farther and whispering something. My chest tightens. What if he doesn't remember? What if he doesn't see through her? I have this horrible image—Regan lying on a chaise longue by a pool at a mansion in Bel Air. It's their mansion, hers and Peter's, and I'm her secretary. It's the only job

I can get. She's dictating letters to me, and I'm correcting her grammar. *"To whom,"* Regan, not *"to who."* Or would I be calling her Mrs. Brooks? I shudder.

"Hey, you made it," Peter says, smiling.

I want to tell him, *Don't do it, don't marry her, she'll only break your heart,* but the words are trapped inside me.

Cluny introduces Greg, and then Peter gives me a hug and a kiss on the cheek. I almost lose my balance, wobbling on my heels, which seem so far away, they could be in Nepal. I feel Regan staring at me as I put my arm around Peter.

"Long time no see," I tell him, and I laugh— maybe a little too loudly. He feels so warm and strong—somebody who's got it all under control. I remember that about him—how he could work a room, even as a teenager, how the teachers loved him, how he could always think on his feet and come up with an answer. Even if it was the wrong answer, he had an answer, and he could usually make it sound pretty good. It doesn't surprise me that he can direct a movie, keep it all together, get what he needs out of everyone—the best of everyone.

When I let go, Regan is sipping her wine, peering at me from over the rim of her glass. "That's quite a dress, Grace."

I thank her, pretending to take it as a compliment, although I'm sure she didn't mean it that

122

way. "Isn't it fabulous? And look at these cutouts! *Trés chic!*"

A server passes by, and I exchange my empty champagne glass for a full one. Regan gives me a disapproving look, but I tell myself not to worry, she's just jealous. She probably wishes she had these curves. I'm feeling so good, I'm even reconsidering those olive crostini.

"This is some party," Greg says.

Peter looks around. "I can't take any of the credit. It was the production company that did it. Although my assistant, Cassie, is the one who got the cake. She said we had to do something to celebrate my birthday."

His birthday. How could it be his birthday? He was born in . . . Oh my God. His birthday is in June. That's now.

"It's your birthday?" I say.

"Yeah. Guess I'm getting to be an old man."

The group laughs. Everybody except Regan, who puts her hand under Peter's chin and says, "Why, darlin', you don't look a day older than sixteen." She bats her eyes, and I'm surprised she doesn't knock him over with the sheer force of her lashes.

Peter's cheeks turn pink. I can't believe how obvious she is.

"I hope you like my gift," she tells him. Then she leans toward me. "I brought him a little present. A set of Marilyn Monroe movies. Don't you remember how much he loved Marilyn? Or maybe he just loves blonds." She laughs and brushes her flaxen hair behind her ear, revealing a large diamond earring in the shape of a cheetah.

Marilyn Monroe movies? I'm afraid I'm going to cry. How did Regan even know it was his birthday? How did she know he likes Marilyn? I was the one he took to the Fifties Film Festival at the Dorset Playhouse. I was the one who went with him to see *Some Like It Hot* and *How to Marry a Millionaire*, not Regan. I can't believe the two of them are that chummy.

"You know," I tell Cluny, grabbing her shoulder to steady myself, "I would have brought him a gift. But nobody told me it was his birthday. Nobody told me." I'm getting teary.

"It's okay, Grace. You didn't need to bring anything. Who cares about a bunch of old Marilyn Monroe movies, anyway?"

"Are you sure? I think I should have maybe brought him something." Regan knew, but I didn't remember. I really think I need to give him a gift.

A woman in a black chiffon dress walks over and asks to get a selfie with Peter. As she's getting ready to take the shot, Regan squeezes in between the two of them.

"I have to give him something," I whisper to Cluny, holding on to her arm so I don't fall. "Can't not give him something."

"Grace, you don't have a gift. Forget about it."

"Well, then I need to think of one. I'll give him . . . I'll give him a gift from my heart." That's right. Not some stupid movies anybody can buy on Amazon. "Yeah, something real," I say, leaning into Cluny.

"Are you okay? You seem kind of—"

"Fine. Absolutely fine."

I hand my empty glass to her. Then I walk toward Peter, very carefully, in my high heels. I feel as though my legs are replacements that have been brought in to do the job of my real legs, but they don't quite have the hang of it yet.

"I have a birthday gift for you," I tell him.

"Grace?"

Cluny is behind me, tapping my shoulder. I ignore her.

I look at Peter, and all I can see are his eyes. His blue, very blue, eyes.

"Aw, Grace, you didn't need to do that," he says.

"Oh, I know, I know. But I wanted to."

"Um, Grace, I think maybe—"

It's Cluny again. I wave her off.

"I prepared this just for you," I say, pointing to Peter and rocking back slightly on my heels. "Hope you like it."

I clear my throat. Then I begin to sing, in a low, slow, breathy sort of way. I sing "Happy Birthday to You" the way Marilyn Monroe sang it to President Kennedy for his forty-fifth birthday at Madison Square Garden. She wore a very tight, nude-colored dress. It was even tighter than mine. And it had twenty-five hundred rhinestones on it. Twenty-five hundred. I've seen pictures. It was so tight, she couldn't even wear underwear. Just the dress.

I'm thinking about Marilyn and the twenty-five hundred rhinestones as I sing. *"Happy birthday to you, happy birthday to you."* I think my voice sounds good. I'm pretty sure I'm on key. I don't want Peter to think this is a joke or something silly. I want him to know how much I care, how much I really do wish him a happy birthday. And I want him to want me, not Regan. I try to sound just like Marilyn, with that breathy voice. I feel kind of like her in my own clingy dress, although I *am* wearing underwear, of course. A few people stare into their drinks, but most of them are watching me. *"Happy birthday, Mr. Director, happy birthday to you."*

I think I did a great job.

But I guess nobody else does. A few people clap, but almost everybody is laughing. Even Cluny and Greg and Buddy. They think it was a joke. They think it was funny. They don't understand that I was trying to *be* Marilyn. I swallow hard, my eyes burning. I glance around for the doorway, and then I bolt from the patio, almost knocking a tray of shrimp from a server's hands.

"Grace, wait!" I hear Cluny call after me, but I keep going. I dash through the crowd in the living room and head toward the foyer. The man who was serving wine and champagne when we arrived is gone. I see a half-open door to a powder room, and I dart inside, close the door, turn the lock, and stand there, my heart pounding. Peter must think I'm an idiot. I feel like an idiot. I lower the toilet seat lid, sit down, put my head in my hands, and cry.

I can't believe everything has gone so wrong. For a little while this afternoon, I was actually happy, and I was looking forward to this party. I wasn't dwelling on Scott or my job or my stupid ceiling. Maybe I hadn't totally put them in the back of my mind, but they weren't hovering in the front of it, either. Now they're all back again, staring me in the face. I'm alone, jobless, and stuck in Dorset. And I've just made a fool of myself in front of the one person I wanted to impress.

I grab a tissue off the counter and decide I'd better go find Cluny and see if she and Greg will take me home. And I make a promise that if I can get out of here without embarrassing myself further, I'll give up this ridiculous fantasy of getting back together with Peter, of believing he'd even want to be with me. I'll stop reaching for the stars and go back to being Grace Hammond, the technical writer, who is returning to Manhattan in a few weeks—alone.

As I wipe my eyes, I look around. The room is

tiny, but it's quiet, and the muted light is soothing. I study the curved pedestal sink, the cream-colored walls, the sloped ceiling. It's a peaceful retreat. The tiny mother-of-pearl tiles on the sink's backsplash glow with a pale iridescence, and I wonder how many pieces it took to fill that space.

There's a knock on the door, and I freeze, not wanting to give up my haven just yet. "I'm going to be a while," I call out. "Lost a contact lens." A few minutes later there's another knock. "Trying to find my contact lens," I say. "Think I'll be in here for a bit."

I look around the bathroom again. Something about the ceiling catches my attention, and then I realize the bathroom seems familiar, and now I know why the house seems familiar. I'm pretty sure my mother was the architect and that she brought me here a few times when the house was being built. If I'm right, there's a little room upstairs that wasn't originally supposed to be there—one of her shrines.

I sit up, feeling more alert, more sober, and more in control. I splash cold water on my face and dab it with a little towel. I need to see if that room is here, find out if this is the house. Opening the bathroom door a crack, I watch as a group walks through the foyer and leaves the house. The room is empty now. I glance at the stairway, which ascends to a landing and then doubles back and continues to the second floor. An antique pewter chandelier hangs from the ceiling, high above me, glimmering like a star sailors would use to find their way home.

Holding the banister, I start up the stairs. After a few steps I pull off Cluny's heels and leave them behind. At the top of the staircase, a long hallway lit by sconces and decorated with oil paintings of old sailing ships stretches before me. Music drifts through ceiling speakers—the Beatles, singing "Here Comes the Sun."

The hallway is lit, but the rooms are dark. I poke my head into each one, zigzagging from one side of the hall to the other, turning lights on and off as I go. A bedroom, another bedroom, a study, a third bedroom, a laundry room, an office, the master bedroom. Finally, I come to the end of the hall, and, even in the near darkness, I can see there's a room that's not a bedroom.

I flip the wall switch, and the space floods with light. Flowers are everywhere, color bursting around me. A little cry escapes my lips. It's a corner room, with the two outside walls and ceiling made entirely of glass. A greenhouse. This is it. Mom's shrine. I remember wondering why anyone would want a greenhouse upstairs and later finding out it was because Mom wanted it. For Renny. I take a long, deep breath.

There have to be at least two hundred orchids in here, most in baskets made of wooden slats. The baskets are suspended from the ceiling by wires, and the long, green roots of the orchids are growing through the slats, hanging down like Rapunzel's hair. More orchids are in pots, arranged on a large glass table in the middle of the room.

I spot phalaenopsis with blossoms of white and pink and purple; cattleyas, the traditional "corsage" orchid, with flowers of pink and white and yellow; cymbidiums of gold, red, and cranberry; dendrobiums with pale yellow petals; and vandas with blossoms of blue and pink and purple, so big the flowers barely seem real.

The scent is so sweet, I want to swoon, and the colors are almost blinding, from the softest pink to the brightest orange. I wish I could put my arms around the whole room. It's like something from a fairy tale. My heart is drumming, happiness rushing through me.

There's a wicker chair in the corner where the two glass walls meet. I walk over to sit down, to take it all in, to steady myself. That's when I see him, standing in the doorway, wearing a pale-gray shirt open at the neck, jeans, and a black jacket. I jump. It's Sean Leeds.

"Didn't mean to scare you," he says. "Are you all right?"

"Me? Oh, sure, I'm fine." I can feel my face turn pink, my heart race, and a prickling sensation go up and down my arms. Cluny's never going to believe this. Oh God, I hope he wasn't there to witness my singing debut downstairs.

He steps into the room and glances around. "Just checking. When you locked yourself in the bathroom for twenty minutes, I thought—"

"How did you know I was in the bathroom?" I try to steady my breath.

"I saw you go in. I came by a couple of times and knocked." He pauses and raises an eyebrow. "Did you find your contact lens?"

"My contact . . . Oh, yes. Yes, I did." I point to my eye. "Thanks."

Sean leans over the table and picks up a pot holding a cattleya. The orchid's yellow-and-pink blossoms look like bells attached to five-pointed stars. "I figured if I didn't follow you up here, I'd never get to talk to you. I've been trying to get your attention all night." He turns the pot around, viewing the blossoms from all angles, and then sets it back on the table.

My head suddenly reconnects with my body. "Really?" I manage to utter, a dry little croak.

"Sure. From the second I saw you in that dress."

I freeze. Oh, no. It's not what I thought at all. He's going to give me some brotherly advice on what is and isn't appropriate to wear to a New England version of a Hollywood party.

"Yeah, I know I made a bad choice." I look away at the spidery blossoms of an arachnis. The plant is teeming with flowers, bright yellow spotted with orange.

Sean walks toward me and puts his hand on

my shoulder. "Are you kidding? You look dynamite in that dress."

I can't believe he's saying this. I can't believe Sean Leeds is touching my shoulder. I'm sure he's just being nice. Or looking for a little attention. I don't blame him, his breakup with Sydney Parker having been splashed all over the tabloids.

"Oh, you're just being nice," I say.

"You don't think you look dynamite?"

"Uh, no. Just the opposite. Someone like Regan Moxley could pull this off with no problem, but not me."

"Whoa, whoa." His hand slides down my arm. "Who is this Regan Moxley?"

I feel every part of his warm hand on my cool skin, as though each of his fingers is breathing new life into me. "She's been hanging around Peter all night. Tall, thin, blond." I pause. *"Southern."* I pronounce it the way Regan does, with her Texas drawl.

He looks at me, head tilted. "With the toothpick legs and the lion's mane? Are you kidding? You rock that dress. It wouldn't do a thing for her. Besides, she could never pull off that Marilyn Monroe act you did."

Oh, no, he did see it. My stomach plummets, and for a second I don't know what to say. "I should never have—"

"Oh, yes, you should," he says, giving my arm a little squeeze before taking his hand away.

132

"That was the most fun I've had at a party in ages."

I can't believe he really means this, but his expression is sincere. I finally muster up the courage to thank him.

"So, what are you doing up here?" he asks.

I could tell him the long version, but I opt for the short one. "I thought I recognized the house from when I was young. I knew I'd be right if I found this room."

"It's a pretty cool room." He gently touches a cobalt-blue blossom on an orchid next to me. "Look at this thing. Beautiful, huh?"

"That's a vanda."

"A what?"

"A vanda. A type of orchid." I can't believe I'm upstairs at Peter's party, talking about an orchid with Sean Leeds.

"I've seen lots of these before," he says. "But I never knew what they were called."

"You've probably seen those as well." I point to a plant with white blossoms speckled with hundreds of tiny purple-pink dots. It looks as though a painter sat there for hours decorating them with a single hair of a brush. "That's a phalaenopsis."

"It's gorgeous," he says as he bends down to smell the blossoms.

"Oh, those don't smell like anything," I tell him. "Try the one at the end of the table, in that big pot." I point. "The one with the yellow-and-cranberry-colored blossoms."

He leans toward the pot. "Umm. That one smells great."

"It ought to. It's a cattleya."

"A what?" He looks up.

"A cattleya." Then I add, "Two *t*'s."

"Huh?"

"It's spelled with two *t*'s. *C-a-t-t* . . ." I stop because I can't remember what comes next. Is it *ly* or *le?* Neither seems right. My mind is too fuzzy to figure it out. "Yeah, well, two *t*'s. The main thing is that it's beautiful and it smells great."

"Beauty and fragrance," Sean says, glancing at me before inhaling the flower's scent for a second time.

"That one over there." I point to one of the large hanging pots. Long, narrow leaves and clusters of blooms cascade over the side. "That's a cymbidium. *C-i* . . . No, *c-y* . . . Oh, never mind."

Sean gives me a puzzled look. "How do you know so much about orchids?"

I step toward the cymbidium, conscious of putting one foot in front of the other, making sure I don't trip or do some other stupid thing. The orchid's peach-colored petals, gently striated with darker peach, are almost hypnotic. "My mother and my sister used to grow them. They had a little greenhouse. When the orchids bloomed, they used to bring them into the house and make arrangements."

"You never got into it?" Sean says, coming over to stand beside me.

"I learned enough by osmosis."

"I guess you did."

I'm staring at the orange blossoms, and I can feel him staring at me. Finally, he says, "So, what was it like growing up here?"

I look at him. "In Dorset?"

"Yes."

"Oh, well, you know. It was like growing up in any small town, I guess. When I was a kid, we skated on the pond behind the firehouse in the winter, rode bikes in the summer, went to concerts on the beach. You kind of knew everybody, and everybody knew you. It hasn't really changed much, especially in that way. That part can also be a real drawback, though."

"I think it sounds pretty nice, people really knowing one another. I'll bet they look out for each other."

"Yeah, I guess that's true."

"Your friend Cluny still lives here. That says something."

"I suppose so. It's a good place to raise kids." I step away from the cymbidium.

"You know, you're lucky," Sean says. "Being from a place like this, knowing this kind of life. L.A. is a completely different story. There's never any privacy. Too many tabloids and blogs to fill. And there's so much pressure to be part of the scene—to go to parties with people you'd rather not even be around, to live a lifestyle that becomes so second nature, you don't even blink when someone down the road puts a vineyard on their estate or surrounds their house with a six-pool moat." He picks up a yellow and pink cattleya blossom that's fallen onto the table. "I grew up in L.A., and I can tell you, Hollywood is like quicksand. By the time you realize you've been sucked in, it's too late." He gazes at the blossom between his fingers. "It's too late for me, anyway."

I don't tell him I'd trade the life I have in a second for a chance to go to L.A. and start something new. "That sounds a little dramatic," I say.

He laughs. "Sorry. But I *am* an actor."

"I'm sure there are a lot of great things about L.A. you're overlooking because you're just too close to it."

"Maybe," he says, but he looks unconvinced. He's silent for a moment, and then he says, "Does your family still have the greenhouse?"

I run my finger down the skinny leaf of a dendrobium. "Oh, no. That was a long time ago."

"No more orchids?" He looks disappointed.

"No. Mom doesn't grow them anymore. She stopped after . . ." I take my hand away. "She just lost interest." I close my eyes for a moment, and when I open them Sean is standing before me, very close. Neither one of us speaks.

A quiet piano introduction, with notes like raindrops barely hitting the surface of a pond, signals the beginning of another song, "Silver Springs," by Fleetwood Mac. I lean against the table and listen as Stevie Nicks sings.

"Pretty song," Sean says. "I saw them play it once in concert."

"It's sad, though. Stevie Nicks wrote it about Lindsey Buckingham," I tell him. "When they were breaking up." The words are out of my mouth before I realize what I've said. I was thinking about Peter and what might have been between us. I hope Sean doesn't think I was referring to his breakup with Sydney Parker.

"They say people do their best creative work when they're in pain."

I've always heard that. "Do you think it's true?"

He shakes his head. "I don't know. I'd like to think people can do their best when they're happy. But maybe pain pushes us to reach for things we wouldn't have reached for otherwise."

I wonder about Mom and all of the houses she designed after Renny died, and the houses with the shrines, like this one. Maybe those houses were her best work. Maybe the shrines made them her best work.

Sean steps closer, pushes my hair back, and gently places the cattleya blossom behind my ear.

Then, before I realize what he's doing, he takes me in his arms, and we begin to dance, moving slowly around the glass table and under the hanging jungle, the scent of orchids filling the room. Somehow my feet stay under me as the voice of Stevie Nicks floats over us.

I'm not sure whether this is real or not. Part of me is trying to figure that out, and the other part of me is just trying to take in the moment for everything it is—the weight of Sean's hand on my back, the feel of his fingers clasped in mine, the faint scent of something citrusy on his skin. He dips me, and I laugh. Then he brings me back up.

I feel like Leslie Caron dancing with Gene Kelly in the dream scene from *An American in Paris*. They dance and sway, and Gene twirls her into his arms, all against the backdrop of the City of Light and a misty, blue fog. I'm not sure I'm even breathing, but somehow I'm moving, still drinking in the sensation of Sean's body against mine.

And then I hear a voice.

"So this is where you went. I've been looking all over for you, Grace."

We stop, and I pull away. Peter is in the doorway. He's smiling, but there's something else in his face, just the smallest bit of tension, or maybe it's confusion. I don't think he's happy we're here.

"Ah, we found the greenhouse," Sean says, with

a lightness I could never muster right now. "Hope you don't mind us taking a peek. I heard it was up here, and I thought I'd drag Grace with me to see it."

"Yes, it's stunning," I say. Now I know why he's such a successful actor. I could never have composed myself like that.

Peter's eyes are on the cattleya blossom behind my ear. "Yeah, sure, no problem. I didn't mean to interrupt." He looks as though he's leaving, but then he pauses. "You know, there's a DJ downstairs . . . if you really want to dance."

He's still smiling, but his voice sounds a little clipped. Is he angry because we came up here? Is he jealous because Sean was dancing with me?

"So, are you coming back down now?" Peter asks, as though he doesn't want us up here alone. I could put his mind at ease about Sean in a second. But maybe I won't.

"Yeah, we're coming," Sean says. "Thanks for letting us snoop."

I follow them through the hall and down the staircase. Peter stops at the landing, letting Sean go on ahead. "Sean's going through kind of a hard time right now," he says. "I'm sure you've heard. Just keep that in mind."

I don't know what to say to this. Is he referring to Sean's breakup with Sydney Parker or to something else? Does he think Sean needs to be protected, or does he think I do?

Before I can ask, Peter says, "I wanted to thank you before, for the song, but you ran off. That's the best birthday present I've gotten in a long time."

"Really? You didn't think it was too much?"

"No. I think it was just perfect. Nobody's ever put so much heart into singing " 'Happy Birthday' to me before." He rubs his hand lightly across my cheek. Then he walks me down the stairs, picking up the sandals as we near the bottom of the staircase. "Your shoes, m'lady?" He gestures for me to sit down. His hands feel warm as he takes my right foot, slides it into the sandal, and then does the same with my left foot. Everything inside me tingles.

We stand up, and he looks into my eyes. "I'd love to see you again, Grace—just the two of us."

"I'd like that as well," I say, barely able to speak.

"And you'll have to come to the set. You can see what I do."

The set. See what he does. That sounds wonderful. "Sure. That's a great idea."

"Why don't you give me your number?" He pulls out his cell phone and enters the number as I recite it. "Now I know how to find you," he says. "Although I would have hunted you down if I'd needed to. I know where you are."

He smiles, and I feel as if I'm back in middle

school, in Spanish class, the first time he ever spoke to me. *¿Dónde está tu libro?* he'd asked. *Where is your book?* I'd left my Spanish book at home, a careless mistake that turned out to be a coup because I got to look on with Peter for the entire fifty-minute class.

"Yes, I'm staying with my folks," I say.

"On the point," he says. "I remember." Then, almost as an afterthought, he looks around the foyer, at the staircase with the ebony banister, at the antique chandelier hanging like a planet in orbit, twenty feet above us. He nods. "I remember."

CHAPTER 7

A conjunction connects words,
sentences, phrases, or clauses.
Most parents never stop giving advice
to their children, regardless of whether
the children are young <u>or</u> old.

I drag the beach umbrella from the garage, its yellow and white stripes faded, dust rubbing onto my shorts. Mom picks up the collapsible chairs and puts them in the canvas bag with the water bottles and the sunscreen.

"You know I don't watch much TV," she says as we walk down the driveway, heading for the beach. "But I always did try to make time for *Stat!* I thought the stories were well written, and Sean Leeds . . . well, who could mind looking at him for an hour?"

"Yes, he was on the show for a long time before he got into movies."

We head down Salt Meadow Lane, the beach bag bouncing against Mom's hip. "I saw him in something recently," she says. "On TV. A movie about a man who inherited a bed-and-breakfast and wanted to sell it, but one of the women who worked there helped him keep it going, and then, of course, they fell in love. The story wasn't

all that believable, but it did have its moments."
The road bends, and we pass Mrs. Baylor's house,
where pink beach roses wander through the
white pickets in the fence.

"*Late Check-In*," I say.

"Hmm?"

"That's the name of the movie."

"Oh, right, yes. I think that was it. Well, he is
very handsome. I'd accept his offer if he asked
me to dance, that's for sure." She laughs and her
face suddenly takes on a carefree look and I
glimpse how I imagine she might have looked as
a young woman.

We turn onto a path bordered by bushes and
brambles, sand edging its way onto my flip-flops,
seagulls circling over our heads. The smells of
seaweed and brine float on the breeze. When we
reach the end of the path, I stop to take in the
small beach—the water a bright, fervent blue,
the waves curling like crescents of lace before
breaking on shore. To the left is an outcropping
of rocks Renny and I used to climb, and a long,
flat boulder at the end, where we'd sit and try to
catch minnows with crumbs of bread on the ends
of twigs.

Only for residents of Salt Meadow Lane, Salt
Meadow Way, and Sachem's Cove, the beach is
never crowded. I spot an elderly man reading the
Sunday *New York Times* under a red umbrella, a
woman rubbing sunscreen on the pale skin of two

blond children, a group of teenagers sitting in a huddle on striped beach towels, and a few people in the water.

My mother digs the umbrella pole into the sand, and I gaze at the sound and think about Peter and the feel of his hands when he slipped the sandals onto my feet, the way he smiled and called me *m'lady*. I think about his blue eyes, that little section of wavy hair I'd love to touch, and the way his hand brushed across my cheek. I think about how every time I look at him, all the things we did together come rushing back to me. Eating ice cream cones in the gazebo on summer nights, watching movies at the Dorset Playhouse, making up songs about Mr. Teague's algebra class, daring each other to ride the roller coaster with our eyes closed at the amusement park upstate, swimming in the Banfields' pool. And the kiss on the night of the dance.

Mom opens the umbrella, defining a circle of shade on the hot sand. I sit down in one of the chairs with my copy of *Real Simple* and my water bottle, while she pulls a sketch pad from the beach bag. I watch the mother and children walk down the beach, collecting shells, and then I start to flip through the magazine. After a moment I glance over to see what my mother is drawing. It's an atrium—a circular area containing trees, surrounded by a low wall—inside a contemporary-looking house. "That's interesting."

She looks up. "What? Oh, this?" She sketches a few more lines. "New construction. On Brookfield Lane. I had a brainstorm early this morning, so I'm doing a little redesign."

"What was the brainstorm?"

She pauses, her pencil in the air. "This atrium. I think it will make all the difference in the world."

I feel my throat tighten. I wonder if it's just an atrium or if it's another shrine for Renny. It's got the feel of a shrine to me, the way that loft area did in the drawing of the barn. I thought she'd gotten over all this years ago. I wonder what she'll say if I tell her I was in her greenhouse last night. Will she tell me the truth about what she's doing?

"You know," I say, glancing at her from the corner of my eye, "when I danced with Sean Leeds last night, it was in one of your shrines."

She turns to me. "What's this?"

"The house where Peter had the party. One of your shrines was in there. Upstairs. A green-house."

A shadow crosses her face. "A greenhouse."

"Yes, the house is on Mill Pond."

Mom doesn't move. She doesn't say a word. She just studies the water, as though the house might be forming somewhere out there on the waves. "A greenhouse on Mill Pond." A blue-hulled skiff motors by in the distance, the whine of its engine like a long punctuation mark. "Yes. I remember that house." She puts down the pad.

145

"I remember the people who built it," she says. "I think their name was Adkinson or Atchinson, something like that. The wife saw that I'd put the greenhouse on the plans, and she loved the idea. The husband thought it was a waste of space. She invited me to come see the place after they moved in. She'd already bought a number of plants, and it was really looking nice. I remember some lilies that were especially lovely." The motorboat glides by, and Mom watches it for a moment. Then she says, "That was the last time I saw her. A couple of years later, I heard the house was on the market, that they were getting a divorce. It made me sad. I used to think maybe it was my fault. That if I hadn't built that greenhouse, they might still be together."

I shift my chair into the sun to get rid of the goose bumps on my legs. This is exactly why I worry about her making these shrines. "No, Mom, things don't happen that way. We can't control what other people do."

"I know it doesn't make any sense."

"Whatever happened with those people wasn't your fault. But making shrines for Renny . . . I just don't think it's a good idea. It's not healthy for you."

She looks at me with tired eyes. "I'm sixty-two years old, Grace. I know you're concerned about me, but I can take care of myself. I've been doing it for a long time." Although she doesn't sound angry, her tone hovers between insulted and hurt, and I feel bad.

"I'm sorry," I say. "I just worry about you sometimes."

"You've got enough on your own plate. You don't have to take me on as well." She gives me a melancholy look, and she suddenly seems so fragile.

I watch the teenagers as they get up from their towels and walk down the beach toward the rocks where Renny and I used to play. "They're growing orchids," I say. "In the greenhouse."

Mom's eyes brighten a little. "Really?"

"Yes. There must be at least two hundred. They've got a paphiopedilum you wouldn't believe. Just gorgeous. Tons of bloom spikes on it. The whole place was magical."

"Orchids." Mom nods. Waves break, white foam spreading and disappearing on the shore. At the far edge, the horizon stares back, blue fading into darker blue. "We had a lot of orchids, Renny and I. Do you remember how she used to grow them from seed? I never had the patience." She brushes some sand off her leg. "She was like your father that way."

She's right about that. Renny was patient. Patient and a perfectionist. Maybe not the best combination. "I think you would love how the greenhouse looks," I say. "Maybe I can ask Peter to let us come over so you can see it."

Mom smiles, and she runs her hand over my hair. "That would be nice."

We step from under the umbrella and walk toward the sound, across the line of seaweed and over the pebbles. The tide is coming in, and we wade in up to our knees, the dark water cold but refreshing, the horizon looking a million miles away.

"It's nice that you've run into Peter again, after all this time," Mom says. "I remember him as a kid. He was always friendly, always had something to say. And he was smart. I remember that, too."

I scan the water's edge, and the damp line that swallows the dry sand as the tide comes in. We used to walk along the high-water line here, Peter and I, looking for sea glass, scouring that place where the tide makes its farthest reach and pushes the sea lettuce and kelp and shells to shore.

My mother walks a few steps farther into the water, and I follow. "Relationships are funny things, aren't they?" she says. "We don't always know where or when the right person will come along."

"No, we don't," I say.

"I wasn't at all interested in your father when I first met him," she says as the teenagers run into the water farther down the beach. I know this story, about how Mom was dating a guy named Bill Adler, a lawyer she was crazy about. And how she and a friend enrolled in an evening poetry-writing class at Columbia, and Dad turned out to be the professor.

"Joanie was the one who wanted to take the class, not me," Mom says, sprinkling water on her arms. I let her talk, even though I know the tale as if it were my own. "I had my hands full working as a young architect in the city. What did I need poetry for? But she persuaded me to sign up with her." A little spray of water hits me in the face, and I brush it off my cheeks.

"Joanie tried to convince me that your dad was interested in me. Oh, sure, I knew he was flirting a little, but I wasn't paying much attention. I was so absorbed with Bill. Everything was Bill. And then one night during class, your father returned one of my poems with a poem of his own attached—'Adjacent to My Heart.' You know the one. He'd written it for me. That's when I just . . ." She pauses to brush a piece of seaweed off her leg. "When I just woke up."

"I love that story," I say, swishing my hands through the water.

"I'm just trying to tell you that you never know where love will come from, Grace. So if you really care for Peter, I hope it works out. I hope he feels the same way. But don't try to plan too much. Let life unfold, or you'll miss the chance to be surprised. Surprises can be wonderful."

I'm touched by her words, especially when I think about Renny's death—one surprise in my mother's life that was anything but good. "Thanks, Mom."

She walks back to the umbrella, her chin tilted up, her hair bouncing on the breeze. I walk as far as the high-water mark, and then I stroll across the beach, keeping my head down, looking for sea glass. Once I found a big piece of teal-blue sea glass here, the only piece I ever found in that particular shade. I brought it home and gave it to Peter, and he tied a piece of fishing line around it and hung it in the window of his room. When the sun was at the right angle, that piece of glass blazed in color, like the Caribbean Sea. I wonder if Peter still has it. I wonder if they have sea glass in L.A.

That afternoon, Dad and I drive to the garden center to pick out a tree to commemorate Renny's birthday, something we do every year. It's a belated commemoration, as her birthday was in April, but I wasn't here then.

We walk through the parking lot, which is full of people carrying flowering plants and hauling bags of soil and fertilizer to their cars. I stop to admire some bright-pink impatiens and follow Dad up a little slope, toward the nursery.

"Your mom said she needs to come here to pick up more flowers for the yard," he tells me. "She didn't trust me to get them. She's got a certain color in mind."

"I think the yard looks great already."

"So do I, but you know your mother. There's some spot that's not quite right. She wants everything to be perfect for the party."

"Maybe Mom will be a party planner in her next life," I say as we stop at the first row of young trees. I look at the tags—birch, cedar, honey locust. "I think she likes doing it."

"She'd be good at it," Dad says.

I brush my hand over the leaves of a red maple, and I can picture the tree in a couple of months, glowing in the orange and crimson hues of autumn. "What would you be, Dad? If you weren't a poet?"

He laughs. "I don't know. I've been a poet for so long, I can't imagine doing anything else. But I guess, if I had to do it differently, I might want to be a photographer."

I've looked at many of his photos on his computer, and there are a few on the wall in the hallway upstairs—a street corner caught at dawn when no one is around, a swing set in an empty schoolyard, a grove of birch trees in the middle of winter, snow falling silently. They make me feel as though I've landed in a place where someone has just left or is just about to arrive.

"You're a good photographer," I say. "Although your photos usually make me feel a little sad."

"I don't know how good I am, but I like doing it. It has its own language. And it would give me an excuse to spend more time outside."

I've seen him work on his poetry outdoors when the weather is warm. Sometimes he sits in one of the Adirondack chairs in the backyard, down by the water, scratching lines in one of his notebooks. He'll gaze at the water for a while, and then he'll stare at the notebook and scrawl something on the page. Days or weeks later it might end up as a finished poem of twenty or thirty or forty lines. Or it might end up as nothing.

I walk toward a little area with a sign that says Fruit Trees. The trees are only six or seven feet tall, and none of them are bearing any fruit yet. The labels read Pear, Peach, and Plum.

"Maybe we should get a fruit tree," I say. "We've never done that."

"I don't know how well a fruit tree would do in our yard," Dad says, "being so close to salt water. Didn't we look into this once before and figure out we wouldn't be able to grow them very well?"

I have a vague recollection of this. "Maybe they've created some new hybrids that will work," I say, sounding as though I know something about trees when I don't know a thing. I guess it's no worse than my father pretending he knows about cars.

"I'll see if I can find somebody to help us," he says, and he walks away.

I stare at the pear tree, wondering how tall it will be in a year or two. Or in another seventeen years. On the first anniversary of Renny's birthday, my parents planted two holly trees—two because you need a male and a female to cross-pollinate and create the berries. Mom thought the red berries would look cheerful in the middle of winter, and they did. Those trees are huge now. It always makes me a little wistful to see how much they've grown since that first year Renny was gone, and to know that they're still here and thriving.

Dad walks toward me, a tall man in a Martin's Garden Center polo shirt in tow.

"You're looking for a fruit tree?" the man asks. "And you're on the water? I'll tell you what should do pretty well." He walks about ten feet down the path, extends his hand, and grabs the trunk of an eight-foot tree as though he's making its acquaintance. "This black cherry here. They're pretty salt tolerant. It'll be another several years before it bears fruit, and the fruit's a little tart, but the animals love it—especially the birds and the squirrels."

"Black cherry?" I look at Dad.

"Your choice," he says. "We could get something other than a fruit tree if you want to."

"No, I like this. And Renny would have loved the idea of fruit for the animals." Every winter she put out seeds and nuts for the birds and squirrels.

"Okay," Dad says, and he tells the man we'll take it.

We walk toward the store—a white, shingled building with pots of flowering plants lined up against the outside. While Dad goes to the counter, I browse through the aisles, looking at the hoses, bug sprays, and aprons, picking up pruning shears and gloves. I stop at a display rack filled with seed packets—beets and string beans and squash and corn. I pick up a packet of carrot seeds and look at the picture of the bright-orange carrots on the front. I can see myself at eight years old, standing at the edge of a patch of dark soil, a little vegetable garden Renny and I once had in our yard. We're sprinkling carrot and zucchini and cucumber seeds into the shallow troughs we've dug with our trowels.

Dad walks up to me. "They're going to deliver the tree this afternoon."

"That's great."

"We can plant it later—the three of us. We'll pick out a nice spot. The man says it needs a lot of sun." He looks at the packet of seeds in my hand. "What have you got there? Carrot seeds?"

I nod. "It made me think about that garden Renny and I had."

He smiles. "You were so proud of that garden. You used to go out there every day and water those plants, pull the weeds."

"I guess I got that from Mom."

"I remember one morning, you went out there and came back in tears. You said you saw a rabbit and he'd eaten all of the little string-bean shoots that had just come up. You were so upset. And then Renny told you rabbits had to eat, too, and after you thought about that for a little while, you stopped crying."

I'd forgotten all about that. I place the packet of seeds back in the display. "Didn't I write a story about it? I think I did. And I drew a picture of the rabbit."

Dad looks at me and smiles. "You did. We probably have it somewhere."

I'm sure they do.

CHAPTER 8

A proper noun names a specific person, place,
or thing and begins with a capital letter.
*Restoring an old <u>Schwinn</u> can be
an expensive proposition.*

I'm back at the Bike Peddler at eleven thirty
Monday morning. The young guy with the hoop
earring is there. His hair and beard are the color
of espresso, and his face is reminiscent of the
lead singer's in an old British rock group called
Hedgehog. I walk to the counter and wait while he
rings up a man and a woman who are renting
bikes and then opens the door as they push the
bikes outside.

"Need some help?" he asks, walking toward me.
I notice a tattoo on his left wrist, but I can't tell
what it is.

"I'm Grace Hammond. I dropped off an old
Schwinn a couple of days ago. A.J. called me
earlier this morning and told me to come in. He
said Mitch wants to talk to me about the bike."

"Yeah, I'm A.J.," he says, grabbing a Dunkin'
Donuts coffee cup from the counter and taking a
sip. "Hold on a sec. I'll see if he's back."

A.J. walks through a doorway to the left of the
counter, and I hear muffled voices. When he

returns, he's trailing not only Mitch but also an older man who looks well into his seventies.

The older man's hair is thin, and what's left of it is white. He's wearing a blue chambray shirt and khaki slacks that seem to hang on his lanky frame. His face is grooved and wrinkled with cracks and lines that run in every direction, as though they're trying to escape their owner. There's something about him that looks familiar. Maybe he just reminds me of a character actor I've seen in movies or on TV.

"Morning," Mitch says with a little smile as he comes around the counter, the older man behind him. "Found any good typos lately?"

I feel myself blush. "There *are* no good typos."

He gives me a nod. "Touché." Then he adds, "I'd like to introduce you to my dad, Scooter. He loves old bikes, and he wanted to see who was fixing up the Paramount. That's why I had you come in."

Now I know why the older man looks familiar. He owned the store when I was a kid.

"I remember you," I tell him, happy to make his reacquaintance. "I'm Grace Hammond." I extend my hand. "You owned this place when I was growing up." I look at Mitch again, and now I see the resemblance—matching brown eyes, smiles that tilt upward a little more on one side than the other, and hair parted on the right, although Mitch's hair is thick, and a section of it always seems to want to fall onto his forehead.

Scooter clasps my hand and gives it a warm shake. "I still do own it," he says. "Mitch just works for me in the summer, when he's not teaching."

Teaching. This catches me off guard. I glance at Mitch, who is headed to the door, where a delivery man approaches with a hand truck piled high with cartons. "You're a teacher?"

"At Thatcher," he says, opening the door.

I wonder what he teaches. I've never been to Thatcher Academy, even though it's only forty miles west, but I've seen pictures of it over the years, mostly in magazine ads. The copy always includes the phrase *One of the oldest preparatory schools in the country,* or something like that, and there are photos of old redbrick buildings, wide, green lawns, and eager, smiling students.

The delivery man wheels the hand truck toward us, slides off the cartons, and waits for Mitch to scrawl his signature on an electronic pad.

"I just do this over vacation," Mitch says, "to help Dad out a little." He glances at his father and then adds, "Not that he needs it."

"Oh, I sure do need it." Scooter laughs and puts his arm around Mitch's shoulder.

"What do you teach?" I ask as the delivery man wheels his empty dolly out the door.

"History," he says, placing one of the cartons on top of the counter and taking out a box cutter.

"Mostly American history. You know, the world wars, the Civil War and Reconstruction, government and culture, history and myth."

"He's always been a history buff," Scooter says, wheeling a bicycle toward the front of the store.

Government and culture. History and myth. That's not what I expected. I expected that a guy working in a bike shop might teach something like woodworking or engineering. Something that involves putting parts and pieces together. I'm guessing they don't offer those subjects at Thatcher. I feel a little embarrassed, thinking of how I stood here with my Sharpie, correcting his flyers.

"You look surprised," Mitch says as he positions the knife at the corner of the box and expertly slices through the top.

I pick up a battery-operated headlight from a display on the counter and pretend to look at it as I try to shake off whatever surprised expression I might be wearing. "Oh, no. It's just that—"

"It's just that you figured me for a jock." He smiles. "And you'd be right. I do happen to love sports, especially biking, of course. And soccer. And tennis. I thought about coaching, but I really didn't want to be a coach. I'd much rather teach history. Where we've come from, who we are."

I look away, avoiding his eyes. "I didn't figure you for a jock. I just . . ." I pause, because I'm not sure how to word what I'm really thinking or if I *can* word it. He doesn't fit the mold of any history teacher I've ever had. "Frankly, all the history teachers I've had were either intellectual snobs or kind of goofy," I say.

Scooter laughs as he slides the bike into one of the racks.

"So you don't consider me an intellectual," Mitch says, opening the top of the box.

I can't tell if he's kidding or not. "I didn't say that." I put the headlight back in the display.

"Oh, so you *do* think I'm an intellectual." His expression is completely serious.

"Well, I don't know," I say, feeling a little flustered. "I mean, I only just met you."

He pulls a sheet of paper from the box, followed by a half-dozen cycling shirts made from bright, stretchy-looking fabric. "Or maybe you think I'm—how did you put it? Kind of goofy?"

"No, no," I tell him, wishing I could take it all back. I hadn't meant to hurt his feelings. "What I was trying to say is that you don't fall into either of those categories."

He removes the last of the shirts and glances at me. "You thought I was a jock."

I'm about to protest again when he adds, "And when you said you only just met me, that's not exactly true."

Oh, no. I hope he's not about to tell me I've been introduced to him several times at Dad's poetry readings or something like that.

"I remember seeing you in here a couple of times when we were young," he says. "I used to come in and help out. One day you were looking at the baskets."

"Really. When was that?"

"Oh." He tilts his head and glances toward the door. "I was probably sixteen. I'm thirty-seven now, so you can do the math."

I do a quick calculation. "I would have been twelve."

"You took about a half hour trying to figure out which basket to buy."

I laugh. "That sounds like me."

"I guess that's why it stayed in my mind all these years. That, and the freckles. I remember your freckles."

"So you helped me with the basket?"

"Yes, I did. You said your name was Grace, and you told me you'd ridden from Salt Meadow Lane."

I have no memory of this other than a vague recollection of a white wicker basket.

Scooter taps me on the arm. "Would you like to come with me and we'll talk about your bike? She's in the workroom." He glances at Mitch. "We'll be right back. Oh, and can you call Marge Ellis and see if she still wants that Cannondale?"

Mitch gives his dad a thumbs-up, and then, just as I'm about to leave, he says, "By the way, I've been checking the mail, but I still haven't gotten that party invitation."

I'm not sure if he's kidding or serious. "Oh, right." I snap my fingers. "I was going to add you to the list."

I follow Scooter into a cluttered, windowless room that smells like oil, old parts, and WD-40. It's a small, rectangular space with a wooden workbench that runs along the left and back walls.

The bench is covered with wheels, pedals, gears, and other bicycle parts, along with cans of spray paint in dozens of colors, and tools piled on top of one another. Above the bench is a row of plastic boxes with little compartments for storing small parts, and above the boxes, shelves packed with cans and jars and plastic containers reach almost to the ceiling. "You've got a lot of stuff in here."

"This is where the work gets done," Scooter says.

I look around the room, and I'm almost dizzy from the clutter—the high tool chests with their metal drawers, the plastic bins overflowing with bike parts, the pegboard with rods that hold small bags of parts and pieces. Clusters of silver wheels gleam in overhead racks, and bicycle frames dangle from hooks. Four coiled yellow air tubes, connected to an unseen compressor, snake from the ceiling to the floor, and in the middle of the floor are two bicycle-repair stands. One holds a black mountain bike; the other holds Renny's red Schwinn.

"How can you find anything in here?" I blurt out, trying to imagine working in such a mess. "I could never function in a place like this. I'm such a stickler for organization. I'd go crazy in five minutes."

Scooter nods solemnly, as though he's heard this before. "Occupational hazard," he says. "We're good with fixing things, not so good at keeping things in order. Especially in this room."

We walk to the bike stand, where Renny's Schwinn is suspended a couple of feet off the ground. "Okay, let's talk a minute." Scooter rests his hand on the cracked leather seat. "Mitch looked up the year she was built, from the serial number. Nineteen seventy-seven." He scratches his head. "Were you even born then?"

"Well, no," I say, feeling a little embarrassed that I'm younger than the bike.

"This bicycle was made at the Schwinn factory in Chicago. That's back when Schwinn owned the company." He rubs a rust spot on the metal tube that goes from just below the seat to the handlebars. "Back when they made their bikes right here in the good old U.S. of A."

I nod, trying to imagine what was apparently a golden age, as far as Scooter is concerned.

"I'm guessing Mitch already told you this was a top-of-the-line bike for its time."

"Yes, he did. That's how we got onto the subject of doing a restoration."

"The restoration. Right." He looks as though he's about to say something, but then he checks his watch. "Tell you what. It's almost lunchtime. Why don't you and I go out and grab a sandwich? Then we can talk more about the bike. My treat."

The bagel I ate this morning is still sitting in my stomach, but Scooter's offer is so sweet, and his eyes have such a kind sparkle in them, that I can't say no. "All right," I say. "But you don't have to treat."

"Nonsense," he says, straightening the collar of his shirt. "How often do I get to take a beautiful lady to lunch?"

This makes me smile. "Okay, you're on."

"Is Tulip's all right?"

"Tulip's is fine."

Tulip's, a little deli with a handful of tables inside and another cluster out front, has been around forever. When I was young the rumor was that Tulip, the owner, got her name by being conceived in a bed of tulips. I found out years later that her parents were just avid gardeners.

"We could walk over there, grab some food, and take it across the street to the green," Scooter says.

"That sounds great." I follow him from the workroom into the store, where Mitch is standing next to a young boy, discussing a flat tire on the boy's bike.

"I'm taking Grace to lunch," Scooter says.

Mitch looks up, his eyes flicking from Scooter to me and back to Scooter.

"You want to join us?" Scooter asks.

Mitch checks the clock above the counter. "I'd better not. I've got to get those Zullos finished for Watson and Crick. They're coming in this afternoon."

"Watson and Crick," I say. "You know people with those names? Like the guys who figured out the DNA double helix?"

"Well, kind of," Mitch says. "It's a husband and wife. Their last name is Creek, but they do some kind of medical research, so we nicknamed them."

"Yeah, but we don't call them that to their faces," A.J. says as he stands behind the counter, looking alarmed.

"No, not to their faces," Mitch says.

"Come on." Scooter gestures toward the door. "We'll let these guys keep working while we goof off. That's the advantage of being the owner. You can tell everybody else what to do." He winks at me.

Outside, the sun is bright, casting crisp shadows, like alter egos, on the sidewalk. We walk past Ellis Antiques, Hayes Florist, and Ames & Trodden, CPAs, with their mullioned windows and perky dormers. We approach a small, whitewashed brick building with a yellow awning, where a clothing store Mom loved, called Tracy Callen's, used to be. When I was here last fall, the place was full of construction workers. Now the new business is open.

I read the sign. "Paradise Day Spa. Don't we already have a couple of those?"

Scooter shrugs. "Guess they think they can make a go of it."

"Like that gluten-free bakery that opened in the spring. I can't believe there are enough people around here with gluten problems that we needed a gluten-free bakery. I mean, how many people in Dorset have celiac disease?"

A little farther down is Tulip's, a tan, shingled building with white shutters. On the bulletin board inside, I spot an ad for the Dorset High School summer theater production of *Legally Blonde*. Next to it is a photo. A note scrawled in the corner says: *To Tulip, A Rare Flower Indeed. xox, Sean Leeds.*

"Well, what do you know," I mumble, pointing to the photo.

Scooter steps closer to take a look. "Is he that actor? The one all the women are crazy about?"

"Yeah, he's the one."

"A customer told me she got his autograph the other day. Said she saw him at Thirty-Two Degrees getting ice cream."

"Oh, really." I look at the picture again, and my mind races back to our dance. "Well, I met him." I wait for that to sink in, and then I add, "At a party the other night."

Scooter walks toward the long deli case, and I follow. He doesn't look as impressed as I thought he'd be. I examine the bowls and platters of prepared foods—tuna salad with green olives and artichoke hearts; Asian sesame noodle salad with shredded carrots and sliced cucumber; chicken salad in a honey dressing with raisins, currants, and walnuts; maple-glazed grilled salmon, the grill marks like hieroglyphics decorating each piece of fish; and beef tenderloin, seared on the outside and, judging by the slices already cut, perfectly rare on the inside.

Scooter glances at me. "A party? Hmm. So, Grace Hammond, now you're hanging out with the actors and the movie stars."

"Well, not really. But I am a close friend of Peter Brooks, the director. He and I went to high school together. We were kind of in love back then."

"Ah." Scooter smiles. "A high school romance."

I gaze at the dessert case, full of coconut squares and maple cupcakes and Tulip's own apple crumb pie, and I get a feeling of weight-lessness when I think that it might be more than just a high school romance.

We take our place in line, and I study the items written on the three blackboards. One sandwich has a blue star next to it.

"Leed On," in honor of Sean Leeds,
who ordered it here!

Fresh-roasted turkey, tomato, avocado,
and sprouts, with Dijon mustard
on twelve-grain bread.

So Sean's been immortalized on Tulip's menu. I can only imagine how Tulip is talking up that visit. I'm surprised she hasn't enlarged his photo to the size of a billboard and pasted it over the front of the building.

I'm laughing to myself, picturing this, when Scooter says, "Let me ask you something. Do you remember what your Paramount cost when you bought it?"

The line moves forward, and I recall again the fat wads of cash Renny and I brought into the Bike Peddler. I can't remember, however, what the bikes actually cost. "No, I don't. But it came from your store. I know that. We always bought our bikes from you."

Scooter rubs his chin. "We never sold too many secondhand bikes. Only as a favor for a good customer, and only if the bike was in great condition."

"Well, that one was in great condition."

"I guess so," he says.

A girl in a striped apron takes our order—a turkey wrap for Scooter and a chicken-salad sandwich for me.

"You know," he says, "Mitch went on the Internet and found the old catalog for your bike. You might not believe this, but that bike cost almost seven hundred dollars new—back in nineteen seventy-seven. Of course, when you bought it, secondhand, it would have been a lot cheaper."

I'm shocked. I can't imagine what the equivalent of seven hundred dollars would be today—probably thousands. "Wow, that's a lot of money, especially for back then." I'm guessing the bike must have cost Renny what I paid for my new Raleigh.

Our names are called, and we grab our sandwiches and walk to the register, where Tulip is scanning items, clicking the register keys, putting food in bags. In her sixties, Tulip is a large woman with dark-gray hair streaked with lighter gray. She's wearing a pink dress, the only possible tribute to her name, and sneakers. Tulip always wears sneakers.

"Hey, Scoot," she says as we get to the register. "How ya doin', hon?"

"Just fine, Tulip. Hey, I see you've got movie stars coming in now."

"We sure do. Movie stars, fellas from the crew, you name it. We've been *bus-y.*" She winds out the word, putting the accent on the second syllable. "I guess all the restaurants have. A friend of mine saw the director and his buddies at Ernie's last night around eight o'clock, having dinner. The bartender told her they were there the night before, too."

"Good for Ernie," Scooter says.

"Oh, and the *Dorset Review* came yesterday and interviewed me," Tulip says, playfully fluffing the back of her hair.

"Ah, Tulip. Will you still talk to me after you're famous?"

"Scooter, I'll always talk to you, no matter how famous I get."

A blush blooms on his cheeks.

Tulip hands him the bag. "I threw in a couple of extra pickles."

"Thanks. Hey, you know Grace Hammond, right?"

She looks at me. "Oh, sure. Hi, Grace."

"I like the photo of Sean Leeds on the bulletin board," I tell her. "And the Leed On sandwich."

"Oh jeez, that man." She starts fanning herself with one of the take-out menus. "He's something else. Whoo! Good-looking, and so nice. Left a big tip in the jar. Oh, and Herbert Tait came in the other day. Saturday, I think it was. You know who he is, right? That old character actor? Used to do a lot of Westerns? Ordered a steak sandwich. A double! With extra fries and my apple crumb pie. I like to see a man with a healthy appetite."

Scooter pays, leaving a five-dollar tip.

"Don't be a stranger," Tulip calls after us. I don't know if she's referring to me or Scooter.

"I think she likes you," I tell him when we step outside.

He looks surprised. "Who? Tulip? Naw, she's that way with everybody."

We cross the street to the village green, where shoppers are buying fruits and vegetables and other goods at the weekly farmer's market. A banner draped over the gazebo announces the Founder's Day celebration being held downtown this Saturday, for the three hundred seventy-fifth anniversary of the founding of Dorset.

As I watch children scamper around the lawn, I remember how Renny and I played tag here on the green. It doesn't seem that long ago that the gazebo, with its filigree railing and gingerbread latticework, was base. Later, in our preteen years, Cluny and I used to sit on the bench inside the gazebo and declare our undying love for our favorite TV stars, John Stamos in *Full House* and Kevin Arnold in *The Wonder Years*. And after Peter and I became friends, he and I used to sit there and eat ice cream cones from the Scoop, which was across from the Dorset Playhouse.

"How about this spot?" Scooter asks, gesturing to a bench.

"Sure," I tell him.

We sit down, and he hands me my sandwich and iced tea. "So, about your bike," he says. "To refurbish her as a proper vintage bike—that means all the parts and labor—it's going to be around nine hundred dollars."

I'm holding my sandwich, but now I've lost my

appetite. "Nine hundred dollars?" How could it be that expensive to fix up an old bike? "Are you sure?" Either it's a mistake, or I've been living under a rock for the past seventeen years. There's no way I can afford that.

"Oh, yes," Scooter says, taking his lunch from the bag. "The price can get up there when you're dealing with a bike they don't make anymore. First there's the labor. We have to disassemble it, every nut and bolt. Take it down to the frame."

I can't imagine taking that whole bike apart and putting it back together. It seems almost impossible. And what if they lose a small part that can't be replaced? The whole idea is giving me a knot in my stomach.

"After that," he says, "we have to clean each piece we can salvage and then get the parts we can't save. Vintage parts aren't cheap because nobody makes them anymore. And then we have to put her all back together."

I look across the green, at the shoppers moving from booth to booth. Maybe it would have been better if I'd never found the bike. What good is it if I can't turn it back into what it once was? I can feel the plan to restore the Schwinn edge away, like a boat that's slipped its mooring.

"I didn't expect it could cost that much," I finally say.

"Well, there's probably a good eight hours of labor alone," Scooter says. "You know, with the rust and everything else. Of course, we can't do it all at once. Just getting some of those parts to shake loose can take a while. But remember," he adds as he puts the sandwich down and picks up his lemonade, "you don't have to do a restoration. You can fix it up with new parts for about a third of the cost."

Rust. The very thought of it makes me feel guilty. I know it's not my fault that Renny's bike was left in the garage, but somehow I feel it's my responsibility to make it right. Who else understands what the bike means—that the time we spent together on our bikes was the last link Renny and I had before things began to change?

A third of the cost sounds better, but it's still a lot more than I expected to spend. And repairing it with new parts isn't what I wanted to do. "I need to think about this," I tell Scooter, but I already know I can't do it.

Scooter wanders through some of the farmer's market booths, and I tag along, pretending to be interested but frantically going through the numbers again and again in my head, trying to figure out how I can come up with nine hundred dollars. I've got my small savings account, but that's supposed to be for emergencies. Fixing a bike isn't an emergency, even if it is Renny's bike.

Scooter buys a bag of peaches and picks out a handful of brick-red beefsteak tomatoes. I trail behind him as he inspects bottles of amber honey and loaves of crusty baguettes. I'm more than ready to leave, but he keeps wandering, past a booth selling fabric tote bags decorated with shells, and signs on bleached wood bearing sayings like *I'd Rather Be Sailing* and *What Happens on the Boat Stays on the Boat.*

We come to a little tent where watercolor paintings, many of them seascapes, are on display. Two are set up outside, on easels. Scooter glances and moves on, but I stop and take a look. One painting features a sailboat in a strong wind, the boat heeling so hard, it looks as though it might capsize. In the other painting, an old house is perched on a rocky point above the ocean. They're both nicely done, and I wonder if the artist used local scenes as inspiration. I step closer to the tent and grab a leaflet from a table out front. *Charlene Francis has been painting for more than thirty years* . . . I read the bio, slowing down when I get to the part that says she's a teacher in the Dorset public school system. Charlene Francis. *Miss* Francis? My tenth-grade art teacher?

Two women are in the tent, talking. I eavesdrop until one of the voices begins to sound familiar. It belongs to a woman with a short, bobbed haircut, turquoise earrings, and sunglasses that hang from a yellow cord around her neck. She looks mid-fortyish and a little plumper than I remember, but it's Miss Francis, all right. Or maybe Mrs. by now.

I wait for the other woman to leave, and then I step inside, where Miss Francis is straightening one of the paintings. I don't see a wedding ring, which answers the question of what I should call her. At least I hope it does.

"Miss Francis? Do you remember me? Grace Hammond? I was one of your students."

For a second, she looks dazed. Then she gasps. "Grace. I sure do. You were in one of my high school classes, weren't you?" She walks toward me.

"Yes, tenth grade."

She clasps my hand and smiles so hard, her eyes crinkle and almost disappear. "Of course I remember. Your dad's the poet. Sure, sure. But what year was that?"

I tell her it was 1998.

"That long ago."

I nod. "I was sixteen."

" 'Ninety-eight," she says, angling her head as though she's trying to grab the memory from some rough-edged spot in her mind. Then she laughs. "That was only my second year teaching. You were one of my guinea pigs."

Her second year? That can't be possible. I thought she was so much older when I had her, but she must have only been in her twenties. It's odd to think that she's probably not much more than ten years my senior and that she was new to teaching when I was in her class.

"I never would have guessed you were a new teacher back then," I tell her. "I always thought you were—well, you know, really experienced."

She waves her hand. "Oh, no, I'd made a career change. From accounting, if you can believe that. Because my parents were accountants." She puts her hand on the side of her mouth as though she's going to impart some top-secret information. "Rule number one. Don't ever listen to your parents about career advice."

"I already know that," I say.

"Well, then you're in good shape."

"Yeah, my father thinks I should be doing something more with my writing. Maybe he wants me to write the great American novel. I guess Mom would be fine with that, too, as long as I'm planning a wedding at the same time."

"That's their job, sweetie. They've been through it, so they think they know best. But, really, they're probably just trying to save you the heartaches of their mistakes."

A man stops and looks at the painting of the sailboat and asks how long Miss Francis will be around.

"Until three," she says, giving him her business card before he walks off.

"Do you have any children?" I ask.

"Not me," she says. "But that's because I'm

never married long enough." She gives me a sideways grin. "Been married four times. I practice the catch-and-release method." She pantomimes throwing out a fishing line and reeling it in.

I laugh, relieved she didn't give me some corny line about how the students are really her children. "Are you still teaching?"

"Still at it," she says. "Painting and drawing."

"Your paintings are beautiful," I tell her. "I never realized you were an artist yourself."

She draws her head in, brows connecting. "Oh, you thought I just *taught* art?"

"Yeah, I guess so," I say, feeling a little stupid. I suppose I should have known better. It's like someone assuming my father just teaches poetry, not realizing he's got several volumes of his own work and a prestigious Northeastern Poetry Society Prize under his belt.

"I'm sorry," I tell her. "You don't always know these things when you're a kid."

"It's all right," she says, waving to a couple of women passing by. "I get it."

A man in a gray suit comes into the tent and starts to browse. "So, are you keeping up with your own art?" Miss Francis asks.

For a second, I think she must be talking to the man in the suit, but she's looking at me. "Who, me?"

"Yes, you. I always remember the students who were especially talented."

She excuses herself and approaches the man, asking if he needs help, prompting a conversation about a painting of a lighthouse. I'm left to ponder Miss Francis's remark, which hangs in the air like a balloon of dialogue coming from a cartoon character's mouth. *I always remember the students who were especially talented.* How can she think I was talented? Especially talented? Sure, I used to sketch and sometimes fool around with pastels, but my drawings were never very good. At least, I didn't think so. Renny was the one with the talent. She could do almost anything.

Miss Francis takes down the landscape, wraps it in brown paper, and writes a receipt for the man, who hands her a check.

"I think you're confusing me with my older sister, Renny," I say after the man leaves. "She was good at everything."

Miss Francis looks at the check and slowly folds it in half, creasing it carefully between her fingers. "I remember your sister. I taught her the same year I taught you. Nice girl, pretty, popular, athletic, I think, wasn't she?"

"Yes."

"Uh-huh. I remember that she *went* for everything. She tried everything. She was—well, *enthusiastic,* I guess, would be the way to put it. But you were a much better artist. I'm not being critical of your sister, you understand." Her voice slows, and she looks down. "Especially in light of what happened." She runs her fingers over the crease of the check again. "I'm just being honest. Effort can sometimes trump talent, but not usually. You had—have—talent. You just didn't have the confidence."

This doesn't make sense. Renny had staked her claim to pretty much everything except maybe the written word, which was my little domain. I tried art, music, all the creative stuff, but I always felt as if I was following in her footsteps and, even then, that those footsteps were disappearing as soon as I got to them. Could what Miss Francis is saying be true? I don't know.

"I always felt kind of afraid for her."

I look up. "Excuse me?"

"I'm sorry. I shouldn't be saying this."

"No, say it. What do you mean?"

"Oh, it's just that . . . you know, I could see she was hanging around with some kids who were pretty wild. And I had the sense she was a bit lost. I worried about her. All that talent. I'm so sorry about what happened."

I feel the chicken salad rumble in my stomach. I don't want to have this conversation. "Yeah, thanks," I say. I look at my watch. "I need to go."

She reaches toward me. "I didn't mean to—"

"No, it's fine." I step back. "I just need to be somewhere."

"All right, Grace. Well, it's nice to see you," she says, and I can tell she feels bad now, but all I can do is turn and leave.

On the way back to the Bike Peddler, Scooter pauses at the corner of Main and Mockingbird. "Do you mind if I run into the pharmacy? I was pulling weeds yesterday, and now I've got this backache."

"I don't mind," I tell him. "I'll just wait outside."

There's only one pharmacy downtown. It's around the corner, and it's Woodside. I haven't been in there since before Renny died. Before the evening she went in and bought a bottle of shampoo and got back into Mom's Acura for the last time. Before she misjudged the curve and hit the tree. The police found the bottle of shampoo on the floor of the car. *Intact.* That's what the report said. The bottle was intact. But the car wasn't. And Renny wasn't.

We turn the corner, and I see the sign— Woodside Pharmacy, green letters on a white background.

"I'll be right out," Scooter says.

I hover by Grove Lighting, next door, reading and rereading the first paragraph of a faded magazine article taped inside the window, about how the right lamp can change an entire room. Can it really? I wonder. Is it that simple to change a room? Is there an easy trick like that for changing a life?

Scooter comes out, and we walk back toward Main Street. "I'm not going to fix the bike," I tell him. "At least not right now. I can't afford it." There. I've said it. I've told him, and I feel relieved. It's embarrassing, but it's not the end of the world.

He looks at me, his eyes gentle behind his gray glasses. "We could fix it with new parts. Like I said, it won't cost nearly as much."

"I just can't do it right now," I say. "I didn't realize it would be so expensive. I'm sorry I wasted your time."

He gives me a sympathetic glance. "It would never be a waste to spend time with you, Grace Hammond, or to look at that bike. Those are two of life's little pleasures." He puts his arm around my shoulder, and for a moment I almost think I'm going to cry.

"Thanks," I tell him. "I'll take the bike home today."

"There's no rush," he says.

But I know I have to get it out of there. I'll get Cluny to come with her Jeep and help me. I just wish I hadn't gotten my hopes set on making the bike beautiful, making it run, making it Renny's bike. Now I feel as though I'm letting her down. Again.

"Well, if you change your mind, we'd love to do

it anytime," Scooter says as we turn onto Main. "Seems like the bike means a lot to you. Good memories and all."

"Yes, it does," I say. And then I add, "The bike isn't really mine. It belonged to my older sister. We used to ride together when we were young, when we were really close. Before things changed. Before she started to . . ." We stop at the end of the block. "She was in a car accident," I blurt out. "When she was eighteen."

Scooter looks at me, and I can feel the questions that are on his mind. "It happened here in town," I say. And, after a moment, I add, "She died."

The muscles in his face drop, as though they are traveling south en masse. He gazes at me with quiet eyes. "I'm awfully sorry," he says. I mumble a thank-you, and we walk half a block in silence. Then he stops. "Your last name is Hammond. I just realized . . ." The grooves around his mouth seem to sink a little deeper. "Is your father the poet?"

"Yes, D. H. Hammond."

"Of course, you're *that* Hammond. Yes." His face takes on another look, one of recognition, as though he's fished something he never expected to see again out of a deep well. His eyes meet mine, a level playing field. "I remember her," he says.

Scooter lets out a sigh and gazes around the cluttered workroom. I wait for him to walk to the stand and take Renny's bike down. But he puts his hands in his pockets, and he doesn't move. "Let me ask you something," he says. "What you said earlier, when I first brought you in here, that you're a . . . what was it? A stickler for organization?"

I think back to my comment and realize I must have offended him. "I'm sorry. I didn't mean to criticize. It's just that I have this thing about crossing the t's and dotting the i's. I think it drives people nuts."

"No, no, you're right," he says as we stand inside the doorway. He takes another look around the workroom, as though he's evaluating a friend whose gradual changes, unnoticed over time, have finally become all too apparent. "I used to have this place in shape, although you might not believe it. And I mean the whole store, not just the workroom. But it's harder for me now. I'm older, and I can't do as much as I once did. And with three other guys working here, things get a little out of hand. We could use some help." He picks up a can of spray paint from the table and moves it to a shelf packed with other paints. "So, what do you think?"

I'm not sure where he's going with this.

"Here's my idea. Maybe you could help us for a couple of weeks and get the workroom organized again." His eyebrows lift in anticipation.

"You mean, you want me to work here?"

"I'm thinking we could do a trade," he says as he picks up an empty bottle of salad dressing from the back of the table, shakes his head, and throws it away. "You organize the workroom, and we'll fix your bike. We'll even do the restoration."

He'll do the restoration. For a moment, that's all I hear. The bike is going to be fixed. No, better than fixed. It's going to be transformed into its former self. Just the way it looked during its glory days, the days of Renny. And that all sounds fantastic. But then I realize I don't know the first thing about bikes. I'd be a fraud to accept this job.

"Scooter, I appreciate the offer," I tell him. "I really do. But, aside from riding bikes as a kid, I really don't know anything about them. I don't even know how to change a tire or take off a wheel."

"Exactly," Scooter says, raising his hands. "That's just my point. You'll come in here with a clean slate. You can come up with some fresh ideas." He smiles, and the gray frames of his glasses move just a millimeter.

I don't think it's a good idea, and I try to interrupt, but he pushes on.

"And if we need new supplies—you know, bins, boxes, hangers—we'll get them. I want you to make sure that every single thing in this room, from a quick-release spring to a star nut, gets into the right place. The guys will help you."

"This sounds like a pretty tall order," I tell him. "I don't want to start something I'm not certain I can do."

"I think you can do it. Will you take the job?" he asks.

I'm about to say no, but then I see a faint weariness in Scooter's eyes, something that tells me he really wants the help. And when I glance at the bike, I see Renny, riding ahead of me, down Bluff Hill, past the Madisons' house, with the apple trees in the front yard, and around the bend, to the big stone barn, and then to the bottom, where we turn onto Harbor Road and breeze past the Sea Shanty bakery and the boatyards and, finally, stop at the Hickory Bluff Store for candy. It's a ride we took over and over again, on days when Renny could have done anything, when she could have been with friends her own age. But she chose to be with her younger sister. The old days. The good days.

"Yes," I tell Scooter. "I'll take the job."

CHAPTER 9

Correlative conjunctions are pairs of
conjunctions (such as *either/or* and
neither/nor) that work together.
<u>*Neither*</u> *he* <u>*nor*</u> *she expected things
to escalate so quickly.*

I walk into Ernie's that night at eight o'clock. It's been only two days since I saw Peter at the party, and I know I shouldn't get anxious, but he hasn't called. So of course I'm anxious. I know it's a long shot that Peter and his entourage will have dinner here three nights in a row, but it can't hurt to be around if they do.

I'm wearing my favorite jeans, faded to perfection, a powder-blue sweater that brings out the blue in my eyes, and a dab of the old Chloé Innocence perfume I used to wear in high school, a scent Peter always liked. I know what Cluny would say—that it's no accident I happened to find that bottle of perfume while I was looking for some deodorant—but I'm sure it was just luck.

Ernie's looks the same as always, like a friend who doesn't change with fads or fashions. I scan its dimly lit interior, decorated in the style of an English pub, with hand-hewn beams running across the ceiling and round wooden tables surrounded by chairs with green, leathery seats. A dark mahogany bar extends two-thirds of the way down the left side of the room. As usual, there's the slightly sour scent of beer in the air, and British rock is playing, the old Rolling Stones tune "Ruby Tuesday."

I don't see Peter at the bar or at any of the tables, and no one here looks as though they have anything to do with making a movie. I do see Susan McClusky, sitting with a man who is either old enough to be her father or is her father. I raise my hand in a tepid wave. I haven't completely forgiven her for stealing my fifth-grade science homework on the water cycle.

The bartender, a man with a fringe of gray hair around an otherwise bald head, wipes the counter in front of me as I take a seat at the bar. "What can I get you, miss?" he asks.

I tell him I'd like the fish and chips. "I might need it to go, though," I say. I'm not staying if Peter doesn't show. I don't like to eat alone in restaurants.

"Anything to drink?" he asks. "We've got a special tonight on the Brittini."

"What's the Brittini?"

He points to the mirrored wall behind the bar. A wooden sign that's been there forever says *Free Coaster with Every Drink.* Next to it is a homemade sign on a piece of shirt cardboard: *Dorset Loves Brittany Wells! Try Our New*

Brittini! "It's kind of like a martini mojito," the bartender says. "She loves them."

I'm relieved to know Brittany Wells doesn't exist entirely on lemon water. "I hear they've been in here," I say. "The movie people." I try to sound nonchalant, as if the sole purpose of my being here isn't to stalk Peter.

"Couple of times," the bartender says, placing a coaster in front of me. He produces a cell phone and proceeds to scroll through his photos. "Here, take a look at this." He tilts the phone toward me. There's a picture of the bartender with his arm firmly clamped around Brittany's tiny waist.

"Very nice," I say.

"Look how little she is. I thought she'd be a lot taller."

"Yeah, I've heard that."

I order a Corona Light, the only thing I ever drink with fish and chips. I'm not about to start bucking tradition. As the bartender pours the beer, I hear someone call my name. It's Buddy, at a table with his wife, Jan.

"Hey, Grace!" He flaps his arms like windshield wipers as I walk to the table. A plate of sausages and mashed potatoes sits in front of him.

"Bangers and mash?" I ask.

"Still my favorite," he says, standing up and clapping me on the back.

I say hello to Jan, who is half Buddy's size—

petite and barely five feet tall. "We missed you the other night at the party."

She shakes her head and looks toward the ceiling. "Not as much as I missed being there. Our sitter canceled at the last minute."

"Yeah, Buddy told me."

"Have a seat." She pulls out a chair and pats the cushion. "I got the whole play-by-play on the party from Bud. He said it was really something. Told me all about your dress, too, and the Marilyn Monroe act."

I wince and sit down.

"And Sean Leeds!" Jan adds. "I heard he's really taken with you, Grace. A small-town girl and a big movie star. Wow."

"It's pretty romantic, you gotta admit," Buddy says.

"We're not having a romance."

"Not yet," Jan says. "Did he ask you out, though?"

"No, he didn't ask me out. He doesn't even have my number."

"Aw, Grace, you should have given it to him," Buddy says. "Tell you what, if I see him again, I'll let him know he needs to call you."

"Buddy, please don't do that."

"We just want to help," Jan says.

"I don't need any help. Really, guys."

The front door opens, and I watch several people walk in, but Peter isn't among them.

"Are you meeting someone here?" Buddy asks.

"I was kind of looking for Peter. I heard he showed up the last couple of nights."

Jan grins. "Maybe he's with Sean Leeds."

"Why don't you eat with us?" Buddy asks. "You can ditch us if Peter shows up. We won't mind."

Buddy retrieves my beer from the bar, and I take a seat. "I heard they're going to be shooting downtown soon," he says.

"Really? Where?" Jan asks.

"Main Street, I guess." He cuts a piece of sausage and dips it in mustard. "Man, I really hope Pete keeps my sign in that scene."

"You and your sign," Jan says as a waitress brings my fish and chips to the table.

"Hey, it could lead to some new customers. You never know."

I cut into the fish, still steaming hot, and take a bite. The outside is crispy and crunchy and the inside, white and flaky. I wonder what kind of fish Ernie's is using tonight. Probably haddock or cod. The French fries look good—they're the big, crinkle-cut kind, great for soaking up ketchup. And there's a side of coleslaw, another Ernie's staple. I don't know how they make it, but the dressing is light and tangy without being too sweet or too sour.

"Hey, get out of there," Jan says, slapping Buddy's hand as he steals a fry from my plate.

"Leave him alone, Jan," I tell her. "He's a growing boy."

Buddy pats his stomach and sighs.

We finish dinner, and Buddy and Jan order coffee. Ernie's is crowded now, but there's still no sign of Peter, and I feel foolish for coming. I wander to the back of the restaurant, past the pool table that floats under the yellow haze of a Tiffany-style lamp, to the floor-to-ceiling bookcases known as the lending library. I peruse the shelves while two men play pool, the balls clacking against one another and landing with heavy *thunk*s in the pockets of the table.

I scan the spines of mysteries, biographies, travel guides, pet care books, cookbooks, history books, and books in languages of countries I've never heard of, all of them mixed together haphazardly on the shelves. I pull out *Breakfast at Tiffany's*, which is next to a James Patterson thriller, and, even though I've read the story of Holly Golightly's Manhattan a million times, as soon as I see the first page I'm immediately drawn in again. I set it aside to borrow.

And then I can't stop myself from doing a little rearranging. I begin pulling out the books on one shelf and reorganizing them by subject. Soon I've got piles of books on the floor, including one with a bright-yellow cover that catches my eye—*Woodworking for Dummies*. I think of my father and smile. I'm scanning the table of contents—"What's All the Buzz about Woodworking? Selecting and Setting Up Your Equipment"—when someone pulls the book right out of my hands. I look up.

"*Woodworking for Dummies.* You planning on building something?" It's Mitch, from the bike shop. At first I don't recognize him, because he's not wearing his usual jeans and T-shirt. He's dressed in khakis and a pale yellow polo shirt.

"Me?" I shake my head. "Oh, no, I couldn't build anything to save my life. I was looking at this for my father."

He turns the book over and scans the back. "Oh, your dad's into woodworking?"

I picture my father and burst out laughing. "No. He's terrible with hand tools. It's sort of a running joke in my family. I was thinking I might buy it for his birthday."

"Ah," he says, handing *Dummies* back to me. "A gag gift."

"Yes, exactly."

"And what's all this down here?" He points to the stacks on the floor, a Euclidean-geometry book on top of one pile. "Are you planning to read all of these?"

"No, I was just doing some organizing. These shelves are ridiculous. I mean, *The Iliad and the Odyssey* is next to *Simplified Boatbuilding.*"

Mitch tilts his head and one side of his mouth goes up. "Well, they're both about sailing."

"That's a stretch," I say, although I have to admit, I'm intrigued by his approach. "With all of these books, they need a system. I could do a real bang-up job if I knew the Dewey decimal system."

"I'm sure you could," he says, and that smile appears again. "I assume you're checking these for typos as well?" He picks up the geometry book and looks at the cover, full of brightly colored triangles and trapezoids and shapes whose names I've long ago forgotten. "Where do you want this?"

"Hmm, let's see. Math. Why don't you put it here?" I point to the far left side of the shelf. "That can be the miscellaneous section. And, no, I'm not checking for typos. Not tonight."

"Ah, so you *have* done that before." He reaches across me and puts the book on the shelf.

"No. I've never come here and checked the books for typos. Although the last time I was here, I kind of got into an argument with the waitress over an apostrophe on the menu."

"An apostrophe? You argued with somebody over an apostrophe?" He's trying not to laugh.

I hand him a P. D. James novel. "Mysteries are on the far right. And, as for punctuation, don't you think if you're putting Mom's Meatloaf on the menu, the *Mom's* deserves to have an apostrophe?"

Mitch puts the book on the shelf. "Yes, Grace. It deserves to have an apostrophe."

I can't tell if he's serious or if he's making fun of me.

"Anyway, that waitress isn't here anymore," I add. "So maybe that says something."

Mitch gasps. "You mean you got her fired? Over grammar?"

I raise my hands. "No, no, that had nothing to do with it. She was fired a lot later. Months later," I insist, trying to recall the exact timing of the apostrophe battle and when I learned the waitress was gone. "At least, I don't think that had anything to do with it." Now he's got me worried.

"Relax," he says, a glimmer in his eye. "I was only kidding."

He's got a good sense of humor. I smile and shove another book at him. "You can put that one over here," I say. "Biographies."

He looks at the cover and lifts the book, pretending to be overcome by the weight. "*Einstein.* No wonder it's so heavy." He places it on the shelf. "Do they have any sports books here?" he asks. "Maybe you can find something on cycling, to help you get ready for the outing on the Fourth."

The bike outing. I haven't even thought about it since the day I signed up. And I did it only because of Regan. Fifty miles. There's no way I can ride that far. I'm not going. But I'm not about to mention it to Mitch. I don't want it to get back to Regan that I'm canceling.

"I haven't come across any sports books yet," I tell him, "although I've only started sorting. Anyway, I already know a few things about cycling. I've seen plenty of cycling movies."

"Movies. Oh, Hollywood again." He takes a book on vegetable gardening from the pile. There's a bright-green head of lettuce on the front cover. "What movies? *Breaking Away?*" He says the name with the tiniest hint of disdain.

He's right. That's the first cycling movie that came to mind. "Yes, I've seen that," I say with a casual tone, in case it might be considered cliché by hard-core cyclists.

"No surprise. That's the one cycling movie everybody's seen." Mitch removes a piece of paper that's sticking out of the gardening book. Someone has written *Tips for Growing Radishes* at the top.

"Oh, I'm sure," I say. "But I do think it's a good movie. You know, production-wise, acting-wise." I leave out *script-wise,* because I don't want to get caught in a trap about how accurate the story is with someone who knows a lot more about cycling than I do. Trying to sound blasé, I add, "I've seen others."

Mitch looks at me. "Oh?"

"*American Flyers*, for one." Maybe he hasn't seen that. I hope he hasn't.

"Kevin Costner?" he says, with a bit of a snicker. "Not very good." He looks at the back of the gardening book. A photo shows a woman holding a bowl of red chili peppers.

No, *American Flyers* wasn't that good. He's right about that, too. Damn. "Well, there's *The Flying Scotsman*, of course." Now I'm getting a little more obscure. I'm confident I can stump him with this one.

But I don't.

"Pretty good movie," he says. "Graeme Obree was quite a racer."

Damn again. "Yeah, he was." I struggle to remember what other bicycling movies I've seen that he probably hasn't. Then I think of one. "I liked *Two Seconds*," I say, trying to sound as if I'm not even interested in the conversation anymore.

"What's that?"

A warm feeling begins to settle over me. "Oh. You don't know that one?" I pretend to be surprised. "It's about a girl who's a professional racer. But she gets kicked off the team, so she becomes a bike messenger. It's in French. With subtitles." I grab the next book in the pile, something called *When Your Inner Self Wants to Be Your Outer Self.*

"Subtitles? French? That's too much work."

Mitch and I reach out to shelve our books at the same time, and for a second, our hands collide.

I think about the other day in the bike shop, the tug-of-war over the flyers. I move *Inner Self* over a couple of inches.

"So you wouldn't invest the time in a good movie just because it has subtitles?"

"I don't know," he says. "Probably not. I wouldn't put that much effort into a movie." He leans against the bookcase and crosses his arms. "In fact, I'll be glad when that whole film crew leaves town. Kevin and A.J. at the shop—they won't shut up about wanting to get autographs from Brittany Wells and Cici Thorne."

"A lot of people are excited about having them here," I say. "I sure am. I think it's great for the town." I run my hand along the spines of the books, making them even. "The director, Peter Brooks, is a very close friend of mine. We went to high school together. He invited me to watch some of the filming."

"I think it's nuts," Mitch says. "It distracts everybody from doing their work. And I got stuck in traffic for twenty minutes the other day because the streets around St. John's Church were all blocked off for filming."

"Oh, come on. It's only for a few weeks. And won't it be fun to see the places we know in a movie?"

"I think people are getting too carried away," he says. "The lady at the post office said the Dorset Inn is going to give tours of all the spots where the movie's being filmed. Who'd want to go on that?"

"You'd be surprised. Tons of people would. I'm sure they're counting on it bringing in business." There are two books left on the floor. I pick up *The Latitude and Longitude of Love: Where to Find Your Perfect Match.*

"Yeah, well, I think it sounds ridiculous. Driving people around in a little van, pointing out Rance Marina and the Sugar Bowl and—"

I gasp. "They're filming at the Sugar Bowl?"

"I don't know if they're filming there. I was just using it as an example."

"Oh. But maybe they will. Wouldn't that be great? Having the Sugar Bowl in a movie? Maybe it could become famous, like Mystic Pizza. I wonder if the waitresses would get walk-on parts. I wonder if they'd change anything. You know how movie companies sometimes make a place look really different for a film?"

Mitch looks at the ceiling. "Enough about the movie already."

"Sorry," I say as I place *Latitude and Longitude* next to *Inner Self.*

He picks up the last book, a collection of poems by Mary Oliver, and starts to put it in the gardening section.

"That doesn't go there. It's poetry."

"It could go there. Have you read her poem " 'The Gardener'?"

Actually, I have read that poem. I think about the first couple of lines, the narrator questioning the way in which she's lived her life. I look at Mitch, holding the book, looking at me. "Yes, I have," I say with a smile. "Okay, then. Put it there."

"You mean, you want to play pool?"

"Yeah, that's what I mean," Mitch says.

I gaze at the green surface of the pool table and the balls arranged neatly in the triangular rack. The wooden edges of the table gleam under the glow of the stained-glass lamp. I've only fooled around at pool tables a dozen times in my life, at most, but I've managed to hit some pretty good shots. In fact, I think I might even have a natural flair for the game. I wonder if he's any good. "Do you play?" I ask.

"Just a little," he says, leading the way to the table.

Perfect. That means I can probably beat him. Let's face it, the whole game is nothing more than pushing a ball around with a pole. "Sure, I'll play."

"Okay, Hollywood. Pick your stick."

I glance at the cue sticks lined up in the rack. Most of them are long, made for men. I choose the shortest one. It's black at the large end, tapering to light blue, then to yellow, and finally to a cream color at the narrow end. I like the way it feels, the wood smooth and cool in my hands.

"I'll bet you didn't know," Mitch says, taking a stick from the rack, "that pool was originally a lawn game, like croquet." He picks up a blue cube of chalk. "In the fifteenth century it was played by people in northern Europe and probably in France." He rubs the chalk over the tip of his cue stick, a fine veil of dust falling through the air. "When the game was brought indoors, it was played on a table with green cloth so it would look like grass." He hands the chalk to me.

"I know you're a history teacher, but I didn't know you taught History of Pool."

"Oh, sure," he says. "It's an advanced-level course, though. Juniors and seniors only." He walks to the triangular rack on the table and adjusts a couple of the balls. "Do you know how to play eight ball?"

That's the only game I do know. You have to sink all of your balls as well as the eight ball before your opponent does. "Of course," I tell him.

"All right, then." He slides the rack back and forth, the balls forming a more compact triangle.

I watch as his hair flops over his forehead and he sweeps it back with a quick gesture. He picks up his cue as if he's been hanging out in smoky pool halls his entire life rather than teaching history. I know exactly what he's doing. He's showing off. And if he thinks this is going to intimidate me, he's wasting his time. He pulls the rack away with a swift movement, like a magician lifting a cape. "Shall we flip a coin to see who goes first?"

"Absolutely," I tell him. "I'll take heads."

He pulls a nickel from the pocket of his khakis and flips it. "Heads."

"Okay." I pick up my cue stick and move toward the end of the table opposite the balls. I lean over the edge of the table the way I remember Tom Cruise doing it in *The Color of Money*. I'm ready to take my break shot when Mitch says, "Wait a minute. Time out. You can't hold a cue stick like that."

I turn my head, the rest of my body still hovering over the table. "What?"

"Let me show you how to hold it."

"Hey, I was right in the middle of my shot. Do you think I'm one of your students?"

He laughs. "I think I could teach you a few things."

"Oh, really?" I say.

"Really." He walks over and stares me straight in the eye. He takes the stick from my hands. "Here's how you hold it." He leans over the table, positioning the narrow end of the stick so it's floating in the crook between his thumb and index finger.

"That's how I *was* holding it," I say. "You're doing exactly what I was doing."

"No, I'm not," he says. "You were doing some crazy thing with it. Here, I'll show you." He stands beside me and places the stick in my hands. I feel his shirt brush against my bare arm. It's soft, as though it's been washed a thousand times. He smells like fresh soap and clothes hanging outdoors on a line.

"Or you can hook this around," he adds, raising my index finger so it forms a loop around the cue stick. "Whatever's more comfortable."

For an extra second or two, he stands there, next to me, with his hand on mine. "Okay, I think I've got it," I say at last, leaving my index finger around the cue stick.

Mitch steps away. I take a deep breath and exhale. I bring my stick back and then forward, giving the ball a serious jab. It flies across the table and, with a loud *crack,* hits the balls at the other end. They scatter, spinning and clacking, colliding with one another, bouncing off the rails, and rolling around in search of places to land. One disappears into a side pocket with a resonating *thunk,* and another drops into a corner pocket, followed by another *thunk.* It's a satisfying sound.

I can't resist clapping. "Wow, I got two in!" I'm proud of myself.

"Not bad," Mitch says, looking at the table. "You sure you haven't played much before?"

"Well . . ." I look down and pretend to fidget.

"Actually, I spent most of my childhood in pool halls. My father tried to make a living at it, and we traveled from town to town, going from one seedy hotel to another, so he could play in tournaments." I look up and gaze across the room. "It was tough." I let out a sigh. "I was just too embarrassed to tell you."

Mitch snaps his fingers. "I *knew* you were trying to hustle me."

I point to a solid-yellow ball close to a corner pocket. "I'm going for that corner."

"Then you'd say, *One ball in the corner pocket.* Didn't your father teach you the rules?"

"Of course he did. I was just testing you. I happen to be one of those people who like to follow the rules."

"Ah," Mitch says. "So you'd never be an anarchist."

"Oh God, no," I say as I get into position for the shot. "At least not unless it was the last job available and the benefits were really good."

I hear him laugh as I line up my shot. I slide the stick back and forth a couple of times and then gently tap the cue ball. It creeps toward the yellow ball, and there's a quiet *clack* as the yellow ball slides into the corner pocket. For a moment it looks as though the cue ball will follow. I clutch my stick, anticipating the worst, but the cue ball stays on the table.

"That was so close!" I throw my hand over my

heart, an unexpected rush of excitement pulsing through me.

"You saved it," Mitch says. "Great shot!"

I hear applause. Buddy and Jan and Ruth and Keith Frye, who own Frye Sporting Goods, are standing by the sofa, watching me.

"She's a hustler," Mitch says, crossing his arms.

Jan gives me a thumbs-up. "You go, girl. Maybe you'll beat him."

"If you beat me," Mitch says, "you'd better be prepared to play again. Grudge match."

"Not tonight," I say. "I need some sleep. I start work tomorrow, remember?"

He looks surprised. "Oh, you got a job?"

"Well, yeah," I tell him. "I'm starting in the workroom tomorrow morning." I study the pool table for my next move, but I don't see any easy shots.

"What's the workroom?"

I turn to him. "*Your* workroom. At the shop. Your dad hired me?" I say the last part like a question because I guess now it is in question.

"Hired you. To do what?"

"To organize it." I walk around the table. There's a red ball very close to one of the corner pockets. "In exchange for restoring my bike," I add. "I'm going to be working there for a couple of weeks. Didn't he tell you?"

"No, he must have forgotten," Mitch says as he

holds his cue stick in a vertical position, like a spear.

"Three ball to the corner pocket," I say. But this time, I don't make the shot.

"Oh, too bad," Ruth says.

"Yeah, well, I guess that's it for me." I've lost my turn.

Mitch picks up his cue stick and walks around the table, his eyes never leaving the green surface. "So, when was this arrangement made?" His voice has taken on the tone my mother used to adopt when I didn't put my dishes in the dishwasher for the third time in one day.

"We arranged it today," I say. "I'm sure your dad meant to tell you. It happened just this afternoon."

He points across the table with his stick. "Ten ball in the corner pocket." His tone is all business.

I look at the shot he wants to make, and I wonder if he's going for a bank shot. That seems like the only thing he can do, but even I know that's not an easy shot for a beginner. He'll never make it.

He leans over the table, positions his cue stick, and lets it go. The cue ball crosses the table, hits my side, returns to Mitch's side, and knocks the ten ball right into the pocket. *Thunk.*

Wow.

Buddy and Jan and the Fryes clap. I'm about to

clap as well when Mitch looks at me from across the table and says, "So what is it you're supposed to be doing in the store?" His tone is almost accusatory, as though he's cross-examining me. My mind is racing, trying to figure out why he's getting upset. I don't want to be in the middle of a father-son conflict.

"Your dad just wants me to organize the workroom," I say. "And I thought maybe I could even do a little tidying up in the store as well. Your dad said—"

"My dad doesn't always know what he's saying." His voice is louder now.

I take a step back. "Excuse me?" I try to gather my thoughts. I know I need to come to Scooter's defense, but this is all moving so quickly. I feel as if I'm losing control of the situation. "I think your father knows exactly what he's saying," I finally say.

Ruth and Keith Frye slip away, and I'm guessing Buddy and Jan probably want to do the same. But then Buddy comes to my defense.

"I've known Grace a long time," he says. "She's good at organizing stuff. Really good. I remember her notebooks in high school. Her notes were so neat, they looked like she typed them."

"I did type them."

"See?" Buddy says. "She did type them."

Mitch picks up his cue stick again and walks

around to my side of the table. "Fourteen ball in the side pocket," he says, and he takes his shot, the green and white ball rolling obediently into the pocket. *Thunk*. "Twelve ball in the corner," he says. His stick flies, the twelve ball ending up in the corner pocket. *Whack*.

I'm speechless, both at his talent with a pool stick and his sudden anger toward me.

"I think I know my father a little better than you do," he says, chalking his stick again. "He never should have made that kind of deal with you." He steps closer to me. "No offense. But you don't know the first thing about bikes, so how could you possibly organize anything in a bike shop? It's like somebody asking me to organize a dentist's office." He's standing very close, and the fresh-air smell is gone, replaced by something a little stale.

"Well, *I* could organize a dentist's office," I say, not backing away.

"Oh, okay, great. Remind me to give you Dr. Howard's number so you can go over there after you do our place."

This is ridiculous, the two of us sparring like children. "Why don't you just talk to your dad about this whole thing?"

"Oh, I will," he says, the edge still in his voice. "I'll definitely discuss it with him. I'm tired of people taking advantage of him."

I clutch my cue stick. "What?"

"You heard me. Telling him you can redo the workroom so he'll fix your bike for free. Admit it. You're doing this to get a free repair. You're taking advantage of an old man."

"Mitch, you don't really believe that," Jan says, stepping closer to me. "Come on. That's not like Grace."

"Yeah, that's crazy," Buddy says. "She would never do that. You're getting carried away here."

I glare at Mitch. The light above the table casts an eerie orange glow over his face. I feel a vein in my neck start to twitch. "I'll tell you what," I say, my tone cold and clipped. "When I come into the shop tomorrow, I'll ask your dad what he wants to do. As far as I'm concerned, it's his decision, not yours." My hands shake as I lay the cue stick on the table. "But you're totally wrong about me. And, from the looks of your pool game, I'd say the only hustler around here is you!"

CHAPTER 10

A possessive noun shows ownership.
*The <u>woman's</u> persistence
cannot be underestimated.*

My mind reeling, I race through Ernie's, and when I step outside I plow straight into a man on his way in.

"Sorry," I say. "That was my—"

"Grace, it's you." He smiles.

"Peter." I let out a deep breath, and then I throw my arms around him.

"Hey, are you all right? What's the matter?"

"I'm fine, I'm fine," I say, letting go. "Just glad to see you." I feel a little embarrassed, but his kind face is such a welcome sight after that Mitch. And he looks so handsome in his jeans, his faded green T-shirt, and his brown cowboy boots. It must have taken someone a year to tool the detail on those boots.

"I was going to call you today," he says. "But I was in the middle of a thousand disasters, and the time just got away from me." His eyes light up. "And now here you are."

I'm caught in his smile, and I think how wonderful it feels to have him back in Dorset, to see him in front of Ernie's. And this time he's alone. "I'm sorry you had a bad day," I say. "What happened?"

He frowns. "It's more like what *didn't* happen. The producers were giving me grief about Cici Thorne, telling me she's expensive and she's not in enough of the scenes." He blows a puff of air through his cheeks. "Believe me, she's in enough of the scenes. And then a company that paid for a product placement, supposedly with no strings attached—now they also want us to *mention* the product. In the middle of a scene where Sean and Brittany are kissing on the beach. It's antifreeze. For cars. How do you write that into a love scene?"

I can't help but laugh. "I can think of a couple of ways you could get it in there. Metaphorically, of course."

"They don't want metaphors."

He glances at the door, and I try, subtly, to block his way. I can't go back in there. I don't want to run into Mitch again. "It sounds like a horrible day."

"Yeah, on top of all that, we had a ton of rewrites, so we ran way over."

"Rewrites?" I ask, pretending I don't know what he's talking about and wondering how long I can keep him out here.

"Script rewrites."

"Got it."

He glances at the door again. "Are you going back in?"

"Uh, no, I wasn't planning to. Why, are you?"

He looks a little confused. "Well, yeah. That's why I'm here."

"Oh, right." I move away from the door. "You know, it might not be such a good idea to go in there."

"Why not? What's wrong with Ernie's?"

"It's crawling with people tonight. You wouldn't get a minute's peace, with all the fans."

"People don't tend to recognize me, Grace. Not the way they do Sean or Brittany."

"Oh, no, they would. In fact, I overheard a lot of people say they wanted to get your autograph or get a selfie with you."

"Really?" He smiles and glances around, as though some of them might be out here right now. "Well, I don't mind that. This is my hometown. If people want autographs or selfies, they can have them."

"Yes, but it's so crowded. You wouldn't be able to get your food for at least an hour."

He looks as though he's considering this. Then he says, "But it's Monday night. How crowded can it be?"

"Oh, extremely crowded," I say. "There's a . . . a motorcycle gang that always comes on Monday nights. From up north."

He gives me a skeptical glance. "A motorcycle gang?"

"Yes, so it's crowded *and* dangerous. You really shouldn't go in there."

He looks toward the parking lot. "I don't see any motorcycles."

"Well, the thing is, on Monday nights they like to walk."

"The motorcycle gang members walk?"

"Absolutely. That's how they get their exercise."

He scratches his cheek and studies me. "Ah, well, I think I'll take my chances. Come on, I'll buy you a drink if you've already had dinner." He reaches for the door.

I block the way again, this time not so subtly. "Okay, but there's something else."

He steps back. "Now what?"

"Well, it's . . . the food." I grimace. "It's not what it used to be. I really think we should go somewhere else."

"But I was here just last night. And the night before. The food was great."

"That may be." I give him a concerned look. "But it's like Russian roulette. You never know when you're going to get that bad meal. I heard a guy had to get his stomach pumped last week."

"From eating here?" He looks alarmed.

"Just saying."

Suddenly the door swings open and bumps against us. It's Mitch. He looks at me as if he's surprised I'm still here, and then he glances at Peter.

"Excuse me," he says gruffly as he steps between us.

Peter watches him walk across the street. "Who's that?"

"Just a guy I know."

Mitch stops and glares at me. "Yeah, I'm the pool hustler!"

"I didn't say that."

"Oh, yes, you did!" He heads toward the parking lot.

"That must have been some game of pool," Peter says.

I take a deep breath and step toward the door. "Okay, shall we go in?"

"I thought you said the motorcycle gang is in there."

I glance at my watch. "They're probably gone by now. Out the back way. I forgot, they come in for the early-bird special."

"What about the food? Russian roulette? Stomach pumping?"

I laugh and roll my eyes. "Oh my God, I was just kidding. The food's great here." I open the door before he can say anything else.

Sitting at the bar for the second time tonight, I study the list of desserts while Peter scans the dinner menu. There's a blackberry and apple crumble, which has a fruit filling and a crunchy topping; a treacle tart that's kind of like a pie, with buttery pastry and a thick filling made with syrup; trifle, with layers of custard, sponge cake, jelly, and whipped cream; and a few strictly American desserts, including a hot fudge sundae. Peter orders the fish and chips, and something warm stirs in my heart. It's just like old times. I order the sundae.

"They still have that?" Peter says, lowering his voice and placing his hand on my wrist. "With the walnuts and that really great whipped cream?" He stares straight into my eyes, as though this is the most important question in the whole world. I know he's just kidding around, but I feel as though I'm on fire.

"Yes, they do," I reply, my voice low and husky. And then I add, barely above a whisper, "With the walnuts and whipped cream."

"Mmm," he says. "And the homemade fudge sauce they used to serve in the little gravy boat?" He tilts his head. "They still have that, too?"

I'm trapped in his gaze. "Yes. They have the homemade fudge sauce."

"And it's the same?" His hand lingers on my wrist. "Just the same?" he whispers.

"It's exactly the same," I whisper back, hoping he won't let go. "Some things never change."

He leans in a little closer. "That's good to know."

I think maybe he's going to kiss me, but then the bartender comes back. "Did you say you wanted coleslaw with that order, sir?"

Peter pulls away, releasing his hand from my

arm. "Oh, sure, yeah," he says. "Coleslaw would be good."

I can still feel the warmth of his hand and his face so close to mine. I want to get him out of here. I want to go somewhere quiet, where we can be alone.

"Why don't we take the food to my house?" I say. "My parents are having dinner at a friend's, and we'll have a much more comfortable place to talk."

"I'd love to," he says, without a second's hesitation.

I can barely sit still waiting for our food. Finally, the bartender hands Peter his bag of fish and chips. Then he puts separate containers of vanilla bean ice cream, whipped cream, candied walnuts, and hot fudge sauce in another bag for me.

"Do you remember where the house is?" I ask when we step outside. "At the end of Salt Meadow?"

"Of course," he says, and I realize I'd forgotten how his eyes get just a little crinkly when he smiles. I'd forgotten how his nose has the tiniest angle to it, as though it's positioned one or two degrees off kilter. It's something you'd never notice unless you looked closely.

"Okay, then," I tell him. "I'll see you there."

I watch him walk to a light-blue Audi convertible and open the door. I can't believe he's getting into his car and coming to my house. It's been so many years. My mouth is dry.

I'm parked farther back in the lot, and when I drive to the front, I see that Peter is waiting for me, his headlights throwing halos on the pavement. I drive around his car, and he follows me. As we leave Main Street, I roll down the windows and breathe in the night air. The temperature has dropped to about seventy degrees. At a stoplight, crickets chirp a steady rhythm, the heartbeat of summer. It's the same sound that hummed around the two of us on nights just like this, when we'd sit on the village green and talk about rock bands and where we wanted to live when we grew up and how our parents didn't understand anything. And now it's all coming around again.

We arrive at the house a few minutes later, and Peter opens my car door and escorts me up the front steps, where moths bat at the lanterns. When we step inside, the sconces in the foyer cast a warm yellow glow over the mirror, the Chippendale chest, and the hooked rug of lavender snapdragons. The house has its own peculiar scent of salt air, well-worn wood, and a hint of lemon that I think comes from the dusting spray the housekeeper uses. I wonder if Peter notices it, too.

He looks around, taking in everything. "I remember all this. The stairway, this foyer." He taps the top of the chest. "Even this Chippendale chest. Didn't your parents used to keep batteries in the top drawer? I remember getting some for a flashlight one night during a storm when the power went out and we were doing our homework together."

I open the drawer. He looks inside and picks up a package of triple As. "Still there," he says.

"Not much has changed," I tell him. "They've bought new furniture here and there, of course, and they renovated the kitchen and bathrooms last winter, but the bones of the house are the same." We walk down the hall, toward the kitchen. "It's kind of surprising my mother didn't go blasting through the walls, the way she does in other people's homes. I'm sure she would have if it weren't . . ." I let my words hang in the air. *If it weren't for Renny.* That's what I was going to say. That she likes to keep the house pretty much the way it was when Renny was alive. But I say nothing.

"Is your mom . . . ?" He pauses as he stands in the kitchen doorway. "Wasn't she an architect?"

"Yeah, she still is." He hasn't forgotten a thing. I wonder if he knows how fast he's running away with my heart, right here, right now.

He takes a couple of steps into the kitchen, stops, and looks around. "Wow, I remember being in this room so many times."

I put the food on the table.

"How many bags of popcorn did we microwave in this kitchen?" he asks.

I laugh as I take a plate and a couple of

bowls from the cabinet. "I couldn't even guess. A hundred?" I put his fish and chips on the plate.

"Remember that science project you and I worked on in here?" He looks away. "Something to do with magnesium and the growth rate of plants. Your mom was really interested in it. Didn't she love gardening?"

I can't believe he remembers that science project. I haven't thought about it in years, but now a vision hovers in front of me—green barley seedlings, like little sprouts of grass. "I think that was in Mr. Tomasino's class. Chemistry or biology, maybe. Wasn't it?" I pull out a couple of chairs.

"Yeah, Tomasino," Peter says as we sit down at the table. "Remember the bets people had about whether or not he wore a hairpiece?" He cuts into a piece of fish, and I watch the steam rise.

"He definitely wore a hairpiece."

Peter nods. "I'm with you on that one."

I remove the containers from the ice cream sundae bag and I open each one. Then I dip the tip of my spoon into the whipped cream. "Wow, that's as good as ever." I can't help but marvel at how thick and sweet it is.

I spoon some of the ice cream into one of the bowls. Then I grab a handful of walnuts, which look as if they've been seared in brown sugar, and drop them on top of the ice cream. I follow that with fudge sauce and a mound of whipped cream.

"Oh my God, it's fantastic," I say after taking a bite. I glance at Peter, but he's looking toward the windows, at the sapphire darkness beyond. A motorboat glides by, its green starboard light winking at us.

"Dorset High," he says, his voice far away, as though he's tunneled deep inside an old memory. "We had some crazy times at that place." He shakes his head and watches the motorboat until the light is gone. "I really hated to leave here when we moved. I was so angry at my parents for taking us away. And I couldn't stand Arizona." He puts down his fork. "It probably wasn't a bad place, but I hated being there because everyone I cared about was here."

I wonder, is he talking about me? "It had to be hard to leave the place where you grew up," I say, rushing to fill the silence.

He looks at me. "I'm sorry we moved at such a bad time, Grace. So close to Renny's . . ." He pauses for a second. "Renny's accident."

Fifteen days, I want to say. *You moved exactly fifteen days later.* But I don't say it. "It wasn't your fault you had to leave then."

"No, but I should have been better about keeping in touch." He gazes at the copper pots dangling over the island. "With everything you must have been going through, I should have done more. I just didn't know what to say." He reaches out and touches my hand, runs his fingers

219

over mine. "I really didn't know what to say." His voice is so quiet, I barely hear the words.

"Of course you didn't, Peter. How could you? I'd shut down. With everybody. My parents, you, Cluny. Everybody." My chest aches. I feel as if everything is slowing down around me.

He takes my hand in his, and my fingers begin to perspire. "You know, that day we said good-bye?" I ask, trying to steady my breath. "I was angry. I was angry at Renny. I was angry at myself, my parents. I was angry at the policeman who came to the house and told us, and I guess I was angry at you, too. I know it doesn't make any sense." I feel tears coming on, and I do my best to hold them back.

"It's all right. I get it, Grace. I know." He leans in, a little closer. "It was an awful thing that happened. She was your sister."

No, it was more than that, I want to say. *It was a lot more than that.* I wonder if everyone walks around feeling guilt over the death of a loved one. *If only I had (fill in the blank), if only I was (fill in the blank).* They're like boulders, these thoughts, weighing me down. But if I tell him what really happened, what will he think of me? *The truth will set you free.* People say that all the time, but does it really work that way?

"Yes," I say. "She was my sister."

We sit there for a while, the house creaking and settling around us, katydids buzzing in rhythmic bursts beneath the open windows. The bell on a buoy rings in the distance.

"You want to know the really weird thing?" Peter says.

I look at him.

"My dad had to leave right away, to start his new job in Phoenix, but my mom and Randy and I could have stayed here a while longer. Mom could have taken her time moving." He picks up a spoon and absently turns it between his fingers. "The reason why she insisted we pack up every table, bookcase, plate, and toothbrush and go out to Arizona with my dad was because she thought he was having an affair with somebody in the Phoenix office. She didn't want him out there alone." He takes the spoon, slowly stirs the river of ice cream and fudge sauce in my bowl, and then lets the spoon drop. It hits the bowl with a *clank.*

"Oh, no," I say, and I can't help but see the sadness in his eyes. That famous Brooks smile is gone.

He leans back in his chair. "My poor mom. She should have just let him go. I mean, he *was* having an affair, and they ended up getting divorced anyway. So all of us leaving Dorset and rushing out there was for nothing. I guess I still haven't forgiven him for that."

"I'm sorry," I tell him. "That must have been really tough on you and Randy."

"We wanted to come back here," Peter says, his eyes returning to the window. "But Mom was so demoralized. Said she needed a fresh start. That's how we ended up in California. She had a friend in L.A., who got her a job at a post-production company."

"Is that how you got into making movies?"

"That was a lot of it, yeah."

I wait for him to go on, but he doesn't. After a minute, he gets up and walks to one of the windows and presses his face to the screen. "I remember you had a great view from here, being on the point and all."

"Yeah, it's hard to see much now. It's pretty dark out there. We do have lights, though."

I walk to the wall and press a switch, illuminating the oak and maple trees on the lawn behind the house, sending a glow down the yard, past the place where we used to hang the hammock, all the way to the sound, where the light ruffles the water. A crescent moon, like a thin scrap of silver, shines in an ink-black sky.

"That's nice," he says. "Really pretty."

I stand beside Peter and gaze at the view. "We used to have a hammock between those two maple trees." I press my finger to the screen. "It was right there. I used to love to nap in it on summer afternoons. There's always a nice breeze from the water."

"You know, I don't remember the yard being

this big. It's pretty dramatic, the way the lawn slopes down to the water like that."

"You sound like a movie director."

He looks at me and smiles. "You guys had a float out there. Do you still have it?"

"No, that was a long time ago. It got old, and my parents never replaced it." I look straight out, to where the float was once anchored, and I can almost see it bobbing in the waves under an orange sun, feel the hot, gray paint flaking under my feet. "Renny and I used to love jumping off that thing when we were kids. She was a great swimmer."

I turn to Peter, and our eyes meet. "She was a talented girl," he says. "A good athlete. I remember that."

I look away as my eyes mist over.

He chuckles softly and says, "You know, I was always a little jealous because you guys lived right on the water and had a float. I mean, how many people had a float?"

"You were jealous over a float?"

"Sure."

"Well, now you have a house on the beach, in Malibu."

"Yeah, but I don't have a float."

He gives me that crinkly-eyed smile, and I have to laugh. "We have an old picture of me and Renny on the float. It's in the family room. Do you want to see it?"

"Sure, I'd love to. Will you show me the rest of the house, too?" He looks around the kitchen again, even studying the ceiling, and I remember his penchant for details.

"Of course," I say. "Follow me."

I lead him through the dining room and the living room. In the library, he stops to admire the fireplace. He walks toward one of the two bookcases full of photographs. "What's this from?" He points to a photo of me in an old green-velvet ball gown Mom found at the thrift shop. My neck is draped in fake jewels.

"That's when I played Ophelia, in *Hamlet*. Senior year."

He grins. "Love that costume."

"I was trying to copy what Helena Bonham Carter wore in the movie."

He turns to the coffee table, where the border of a large jigsaw puzzle has been partially assembled. The photo on the puzzle's box shows the Grand Canal in Venice—motorboats and gondolas on a river of green-blue, bounded by ancient buildings that sparkle, orange and golden, in the sun.

"My dad does those."

"Impressive," Peter says. He picks up a puzzle piece, bringing it closer to his eyes. "What's this? It looks weird. And it's not made of the same material as the others."

"I know. It's some kind of lightweight wood.

My mom gets the puzzles at the thrift shop. She likes to buy things there and give them a new life. You know, reduce, reuse, and recycle? If there's a piece missing, she makes her own replacement."

I think about the pair of carved wooden peacocks, originally in eye-numbing purple, that Mom transformed into lifelike creatures. They grace the dining room today. And the old wooden picture frames she restored and made look like cherished antiques. They hang in the upstairs hall, filled with family photos—all except for the two frames that still display the pictures that came with them, faded 1940s-era strangers.

"So she made this part for the puzzle?" Peter asks, becoming suddenly still.

Now I wish I hadn't tried to explain. He probably thinks she's nuts. "I know it's kind of weird, but she—"

"That's pretty inventive," he says. "Really inventive."

"Yes, I guess it is," I say, relieved. I give a little tug at the sleeve of his T-shirt, my hand brushing his arm. "Let's go into the family room. That's where the photo is. The one of the float."

I lead him down the hall, and when we step into the family room, he stops and stares straight ahead, at the far wall. "Whoa. I do remember that—the Steinway." He rubs his hands together and approaches the baby grand piano. "Nice." Pulling out the bench, he takes a seat and runs his palms over the fallboard covering the keys. "Does anybody play?"

"No, not since Renny died," I tell him as I stand beside the piano. "She was the one who really played. I tried, but I was never very good. A little 'Für Elise,' a little 'Moonlight Sonata.' Just the first movement, though."

"Nothing wrong with that."

"Do you still play?"

"Not very often." He starts to open the fallboard but then hesitates. "Do you mind?"

"No, go ahead."

He looks at the keys for a moment, as though he's admiring them or maybe just getting acquainted with them. Then he sits down and plays a few arpeggios, the notes singing up and down the keyboard, and I wonder how someone who doesn't play very often can sound that good. "I don't think it's out of tune," he says.

"That's because my mom has it tuned. I said it never gets *played;* I didn't say it never gets tuned."

"Ah, I understand," he says.

And then he does something incredible. He starts to play "Claire de Lune." A memory wells up inside me—ninth grade, the empty Dorset High auditorium, and Peter seated at the grand piano, playing this same piece of music, while I'm standing in the doorway, listening. He doesn't know I'm there, but he's hypnotizing me, the notes cascading up and down the keyboard, out into the auditorium, carrying me away to some distant place, a garden of moonlight and wisteria.

I'd heard him tinker around on the piano plenty of times before that day, mostly with jazz compositions and bits and pieces of blues tunes he was practicing. But that was the first time I heard him play something seriously, from start to finish, and I remember thinking that anyone who could play like that would own my heart forever. Maybe he does. By the time he gets to the end of the piece, the final notes whispering through the upper register of the keyboard, I've got tears in my eyes.

"I think I played it better in high school," he says.

I look away and wipe my eyes. "No, it was beautiful."

"Ah, you're just an easy critic." He runs his hand gently along the tops of the keys, and, although there's no sound, it's as though he's divining something from them, some information only he can glean. Then he stands up, steps toward me, and holds out his hand. "I need to show you something."

I can't imagine what he wants to show me, especially in my own house. I feel a little nervous as I put my hand in his, but then he takes me in his arms, and we start dancing.

"You know, I wanted to be the one to dance with you the other night," he says as he leads me around the room, a gentle smile playing on his face.

I smile as well, but I don't say a word. I just melt into the rhythm, and after a minute I can almost hear the music of Debussy. It's just me and Peter. Maybe this is the way it was always meant to be. I have such a weightless feeling, I think I could float away.

"I remember the last time we danced," he says. "That was a long time ago. The Cinderella Ball." He adjusts his hand on my back, sending a tremor up my spine, and he pulls me closer. "Do you remember?"

I feel his breath on my neck. "Of course I do."

"That dance with you was my only dance all night," he says.

I think about the words of the song, how life has started from this moment, and I remember how true they felt that night. "It was my only dance, too," I tell him.

He sways me from side to side. "And we kissed."

"Yes," I whisper, as I rest my neck against his cheek, feeling as though I could stay this way forever. "Our one and only kiss."

"I remember I got there a little late, and I was worried you might have gone. And then I walked in and saw you."

He was worried I'd gone. I never knew that. I can barely feel my feet touch the floor as he leads me across the room.

"The Dorset Yacht Club," he says. "The room was decorated in white and gold and—"

"It was silver," I tell him. I remember the room. I know every detail. "It was silver and white. They had tons of balloons hanging from the ceiling in silver and white."

"Yes. That's right," he says, spinning me and drawing me back into his arms. "Lots of balloons."

"And streamers," I add. "Made from something silvery and gauzy. Fabric, I think. They were beautiful."

He holds my hand a little tighter. "Streamers?"

"Yes. They started in the middle of the ceiling and the other ends were attached further out so they draped over the room. It was kind of like a maypole effect. Remember?" My hand is on the back of his neck. His skin is warm. I run my fingers through the ends of his hair.

"And Cinderella table decorations," he says.

I close my eyes so I can see the room again. "Yes, white tablecloths. With little glass slippers on the tables. And, oh my God, silver magic wands," I whisper. "I almost forgot about those." He leads me across the room, toward the piano, his body pressed close to mine. "Do you remember?" I ask.

"Of course I remember." He dips me and slowly raises me up. "Now, admit it. I'm a much better dancer than Leeds, right?" He smiles.

"You're pretty good."

We stop and stand by the piano. His eyes meet mine, and he brushes his hand over my hair. He's still gazing into my eyes, and I know he's going to lean in and kiss me. I'm waiting for it, wanting it to happen, wanting him to press his lips to mine. And then he does. He moves in closer

and he kisses me. And he's the boy I knew, but he's also the man I'm beginning to know. That teenage kiss we shared is still there, in our history, but the one we're sharing now is something new, something bigger. He pulls me in even closer, his arms around my back, his skin smelling of cedarwood and that faint trace of rosemary.

And that's when I hear her.

"Honey, are you home? Who's here?" It's Mom, down the hall.

We pull apart. Peter smooths his shirt; I fix my hair. We walk through the room and meet my mother in the hall.

"You remember Peter Brooks, Mom."

"Of course I do," she says as she smiles and extends a hand. "This is a surprise."

"It's nice to see you again," Peter says. "It's been a long time."

"We got takeout at Ernie's," I tell her. "I was just giving Peter a tour of the house."

"Yes, it's beautiful," he says. "Brings back memories."

"Well, don't let me stop you," Mom says. Then she adds, "I'm going upstairs to check on Dad. We had to leave early. He's getting one of his migraines." She turns to Peter. "Good luck with the movie. I hope it goes well."

"Thanks," he says, and she walks down the hall.

Peter glances at his watch. "I'd better get going, Grace. We've got an early start tomorrow."

I don't want him to leave. "All right," I say, trying not to sound disappointed. I follow him into the foyer, and we stand at the door. He kisses me again, briefly. Then he brushes a lock of hair from my face. "Come to the set. We'll be downtown tomorrow. Main Street."

"Okay," I tell him, wanting to commit to memory the feeling of his hand on my skin.

And then he's gone. I watch him get into the blue convertible and close the door. He starts the engine, and the car heads down the drive, gravel rumbling under the tires. I watch the taillights until I can't see them anymore. I listen to the engine until all I hear is a faint whine somewhere far down Salt Meadow Lane. And then that's gone.

The moths are still tapping around the lanterns when I walk to the door. Inside, I head down the hallway and into the family room, where I close the fallboard on the Steinway, sending the eighty-eight keys into exile once again.

CHAPTER 11

The present tense of a verb describes
things that are happening now.
She hopes she is up to the task.

I hardly sleep that night, thoughts of Peter whirling in my head. We're at the kitchen table, with the fish and chips and hot fudge sundae between us. We're at the window, our faces pressed to the screen, the lights in the back-yard flickering over the water. He's leading me across the family room, "Claire de Lune" playing in my head, my feet barely skimming the floor.

At seven thirty I get up, put on my white jeans, a pale-blue top, some makeup, and the good-luck necklace Mom and Dad gave me when I went to college—a gold *G* on a chain. I think I'm going to need some luck. After last night, I'm not even sure I still have a job.

There's coffee left in the pot, but my stomach is too jumpy to drink it. I pour myself a glass of water and stand at the sink. What if Mitch is right? What if I *am* in over my head? Maybe this whole thing will be a huge failure. I feel a twinge in my chest as I think about it. And then my cell phone rings.

"What are you doing?" It's Cluny, and she's using that same, animated *I've got a mystery for you!* voice I remember from our Nancy Drew days.

"I'm about to leave for work."

"Good, I'm glad I caught you. Have you seen the paper?"

"Not yet."

"Find page seventeen. It's your horoscope."

"Oh, Cluny, not that again." I glance at the table, where the pages of the *Dorset Review* lie scattered. "I can't, I've got to go." I sling my handbag over my shoulder and, as an after-thought, grab one of Dad's new spiral notebooks from the end of the counter.

"You have to be careful," she says.

I head down the hall, toward the front door. "What are you talking about?"

"Mercury is going retrograde. We all need to be careful."

"What does that even mean?" I slide my car keys off the Chippendale chest.

"It means when you look at Mercury in the sky, it looks as though it's moving backward, although, of course, it really isn't."

"So, what do I care?" I check my makeup in the hall mirror.

"You should care, because Mercury going retrograde can cause all kinds of problems, Grace. With travel, for one thing."

"I'm only driving downtown."

"And also with communication."

I peek into my handbag. "I've got my Sharpies."

"You're not taking this seriously. I'm telling you, be careful—with your new job, with Peter. Where you go, what you say."

"Cluny, all Peter and I did last night was kiss. How could I possibly be more careful than that? And just because some planets are moving back and forth and sideways doesn't mean it's going to have any effect on me. Look, I'm going to be late. I'll talk to you tonight."

I head down the driveway, "Claire de Lune" playing on my phone. But it takes more than twenty minutes just to get near Main Street. A few of the intersections are blocked, and traffic is at a crawl. As I cross Mason Street, I see a long line of white box trucks and tractor trailers parked by the side of the road. Standing out among them is a bright-red tractor trailer with the name Panavision emblazoned on its side. Hollywood has come to Dorset.

By the time I park in the lot behind the stores and run around to the front door of the bike shop, my blouse is fused to my skin with perspiration, and I'm pretty sure I've got sweat stains under my arms. Mitch is crouched at the back of the store, near the counter, spraying WD-40 on the chain of a white mountain bike when I walk in. He glances at me. Then he looks at the clock on the wall, above the counter. "Fifteen minutes late on your first day?"

"I know. I'm sorry." I walk toward the counter.

He stands up and grabs a rag. "Look, I'm not in favor of this plan, but if my father wants to hire you, I won't get in the middle of it. It's his store and his decision. I'll give you a chance. But you need to be on time."

"I will be. I'm sorry," I say, looking around for Scooter. "It couldn't be helped, though. They have the roads blocked off for the movie, and I couldn't turn onto Main. And when I finally could, the traffic was all backed up."

He crouches by the bike and rubs the chain with the rag. "Well, it's going to be a mess until those movie people leave, so you'd better plan your time accordingly. I don't know why the town ever agreed to it."

I glance at a display of cycling gloves to the right of the counter and notice a pair of gray Giros in the wrong place. "Oh, I think shooting the movie here is a good thing. It's putting Dorset on the map."

Mitch looks up. "For what? Being overcrowded and congested? I read that business has doubled in the restaurants here because people are coming in from other towns to try to get a glimpse of the actors. They're all a bunch of Hollywood phonies, anyway, with their mansions and their handmade cars. Why do you think they call it Tinseltown?"

I pull the gray Giros from the display and put them where they belong. "Dorset will be on the map for having a famous director in our midst. Peter Brooks. And he's certainly not a phony. He and I were very close friends. We still are." Peter's blue eyes flash through my mind.

"I know," Mitch says, sounding unimpressed. "You've told me."

"Oh, right. I guess I have. Well, he invited me to stop by and watch some of the filming, so I'm going today. I've never been on a movie set."

Mitch's eyebrows tick up. "Oh, hanging with the stars, are we?" He sounds a little sarcastic.

"I'm not hanging with the stars. I'm just going to visit Peter."

"Right." He goes back to the bike chain.

I look around. "So, what do you want me to do first?"

"Kevin's going to show you around the workroom," he says. "Explain how we do things, where we keep everything."

I follow Mitch into the workroom, where a guy who I'm guessing is in his mid-twenties tinkers with a green Cannondale suspended from one of the repair stands. His long, blond hair is sun-bleached in places to the color of white corn; his green Downey's Pickles T-shirt sports a drawing of a pickle jar. He's pulling a wiry cable from one of the hand brakes. I glance around the room, at the boxes and bins, the rims and frames overhead, the table of tools and parts. It feels as though the mess and clutter have grown overnight. Or maybe it's just worse than I remember.

"Kevin?" Mitch says.

The blond guy turns. "Oh, hey. What's up?"

"This is Grace. She's the girl who's going to be working here for a couple of weeks." He pauses. "Organizing us." He glances at me, and I feel a sudden sense of responsibility. I need to do a really good job on this.

"Oh, right," Kevin says.

"So I told her you'd show her what's here." He motions across the room. "Explain how things are set up. She can watch you work on some bikes, too. Then we'll go from there."

"Yeah, okay. Sure," Kevin says, and Mitch leaves.

Kevin looks me up and down, and I realize I'm way overdressed. I should be wearing a T-shirt and blue jeans, like the guys are. I put my notebook on the table and stash my handbag on the shelf underneath.

"So, what bike shops have you worked at?" he asks.

"Bike shops? Me? Oh, no. I haven't worked at any. I mean, this is my first."

"Oh. Are you a racer or something, then?"

I laugh. "No, I'm not a racer."

"But you ride a lot." He says this in a hopeful tone, and I feel bad about disappointing him.

"Uh, not technically," I say. And then I add, "Although I did sign up for the Dorset Challenge." I don't need to tell him I'm probably not going to ride in it. That I must have been out of my mind when I signed up to ride fifty miles.

He peers at me. "Then how do you know about bikes?"

I start to line up the cans of spray paint on the worktable. "Well, I don't *exactly* know about bikes. But I do know about organizing things. I'm pretty good at that. And I really think I can help here, make it easier for you guys to do your work."

"Hmm," he says, opening one of the brakes of the Cannondale and threading the cable through it. "So why are you working here, anyway? I mean, if you're not into bikes?"

I throw an empty spray can into the trash. "Scooter and I are doing a trade."

"What kind of trade?"

"Scooter said if I worked here for a couple of weeks, he'd have my bike restored. It's that Schwinn over there." I point to Renny's bike, leaning with three others against the wall.

"Oh, that one. Yeah, I was checking it out yesterday. It's cool. Pretty old. What year is it?"

" 'Seventy-seven."

"Was it your dad's or something?"

I walk to the bike and run my hand over the word *Paramount* on the top tube. "No. It belonged to my sister. She died when we were young."

Kevin looks up. "Oh man. Sorry." He looks away. "Really sorry."

"Thanks," I say, staring at the deflated tires and rusty spokes.

"It's going to need a lot of work."

"I know."

He shifts the Cannondale's gears with one hand and uses his other hand to pedal the bike. "Just give me a minute to finish this, and I'll try to explain what's here." He removes the pedals with a wrench, and the bike looks odd, like someone missing a pair of feet.

"What are you doing?" I ask.

"I'm replacing the cassette."

From the worktable, he takes an object that looks like a shiny metal funnel with rows of tabs on the outside. "This is a cassette." He hands it to me. "It's also called a cog set. It works with the derailleur."

I turn the cassette over, running my fingers along its bumpy surface.

"I know what the derailleur is. It's the thing that switches the gears."

"Uh, sort of," he says, taking the cassette from me. "Okay, see, even though people call them gears, they're actually sprockets—these things here." He rubs his thumb over the metal tabs. "Because they're driven by a chain."

"Sprockets. Chains." I need to remember this. I jot down a couple of things in the spiral notebook. Then I rub a spot of dirt off my pants.

"You know," he says, "white pants aren't too good in a bike shop. Jeans are better."

"Yeah, I think you're right."

He flicks his hair from his face. "And you might want to spend a little time learning about how a bike works. It'll make it easier for you."

"Do you have any suggestions?" I can hear Mitch and A.J. out front, talking to customers.

"Sure. There are some dynamite YouTube videos. I can forward them to you if you want." He pulls a dog-eared paperback from the pocket of his jeans and hands it to me. "And you might want to check this out."

"*You and Your Bike*. Catchy title," I say as I flip through the pages, stopping at diagrams of bicycles, sketches of tools, tables of God knows what. "This looks pretty thorough." I don't think I could ever learn all of this, and I'm hoping I won't need to, but, at the same time, I'm touched by his thoughtfulness.

"It's a little worn out," he says. "But the pictures and drawings are decent, and it's a pretty short book."

"Brevity is good."

"What?"

"Um, being brief," I say. "Being short. It's a good thing."

"Oh, yeah. Sure."

"Thanks, Kevin," I say. "I really appreciate this.

I'll give it back to you when I'm done." I smile, and he starts to blush.

"Dude," he says. "You can keep it."

"I'm going to Eastbrook to drop off a bike," Mitch tells me as he walks into the workroom later i the morning. "I thought you could come with me. I'll be driving over part of the route for the Dorset Challenge. You can see what it looks like."

I don't really care about seeing the route for a ride I'm probably not going to do. On the other hand, he's being nice. I shouldn't turn him down. I look at the blue notebook, filled with my scribbles. "Are you sure you don't want me here working?"

"You will be working. We're delivering a bike." He jingles the keys. "Come on. Let's go." I follow him as he wheels a teal-blue beach bike out to the parking lot and loads it into the Bike Peddler's van. "Hold on," he says, and I watch him go through the back door to the shop and return with two bottles of iced tea.

I step into the van, trying to avoid the junk on the floor—empty coffee cups, half-filled water bottles, catalogs, plastic grocery-store bags, and a baseball cap with *Falcon Sports* on the brim. I take a seat, tossing the cap into the back and nudging the cups and bottles away with my foot.

"You know," I say, looking down, "you might want to throw away all this trash." I realize too late that I shouldn't have said this. He'll probably have me clean the van next.

He pulls out of the parking lot. "You always seem to be concerned about the state of other people's stuff. First it's our flyers, then the workroom, now the van. What's next?" He peers at me out of the corner of his eye.

"Sorry. I just think there's a lot to be said for being neat. And organized."

"I can see why a job correcting computer translations, or whatever you said you did, is perfect for you. You get to fix all the mistakes."

I think he's getting back at me for insulting his van. "That's not all I did. I wrote promotional materials, product manuals, things like that." He doesn't say anything. "I don't have the skill to be a poet or a novelist or that kind of writer," I say, jumping in to fill the silence. "There are practical considerations, you know." Something jabs my thigh, and I realize I'm sitting on a small pair of pliers. "Anyway, I think being organized makes it easier to get things done. If everybody was organized, the world would be a better place."

Mitch gives me a skeptical look. "Why would the world be a better place?"

"Because things would move more efficiently, more quickly."

We stop at Thistle Lane to let a man walking three Irish setters cross the street. Mitch rolls down the window and rests his elbow on the sill.

"Don't you think the world moves fast enough already?"

"Maybe it's fast enough, but it's not *orderly* enough."

"So you think there should be order for its own sake," he says, stepping on the gas again.

"Well, sure. We need rules. Rules are the mark of a civilized society. Without them, everything collapses."

"Look, I'm not advocating anarchy here. I'm just . . . Well, haven't you ever heard that saying *If you obey all the rules, you miss all the fun?*"

"Of course I have. Katharine Hepburn said it. I thought you didn't like Hollywood."

"She's different. She was her own woman. She was never the Hollywood type. You know, she lived in Connecticut, not that far from here."

"Sure, I know." Any self-respecting resident of Dorset knows where Katharine Hepburn lived.

"Anyway, she was right." He glances at the floor, where I've somehow managed to find a place for my feet amid the clutter. "So if the van's a little messy, well, okay. And if the workroom's a little messy—"

"A little? The workroom's more than a little messy. Maybe you just don't see it, but if you guys kept that place neater, I guarantee you'd get a lot more done."

Mitch doesn't say anything. He turns onto Plum Ridge, and as we head away from Dorset, it feels as though the temperature in the van has dropped a few degrees.

"Look," I say, "I didn't mean to criticize."

He stares straight ahead. "It's fine."

But I know it's not. I can tell by his voice. "Okay, I guess I *did* mean to criticize. I'm sorry. Sometimes I get a little carried away."

"So you said the day you corrected the flyers."

I feel my face getting warm.

"But," he adds, "I accept your apology." He's quiet for a minute, and then he says, "In fact, I wanted to apologize to you for last night. At Ernie's."

I didn't expect this.

"I was out of line," he says. "I know that. I was just frustrated. My dad loaned money to someone yesterday, and I know he'll never see a penny of it. People take advantage of him because he's such a good guy. But that didn't have anything to do with you. I shouldn't have said what I did."

"It's okay." I roll down my window. "And you're right. Your dad is a good guy. I can see why you'd want to protect him."

The breeze catches my hair, sending it dancing around my face. The road narrows, and we cross an estuary, where water snakes through tall, yellow-green marsh grass. A giant white egret takes off in front of us, wings extended, long legs dangling beneath its slender body. I grab my handbag and hunt for my phone so I can take a picture, so I can remember what an egret looks like when I'm back in the city. By the time I find it, the bird is gone, a speck against the sapphire sky.

We leave the bike with Mrs. Rudolph, a woman in her forties who bought it for her twelve-year-old daughter. On the way back, Mitch makes a detour to Miller's Orchards so he can get a peach pie for Scooter. As we turn into the driveway, the van wheels rumbling over dirt, I try to remember the last time I was here—five or six years ago, maybe. I came with my parents to get their Christmas tree, something we always used to do when Renny and I were young.

Mitch parks in front of the store, a long, red building with white trim. Clay pots, bursting with purple and white impatiens, form a border along the wall. Behind the store are one hundred and fifty acres of apple trees, row upon row of assorted varieties.

We step inside the store, and I stare at the long tables packed with bushels and crates of corn and cucumbers, tomatoes and string beans, peppers and zucchini. There are endless boxes of straw-berries and nectarines and packages of rhubarb. And there are pies—cherry and blueberry and peach and raspberry, with flaky, golden crusts—and freshly baked coffee cakes with crumbly toppings.

Shelves crammed with jars of local honey in varying amber hues, and glass bottles of dark, mysterious-looking maple syrup, catch my eye. There are cupboards overflowing with fruit butters and jams and jellies and boxes of fudge. Framed prints of country scenes—red barns, covered bridges, horses in fields, hills of sunflowers—adorn the walls, along with an assortment of painted signs for sale: *No Whining, It's Good to Be Queen, Grandpa Knows Best, Bad Decisions Make Great Stories.* I don't remember the signs or the prints or the other home-decor items I see, but everything else looks pretty much the same.

Mitch selects a pie from the table and carries it to the counter. A woman with plump, pink cheeks packs the pie in a box and wraps the box with red and white checked ribbon. Outside, Mitch puts the pie in the van, but he doesn't get in. Instead, he stands quietly, gazing at the sloping hills of the orchards.

"It's pretty here," he says finally.

I nod. "It sure is." Somewhere behind us, a bird sends a three-note song into the air, and another bird answers.

"You know, only two different families have owned this property during the past two hundred years."

"Really. That's amazing."

"During the Revolutionary War, the owners had

two sons in the militia, and both of them were killed."

"You're quite the local historian."

"Not really. Just bits and pieces. Arcane stuff." A man walks out of the store carrying a grocery bag, corn husks peeking from the top. "Do you want to take a walk? Up there? See the view from the top?"

"Yeah, sure," I say. "I haven't been in the orchards in a long time."

We make our way across the parking lot to where the grass begins, and after a hundred feet or so, we enter a wide path between two rows of trees, where the land starts to slope gently upward. Green leaves and tiny, yellow-green apples cloak the trees' branches, and fallen apples lie scattered on the ground. Most are no bigger than acorns, but I know in a couple of months, maybe sooner, some of the apples will be ripe enough to pick.

"We used to come here a lot," I say. "When I was little." I reach out and touch a branch as we walk by. "Apple picking in September, pumpkins in October, Christmas trees in December. Did you come here as a kid?"

"Yeah," he says. "My dad used to bring me."

"I liked apple picking the best," I say. "When the fall weather was crisp but the sun was still warm."

He nods, and we continue up the slope. Birds chatter, their songs piercing the blue silence. I think about Renny and myself and my parents, riding over these hills in the hay wagon, a long, red cart with rails on the sides and hay on the floor, pulled by a throaty tractor. The driver, an old, whiskery man with a red cap and a plaid shirt, would stop at each orchard where the apples were in season. Riders would jump off to pluck apples from the trees and scoop them from the ground and walk back to the store or catch the wagon on its return trip. McIntosh, Macoun. Honeycrisp, Red Delicious. Cameo, Jonagold. Renny and I used to study the people in the hay wagon and ask each other, *If they were apples, what varieties would they be?*

Mitch stops and turns and looks down the path. I stop as well. "I used to love the hay wagon," he says, as if he's read my mind.

"Me too." I gaze down the hill at the rows of trees, and I can almost see the wagon making its rounds, almost hear children laughing.

"I remember coming here once on a school field trip," Mitch says. "I think it was third grade."

"Where did you go to school?"

"Howe Elementary," he says.

"Oh my God. You went to Howe? Me too, but I don't remember seeing you there."

"I don't think our paths would have crossed. Don't forget, I was in fourth grade when you were in kindergarten."

I have a sudden flash of myself as a kindergartener—straggly hair and a couple of crooked front teeth—and I give a sheepish smile. It's doubtful any boys would have wanted to hang out with me. "So then, you were at Baxter Middle School," I say as we start up the hill again.

He nods. "Oh, yeah. Was Mrs. Hawes still the principal when you were there?"

"Yes. She was nice. But I couldn't stand Mr. Sulio."

"The assistant principal?" Mitch asks. "He was mean. Maybe they had a good cop–bad cop thing going."

I laugh and watch an oriole hop across the path ahead of us, its bright-orange plumage a beacon in the grass. "You must have gone to Dorset High, then."

"No," Mitch says. "Actually, I went to Thatcher."

"Thatcher?" This surprises me. I didn't realize his connection to the school ran so deep. "So you were a student there, too?"

"Yeah, my aunt wanted me to go. She paid for it."

"That's very nice."

"Well, she kind of felt she needed to step in."

I wonder what he means by that, but he doesn't explain, and something about his tone tells me I shouldn't ask.

"My sister, Renny, loved this place," I say as we walk through speckled patches of shade cast by the trees. "When we were kids, she used to run up and down the hills for what seemed like hours. My father wrote a poem about it."

"I'm sorry about your sister," Mitch says. "My dad told me."

"Thanks." I pick up an apple from the ground. There's a dark spot on one side where it looks as though it's starting to rot.

"How old were you when she died?"

"Sixteen."

"What happened?" he asks, startling me with the directness of his question. People usually couch the query or wait for me to share something more on my own.

"She died in an auto accident. But I guess your dad probably told you that."

"Yeah, he did."

I wonder if he can sense how much it still hurts me to talk about it this many years later. That there's a physical ache in my chest. I picture her on that last night of her life, sitting on her bed, the movie poster from *Titanic* on the wall behind her. I remember thinking how ominous that poster looked—Jack and Rose, the movie characters, oblivious to the approaching tragedy. That was moments before Renny and I began arguing, just before she went out the door for the last time.

"It happened on Crestwood," I say as we climb higher into the hills.

Mitch looks at me.

"The accident. That's where it happened. On

Crestwood, close to Middle Road." I hear a tractor in the distance, and I listen for the sounds of children, but the only noise is the sputter of the engine. "The kids from school left things at that place for weeks afterward. Flowers and teddy bears, crosses and letters."

"That's so sad," Mitch says.

I run my finger over the dark spot on the apple and think about being in my room that Saturday night, trying on clothes, deciding what I was going to wear to see Peter the next day. The doorbell rang, and when I walked into the hall and looked down the stairs, I saw my mother open the door. It was dark outside, but the lanterns were on and the moths were fluttering. I could make out his blue uniform through the screen. *Mrs. Hammond, I'm Lieutenant Belforth, Dorset Police Department. May I come in?* I knew right away something had happened. It was right there in his voice.

I toss the apple as far as I can, over the trees. A cloud drapes itself against the sun, turning the June afternoon gray, the air still.

"I lost someone, too," Mitch says. "I lost my mother. When I was four."

I stop walking. "She died when you were four?"

"No, she didn't die. She left us—my father and me."

I watch the breeze ruffle the grass ahead of us. "You mean she moved out?"

"Yeah, so she could be with another guy."

I feel as though I've just kicked a rotted log and let loose a thousand bugs. "That's terrible. I'm sorry."

"I'm not," he says, his voice empty of emotion. "My dad told me years later that she said she was hoping for a different life."

"What kind of life did she want?" How could a mother leave her four-year-old child?

"I don't know. The guy she ran off with was some small-time soap opera actor from New York. That's all I know about him. He wasn't any big deal, but I guess she thought he was something special."

"I can see why you're not a fan of people in show business."

"That's part of it."

"Did you see her after that?"

Mitch bends to pick up a branch from the ground. It looks brittle, like something left behind by the winter. "No," he says.

"Not ever?"

He shakes his head.

"And you never heard from her?" I ask. "No phone calls? No letters? Email? Anything?"

He snaps a piece off the branch and tosses it to the side of the path. "There were some letters. They started when I was older. Fifteen, I think."

"What did they say?"

"Oh, you know. What you'd expect, I guess. She

wanted to see me. *I was young, I was immature. I don't expect anything from you. I'd just like to meet my son.* That kind of thing."

"And what did you say? What did you tell her?"

He looks straight ahead, up the hill. "Nothing."

"Nothing? You mean you didn't answer?"

"No. Why should I? She had her opportunity to be my mother, and she gave it up."

"I don't know. It's just—it's not every day people ask for another chance. Or get one. Maybe you should give that to her."

"She doesn't deserve another chance." He flings the stick across the grass. "I used to think I missed having a mother. But you can't miss what you never had." He looks away, and I wonder if that's how he really feels.

We sit on the side of the path, by the trees, a dozen tiny apples on the ground around us. "I remember the first time I ate an apple right off a tree," I say. "It was here, in these orchards. I was surprised how hard I had to pull to get it off the branch."

"What kind of apple was it?" Mitch asks. "Do you remember?"

I look around, as though I might recognize the type of apple if I saw it again. "No, I don't. It might have been a Cortland or an Empire. Or it might have been a regular old McIntosh. Whatever it was, though, I just bit right into it. Didn't give a damn about washing it, like I would now."

I run my hand over the trunk of the tree beside me, feeling its rough texture, its knots. "That was a great apple. So crisp and sweet. So fresh. It wasn't like any apple I'd ever eaten. I remember standing there, thinking, *I will always remember the taste of this apple, as long as I live.*"

Mitch picks up one of the apples and turns it to reveal a blush of pink. "Those are great moments," he says. His eyes are soft, quiet. A little piece of hair hangs over his forehead. "When you have this feeling that what's happening is really special and you know you'll always remember exactly what took place. Every detail."

"Yes." I turn to him and smile. "That's how it was."

CHAPTER 12

An indefinite pronoun does not refer to
any specific person, thing, or amount.
Everything is funny as long as it is
happening to somebody else.

When I step outside the bike shop, the street is
bustling with cars, kids on bikes and skateboards,
and people darting in and out of stores. The flag
by the door of Copper Kettle Cookware flutters
in a warm breeze, sending shadows dancing on
the building's redbrick exterior.

A few blocks up, there's a huge group of people
standing in the road, and my heart does a little
dance, because I know they must be gathered
there for Peter's movie. I stride toward them,
past the display of vintage decanters in the
window of the liquor store and the claw-foot
table and teapots in Laurie's Antiques.

I cross Leeward Avenue and walk another block.
To the right, down Mason Street, half a dozen
white box trucks and several movie-set trailers
are parked. As I walk farther up Main Street, huge,
round lights on stands and rectangular screens
in black-and-white rise in the air like sails. There
must be a hundred people in the street—joggers
in spandex shorts, mothers holding the hands of

children, men in business suits, college students, grandmothers. There's an excited buzz going through the crowd, and it's all about the movie. *I got a selfie with Brittany Wells. I sat two tables down from Sierra Benson at the Sugar Bowl. My friend was an extra, and she got to say a line! I saw Herbert Tait at the bank, getting money from the cash machine!*

I peer over the heads of the people in front of me so I can see what's going on, but I'm too far back, and I'm too short. "Excuse me," I say as I begin to squeeze my way toward the front. Pushing through the crowd, I notice a number of women holding small, gold bottles, but it's not until the cloying scent of jasmine hits me that I make the connection. It's that perfume, Catch Me!, that fans are spraying around Sean.

When I finally press through the mass of onlookers, I stop. I lean against the barricades set up by the crew and take in the scene. Cables snake up and down the street, and twenty men are moving equipment and arranging lights and metal stands. Two women are inside a huge trailer full of clothes, and a handful of people are hanging out by a little tent where food and drinks have been set up. Several twenty-somethings are scurrying around, most of them talking on cell phones and walkie-talkies. One guy, who must be a production assistant, stands guard on the other side of the barricades, a megaphone in his hand.

To the far right is a cluster of director's chairs, with the name By Any Chance printed across their blue canvas backs, and in front of the chairs are two video monitors on stands. The block doesn't look like the Main Street I know. It's been completely transformed.

Halfway down the sidewalk there's an old-fashioned clock with a big, round face and a black iron stand. It looks just like the clock that was here on Main Street when I was young. And parallel parked by the curb is an old, red Toyota Camry. With its simple grille and plain wheels, the car seems boxy and antiquated, compared with the flashier, more curvaceous version of the model that's on the road today. A silver Lincoln Continental is parked in front of the Camry. It reminds me of the car my aunt Cordelia used to drive, back in the nineties, when she'd come from Boston to visit us.

"Look at the parking meters," a man behind me says, and I notice that someone has placed trees in front of the electronic meters in order to disguise them, and put up the old, coin-operated silver meters, the kind with the rounded tops and glass windows and little arrows showing how many minutes remain.

Several shops have been temporarily transformed to resemble businesses that long ago closed their doors. The Art Barn has been turned back into Zodiac, a store that used to sell trendy clothes, and the old, white house where Dorset Golf & Sportswear is located is once again Seaside Video. It seems strange that there ever was a place in town where you could rent DVDs and, before that, videotapes. A Shore Realty sign has been placed in front of the brick building where the paint-your-own-pottery studio is located, and I think about Alice Howe, a classmate of mine whose grandfather started the real estate company and ran it until he died.

And then there's the Sugar Bowl. Its blue and white striped awning is gone, one with yellow and white stripes having temporarily taken its place. And the sign I remember from my teen years is back: a red coffee cup with little, wavy steam lines rising to meet the words *Sugar Bowl* in hand-scripted letters above it. Outside the restaurant, huge lights and reflectors have been set up, and the windows are covered with what appears to be orange cellophane. Mitch was right when he predicted they would be filming in there.

I feel as though I've stepped back in time, to the Dorset of my youth. I almost believe if I walked into Seaside Video, I'd be greeted by wall-to-wall shelves of DVDs and a little area by the counter stocked with popcorn and candy.

I'm jostled by a woman standing next to me, dressed in gray sweatpants. "I think I'll faint if I actually see Sean Leeds in person," she tells her friend.

"You'll faint? I'll faint," the friend says. "I'd love to get his autograph on this." She holds up a bottle of Catch Me! "My cousin's wife's sister, Eugenia, actually got his autograph."

"No!" the lady in sweatpants says.

"Yes, but Eugenia didn't have the perfume with her, so she had him autograph the bottom of her grocery list. And then her husband threw it out by mistake."

The sweatpants woman groans. "I would kill Gary if he did that." She takes her Catch Me!, spritzes a shower of jasmine in the air, and they both laugh.

My God. These women are talking about fainting just from seeing Sean, and I danced with him. He might have even kissed me if Peter hadn't come in. I touch my fingertip to my lips, wondering what it would have felt like. If anybody fainted, it should have been me, and it should have been then. But Sean just seems so nice and normal, like a regular guy who just happens to be in the movies, exactly the opposite of what Mitch would call a Hollywood phony.

A woman nearby whines, "I can't believe we've been here for four hours."

I turn and take in her short, blond hair and perfectly plucked eyebrows. She's wearing a silk blouse and a chunky gold necklace, and she's standing with another woman, dressed in a Pucci top and carrying an oversized Prada handbag.

These must be two of the ladies who keep the new spa in business.

"You've been waiting for four hours?" I ask the one with the eyebrows. "To see Sean Leeds?"

She checks her watch. "Yes. Four hours and ten minutes, to be exact."

"Four and a half," says her friend. "I got here before she did." Then she adds, "But it'll be worth it if we get to see him."

Four and a half hours, just to get a glimpse of Sean. Wow.

"How about you?" the eyebrow woman asks me.

"I just got here."

"And how long are you planning to wait?" Pucci top asks.

"Wait? Oh, I'm not going to wait."

Pucci top gives me a curious look. "Then what are you doing here if you're not waiting to see Sean Leeds?"

I lean in and lower my voice. "I've been invited to watch the filming."

"Invited?" they ask in unison.

"I know the director," I explain. "We're old friends. Very close friends." And then, because I can see how excited they are, I add in a half whisper, "I know Sean, too."

"You know the director *and* Sean Leeds?" Pucci says, so loudly that several people turn to stare at us.

"Peter Brooks and I went to Dorset High together," I tell her.

"Fabulous!" Pucci says. "Can you get Sean to sign our perfume bottles?"

Word begins to travel through the crowd. *She knows Sean Leeds. Friend of the director.* I can feel everyone looking at me, sizing me up, waiting for me to do something. And I guess I can. I'm the director's . . . well, good friend. Very good friend. And, after that kiss, who knows what's next? I could be on the way to becoming his girlfriend.

Yes, I'm probably almost his girlfriend. It's a great thought. Such a great thought, in fact, that for a moment I forget I'm standing outside the Sugar Bowl in Dorset, Connecticut. I imagine, instead, that I'm in front of a movie theater on Sunset Boulevard in Hollywood, my arm linked firmly in Peter's, my six-inch Jimmy Choo heels kissing their way along the red carpet. Camera shutters pop and wind and strobes flash as we approach the theater entrance. Paparazzi shout, "Peter, Peter, over here!" Peter turns, obligingly, and gives a little smile, a little wave. I turn to my good side (do I have a good side?) and do the same.

The fantasy comes to a jarring halt when somebody shoves an elbow in my back. There's a murmur behind me. *She knows the director. Sean Leeds's friend.* I edge to the left, just a little, and now I'm only a couple of feet from the production assistant. I'm about to give him my name so he can let me through the barricade when he picks up his megaphone and tells us to clear the street because a limousine is coming through.

A limousine. It must be one of the actors. I shuffle aside with the crowd, little sputters of electricity and speculation about who's inside the vehicle traveling from person to person. But the woman who emerges from the limousine isn't one of the actors. She's tall and has a head of thick, wavy yellow hair. She's dressed in a white knit top with black skinny jeans and short, black boots. It's Regan Moxley. My stomach lurches. What's she doing here?

Everyone goes wild. People applaud, whistle, shout for selfies, and a few of the men make catcalls. They think Regan is in the movie. I can't believe this.

"She's not an actor!" I scream. "She reads SparkNotes!" I look around, hoping to get someone's attention, anyone's attention. But no one hears me.

Regan tilts her head upward, flicking her hair as the driver of the car closes the door behind her. I watch her walk up to the production assistant, lean in, and whisper in his ear. He says something into his walkie-talkie, and soon a young woman with long, blond hair appears. I think I remember seeing her at the party. She escorts

Regan down the street and into the Sugar Bowl. And that's it. She's in.

I stamp my foot. Why is Regan Moxley always in the way? Why is she always trying to steal my thunder? Trying to steal Peter? I feel my blood pressure rising, but I tell myself to remain calm. Maybe I didn't arrive in a limousine, and maybe I'm not six feet tall and wearing skinny jeans, but I'm going in there just the same way she did.

I walk up to the production assistant. "Excuse me." I flick back my own hair, although I suspect the effect isn't the same. "I'm Grace Hammond. I'm a friend of Peter Brooks." I let that sink in. "And a friend of Sean Leeds." I pause here as well. Then I smile, hoping to indicate that even though I'm friends with these two very important people, I myself am still a regular person, just like him.

He scratches his neck where it looks as though he's been bitten by a mosquito. "Yeah?"

"I'd like to go inside the Sugar Bowl, please."

"Sorry," he says. "They're filming." He brushes something off the front of his black *I Got Crabs at Ernie's* T-shirt.

"Yes, I know they're filming," I say. "But Peter told me I could drop by the set."

He rubs his eyebrows, which are dark and thick and almost meet in the middle. "What did you say your name was?"

"Grace Hammond."

He picks up his walkie-talkie. "I need Doug." He adjusts his sunglasses. After a moment he says, "I've got Grace Hammond out here. Can she go on set?"

I feel the crowd watching me as I wait to get the word to enter. A little squawk comes through the walkie-talkie. The production assistant shakes his head at me. "Can't do it. You're not on the list."

What? How can that be? I hear a few snickers and some muttering behind me. "Can't you just call Peter on that walkie-talkie? I'm sure he'll tell you to send me right in."

"They're filming."

"Yes, I realize that." The sun is beginning to burn the back of my neck. "But Peter is a very close friend of mine. In fact, I'm . . ." I pause, wondering if I should give it a spin. "Well, I might almost be his girlfriend."

The production assistant pulls back and peers at me, his eyebrows having completely merged now. "I don't care who you are, ma'am. The office says you're not on the list. Sorry."

What is this list? And why is he calling me *ma'am?* I'm not a *ma'am.* I've never been a *ma'am.* I'm barely older than he is.

I point toward the door of the Sugar Bowl. "But that *other woman*"—my lips curl with the words—"she just went in."

"She's on the list."

"*She's* on the list?"

"Look, I'm sorry, lady. I don't make the rules."

Behind me, there's more muttering and whispering and some outright laughter. *The girl who said she knew Peter Brooks can't get in.* The crowd is turning against me, relishing my downfall. *Sean Leeds's friend . . . they're not letting her inside.* I want to disappear, to vanish into thin air. I want somebody to beam me up, like in *Star Trek.* Beam me up, Scotty. Get me out of here. Now!

But I can't do that. I have to walk through the crowd to go back down the street. There's no other way. Heat radiates from my face as I turn away from the production assistant. Everyone is staring at me. I push my way back through the group, aiming for a small opening between two women. One is in a pair of black exercise shorts and a black top, and the other is in jeans and a T-shirt. The two of them are talking and laughing, and the one in the exercise shorts is holding a huge bottle of Catch Me! and spraying it. *Spritz, spritz.* The air reeks of jasmine. I feel a little sick.

"Excuse me." I move closer, eyeing the space between them.

"Sean Leeds, I love you!" the exercise woman screams. She holds the bottle high, like the Statue of Liberty with her torch, and sprays a thick mist of perfume, most of which falls on me. I can taste it, acrid, metallic. My stomach churns.

"Do you mind?" I nod toward the bottle while I try to rub the perfume off my arms.

The exercise woman looks at me, her eyes like pebbles. "I'm not bothering you."

"On the contrary," I say. "You just sprayed me with that atomizer." I point to the bottle.

"Oh, I'm sorry. You don't like jasmine?" She and her friend laugh, and then she lowers the bottle, and, with a long *spritzzzz!* she sprays me right in the chest.

"Hey!" I try to step back, but the crowd is so dense, there's nowhere to go. "What's wrong with you?"

"What's wrong with *you?*" she says, unleashing another cloud of perfume in my hair.

"Give me that!" I try to scream, but there's perfume in my throat, and the words come out like a croak. I lunge for the bottle. I've got the top and she's got the bottom, and I'm pulling as hard as I can. Someone behind us yells, *Catfight!* and the next thing I know, the atomizer comes off right in my hand, releasing a gush of yellow perfume all down the front of my blouse.

I shriek, and the crowd backs away while the two women stand there and laugh. "You don't know Sean Leeds," the exercise woman says. "You're probably not even a fan!"

"Of course I know him. I danced with him at a party—something you'll never do. You and your aerobics getup and your perfume and your . . ."

266

I'm trying to think of a good insult. I finally scream, "Your porcine thighs!"

"What?" she yells. Her face is brick red, splotched with little bullets of crimson.

"Porcine," I say, pointing to her lower half. "It means *fat*. You have fat thighs."

"I work out!" she yells after me, as I turn and flee into the crowd. "I do yoga! These are muscled thighs—they're not fat!"

I'm drenched, reeking of jasmine, and stinging from humiliation. I break free of the mob and don't stop running until I reach the end of the block.

"Mommy, what's that smell?" a little girl asks as I stop to cross Mason Street.

"That lady's wearing way too much perfume," her mother says. "Some people just don't know when to quit."

"They sprayed me," I say, looking down at my stained clothes. "It's not my fault." The mother grabs her daughter's hand and pulls her close, as though I could be a criminal—maybe some kind of perfume addict.

I move along, an outcast in my own town. How is it that Regan got in and I didn't? What's so special about her? Could Peter be dating her? And why did that crazy woman douse me with perfume? Sean ought to know how dangerous his fans are. There must be someone at his fan club I can call to report this.

As the Bike Peddler comes into view, I panic. There's no way I'm going in through the front door looking like this. I run around to the parking lot and to the back door, thinking I can sneak into the workroom, grab my handbag, and make a quick getaway. On the way home, I'll call the shop and say I'm sick. A sore throat. No, malaria.

I put my hand on the knob and try to turn it, but the door is locked. Why is the door locked now? It was unlocked before. I give a quiet knock, hoping Kevin will hear it from the workroom. Then I count to ten. Nothing. I knock again, a little louder. Still nothing. I wonder if I could open the door by sliding a credit card between the door and the jamb, the way detectives do in the movies. Or maybe it's spies who do that. Then I remember I don't have a credit card because my handbag is inside. I consider trying to force open a window, but there aren't any windows in the back. I knock again a couple of times before finally giving up. I let out a moan and lean against the building, the warm bricks and my own humiliation burning through me.

That's when the door opens. "Hello?"

The person who pops his head out isn't Kevin, however. It's Mitch. He looks around, sees me, and steps back. "What the . . . ?"

I take a deep breath. "I was attacked." I brush by him and head inside.

"Attacked?" He follows me.

"Yes." I dash into the workroom to get my handbag. "By a woman with porcine thighs."

"A what?"

"Porcine thighs."

"A lady with fat thighs came after you?"

"Exactly," I say as I look on the shelf under the workbench. I don't see my handbag. I could have sworn I left it there. "I need to go," I say. "I need to leave."

"Wait a minute," Mitch says. "Just calm down. Where did this happen?" His brown eyes soften with concern.

"Right down the street." I don't want to relive the whole thing. I just want to find my keys and get out of here. I scan the room. No handbag. No keys.

"Here in town?" he says.

"Yes, outside the Sugar Bowl."

He looks startled. "Well, my God, you've got to call the police. Or I'll call them. But we have to report it. You can't have someone attack you like that and get away with it. Are you hurt?" He puts a warm hand on my arm.

"No, no. I'm not hurt. And I don't think it's a matter for the police. Really." I can't have him call the police. The episode would end up in tomorrow's paper. POET'S DAUGHTER ENTANGLED IN PERFUME BRAWL. I can just see it. "No, let's not call them. It's not that big a deal. It was just some crazy Sean Leeds fan."

"A fan of Sean Leeds." He tilts his head and sniffs the air. "What's that smell? Perfume?"

"Yes. It's jasmine."

"You bought perfume while you were out, too?"

"No, she attacked me with it!"

"Who?"

"Porcine Thighs. She came after me with her perfume."

A smile dances across his face. "She attacked you with her perfume?"

I can't believe he thinks this is funny. "This is not amusing. The woman *sprayed* me. She held the bottle in the air." I hold up my hand. "And drenched me. On purpose. An unprovoked attack. It's assault and battery."

Mitch's lips are pressed together as though he's trying not to laugh. "A perfume attack."

"I could have been seriously hurt. The lady was in shape, and she was huge."

He grins. "I know, you told me. Porcine thighs."

I stare at the highest shelves in the room to see if my handbag might have magically floated up there, but there's only a fire extinguisher. "She was a lunatic. I'm lucky to be alive."

"Absolutely," he says. "I don't know how you survived. I think you were very brave."

"Look, I just want to get out of here. It's been a long day."

He looks at his watch. "What do you mean? It's only two fifteen."

"Metaphorically speaking."

"Metaphorically speaking?"

"Yes. It feels a lot later than two fifteen to me. I've just had a very traumatic experience." I stare at the worktable, trying to remember what I did with my handbag. "I need to go home now. Unless you want your whole store to smell like this."

Mitch sniffs the air again. "Actually, it's not that bad."

"Stop! This isn't funny. You're not the one soaked in jasmine. You don't understand how awful it was."

His expression becomes more serious. "Grace, I'm sorry," he says. "It's just that when you tell me you got attacked with perfume by some crazy fan of Sean Leeds, it sounds like something right out of a movie itself."

"Just let your dad know I'll be back tomorrow," I say.

"I'll let him know."

I turn around, scanning the room once more. How can my handbag have disappeared? "Oh God, where the hell is it? Why can't I find that thing?"

"What are you looking for?" Mitch asks.

"My handbag. I thought I put it on the shelf under the workbench, but it's not there."

"Your handbag. Why didn't you say so? I stuck it in the top drawer of that file cabinet." He points to a tall, gray cabinet, its drawers covered by half-removed stickers with names like Bontrager, Huffy, and Razor on them. "I put it there so it wouldn't get dirty."

"Oh, for God's sake." I don't know whether to thank him for doing something nice or scream at him for making me search for it. I open the drawer, pull out my handbag, and grab my keys. "I'm out of here," I say as I head for the back door.

Outside, the sky is a sheet of blue. Three teenage girls walk by, dressed in denim short-shorts, cans of soda in their hands. I take a few steps toward the parking lot, and then I hear a door open behind me.

"Grace. Hey, Grace."

I turn.

Mitch is standing in the doorway. "Just wanted to say, jasmine is one of my favorite scents. I hope you'll wear it again sometime."

I can't believe this. Nothing like being kicked when you're down. I raise my key and point it at him. "I swear, Mitch, if you say one more word, I'll . . ." But I don't know what I'll do, so I just turn and walk to the car and drive away.

CHAPTER 13

The past tense of a verb describes things
that have already happened.
They <u>discussed</u> the topic on numerous occasions.

The shower is hot. Very hot. I stand there, letting the water run over my head and down my body for a full minute before picking up the bar of organic soap Mom special orders from some place in Oregon. The smell of jasmine is an irritant, continuously released as the water soaks my hair and trickles down my skin. It's a scent I'll never want to wear. I place the tan bar of soap under my nose. It doesn't smell like anything, which is fine by me. In fact, it's perfect.

After I've scrubbed off the jasmine, I lie on my bed for an hour and a half reading *You and Your Bike*, flipping through diagrams, learning about maintenance and tools and repairing common mechanical problems. That's one thing about bikes—if you maintain them they won't let you down. Unlike men. At least, unlike the kind who cheat on you for two weeks before letting you know they've moved on.

Later, I head downstairs. I find my father in the library. He's dressed in a pair of gray slacks and his favorite blue sweater, with the right arm unraveling at the wrist. He's sitting where he always sits—in the brown leather chair that's worn smooth in spots and covered with faint cracks in others. On the coffee table in front of him is the jigsaw puzzle of Venice's Grand Canal.

He calls to me. "Come on in, Gracie. Come join me."

"All right," I tell him.

The threads of the Persian rug are soft under my bare feet as I cross the room. The evening light is silky and faded against the caramel walls. Birds that haven't settled down for the night are calling, their quiet chatter drifting in with the cool air through the open windows. The muted sound of a foghorn blows in the distance.

I look around, and I can't help but replay last night: Peter in this room, marveling over Mom's puzzle pieces. And then in the family room, coaxing the Steinway's voice back to life, telling me all the things he remembered from the dance, kissing me, inviting me to the set. And today I find that I'm *not on the list.* How could he let that happen? Was it all just a lot of Hollywood schmoozing? Maybe Mitch is right. Maybe Peter is a phony, and maybe I'm a fool to believe he'd really be interested in me.

A book of plays by Eugene O'Neill is on the love seat. I move it to the table and sink into the cushions, pulling my legs up onto the sofa.

"Why the long face?" Dad asks.

"Just tired," I say as I study the walnut book-cases that bracket the fireplace. I locate the shelf where his poetry collections reside. All seven volumes are there, including my favorite, *Crossing Rivers*, which was published when Renny and I were young, when Dad's voice as a poet seemed a bit less solemn than it became in later years. "I've had an exhausting day."

"Something I can do to help?" he asks.

His hair looks whiter today, and the little creases around his mouth appear just the tiniest bit deeper than they did the last time I noticed them. I remember the party Mom gave him when he turned fifty-five. It seems like it was yesterday, and it's hard to believe that ten years have passed since then.

"No. I'm fine," I tell him. "Thanks."

He sits back to view the jigsaw puzzle the way a painter might stand back to evaluate the progress of a painting. "Do you think I've taken on too much with this one?"

I gaze at the puzzle. The borders are complete now, and I can see how big the finished picture will be—about two feet by three. The top of the puzzle box, with its colorful photo, rests against a glass containing half-melted ice cubes—the remains of a gin and tonic. Two Thousand Pieces, the label reads.

"I'm sure you can do it," I say. "You always manage to conquer these things."

He sighs and nudges a yellow piece into position. "I think I could use a little help." He gives me a pretend grimace as the sounds of Mom making dinner in the kitchen drift toward us in a language of their own—the clanking of pots and pans, the pale whir of the electric can opener, the running of water. I smell garlic and onions, but I'm not hungry.

There's an assortment of blue pieces in front of me—the ones he's culled from the general population of two thousand. I pick through them, settling on a piece that looks as though it's part of the water. I search for a place where it might fit. Finally, I cast it aside in frustration. "Forget it."

My father's eyes dart from me, to the picture on the box, to the skeletal outline of the puzzle on the table. He chuckles softly as he picks up another piece. "You never did like doing these. I remember, when you were a child, you always wanted the puzzle to be finished. You didn't have the patience."

"I just wanted to see the picture all put together."

"Exactly," Dad says, his hand hovering over the puzzle, like a divining rod searching for water. "You always wanted to keep moving, finish one thing, get on to the next. No lingering."

"I'm still that way. That's why I can't do these."

He presses the piece into place, raises his

eyeglasses, and gives me a probing glance. "You really do look exhausted, Grace."

I am exhausted. I'm exhausted just thinking about how that awful woman sprayed me, how I never got to see Peter, and how Regan showed up in her skinny jeans. "I just need a good night's sleep."

"Your mother told me you were working at the bicycle shop today. Looks like they wore you out."

"No, that was okay." I'm not about to tell him what happened. He would definitely want to call the police. And probably dash off some silly poem about the unfairness of it all and send it to the editor of the *Dorset Review.* I can just imagine it.

They gather there, the fans of Sean
To cast their eyes upon his form
And in his shining presence ask
For selfies or for autographs.
But holding bottles in the air
They spray the crowd without a care.
The scent no longer seems so fine.
Those thighs! I think they are porcine!

Dad shuffles through more puzzle pieces, finally picking up a green one. "I still don't understand why you would want to work in a bike shop." He has this habit of recalling what he wants to recall and forgetting the rest.

277

"Remember I told you we're doing a trade? I'm helping them organize things, and they're fixing Renny's old Schwinn. Restoring it."

He looks up. "Are you really planning to take that bike back to New York? Can you ride it there? Isn't that kind of dangerous?"

"Sure, I can ride it there," I say. "I'll ride it in Central Park."

"And you want to expend all that effort on this bike because . . ."

"I don't know. I guess maybe it's a metaphor."

"Ah," he says, leaning back in his chair and putting his arms behind his head.

"For the good times Renny and I had together before everything started to change. Before she started to change."

"As long as it's just a metaphor, Grace. It won't bring her back, you know."

I don't say anything.

"Couldn't you just pay them to fix the bike?"

"Not now, when I'm out of work. It's expensive."

"Your mother and I would help you out, you know. If you needed anything."

"Thanks. I know. But this trade arrangement is fine. Really."

He rises from the sofa. "Hmm. Yes, well, I had an idea I wanted to discuss with you." He empties the melted remains of his drink into the copper sink. The ice cubes rattle and clank. Then he screws off the top of a bottle of Tanqueray, an action I've seen him perform countless times, especially after Renny died, and he restocks the glass with ice. He measures the gin in a silver jigger, pours it into the glass, and adds tonic water. Bubbles erupt and fizz over the top; it's like a chemistry experiment gone awry. "Do you want a drink, Grace?"

"No, thanks."

He drops a slice of lime into the glass. "I know some people who might be able to help you get a real job."

For a second, I don't say anything. I thought we already had this conversation a few days ago. Is that why he lured me in here—to go on, again, about my career? "Dad, I know you know some people," I say, my neck stiffening. "But you're talking about poets and novelists and people like that."

He takes a long sip of his gin and tonic, walks back to the chair, and sits down. "Really, Grace, you make it sound as though I'm hanging around with ax murderers."

"No, it's just that I'm not talented enough to work with people like that."

"That's not true. You've got all the talent in the world. And these are good people. I know they'd be happy to help you if they can. I'd like to get you out of the bike shop." He sits down. "And the proofreading."

"It wasn't proofreading," I remind him again. "And the bike shop is only for a couple of weeks."

"Just hear me out. I actually have a lead for you on something." He leans forward, his stomach protruding slightly under the sweater. "Did you ever meet Paul Duffner?"

Paul Duffner. The name doesn't sound familiar. "I don't think so."

"He's a colleague of mine at the university. In the English Department. He's working on a fantastic book, all about the Dutch poet and playwright Joost van den Vondel. Seventeenth century. The Shakespeare of Holland. In fact, Shakespeare may owe a debt to Vondel, if you ask me. And certainly, if you ask Duff. Milton may have even drawn some inspiration for *Paradise Lost* from Vondel's *Lucifer.* I'll bet you didn't know that when you read *Paradise Lost*, did you?"

Should I tell him I've never actually read *Paradise Lost*? Maybe not.

"Well, it's an exciting project, and Duff could really use a research assistant to help him with—"

"Dad, please." I hold up my hand. "I don't think this is for me." I can't imagine doing research on a seventeenth-century Dutch *anything*. Maybe I do need a drink. I get up and walk to the bar, where I pour myself a glass of sauvignon blanc. I take a long sip and then top it off. The idea that

I'm not interested in a job like this probably makes me a big—or, rather, bigger—disappointment to him.

"I'm sorry," I tell him. "But it's just not the right thing for me. And I couldn't do it even if it were. I'm not staying here." I gesture at the room but intend to indicate more than the house. "As soon as my apartment is fixed, I'm leaving. I need to get back to New York and start looking for a job there. Something will come along." I'm not sure I'm convincing him. I'm barely convincing myself. But I don't want my father to think he's my new career counselor.

Dad takes off his glasses and sighs. "Finding something isn't the answer, Grace. It's finding the right thing. You could do worse than work for Paul Duffner for a year. You could learn something new. You might even enjoy studying poetry again."

"I know you're trying to help. But, please, let me do this myself."

He taps his glasses on the arm of the chair. "But, Grace." He pauses. "The bike shop?"

"You know, I actually kind of like it there. I got a good start today, and I think I can really help them. I think I'm doing something they need."

"I'm sure *they* need it," he says. "Who wouldn't want to have a bright, attractive young woman like you, summa cum laude from Middlebury, organizing their store, essentially for free?

They're getting the deal of the century. But what are you getting? You can't put that job on your résumé."

I try to interrupt, but he goes on. "You know, the other night I was looking for that poem you wrote about the garden and the rabbit that ate the string beans. I thought we might have it in the attic. I couldn't find it, but I did find something else—that script you wrote in college. I think you should read it, maybe remind yourself how talented you really are."

Oh, no. Not my college screenplay again. "I don't need to read it," I tell him, recalling the angst I felt trying to come up with the right ending for a story of two sisters, one dying of cancer. "It was mediocre at best."

His mouth goes slack, and he looks at me as though it's him I've insulted. He rubs his glasses with the bottom of his sweater, holds them up for inspection, and then puts them back on.

"Don't you think I recognize good writing when I see it?"

"You're my father. You probably think anything I write is good."

He leans in across the table, closing the space between us. "That's not so. I'm being objective here. Your script is good." He takes another sip of his drink. Flecks of lime swirl in the glass. "Personally," he says, "I can only assume you're stalling for time."

Uh-oh, here we go. It's as though he's flipped a switch inside me, one that runs on circuitry so well established, I can't help but respond. "I'm not stalling for time," I say, my stomach tightening.

"I think you are. Working in a bike shop? That's not real life. When are you going to get started with life, Grace? You're thirty-three. I think you know you're cut out for greater things, but you're afraid to try. So you'd rather inventory handlebar grips or whatever nonsense they've got you doing."

I sit up straighter. "I'm not inventorying handlebar grips, and it's not nonsense. I'm reorganizing the workroom. It's a big task. Lots of responsibility. They're counting on me."

"Honey, you could work for a magazine," he says. "Or a book publisher. I could call Matt Rosenberg. I know he'd meet with you."

"Of course he'd meet with me. He's your publisher." I wring my hands. "That's enough. Why are you doing this?"

"Doing what? I'm just trying to help." He tilts his head, his neck sagging a little.

"No, you're not. You're trying to map out my life, because you can't do it for Renny anymore."

There's a crash in the kitchen, and the sound of something splintering into a million pieces. "Oh, damn," I hear my mother say, quiet and resigned.

Dad gets up and walks to the doorway. "Everything okay, Leigh?"

"Yes," Mom calls back. "Just dropped a plate."

He sits down again. "What are you talking about—mapping out people's lives? Don't be ridiculous. I'm only—"

"I'm not being ridiculous." My stomach is in knots. "I don't need this kind of micromanagement. I'll figure things out."

I feel myself shaking. I'm on the verge of crying, and all I can think about is how this would be the worst day of my life except that there will only be one worst day of my life. It's also the worst day of my father's life and the worst day of my mother's life, and that's the day Renny died. The thought of that makes me angry and sad at the same time, because somehow our lives— mine, my mother's, and my father's—have always been about Renny, and still are about Renny, even seventeen years later.

I stand up. "I'm sorry but I can't be Renny. I'm never going to be her."

My father rubs his forehead. "Nobody expects you to be Renny. That's not what this is about."

"Isn't it, though? Isn't that exactly what it's about? She did what you wanted. Reciting those stupid poems at dinner and poring over all those biographies of writers you love. She wanted to be an English lit major, for God's sake. You can't tell me you weren't behind that."

He raises his hands in protest. "I wasn't."

"I don't believe you. Now Renny's gone, and it's all on me. All the attention you used to lavish on her has nowhere else to go. Well, I don't want that kind of attention. Not now. Don't try to make me be Renny. I'm not her."

I storm out of the room before he can say another word.

It's been a long time since I've opened this door, and I'm not surprised when it sticks. I finally pull hard enough to look inside. It's a small space, tucked under the stairway that goes from the second floor to the attic, a space originally intended to be used as a storage closet but discovered by two young sisters who claimed it as their secret spot. It was a place for them to drag blankets, curl up on the floor, and tell ghost stories on rainy days, a place to keep their favorite books, a place to draw on the walls without fear of being scolded, and, years later, to cover those same walls with pictures—clothing ads, makeup ads, TV stars, rock bands, friends, boyfriends. Although I never asked her, I've always felt that this was the original shrine, the place that inspired my mother to create the others.

I locate the switch inside the doorway, and when I press it, a soft, pink bulb glows from the ceiling like a cotton-candy sunset. It was Renny's idea. She always loved pink. I try to remember how many years it's been since I've set foot in here. Five? Six? Everything looks the same. The two white cushions on the floor, rescued from the old sofa my parents got rid of decades ago; the blue vase in the corner, with its silk tiger lilies; yellow throw pillows Renny dragged in after she redecorated her bedroom in lavender; a book on hairstyles, with a picture of Jennifer Aniston on the cover, circa *Friends*; an old makeup case with a half-used pink lipstick called Dream Girl.

I stare at the collage of photos Renny and I arranged on the wall so many years ago. In one, I'm a year old, and Renny is holding me with a three-year-old's eager, proud grin. In another, we're in the auditorium at Howe Elementary, and my third-grade class has just completed its spring musical program. Something about the pioneers and westward expansion. I still remember the red and white checked dress I wore. I looked like a picnic tablecloth.

There's a picture of Renny and me and Mom and Dad at the pond in Central Park, on the trip we took to New York when Dad was getting the Northeastern Poetry Society Prize. There are people in rowboats behind us and, beyond them, clusters of trees and a huge building with towers soaring into an endless sky. I think that must have been 1992. I was in fourth grade, and Renny was in sixth. I remember the cream-colored sweater she's wearing, with the faux fur around the collar and the pearl buttons. I remember there was a boy she liked back then, and the thought of it scared me. I thought boys were such losers.

There's a photo of us in our driveway, me with my Raleigh and Renny with her Schwinn. We're holding the handlebars, a breeze blowing our hair, Long Island Sound whipping up a little chop behind us, like icing on the water. When I remove the thumbtack to take the photo off the wall for a closer look, I find another picture behind it. It's Renny, on the night of her senior prom at Dorset High. She's standing next to a boy with dark hair and sleepy eyes. It's the middle of May, only a week before she died.

Her hair is long, styled in loose waves that unfurl down her back. She's wearing a pale-blue gown, the most gorgeous thing I'd ever seen. She and Mom bought it weeks before the prom, and as soon as I saw it, I was dying to try it on. One day, when no one was home, I did. But it didn't look good on me. The hem dragged on the floor, and the bust was too big. I felt like a child pretending to be a grown-up.

Smoothing the bent corner of the photo, I stare at Renny. She's beautiful. That's the thing about death. It freezes you in time, locks you into a moment. She'll always look that way. She'll never have a wrinkle, a blemish, crow's feet, a sagging neck. She'll never worry about finding a job or whether the man she's in love with will love her back or what the rest of her life is going to be like.

I gaze at the boy with the sleepy eyes, Elliot Frasier, the former star quarterback of the Dorset Dragons. He dated Renny all senior year, took her to the prom, and then broke up with her just a few days before the Cinderella Ball. What happened the evening Renny died was my fault. I know that. But it started with Elliot. Renny wouldn't have been upset if Elliot hadn't broken up with her. I often wonder about that. If she hadn't been dating Elliot, if she had never met Elliot, if Elliot had never been born . . . There's no stopping how far back I can go.

I saw him only once after that summer, here in town. He was coming out of Tyler's Stationery. It must have been ten years ago. He was dressed in a suit and tie, and his hair was a lot shorter than he used to wear it. He was with a woman in a white dress, and she was carrying a shopping bag. I wondered what was in there. Invitations to their wedding? She was smiling; he was laughing. I wanted to shout, *You have no right to laugh. If my sister had never met you, she might be alive today!* I was about twenty feet away, walking in their direction. I would have run right into them. Instead, I buried those words in my heart and crossed the street. What else could I do? I tack the picture back on the wall, covering it once more with the photo of Renny and me and our bikes.

There's a wicker basket full of magazines, and I sit on the old sofa cushion and grab the issue of *Seventeen* from the top of the pile. In my early teen years, every girl I knew read this magazine, devouring the how-to articles on flirting and dating, columns about "true" embarrassing moments we all knew were fabricated, and sobering, cautionary tales of girls whose best friends had died of rare diseases. This issue, from November of 1995, has a very young Natalie Portman on the cover.

I pick up an April 1994 issue of *YM*, full name *Young & Modern*, although nobody ever called it that. This magazine was my go-to, my staple, back in the day. Drew Barrymore is on the cover, a teenager herself. "Drew: How She Beat Her Bad Rep" is the lead article, followed by stories on acne, the mysteries of men, and "Heather Locklear: Her Shocking Hair & Hunk History."

I pull out a few more magazines, and then I find something a little different—a 1996 issue of *Cosmopolitan* with Cindy Crawford on the cover, and it feels as though someone's just opened a window and let in a blast of arctic air. This is what Renny took from Nutmeg Market the day I realized she'd begun to shoplift. Cluny and I were riding by on our bikes, and Renny was walking out of the market with some friends, one of whom had already turned sixteen and was driving. I saw Renny pull a magazine from under her sweater and hold it up like a trophy right before she got into the car.

When I went into her room that night, I found her sitting at the vanity in her bathroom, trying on plum-colored lipstick. Green Day was blasting on her portable CD player. *Cosmo* lay splayed on the floor.

I pointed to the magazine. "I know you stole that."

She glanced at me in the mirror. "What?"

"I saw you coming out of Nutmeg Market. I know you stole the magazine. You had it under your sweater."

She shrugged, picked up a pair of scissors, and trimmed a few split ends from her hair. "So I take things sometimes. So what?" I think she had second thoughts then, about admitting it, because she shot me a nasty look and added, "Don't you dare tell Mom."

"You shouldn't do that," I said. "It's wrong. And you're going to get caught. Why don't you just buy it?"

"Because I don't have the money."

"Then ask Mom," I said. "Or I'll give you money." I was a better saver back then.

"Grace, butt out," she said. "I can take care of myself."

After that, I worried about anything new she brought home—jewelry, clothes, CDs, magazines, makeup—wondering if she'd bought it with her allowance or if she'd stolen it, wondering when she'd get caught. But she didn't. She never got caught.

There's a knock on the door. I sit still, hoping if I don't make a sound, Dad or Mom, whichever one of them is out there, will go away.

"Grace, are you in there?" It's Dad.

I remember the disappointment Renny and I felt as kids when we discovered that our secret room wasn't as secret as we'd thought—that our parents had known about it for years. When I was ten, I overheard Mom say something to Dad about *the girls' little hideout.* And I knew. Years later my mother told me she had once considered putting shelves in there to store the Christmas decorations, but when she realized Renny and I had laid claim to it, she canceled the plan.

My father knocks again, and I hold my breath. I don't want to talk about Renny anymore. I glance at the cover of *Cosmo* again. Cindy Crawford's brown eyes stare back at me. My parents don't know about the shoplifting. Or anything else. And I'm not about to tell them.

Dad turns the door handle, but the door sticks and rubs against the jamb. I wait for him to give it a little shove, a little more pressure, but it doesn't happen. Instead, I hear his footsteps recede down the hall. I return the copy of *Cosmo* to the stack of magazines, and I sit there on the old sofa cushion, under the pink light, wishing Renny were with me, wishing I'd never done what I did on that last day.

CHAPTER 14

The subject of a sentence is the noun
or pronoun that performs the verb.
*A <u>woman</u> may attract the attention of
more than one man.*

The next morning, on the kitchen counter, I find a manila envelope with my name scrawled on the back in Dad's handwriting. Inside is something I haven't seen in at least a decade—*All She Ever Knew*, my college script from Essentials of Screenwriting, junior year, Mrs. Semple. Clipped to the cover page is a note, written on a little piece of paper with the logo of a chisel and the name *Whorley Tools* at the top:

Grace,
I, more than anyone, know how special and talented you are. Here is just one example, from your college days. Very impressive! Please read this and believe that I believe in you.
With much love,
Dad

Ever since I was little, my father has made a habit of leaving things for me to find at times when I'm upset, especially when I'm upset with him. Once he left a pair of his old eyeglasses on my bureau, along with a poem he wrote about needing to see more clearly. Other times he's left books, usually by obscure but nonetheless talented poets. Once he left a pair of my baby shoes, little pink Reebok sneakers, next to my pillow, with a note that said he would never be more than a few footsteps away. And now he's done it again.

But I'm not sure I want to look at my college screenplay. I don't think it was all that good, and I still feel a bit guilty about the A that Mrs. Semple gave me. She should have given me an incomplete, but I guess she thought she was doing me a favor. She knew how many times I'd rewritten the ending, that I couldn't seem to get it right.

A story about a young woman whose sister has terminal cancer can really go in only one direction. Yet one of my versions included a last-minute, miracle cure developed by a handsome research physician/love interest. Another featured the discovery that the sister's perfectly normal X-rays had accidentally been switched with those of a terminally ill patient. And those endings were the most credible of the bunch.

The night before the project was due, I jettisoned the ending altogether, and the next day I turned in an unfinished script. I remember

Mrs. Semple looking at me with her quiet blue eyes and saying, *Someday you'll write the ending.*

On the way out the door, I put the script on the Chippendale chest. Maybe I'll look at it later. It's sweet of my father to tell me he thinks it's good. For that, I feel grateful.

I spend the morning sorting through piles of stuff on the worktable at the bike shop, asking Kevin and A.J. questions, taking pictures of parts and making new labels with names and photos on them. At noon I run out for lunch. When I return, a dozen women are crowded around the shop's entrance, all talking at once. "I'm getting this framed!" one of them says, pressing a piece of paper to her heart. "Those eyes," another says. "Oh my God. I'd follow him anywhere."

I squeeze by them and open the door. Kevin is near the counter, emptying the saddlebag on one of the rental bikes. A.J. is adjusting the back wheel of a mountain bike while its owner, a gray-haired man, looks on. The usual rubbery smell of the shop has been replaced with something sweet. Almost too sweet. It smells like jasmine and that terrible perfume Catch Me!

"What's going on?" I ask Kevin, trying not to inhale too deeply. "What are those women doing outside, and why does it smell in here?"

"I know," he says, closing the saddlebag. "It's bad, isn't it?"

"It's awful."

He steps behind the counter. "This dude came in a little while ago. He was looking at some of the bikes. Next thing I knew, all these ladies were in here. They were trying to make it look like they weren't paying any attention to the guy, but they were definitely checking him out. I knew something was up. Then I realized it was Sean Leeds. I recognized him from *Bullet Holes*."

"Sean Leeds was here?" Oh my God. How did I miss him?

Kevin shrugs. "Yeah. It was definitely him, except he looks a little shorter in person. Man, there must have been thirty ladies here, all going crazy, asking for his autograph. The dude was nice about it, though. He even did some selfies."

Thirty women. I wonder if Porcine Thighs was here. "Did anybody get rowdy?"

"Uh, well, this one lady . . . she wanted Sean to sign her chest, and she was going to take off her shirt, but Mitch said no way, and he walked her outside. She looked almost as old as my mom. That was scary. And some of them had these bottles of perfume they were spraying, until Mitch got them to stop, because it was really stinking up the place."

"So, did he buy a bike, or was he just browsing?"

Kevin runs his finger along the stubble on his chin. "Uh, nope. He was looking for you."

"Me?"

"Yeah. He asked for you. Said he went to your house first. Found out you were here."

My house? "Did he say what he wanted?"

"No. When Mitch told him you weren't here, he left."

"That's it? He didn't leave a message? A phone number?"

"No, but he left something else."

Kevin bends down, and when he stands up again he's holding a huge orchid in a large clay pot. He places it on the counter. The orchid has a half-dozen long, green leaves and one twenty-inch bloom spike that shoots from its base into a tall, graceful arch. Attached to the bloom spike are nine massive blossoms—white with flecks of maroon.

"Wow."

I step closer. It's some kind of cambria. Not your usual grocery store orchid. Nothing you could find around here, that's for sure.

"There's a note," Kevin says, handing me a small envelope.

I rip it open.

Grace,
Thanks for the dance the other night.
I'm hoping you might start a new collection.
Maybe this can be the first.
Yours,
Sean

I read the note again. *A new collection. This can be the first.* I turn the words over in my mind as I study the tiny dots of color on the orchid's petals. I can feel Kevin staring at me, but I can't stop smiling. Maybe Peter's forgotten about me, but it's nice to know that not everyone else has.

Kevin tilts his head. "So you and Sean Leeds are . . . like, friends?"

"Yeah, we're friends."

The bells above the door ring, and three young women stroll in. "Gotta get to work," Kevin says. As he walks toward the women, I hear him mutter, "Sean Leeds . . . Cool."

I pick up the orchid and head into the workroom, where Renny's bike leans against the wall, untouched. A blue Fuji mountain bike is on one of the repair stands. The front wheel is off, and Mitch is removing the stem, the piece that connects the handlebars to the rest of the bike. I wonder when someone will start to work on the Schwinn.

"You just missed all the excitement," Mitch says. "Hollywood came to the Bike Peddler. And apparently Hollywood was looking for you."

"So I hear." I try to keep my tone casual, as though I'm used to people like Sean Leeds inquiring after my whereabouts. I place the orchid on the file cabinet and drop my handbag into the drawer.

Mitch slides the fork, which holds the front

wheel in place, off the bike. "Course, I could have done without the sideshow. Those women were nuts. Autographs, selfies; some of them were spraying that perfume you were wearing yesterday." He gives me a cursory glance. "I had to put a stop to that. This is a bike shop after all, not Sephora."

"Right," I say. "Without that rubbery smell, people might not know."

"I was afraid the lady with the thighs might be here and I'd have to wrestle her to the ground and confiscate her jasmine."

I laugh. "I heard you did have to escort one unruly fan outside."

"News travels fast. Who told you that?"

I pick up a seat post clamp from the worktable and deposit it in a container where several others are stored. "Kevin did. Something about an autograph on her chest?"

"I guess she ran out of paper."

"Well, Sean does attract the ladies. He's a popular guy." I watch as Mitch taps the fork with a hammer and some metal rings fall to the floor.

"Looks to me like you attracted him."

"What?"

"Sean Leeds. He brought you an orchid." Mitch glances at the file cabinet. "So now you really are hanging with the Hollywood crowd."

Here we go again. "I barely know him. I just had a little talk with him one night." I pick up a round piece of metal that looks like a ring. "What's this?"

"That's a headset bearing. It goes in one of those." He points to the small plastic drawers above the worktable, half of which bear my new labels showing the names and photos of the parts inside. "By the way," he says, "good idea with the labels."

So he noticed the labels. And he likes them. Amazing.

"And the table looks a hell of a lot better."

So he noticed that, too. I feel proud of my work.

Mitch picks up a new fork from the table. "Didn't you dance with him at a party?" he says, and I realize he's still talking about Sean.

"How did you hear about that?" I open and close several unlabeled drawers, looking for the place where the bearing belongs. "Is there an underground newspaper in town I don't know about?"

"Everybody heard about that. This is Dorset, remember. The story is that you danced with him in a greenhouse."

"Oh my God, you really did hear everything. Yes, we were in a greenhouse, with orchids. That's why he got me an orchid." All of a sudden I'm feeling defensive. Why does Mitch make me feel that way?

"So," he says, "you danced with Sean, you're dating the director. I'd say you're in pretty good company there, Hollywood." He slides the new fork onto the bike frame.

"Mitch, I'm not from Hollywood. I live in New York, but I'm *from* Dorset. Just like you. I'm a small-town girl. Not glitzy, not flashy, and definitely not Hollywood." I find a drawer with the word Bearings scrawled on a faded label, and I drop the piece into it. "And, although I wish I were dating the director, I'm not. He didn't even have my name on the list to get into the movie shoot yesterday. After he *invited* me."

Mitch puts the handlebars on the bike. "Maybe they only allow one guest at a time."

"What do you mean?"

"Well, Regan Moxley was there, right? Maybe there's a limit on the number of people who they let come watch."

"There really *is* an underground newspaper here. You knew Regan was there?"

"That was in the real newspaper, Grace. There's a photo on the front page."

"The front page of the *Review*?"

"Yeah. There's a copy on the counter, if you want to see it."

I rush into the store and grab the paper, and right there on the front is a photo that makes my stomach lurch. Peter is smiling and pointing to something on a video monitor. And standing next to him, looking at him with dark, adoring eyes, is Regan.

The headline reads, DIRECTOR REVIEWS FOOTAGE WITH DORSET'S NEWEST ACTRESS. I feel my throat tighten as I read the caption.

Film director and former resident Peter Brooks views a scene from yesterday's filming of *By Any Chance*, with resident Regan Moxley. Moxley, who came to watch the action, was later given a small part in the movie. "She's a natural," Brooks said. "She was born to act."

I throw the paper on the counter. Regan got a part in the movie. An actual part. How is that even possible? He won't let me in to watch, but he gives Regan a part. I feel something start to tear inside me, and I just want to cry.

But I don't. I walk back into the workroom and stand in front of the table, looking at everything I still have to organize. I can feel Mitch staring at me. There's an awkward stretch of silence, and then he says, "Are you okay?"

No, I'm not okay. That's what I'd like to say. I watch as he puts the front wheel back on the Fuji, and I'm about to tell him I'm fine. But then I look at Renny's Schwinn again, and the thing that's tearing apart inside me rips even further.

"Is somebody going to get started on my bike?" My voice is wobbling, and I stop for a second to bring it under control. The last thing I want to do is cry. "I can't take looking at it any longer. I'll work extra hours if I need to, but I'd really appreciate it if someone could begin working on it."

Mitch peers at me, his mouth ajar. "Well, yeah. We'll get it done," he says, his voice soft. "I'll have A.J. start on it tomorrow." He takes the Fuji off the repair stand and leans it against the end of the worktable. "Are you still planning to ride it in the challenge?"

"I don't think I'm going to do the challenge," I tell him. "I haven't really been on a bike in years. I only signed up because Regan was making such a big deal about it. I felt I had to compete with her." I pick up another bearing and let it fall into the plastic drawer. "But obviously I can't."

Mitch walks over to Renny's bike, lifts it up, and sets it in the repair stand.

"Are you going to begin working on it?" I ask, feeling a sudden rush of hope.

"Yeah," he says. "You're doing your part of the deal, so I'll do mine."

"Fantastic," I say, stepping closer to the bike and imagining it with a new seat that's not rotted and peeling, wheel spokes that aren't gray and oxidized, tires that aren't flat and cracked, and a chain that's not coated in rust. "I can't believe you're going to take this whole bike apart and put it back together." The prospect seems daunting, but also thrilling.

He runs his hand along the top tube. "I've rebuilt plenty of old bikes, and it's always interesting. You usually run into some kind of challenge. Sometimes you'll have a nut that's frozen on there because it hasn't been moved for a long time, and it just doesn't want to come off."

I hope that doesn't happen with Renny's bike. "What do you do? I mean, if you can't get it off?"

"Oh, I'll get it off," he says. "With this." He picks up a can of WD-40 from the table. "Sometimes, with a part that's stubborn, you've got to spray it, leave it for a while, loosen it a little, spray it again, leave it, loosen it. It can take a couple of days."

"Just to get one bolt off?"

"Sure, sometimes," he says, putting the WD-40 back on the table. "That's part of the challenge of taking something old apart and reassembling it as something new, something better. Sometimes you need a few days just to get one bolt off, but you've got to have a clean slate before you can put the bike back together."

You've also got to have a lot of patience. My father might, at least if he had the mechanical inclination. I can see him in here, tinkering with a bike the way he tinkers with his puzzles. I'd never have the patience for it.

"So where do you start?" I ask.

"With the wheels," Mitch says. He flips the quick-release lever on the front wheel, removes the wheel, and leans it against the wall. Then he does the same with the back wheel. "Next, I have to get the chain off. Once that's done, I'll start taking off the cranks so I can get to the bottom bracket."

"The crankset is here, and the bottom bracket's there, right?" I point to the parts.

"Uh, yeah. That's right."

"The bottom bracket connects the crankset to the bike and lets the crankset rotate," I add.

Mitch gives me a curious look. "Yeah, right again. Are you taking a class at night or something?"

I laugh, feeling good that I've done my homework.

"Okay, so, now the chain," he says as he picks up a metal tool that looks like a T. He places it around a section of the Paramount's chain. Then he turns to me. "Hey, why don't you do this?"

"Me?"

"Yeah, you. You're learning about bikes."

I move closer. "What do I do?"

"Just turn the top of this tool a few times. Right here." He points to the horizontal part of the T. "It will break one of the pins in the chain."

"Okay." I grab the tool and give it a few turns. The more I turn, the harder it gets.

"Keep going," he says.

I turn the tool again, and suddenly, the old, rusty chain gives way. It breaks apart and falls to the cement floor, landing with a *clank*. I look at the broken chain and think about how many years it was on that bike. It could have stayed on there forever, but then the bike wouldn't work. It had to come off. There's something almost freeing in knowing this is the first step in turning around this bike, in taking it from something run-down and unusable to something vibrant and functioning. I think about what Mitch said. *You've got to have a clean slate before you can put something back together.*

We pedal down Main Street. I'm on a rental from the shop, a black Trek road bike, and Mitch is slightly ahead of me, on his own carbon-fiber Trek. I overheard Kevin say it cost eight thousand dollars. Eight thousand!

"Really," Mitch says, "all you'll need is a little training, and you'll be able to handle the Dorset Challenge. You don't have to do the fifty-mile ride. There's one that's twenty-five."

Twenty-five miles. I'm not so sure I can do that, although the Trek feels pretty good, much lighter and quicker than my old Raleigh. I have a sudden sense of liberation being outside, my own legs propelling me, the freewheel making its soft ticking sound as I coast.

Downtown seems so much different on a bike than in a car—so much busier. Drivers whiz by, people cross in the middle of the street, other bikers race past, tourists move in packs on the sidewalk. But soon we're off Main Street, heading down quiet roads where graceful trees dip their branches and the air is cooler. These are roads I haven't seen from the seat of a bike in years.

We pass a field where a man is riding a lawn mower, and the sweet scent of green, fresh-cut grass fills my lungs. We ride by yards where golden day lilies and yellow coreopsis and purple hydrangeas climb through gardens. Passing a stream, I hear water gurgle over rocks and notice dappled sunlight falling through the trees. Farther on, a black Lab bounds toward me, tail wagging, and races me along the edge of a wide lawn. At the end of the property, he stops and barks, an invitation to return.

Mitch waves me forward, and I ride up beside him. "I think we'll do about ten miles," he says. "Round-trip."

"Are you crazy? That's too far."

"No, it's not. You can do it."

I give him a dirty look, and the image of Mitch as a drill sergeant comes to mind, with me struggling to lift a thirty-pound weight in each hand and him counting, *Sixteen, seventeen, eighteen*—

"Where are we going?" I ask.

"You'll see."

A chipmunk scurries along the shoulder and into the woods. "Just don't take me on a ton of big hills."

"Oh, I won't take you on a ton."

"Or any."

"Grace," he says as we go around a bend, "you can't avoid hills. This is Connecticut, remember. Not Manhattan."

A half hour later we're somewhere just north of Dorset, on a road where houses are tucked back in the trees. I'm winded. We've been up and down a number of hills, some small, some not so small, and Mitch still refuses to tell me where we're going. I don't recognize the road we're on now, and I see another hill ahead of us. This one's big, very big, so big it looks as if it goes straight up. I downshift, and I downshift again, and pretty soon, I'm all the way down to first gear, and I'm still struggling. Mitch, who is ahead of me, finally turns, and when he sees how far behind I am, he rides down the hill to rejoin me.

"You okay?" he asks as he pedals alongside me. He's not even winded.

Huff, puff. "Can I get off"—*huff, puff*—"and walk it up?"

"No, you cannot get off and walk it up. What kind of trainer would I be if I let you do that?"

Huff, puff. "A nice one?"

"Sorry. Keep going. You can do this, Grace."

"You're a sadist," I tell him, panting.

"Only on Wednesdays. You're good for this. I know you are. You're not going to let a little hill get in your way."

A big mountain is more like it. All I can see ahead of me is hill, hill, hill. My legs are on fire, but I keep pedaling.

Mitch pedals on ahead a little and circles back again. "Do you know where we are?"

Huff, puff. "No idea."

"Then it'll be a nice surprise when we reach our destination, because it's really pretty."

The surprise for me will be getting there at all. When Mitch finally says, "Almost there," I manage to pull out my last ounce of energy and make it to the top.

"Oh my God!" I straddle the bike and lean over the handlebars, trying to catch my breath. In the distance, through the trees, I can see the blue of Long Island Sound. I pull out my water bottle and take a long drink. Mitch does the same.

"Come on. You can coast the rest of the way there," he says.

"Where is *there?* Where are we going?"

"You'll see."

I let out a loud sigh, half fatigue and half frustration, and then we fly down the other side of the hill, the tires zipping along the pavement in front of me, trees whizzing by, my hands on the brakes, gently controlling my descent. I tilt back my head and let the breeze cool my neck, wet with perspiration. At the bottom, Mitch turns onto a dirt road marked by a sign: Bratton Point Lighthouse.

"I've never been out here," I say, pulling up next to him.

He looks at me as though I've told him I've never eaten a potato. "How could you never have been to the lighthouse?"

"I don't know. I just haven't."

We ride to the end of the road, where a long, grassy stretch of land juts into the water. An old two-story house stands in the middle of the land, its pristine, white walls blinding against the cobalt sky, its red roof like a brilliant smile. Attached to the right side of the house, and only slightly higher, is a white lighthouse. A driveway leads to the house, and a white picket fence runs around the buildings and part of the lawn.

We leave our bikes in the driveway and walk across the grass, past the house and lighthouse, to where the lawn recedes and turns to boulders and rocks and the water takes over. The sound stretches around us, a small chop licking up a bit of froth.

"You're right. It is beautiful here." I can taste the salt in the breeze as it caresses my face.

"Was it worth the ride over the hill?"

"Every last breath," I say. Then I realize I'll have to do the whole thing again. "But I'm not looking forward to the trip back."

"Oh, we don't have to go the same way," Mitch says. "We can avoid the hill."

"What? Then why didn't we avoid it coming here?"

He smiles. "You needed to know you could do it."

"So you've really never been here," Mitch says as we sit down on a flat rock by the water, the lighthouse to our left.

"No. Maybe I'm just spoiled, growing up on the water and all. It's always been right there, in my backyard."

"You must be a good swimmer then."

"I'm okay. My sister was the real swimmer. She was on a team when she was a kid. She did a lot of team things, a lot of athletics." I laugh. "She tried to coach me in some of the sports we did in school, but it didn't help—I was hopeless."

A seagull glides over the water, its wings spread to catch the air current. "You must miss her," Mitch says. "It sounds like you were really close."

I reach down and pick up a handful of the broken shells that lie scattered among the rocks. "Yeah, I do miss her," I say, studying the shards. We sit in silence, and I listen to the water lap against the rocks. "The thing is," I finally say, "it never should have happened. She shouldn't have been driving. Not when she was upset." I gaze at the water, so dark now, it's almost black. "And not when she'd been drinking."

"What happened?" Mitch asks, his voice quiet.

311

It seems like such a simple question, but the answer is complicated. "It started with a guy," I say. "Elliot Frasier." I wipe my hands, and the shards of shell fall onto the rocks. "They dated all senior year, and then he broke up with her." I glance at Mitch. "But that was only part of it. The other part was that Peter and I were kind of getting together. We'd been friends, but it was becoming more than that. And Renny didn't want to hear about it."

"Because of her own situation."

"Yes. She was angry with Elliot and jealous of me. And she'd been drinking. It was a very bad combination. The worst."

A spray of salt dampens my hair; a breeze blows through the sedges. "I should have left her alone. You know . . . gotten out of her room and stayed out of her way. We got into a fight and said some pretty nasty things. The kind of things siblings say, I guess. But they usually get the chance to apologize."

Mitch looks at me. "I'm sorry, Grace."

"Yeah," I say. "So am I."

"Are we trespassing?" I ask as we walk across the grass and stop at the picket fence in front of the lighthouse. "Does somebody live here?"

"Not anymore," Mitch says. "The light's been automated."

"Oh, right." I gaze at the lantern room, at the top

of the lighthouse, and think about the lives it must have saved over the years, warning boats away from the shoals.

"People used to live here, though," Mitch says as we walk around the perimeter of the fence. "There were lighthouse keepers here starting in 1827, when the owner of the land sold it to the federal government. The government built the original lighthouse and a little residence and hired the former owner as the first keeper."

"Lighthouse keeper. That's a job you don't see advertised anymore."

Mitch smiles. "No, you don't. There were probably eight or ten of them here over the years, including a woman who took over the job from her husband after he died."

"A woman lighthouse keeper," I say as we continue to walk alongside the fence. "She must have been ahead of her time."

"I suppose so."

"And when did the last keeper leave?"

"I think it was around 1987," Mitch says. "That's when the Coast Guard automated the light." He points to the lantern room. "But it still has the original Fresnel lens."

I look at the lighthouse and the attached residence, with its clean white walls, fresh, gray trim, and bright-red roof, and I wonder what it would have been like to live here. "It's such a pretty place," I say. "What a view they must have had."

"Yeah. Incredible view," Mitch says as his gaze goes from the lighthouse to the water.

"There's something so romantic about it, the idea of living by a lighthouse."

"I've always thought so, too," he says. He turns to me and smiles, and all of a sudden he leans in. He looks into my eyes, and I think he's going to kiss me. And I realize I want him to kiss me. I close my eyes, and, as I'm waiting for it to happen, someone calls out.

"Excuse me, are these your bikes?"

I open my eyes. A short, sturdy-looking man stands in the driveway by a green pickup truck. The name Anderson's Lawn & Landscaping is on the door. Three other men step out of the truck.

"Yes," Mitch says. "They're ours."

"You'll need to move them," the short man says. "I've got to pull this truck in here."

Mitch looks at me. "Guess we'd better go."

"Right," I say, but as we walk to the bikes, I'm scrambling to figure out what just happened, trying to wrap my head around it. Was he going to kiss me? I don't think I imagined that. Was I going to let him? I was. I know I didn't imagine that.

I ride in front on the return trip. It's almost five o'clock, and we're cycling down Elm Street, along the back of the village green, when I see Peter leaving Ernie's with a take-out bag in his hand. He's wearing a pair of jeans that fit him perfectly and a charcoal-gray T-shirt, and I just want to kill him for the way he stood me up yesterday.

For a second, all I can see are Peter and Regan, and they're at the Academy Awards again, the two of them seated together, her hand linked in his. But this time it's Regan's name that's called. She gives Peter a kiss and sashays her way up the steps to the stage to collect *her* Oscar statuette. *Best Actress in a Supporting Role.*

No! I pedal faster, until I'm almost alongside Peter's parked Audi. As he's about to open the door, I give the handbrakes a hard squeeze, and the bike skids to a stop beside him.

He does a double take. "Grace? Oh my God. Look at you. What are you doing on that bike?" He's all friendly, as if nothing's happened.

"I'm riding it," I say, pretending nothing's happened as well. "I'm training for the Dorset Challenge."

"What's the Dorset Challenge?"

"You haven't heard of it? It's a very demanding bike ride being held on the Fourth of July."

Mitch pulls up beside me, and before he can say anything, I grab on to his arm. "And speaking of training, here's my trainer." I smile. "Peter Brooks, this is Mitch Dees. Mitch, Peter Brooks."

The two men eye each other. "You're the

movie director," Mitch says as they exchange a perfunctory handshake.

"Guilty as charged," Peter says. "And I guess you're the trainer."

"Ah, I'm not really a trainer. Although I am training Grace. I make an exception for her." He glances at me. "She's special."

I feel myself start to blush.

"That's nice of you," Peter says, but there's a slight edge to his tone. Now he's the one looking at me. "Yes, Grace is special."

"We had quite a ride," I say. "Mitch took me to the Bratton Point Lighthouse. He knew all about its history, the lighthouse keepers, the lens. It was fascinating."

"Oh, really?" Peter says.

"I'm a history buff," Mitch says. "I teach it at Thatcher."

"And he helps his dad at the Bike Peddler in the summer," I add. "He cycles a lot. That's why he's in such great shape."

"I have a bike," Peter says, a little defensively.

"I'm sure it's very nice," I say as I check my watch. "Well, we'd better be going." I slide back onto my seat. Then I smile. "Oh, sorry I didn't catch you yesterday."

Peter gives me a quizzical look. "What do you mean? What was yesterday?"

I keep the smile on my face, although it's a strain. "You told me to come visit you at the set. So I did. I was right outside the Sugar Bowl."

Mitch pulls out his water bottle, leans against Peter's car, and takes a leisurely drink.

"You were there?" Peter asks. "Yesterday?"

"Yes. But your production assistant wouldn't let me in. He said my name wasn't on the list."

Peter's eyebrows draw together. "You're kidding me. I told Rob Nagle to put you on the list."

"Well, I guess Rob Nagle, whoever he is, didn't do it. Although he must have put Regan Moxley's name on there. She walked right in."

"But I—"

"By the way," Mitch says, "there was a nice photo of you and Regan in the paper. Did you see that?"

Peter glares at him. Then he puts his arm around me and pulls me close. His T-shirt feels soft, and it has that Peter smell I've always loved. "Grace, I'm sorry. I had no idea. I thought it was all set up. Why would I invite you and then not arrange for you to be let in?" He shakes his head. "I'll have Rob's ass in a sling. I'll have him fired. How about that?" He grins, and his eyes sparkle.

I feel myself begin to thaw. It was just a mistake. Why did I jump to conclusions? I'm sure there's a reasonable explanation about Regan as well. "I guess firing him would be a good start."

Peter laughs and gives me a squeeze. "Okay, you've got it."

"Grace," Mitch says, looking a little impatient, "I think we'd better be getting back."

"Just one more thing," Peter says, pulling his arm a little tighter around my waist. "I was going to call you, but now I can ask you in person. I'm going to be one of the judges at the apple pie contest at Founder's Day this Saturday, and I was wondering if you'd go with me."

"You're going to be a judge?" I say. "I'm impressed."

"It's not that big a deal," Mitch says as he inspects his front brake. "I've done it before."

"Well, I know about *eating* apple pies," Peter tells me. "But I don't know anything about judging them."

"You'll be fine," I say. "I don't think they'll ask for your judging credentials."

"No, they won't," Mitch says. "I told you, I've done it."

Peter gives him an exasperated look and then returns his attention to me. "So, do you want to go? I can pick you up at noon."

Founder's Day with Peter. I'm jumping for joy inside. "I'll meet you there," I say. Did Mitch's shoulders just slump a little? "I'm going in the morning with Cluny and Greg and their girls."

"Then I'll call you when I get there," Peter says. He leans over and whispers, "I hope all is forgiven."

"Yes," I whisper back. "All is forgiven."

CHAPTER 15

A participle is a word formed from a verb
and used as an adjective.
*In sporting events, <u>competing</u> teams
are not always evenly matched.*

"**C**luny, it's not that good. Please put it back."
She's holding my college screenplay, having
plucked it from the Chippendale chest in the hall.

"No, I want to read it. Let me be the judge of
how good or bad it is."

"But I never finished it." I try to grab the script
from her, but she dodges me and slips out of the
house with it.

"This would be like me paging through some
sketchbook you had when you were in college," I
say as we walk toward Greg's Tahoe.

"I wouldn't mind if you looked at my old
sketchbooks. They're still me. My work was a lot
simpler back then, at least in some ways, but I'm
not ashamed of it. And you shouldn't be ashamed
of yours, either."

"I'm not ashamed. I just . . ." I don't finish the
thought because I'm not sure what the thought is.
Am I ashamed of it? Or am I ashamed that I'm
not doing something better with myself, and the
screenplay is a reminder of that? Maybe it's a

little bit of both. Oh God. Could my father be right? Do I have more talent than I'm giving myself credit for? Am I afraid to try something more challenging? To take a chance?

Cluny's six-year-old daughter, Morgan, grabs my hand as we stroll down Main Street toward the middle of town, where the Founder's Day celebration is taking place. "Aunt Grace, my friend Lilly says they've got funnel cake."

"Really. Then we'll have to get some, won't we?"

Cluny sighs. "You're corrupting her."

"No, I think it's this *Lilly* who's corrupting her. And, anyway, they can't eat carrot sticks all the time."

"What's funnel cake?" asks Elizabeth, who is four.

"What's corrupting?" Morgan asks.

"We'll explain later," Greg tells them.

Up ahead, a blue and white banner hangs over the road. *Happy 375th Birthday Dorset!* It's just crying out for a comma. *Happy Three Hundred Seventy-fifth Birthday.* Pause. *Dorset.* If only I had a Sharpie that big.

The girls skip ahead to catch up with their father. Cluny turns to me. "So, tell me what's *really* going on."

"What do you mean?"

"With Mitch. Miller's Orchards on Tuesday, the

lighthouse on Wednesday. What's happening with you two?"

"Nothing. I told you, we delivered a bike, and he bought a pie."

"And you took a romantic walk in the orchard."

"No, we didn't. It was just a walk."

"Okay, but the next day you rode bikes to the lighthouse."

"He's training me for the Dorset Challenge. He wanted to take me up this monster hill."

"If he made a pass, it sounds as if he's training you for more than the Dorset Challenge."

"Cluny, stop. Honestly. I don't even think he was making a pass. I think I kind of imagined it. And, anyway, everything's great now with Peter. I was so relieved when he told me the whole deal with the movie shoot was just a mistake."

"So you didn't have any other outings with Mitch."

"No, that was it. He wasn't even in the shop the past two days. He went to a bike race, and I've just been working. You should see the cool storage bins and crates I got at Sage Hardware."

"Greg," Cluny calls out. "Elizabeth's sneaker is untied. Can you get that, please?" She gives me an incredulous look. "Most women lust after clothes and jewelry. You're ecstatic about storage bins."

"Oh, I still love clothes and jewelry."

"Thank God. I was worried." She laughs. Then

her expression becomes serious. "So, you're really going to ride in that bike outing?"

"I don't know. There's a route that's twenty-five miles. It's a lot better than fifty, but it still seems like a long way." We walk in silence for a bit. Then I stop. "Hey, would you ride in it with me? Please? It could be a lot of fun."

"Oh, Grace, I can't. I run and do my yoga, but I'm not in bicycling shape."

"Neither am I. Come on, Cluny, *please.* I'd really like to show Regan Moxley I can do it. Wouldn't you?"

She raises her eyebrows and lets out an extended sigh. "Well, I guess when you put it that way . . . Yeah, okay."

"Yay!" I give her a hug.

We walk to the Founder's Day entrance, where a sign reads, *All proceeds benefit the Dorset Historical Society and this year's special recipient, the Dorset Animal Rescue League.* Greg buys the tickets and refuses to take my money.

"Come on, Greg. I'm not a charity case," I tell him.

He looks at me. "Grace, has anyone ever told you that you need to relax a little?"

"Who? Me?"

He laughs. I don't see what's so funny.

A volunteer hands us programs. *Games on the Green, Baxter Middle School Choir, Apple Pie Contest, Vintage Car Parade, Revolutionary*

War Reenactment, Tara Jones Dance Studio, Zip Roddy Quartet.

We pass booths selling oysters, burgers, barbecue chicken, and fried clams. Smoke billows over the food tents, and the smells of hickory and barbecue and fish drift on a slow breeze, making me hungry. I study the people going by: teenagers in ripped jeans, fathers with children on their shoulders, mothers with babies in front packs, toddlers in strollers, dogs in strollers, dogs on leashes, college girls in short-shorts, elderly people with canes. We pass a line of children waiting for their turn in a hula-hoop competition, and a man selling T-shirts that say, *Dorset: Here's to the Next 375!*

At the Dorset Historical Society booth, two women in hooped skirts and aprons are handing out pamphlets about the history of the town. A collie dressed in a Colonial pinafore comes over and sniffs my ankles as I look at a display of old photographs. A sepia-toned picture of Main Street shows a blacksmith's forge where 32 Degrees, the ice cream shop, now stands.

Farther down the street, a line of children and parents snakes around a booth where an artist is offering free face painting. We wait for almost an hour so the girls can have their faces done up like Disney princesses.

Then we're on to the dunk tank. Scott Danzberger, from the town's board of selectmen, sits, dripping wet, on a precarious-looking platform a couple of feet above the water. Greg pays the five-dollar fee, and the second softball he throws hits the target, triggering the lever that dumps Scott into the tank.

"Sorry about that," Greg says. "But it *is* for a worthy cause."

"You'd better vote for me in the next election," Scott calls as we walk away.

Greg offers to take Morgan and Elizabeth to see the red engine on display from the Dorset Fire Department and then to visit the bounce house, their favorite part of any celebration. "You know, once they get into the bounce house, we'll probably never see them again," he tells Cluny.

"That's fine," she says. "As long as they end up in a good home."

It's about twelve thirty when I get a call from Peter telling me he's here. "But they've got us in a tent," he says. "And they're not letting anyone in but the judges."

"Wow. Serious business."

He laughs. "Yeah, guess so. I'll call you as soon as I'm done."

It's close to two when he calls again and tells me the results are being tallied. I arrive at the tent to find dozens of people assembled there. The front flaps of the tent are parted to reveal a long table inside, strewn with the remains of about twenty-five pies. Some of the pie plates are empty, but most still have a few slices on them, and the variety is impressive—traditional crusts, lattice-work crusts, crumbly toppings instead of crusts, and crusts with decorations made from dough, like apples and leaves, red stripes and blue stars.

I spot Peter talking to some people by another table, farther inside the tent. He's wearing a white button-down shirt, dark-denim jeans, and a blue blazer. I've always been a sucker for a blue blazer, and my heart does a little jump when I wave and he waves back.

"Hey, Gracie girl." He walks over and gives me a kiss.

I glance at his hair where he's got that little wave, and I'm dying to touch it. "You look so handsome in your blazer."

"Thanks," he says. "I thought I should dress like a judge."

"Yes, you're very judicial looking. All you're missing is the white wig."

"That's only for pie contests in England, Grace."

"Oh, right. I forgot."

A tall woman with strawberry-blond hair emerges from the tent and raises a microphone. "We have our winners," she tells the group, which closes in around her, people holding cameras and cell phones in anticipation. A bearded, pot-bellied man from Channel 22 News stands in the front with a video camera, ready to capture the moment. "First place goes to Meredith Leonard, for her three-apple pie," the woman announces to loud applause.

Peter steers me away. "Let's go," he says. "I've had about all the pie I can take for one day. I may never eat apple pie again. Or even apples."

"Oh, don't say that." I think of all the trees in Miller's Orchards, all the restaurants in Dorset, each putting its own particular spin on an apple pie in order to lay claim to having the best in town, all the residents who entered their pies in the contest. "It's almost like saying you'll never come back to Dorset."

He gives me a quizzical look. "I didn't mean it that way, Grace."

"Oh, well, that's good." We meander down the street. "So, what's going on? Are things better? With the movie?"

"There are always ups and downs. But overall, things are better. The rewrites are going well, and we're back on schedule. That keeps the studio happy, anyway."

"I'm glad."

We pass a poster listing the day's events. "Hey." I tap his shoulder. "Look at this. The Tara Jones Dance Studio is going to perform in a few minutes. Maybe we should watch."

He grimaces. "No, thanks. She always yelled at me for turning in the wrong direction. I used to get my right and left mixed up. She'd come at me with those long, spindly fingers." He raises his hand, extending his index finger. *"You, young man. Turn the other way!* I can't believe she's still teaching. She must be a hundred by now."

"She always did say dancing keeps you young," I remind him with a smirk.

"All right, folks. That ends the egg toss. Let's get ready for our next event." Peter and I stand at the edge of the village green, where a stout, sun-burned man with a microphone is speaking to a group of about twenty people. A banner over the gazebo announces that the Zip Roddy Quartet will be performing at four o'clock. In anticipation of the event, some fifty people have already set up collapsible chairs and spread blankets on the grass.

"Okay," the announcer says. "I'll need every-body who wants to do the three-legged race right over here." He looks around, waving in the stragglers at the edge of the group. "Don't be shy, folks. Find a partner, tie two of your legs together, and run the length of the field and back. Nothing to it."

"Grace!"

I turn at the sound of my name. Cluny and Greg and the girls are walking toward us.

"Hey, Peter," Cluny says. "How was the pie contest?"

"I survived, although I might need to run a couple of miles later to make up for it."

"We still have room for a few more teams," the announcer says, a hopeful note in his voice. The crowd of onlookers is growing.

"You could run right now," Greg says. "In the three-legged race."

Peter glances toward the green, where the teams are assembling along a horizontal chalk line drawn on the grass. He turns to me. "Yeah, how about it?"

"The race?" I expect him to laugh, but he doesn't.

"Sure, we could be a team."

I can't believe he's serious. "No, no." I cross my arms. "That's not my thing. I mean, you know I'm not very athletic."

"Oh, come on. For old times' sake. It'll be fun."

"Yeah, Grace," Cluny joins in. "For old times' sake."

"What old times?"

Peter nudges me. "We did a three-legged race once at a party. Don't you remember?"

"That wasn't a three-legged race," I remind him. "It was a wheelbarrow race. And you ended up steering me right into the Rickenhouses' pool." I can still feel the chill of that water. End of September. Pool heater off.

He glances across the green as though he's trying to recall the event. "Well, it *was* dark. You can't blame me for not being able to see. And it was still fun."

"Maybe for you," I say. "But, putting that aside, look at those two ten-year-old boys out there. They'll crush us."

"All we have to do is walk fast," Peter says. "And stay in sync."

"It's not that easy."

"Gracie girl. Where's your sense of adventure? And nostalgia?"

I'm racking my brain to come up with an alternative activity—the school choir performance, the vintage cars, anything—when a familiar voice joins the discussion.

"I'll do the three-legged race with you, sweetie."

The Southern accent, the sultry tone. It's Regan. Her smile is outlined in bright-pink lipstick, and she's showing off her tan size-zero legs in black cutoffs so skimpy, I'm not even sure they qualify as shorts. I can feel my jaw muscles tighten like vise grips.

"I'll take him off your li'l ole hands." She smiles and puts her arms around Peter like a lion about to drag its prey into the lair.

Peter shoots me a look that makes me think he's asking for help, but then he laughs. "You're going to run a three-legged race in those?" He points to her platform sandals, which are at least four inches high. "This I've got to see."

"Oh, no, I'll just go barefoot, darlin'." She strokes his cheek.

I can't stand to see her touch him. "No, you won't." I grab Peter's hand. "He's doing the race with me."

"Well, that's a shame," Regan says with a wink. " 'Cause I promise you'd come in first with me, Petey."

Petey? Nobody has ever called him Petey. Cluny and I look at each other, horrified.

"Last call for the three-legged race, folks," the announcer says.

Peter takes off his jacket and hands it to Cluny. "Would you mind holding this?"

Then he takes my hand and leads me to the starting line. A dozen other teams are already lined up—adults, children, and teams of adults and children, which could prove to be the most dangerous of all. The orange pylons on the far side of the green seem as though they're miles away, and I'm beginning to wonder what I've gotten myself into.

"Here you go," the announcer says, handing Peter a cord to tie around our ankles. He steps closer, and I can feel the muscles in his leg, the warmth of his body, as we stand side by side, his blue jeans against my white ones. He ties his right ankle to my left.

"Okay, now, here are the rules." The announcer takes a few steps into the field. "You and your partner have to cross the green and go *around* your pylon." He points and makes a little loop with his finger. "Don't go in *front* of it, or you'll be disqualified. And if you fall down or the two of you get separated, you'll be disqualified. The first team back to the starting line wins. Everybody got that?"

I nod nervously and stare at the stretch of lawn in front of us. *Around the pylons.* I trace a straight path with my finger, adding a little loop at the end. *Don't fall.* I look down, at my left sneaker and Peter's right sneaker, and I think about the walk we took so long ago, after our dance at the Cinderella Ball, on the docks behind the yacht club, where a round, blue moon hung over the water.

As we passed the boats, we called out their names and made up silly stories about how the names came to be. *Reserved Seating* from Dover, *My Girl* from Dorset, *Insomnia* from Dorset, *Lickety Split* from Port Jefferson, *Time Out* from Block Island. And that was when he kissed me, in front of *Time Out.* He tasted like mint gum, and the summer that was almost upon us. He traced his finger along my bare arm, and I felt a current soar through me. Looking at Peter now, his leg pressed firmly against mine, I can still feel that sixteen-year-old hand on my arm.

The announcer raises his microphone. "Just a second, folks. Looks like we have one more team." I look over and I can't believe what I see. It's Regan. And she's found herself a partner:

Mitch. He takes the cord from the announcer, and he and Regan walk to the empty lane to our left. There's only one team between us.

Mitch ties their ankles together, and he and Regan laugh, and there's something about this little scene I find irritating. Maybe it's the way Regan always manages to manipulate the men around her into doing her bidding. I would have thought that Mitch, of all people, was above this. Mitch, who seems to have radar for phonies.

"No, your *left* leg," he says, and Regan laughs again.

"Hey there, Grace," she calls as she links her arm in Mitch's. "Don't we make a great team?" They're almost the same height. Physically, they do look as though they go together, but I'm not about to admit it out loud. "Sorry to hear about your breakup," she says, a false note of sympathy in her voice.

"My what?"

She smiles and glances at Mitch. "He told me."

I'm about to say *Told you what?* And then I realize what she's talking about. She still thinks the two of us were dating. And he told her we broke up!

Peter gives me a puzzled look. "What's she talking about?"

"Nothing," I say. "Just a joke." But as I glance back at Mitch and Regan, I get a queasy feeling in my stomach.

Peter swings his arm around my back and pulls me close. I put my arm around him. "All right," he says. "Let's focus here. Remember, step together. Just think *right leg, middle leg, right leg, middle leg.* That's the key."

Someone yells, *Peter Brooks—go, Hollywood!* and a roar of laughter erupts from the crowd. The announcer raises a starter's pistol, and with a loud crack, the race begins, Peter and I sprinting away from the starting line. He's a horse that wants to gallop, and I'm a rider who wants to trot, and I struggle to keep up with him.

"Slow down or I'll lose my balance!" I yell, our middle leg feeling like the limb of a badly constructed robot.

Peter slows down, but not by much, and I soon realize why. We've gotten a good start, but Regan and Mitch are coming up on our left—Regan, all legs, with her black minishorts, and Mitch, the muscles in his arms flexing as he guides her smoothly over the grass.

I stumble over a dip in the ground, but Peter catches me. *Right leg, middle leg, right leg.* Now Regan and Mitch are breezing along next to us, their strides so in sync, it's almost eerie.

"Good luck catching us! You'll never win!" Regan yells.

"Oh, yes, we will!" I yell back. "Come on, Peter, faster!" He tightens his grip on me, but we're struggling to keep up. I can't stand the fact that she's ahead. If I can't beat her with athleticism, maybe I can at least outwit her. "Hey, Regan," I taunt. "Do you sell SparkNotes at the bookstore?"

"What?" she screams, her eyes blazing.

"Let's go, we're winning," Mitch says.

"You heard me!" I yell back. *Right leg, middle leg.* "SparkNotes. That's all you knew how to read in high school." *Right leg, middle leg.*

"That's not true!"

"Oh, yes, it is. And how about Grover Holland? Are you going to deny that, too?" *Right leg, right leg. Oh, no, I'm goofing up here.*

Regan glares at me. "Who?"

"Come on," Mitch tells her. "We've got a race to win."

"Twelfth grade!" I yell. "You stole Grover Holland from me!"

"Let's go," Peter says, lurching ahead as two teams pass us.

Fall, fall, I chant as Regan and Mitch navigate the orange pylon. But they don't fall. And now they're on their way back.

Peter and I approach the pylon and hobble around it. "Come on, Grace," he says. "They're ahead of us!"

They're way ahead of us. In fact, they're ahead of everybody now, moving so elegantly, they make it look like a dance competition rather than a casual picnic game.

"Damn! They're going to win!" I say as three other teams gain on us.

Peter pulls me forward as if he's shifting into high gear. I almost lose my balance again. The crowd is screaming and cheering. I don't know where Cluny and Greg and the girls are. I can't see anyone. It's all just a big, loud blur. Then I see Regan and Mitch cross the finish line, followed by all the other teams but one, a mother-and-son duo.

"Faster, faster," Peter calls as we barrel ahead, nearing the finish. "Let's not come in last."

"I'm trying," I say, but I can't make my legs move any faster.

In an effort to save our second-to-last place, Peter attempts to leap over the finish line. "No!" I yell as I lose my balance and fall, taking him down with me. We lie in the grass, his arms around me, our ankles still bound by the cord, the finish line under us.

"I think we lost," I say, panting. "Sorry. I told you I wasn't athletic."

He doesn't move. He just looks at me. Then he says, "I don't accept your apology, Grace. I'll only accept this." He slides closer, and I gaze into his eyes. They're blue, like sea glass, with darker blue around the outside. He reaches out and touches my hair, and then he kisses me. His lips are warm and soft. The kiss keeps going and going, and, even though I'm not standing, I feel a little weak in the knees, a little dizzy. When I open my eyes, he's looking at me in a kind of dreamy way. I think he's about to say something. And then I hear a voice above us.

"Well, that was quite a finish."

I look up. It's Mitch. He's holding a trophy with a little gold cup on it. I can feel my face turning red.

"Hey, Mitch," I say as I struggle to untie the knotted cord that binds my leg to Peter's. "Congratulations."

"Here, I'll get that," Peter says, and a moment later we're separated and we stand up. I brush the dirt off my clothes and look around. In the gazebo, the Zip Roddy Quartet is setting up their instruments. A couple of children walk by carrying ice cream cones. Cluny and Greg and the girls come toward us. I look around for Mitch, but he's gone. He's vanished into the crowd, as though he were never there.

CHAPTER 16

The object of a sentence is the entity that
is acted upon by the subject.
She finds <u>herself</u> in the spotlight.

Peter takes my hand, and we walk to the edge of the green and onto the street. I'm still spinning from the kiss when I notice a man waving and coming toward us. I recognize his sandy hair, light complexion, and teeth, which are just a little too big for his face. It's Mark McKechnie, one of the reporters for Channel 22 News. Trailing behind him is the cameraman from the apple pie contest.

"Peter," Mark says, clapping him on the shoulder. "Thanks again for the interview."

"Yeah, sure. No problem." Peter turns to me. "Do you know Mark McKechnie? Channel Twenty-Two?"

"No, I don't think we've met," I say.

Peter introduces us. "Grace also grew up in Dorset," he tells Mark. "We hadn't seen each other in years, and we both ended up here in town at the same time." He puts his arm around me and kisses the top of my head, and I feel a little *zing* go through my body. "Must be fate," he says. He looks at me. "Mark did a little interview with me before the pie contest."

Mark smiles, and his large teeth gleam. "We also got some footage of the race—the winners and . . . uh, the losers. I was wondering if I could maybe get you to say a few words about it on tape. I'm doing a little montage of the whole day here."

Peter laughs. "The race? Oh, I could say a few words about it, all right. But you wouldn't be able to broadcast them. We came in dead last, in case you didn't notice. And it's all Grace's fault." He gives me a playful jab in the ribs. "So maybe you should ask her."

"Right." I jab him back, less playfully.

"Oh, and she lives in Manhattan now, so you can put a nice *small-town girl goes to the big city and comes back* spin on it."

Mark looks at me. "You know what? We could do that. How about it, Grace?"

What? He can't be serious. "You really want to interview me about Founder's Day?"

"Yeah," Mark says. "I'll just ask you a few questions."

He is serious. Oh God, I wonder how my makeup looks. I stare at the grass stains on my white jeans. "No, I don't think so."

"Go ahead," Peter says. "I've done mine. Now it's your turn."

I comb my hair with my fingers and dig into

my handbag for a lipstick. "It's just going to be a couple of questions, right?"

Mark signals to the cameraman, who has wandered over to a fried-clam booth nearby and is chatting with a young brunette. "Willie. Stop flirting and get back here."

Next thing I know, I'm standing on the side of the street, with the village green and the gazebo behind me and the camera pointed at me, a little light on the front glowing red, telling me I'm being recorded. Mark asks when I moved from Dorset, how often I come back, and what I like best about Founder's Day. After that, he launches into a few questions about the race. *Did you have a plan going into it? What is Peter Brooks like as a partner in a three-legged race?*

Then he changes the subject. "So, you're here on vacation?"

"Yes," I say, deciding I'll leave out the lost job, lost boyfriend, and temporarily lost apartment.

"And how are you spending your vacation in your hometown, besides coming to Founder's Day?"

I wonder if he thinks I'm just goofing off—sleeping late, eating ice cream, reading books. Actually, that sounds like what I'd originally planned to do. "I'm working," I tell him, feeling very purposeful.

This elicits raised eyebrows. "You mean you

have a job? While you're here on vacation? That's very enterprising."

"Yes, I have a job. I'm working at the Bike Peddler."

"The Bike Peddler," Mark says. "Now there's a business that's been around a long time. What are you doing there?"

What am I doing? The red button on the camera glows like the eye of a wild animal. Peter gives me a smile and a thumbs-up. I can't let him find out I'm just straightening up a bike-shop work-room. He still remembers me as the girl who won the tenth-grade essay competition and never lost a spelling bee. I've got to make it sound as though I'm doing something more important.

"Well, I'm . . . I'm a consultant. I'm consulting."

"A consultant," Mark repeats. "And what kind of consulting are you doing?"

I glance at Peter again. Little beads of per-spiration trickle down my back. Aren't there consultants who help people organize things? Who go in and sort through . . . stuff? I'm sure there are. I think I've seen ads for them on the Internet. "I'm an organizational . . . um, consultant," I say. "An organizational efficiency consultant." That sounds better. As though it might require an extra degree.

"An organizational effective . . . What was that?" Mark smiles and shakes his head.

"Efficiency. Organizational efficiency."

"And what do you do as this, this consultant to the Bike Peddler?"

"Well, I . . ." I look at the red light again, and my mind starts to unravel like a loose hem. "Well, I have to . . . you know, organize things to make them more efficient . . ."

"So right now there's no efficiency there," Mark says.

That's going a little too far. "I didn't say that. What I can say—"

"So tell us what's going on at the Bike Peddler that they need to hire a consultant from New York."

What's going on? How should I explain this? "Well, you see, I've been going there since I was a kid, and, truthfully, it's always been kind of a mess. It needs a good makeover, for one thing. That would help them move ahead, stay competitive, shall we say? I think they just need to embrace change a bit more."

"Embrace change. So are you saying the store hasn't kept up with the times? That maybe it's a little out of date?"

I hate to sound negative, but what he's saying is true. "Yes, I think that's right. They are outdated. I think they could do a lot better if they took a really good look at everything that's there and reorganized. That would help them become more efficient."

"Efficiency again," Mark says. "I guess in your line of work you must see a lot of businesses that run into problems because of inefficiency."

My line of work? Oh, right. I'm a consultant. "Yes, I do. It's always sad to see. Very sad."

"Well, I'll bet the folks at the Bike Peddler hadn't even realized how far behind the times they are. I'll bet they're glad to have you help bring them into the twenty-first century."

"Well, I didn't mean to suggest they're not in the—"

"There you have it," Mark says, pulling the microphone away from me. "Grace Hammond, organizational . . ."—he looks around nervously for a second—"consultant from New York City, has returned to Dorset. She may have lost the three-legged race, but she's a winner where the Bike Peddler is concerned."

The Zip Roddy Quartet begins to play in the gazebo, doing a cover of the Bruno Mars tune "Just the Way You Are." The lawn around the gazebo is full now, with blankets and folding chairs and people everywhere. Peter and I are sitting on the grass, at the edge of the green, sharing fried oysters and drinking beer.

"We're scheduled to wrap at the end of the week," he says, taking another oyster from the paper plate.

The end of the week? Somehow I didn't realize

it was going to be so soon. "You are?" I say, wondering what's going to happen after that. What it means for us.

"You should come to the shoot on Monday," he says.

"The shoot?" Oh, no, we're trying that again. I take a deep swig of beer as two women walk by pushing strollers.

"Or, wait a minute," he says. "Better yet, come on Tuesday. We'll be at the yacht club. That'll be more fun."

"Will my name be on the list this time?" I'm only half joking. I'm also wondering if Regan's going to be there, but I'm afraid he might say yes, so I don't ask. I wonder if she gets a dressing room.

"Grace, of course you'll be on the list. Don't worry. I'm going to see to it myself."

Thank God. "I'd love to come," I tell him.

"When you get there, call my assistant, Cassandra." He gives me her number and says something about the parking lot. "She'll find you," he says. "There won't be any problems this time."

We listen to the music for a while and then walk to the far side of the green, where there aren't any people—just a small grove of maple trees. He leans me against a tree and draws me in with his blue eyes. They're as deep as the quarry where we used to swim when we were teenagers.

He presses his lips to mine and kisses me, and I think about the Cinderella Ball and the kiss on the docks. I was just a kid then, and now here I am, seventeen years later, with all the flotsam and jetsam of those years still swirling around me, holding me under water: Renny's death, my failed love life, my questionable career. I open my eyes and see Peter looking at me, and I feel as if I've finally come up to the surface.

Outside my bedroom window, the sun is setting, the evening light a whisper against the lace curtains. I'm lying on my bed, propped up with pillows, one of Mom's home-decorating magazines on my lap. But I'm not looking at it. I'm gazing at the ceiling, at a little square patch of light coming from one of the windows. I'm thinking about Peter and the feeling of his lips on mine, his face against my face, the slight stubble on his cheeks, his arms around me.

I watch the sun lower itself toward the horizon, and I slump into the pillows, my eyelids heavy. Two birds are still singing, lone voices in an otherwise silent evening. I'm in that state just before sleep takes over when the ring of my phone jolts me awake.

"Grace, turn on the TV, right away." It's Cluny. "Channel Twenty-Two. They're doing a thing on Founder's Day after the commercials. Maybe they'll show you and Peter in the race."

I sit up and rub my eyes. "What did you say?"

"Channel Twenty-Two. Turn it on. Founder's Day."

I rummage through the drawer of the bedside table for the remote control. "Hold on. I'm getting there." I find the remote and press the Power button. Maybe there will be a little clip about Peter and me losing the race but winning at love. I wonder if they caught that kiss. That's just the kind of thing they do on Channel 22, and I usually think it's corny, but this time I wouldn't mind. The television springs to life with a detergent ad.

Then the Channel 22 News logo pops up, and the anchorman, George Steffans, says a few animated words about Founder's Day, followed by, *Our very own Mark McKechnie was there, and here's what he saw.*

Mark does a voice-over while the camera zooms in on a long table covered with apple pies and then cuts to Peter, standing in front of the tent. *I've always considered Dorset my real home.* There are a few shots of Peter and the other judges at the table, with plates lined up in front of them, a slice of pie on each. "And the winners are . . . ," Mark's voice-over announces, and the scene switches to a crowd of people in front of the tent as the woman with the strawberry-blond hair reads off the names.

After that, there's a clip of the vintage-car parade, and a stop at the historical-society booth, with a shot of the collie in the pinafore. "Even the dogs got in on the festivities," Mark's voice-over says. Then it's on to the fire engine, where a little boy starts to cry and refuses to get out, followed by the Tara Jones ballroom dancers, nine- and ten-year-olds led by Tara herself, who does look like she's a hundred and, judging by the way she's swaying, also looks to be a little drunk. After that, the camera pans across the booths and the crowds in the street, and the piece finally ends with a clip from a speech by First Selectman Scott Danzberger, his hair still wet from the dunk tank.

"Peter looked good," I tell Cluny. "I guess they aren't showing any footage from the race, but maybe that's just as well. I'd rather not relive our loss."

"Oh, but that would have been funny," she says. "To see you and Regan going at it."

No, it wouldn't have. I'm just about to turn off the television when George Steffans says, "Our next story is about one of Dorset's most established businesses and how a very savvy former resident is teaching an old dog new tricks. We go back to Mark McKechnie for that story."

Teaching an old dog new tricks? I don't like the sound of that. I start to get a funny feeling in my stomach, and then I see my face on the screen.

"There you are!" Cluny says.

Oh, no, I look awful. I really could have used

a hairbrush. And I can't believe how high and whiny my voice sounds. But my answers seem okay. That is, until I mention the job. After that, it's a quick and steady decline. *It's always been a mess. It needs a good makeover. They need to embrace change.* By the end of the interview, I've made the Bike Peddler sound like a relic from the Stone Age. I feel as though I've swallowed a bag of cherries, pits and all.

There's a heavy silence on the other end of the phone, as if the cable carrying our conversation has snapped. Finally, in a kind of dazed whisper, Cluny says, "What happened?"

I turn off the television and sit down on the bed. "Wow, that didn't come out the way I'd planned."

"Grace, why did you say those things about the bike shop?"

"I didn't mean to, Cluny. Really. It just got out of control. And Peter was watching. He was standing right there. I was too embarrassed to say I was only cleaning up the workroom. I wanted him to think I was doing something important."

"But it is important. At least, it is for them."

I put the remote control back in the drawer. "Do you think they've seen it?"

"Scooter? The other guys in the shop? Of course. At least one of them will have seen it."

I take a deep breath. "So what do I do now?"

There's another long silence. "I don't know,

Grace. Throw yourself on the mercy of the court, I guess. Go in there on Monday and apologize. What else can you do? Do you remember the time Nancy Drew had to apologize because she was wrong about—"

"Cluny, I'm not ten anymore. This isn't Nancy Drew. This is a serious problem. I feel like a creep, a traitor. I don't want to go back there. I'm too ashamed about what I said."

"You've got to move forward, Grace. That's all you can do."

We hang up, and I fall back against the mattress, my eyes on the ceiling. The little patch of light that was there before is gone.

CHAPTER 17

A transitive verb is a verb
that has one or more objects.
*The paparazzi have a tendency
to chase celebrities.*

I spend Sunday morning at home in my pajamas, dwelling on the TV interview, cringing as I mentally replay the things I said. All I want to do is watch old movies and eat ice cream, but when I check the freezer, there's no ice cream left. I stand there with my hand on the freezer door, the realization hitting me that black raspberry chocolate chip is probably the only thing in the world that will cheer me up right now. So I throw on some clothes and head for 32 Degrees.

As usual, there's a line extending out the door, and it's all I can do to wait my turn. Inside, behind the long case of ice cream, Renée, the owner, and two college-aged girls are busy assembling cones and sundaes and floats while the milk shake machine whirs. I study the list of flavors posted on the wall. Black raspberry chocolate chip is there, thank God, along with about twenty others that sound tempting, including ginger, cinnamon coffee, chocolate hazelnut, peach, and juniper lemon. Now I'm not sure what I want.

The line moves forward, and I move with it. Maybe I'll get a scoop of black raspberry chocolate chip and a scoop of cinnamon coffee. Or maybe I'll go for something strictly fruity on the second scoop. That would be a lot healthier. Oh, who am I kidding? A man and woman ahead of me order the Works, which Peter and I used to get when we were kids—a sampling of eight different flavors of ice cream in a giant bowl. It's no less than a work of art, a precariously balanced sculpture made of heaping scoops of ice cream.

"What can I get you?" one of the girls asks when I finally make it to the counter.

"I'll have a scoop of black raspberry chocolate chip," I tell her. "With a scoop of cinnamon coffee." I shake my head. "No, wait, how about black raspberry chocolate chip with a scoop of peach." I smile, certain I've added some vitamins there somewhere.

"Okay," she says. "So, one black raspberry chocolate chip and one peach. Cone or cup?"

I wave my hand. "Cancel that. Sorry. Um, I think I'll get three scoops. So leave the black raspberry chocolate chip, but I think I'd rather do . . ." I glance at the menu board again. "Let's see . . . how about the butter pecan and the cookies and cream?"

"So, then, you want black raspberry chocolate chip, butter pecan, and cookies and cream."

I nod.

"Cone or cup?"

"No, wait."

The girl looks at the line behind me. I lower my voice. "Tell you what, just give me the Works."

Out front are a half-dozen round tables with umbrellas. I take my Works, which the menu assures me contains a pint of ice cream or my money back, and sit down at a table as far away from everyone else as I can get. Then I methodically sample a spoonful of each flavor, and when I've done that I go back to the first scoop again.

A middle-aged couple sits down at a table near me. She's got short, black, curly hair and big glasses; he's got a potbelly and a gold neck chain. I'm focused intently on my third go-round of the flavors when I get the feeling the woman is staring at me. She whispers something to the man, and the next thing I know, the two of them stand up and approach me.

"Weren't you on the news last night?" the woman asks, her breath smelling slightly of garlic. "I think I saw you on TV." She stares at my giant bowl of ice cream.

This can't be happening. That's the last thing I want to talk about. "On TV?" I try to laugh it off. "No, that's impossible. I've never been on TV." I cover my ice cream with a napkin and hope they'll leave.

"You weren't at Founder's Day?" she asks.

I screw up my face. "What's Founder's Day?"

She points a finger at me. "Yeah, that was you. You're some kind of organizer guru. You're from Dorset, but now you live in New York."

"Actually, I'm from Alaska. And I still live there." I wish they would leave and let me eat my Works in peace, before the whole thing melts.

"Hey, do you do closets?" she asks as more people stream out of the shop and onto the patio. "We could really use somebody like you. And our basement—Mickey likes to collect magnets. I keep telling him to sort them, get them in some kind of order. You know, magnets from different states in one section, countries in another, animals, TV characters . . ." She moves her hand through the air as though she's pinpointing the places where they'll go. "They could be worth a fortune. He's got thousands."

"It sounds lovely," I say. "But I think you're confusing me with someone else." I can almost hear my pint of ice cream melting, all eight individual flavors merging into a homogenized pool of brown slop.

The woman looks away, as though consulting her memory. Then she says, "That's so weird. The girl on the news looked just like you."

"Maybe I have a double," I tell her.

"You must. You could be twins!" she exclaims. "Right, Mickey?"

The man nods, his gold necklace blinking. "Yeah, Marge. Twins."

Marge squints. "You sure that wasn't you?"

I'm about to grab my Works and run when I hear a familiar voice.

"Excuse me, but this woman happens to be *my* organizer, and we're actually scheduled to meet right now."

I look up, and there's Sean. He's dressed all in gray—T-shirt, jeans, sunglasses—and he's sporting a day-old beard.

"Oh, my!" Marge says, brushing her curls from her face and straightening her glasses. "Sean Leeds! I loved you in *Purple Cowboys.* Did you really ride all those horses yourself?"

Mickey nudges her. "They don't ride the horses themselves, Marge. They have stunt people do that. Right?" He looks to Sean for confirmation.

I glance around the patio. It feels as though everyone is watching us, even the people who are clearly pretending they're not. There's a buzz of excitement, people speaking louder than normal, laughing more.

"I bet *he* rides the horses himself," Marge says. "Big, strong guy like him." Her eyelids flutter as she places her hand on Sean's biceps.

Sean gently removes her hand and smiles. "I didn't ride the horses. Your husband is right."

"Aw, well, you looked good, anyway," Marge says with a wink.

"Thank you. Now if you don't mind, I really do—"

"Excuse me, Mr. Leeds." Three teenage girls appear at the table. "Could we please, oh, please, get a selfie with you?" The one in the middle makes a praying gesture.

"Of course," Sean says, and the girls jump up and down, shrieking. They take a few selfies, giggle, and run off.

"Mr. Leeds, Mr. Leeds." It's a group of tanned twenty-something women this time. "We've seen all of your movies," one of them says. "Twice." They take a number of photos, rearranging their positions several times so each one can stand next to Sean, first on his right side, then his left.

More and more people gather, all of them with cell phones in hand, a few with pens and paper as well. One woman holds a bottle of Catch Me!, and the smell of jasmine wafts through the air.

"You might need this," I say, handing Sean one of my Sharpies as he gets ready to sign a napkin. I watch him pose with a family of four and then with two good-looking men who make some jokes about dating him, but I think they're serious.

"Hey, can I get a selfie with you, too?" a young girl asks me. "I saw you on TV last night."

I take a step back. "Oh, no. I don't think so. I mean, I'm not really even anybody. Or a star. I mean, I'm not a star. Thanks, but not right now." Oh God, I just want to get out of here.

There must be thirty people in line now, and more are swarming in from the village green, across the street. Cars are starting to slow down, drivers and passengers gawking and honking and yelling Sean's name.

"Yes, thank you," I hear him tell a fan. "I'm so glad you liked it." He extricates himself from a group and grabs me by the arm. "We've got to get out of here," he whispers. "Any place close by where we can hide out until this blows over?"

"The pond," I tell him as more people try to squeeze in around the tables. "Behind the firehouse."

"I'll follow you," he says. "Let's go right after I sign that lady's perfume bottle. On the count of three."

"Affirmative."

Sean signs the bottle and then grabs my hand. "One, two, three!" he says, and we're off, running down Main Street to the end of the block, where we turn onto Breakwater Road; cutting through the property behind the building where my pediatrician used to have his office, and down the driveway by the Forrester Design Group; and then running across to Hampshire Lane and turning onto the path near the firehouse, through the trees, and then into the clearing.

By the time we reach the pond, where several ducks glide silently on the water, we're laughing and out of breath.

"We left them in the dust," Sean says. "Great getaway."

"Do you have to do that every day?" I ask, still winded. "My God."

"Oh, I could tell you stories," he says, looking skyward.

"You know, somebody back there asked me for my autograph."

"Really. See? That's how it starts. Pretty soon, you'll have to travel under an assumed name."

I laugh. "Speaking of assumed names, I tried to find out where you were staying. I wanted to thank you for that orchid. But the woman at the Dorset Inn said they don't reveal the names of their guests." I put a couple of quarters into a duck-food dispenser, and a scoop of cracked corn falls into my hands.

"I'm not there, anyway," he says. "I'm renting a house."

"Ah, right. I should have figured." I pour half the corn into Sean's hands.

"I'm glad you like the orchid," he says.

"I love it. It's incredible. And my mother went crazy when she saw it." I don't tell him he could have given me a plain old spider plant and she would have been just as excited. "She's a huge fan of yours."

He looks embarrassed. "Really?"

"Yes. In fact, if I don't get my own selfie with you, she'll never forgive me."

The ducks begin to swim toward the bank where we're standing. "We can arrange that," he says.

"I was hoping we could."

"How long are you staying in town, anyway?" he asks.

"At least until my dad's party. After that, it depends on when they get my ceiling fixed." The ducks waddle out of the water, honking at us, and we scatter some corn on the ground for them.

"What happened to your ceiling?"

"There was a leak above my apartment, and part of the ceiling caved in."

"And what's the party?"

"That's for my dad's sixty-fifth birthday. It's on Saturday. My mom planned the whole thing."

"Sounds nice. I mean the party, not the ceiling."

"Yeah. My mother's great at that stuff. It's going to be under a tent, in the backyard, overlooking the water. There's a band coming. And Sunrise Catering is doing the food. They're fantastic. Mom's really thrown herself into the planning, getting the yard in shape and all. It looks beautiful."

We walk toward a bench that faces the pond. "Hey, you should come," I say as we sit down. "I'm inviting Peter, too. I'd love to have you, and my mother would absolutely die if you showed up."

Sean gives me an apologetic look. "We're hoping to wrap before then. Otherwise, I'd take you up on that offer."

I feel myself blush. "Oh, right." I can't believe I invited Sean Leeds to my father's party. Of course he wouldn't want to come. How ridiculous of me to ask. And I'd forgotten that Peter will probably be gone by then, too, an even bigger disappointment. He said they'd be wrapping by the end of the week. "Then I guess Peter will be leaving as well."

"I don't know what his plans are," Sean says. "He seems to keep changing them."

I wonder what that means and if he might be staying a little longer.

"Peter's a good guy," Sean says. "A real straight shooter, which can be hard to find in Hollywood. I consider him a close friend."

"I'm sure he feels the same way about you."

Sean puts his hands behind his head and stretches. I study the reflections of the trees and sky in the pond as a gray squirrel shinnies up an oak.

"God, I love this town," Sean says. "I don't want to leave. I can see why Peter wanted to come back."

"You could always visit."

He turns to me. "Yeah, I could. But I probably won't. You know how that goes. You get busy and . . ."

"I know. I haven't been too good about visiting Dorset myself."

"Really? But you're in Manhattan, right? It can't be that far."

"It's only a couple of hours by train. It's not the physical distance that's the issue."

"Well, if I were you I'd be here a lot. You're lucky to have this place."

I gaze at the pond, the maple trees and the elms, the yellow coneflowers and purple milkweed, the ducks gliding by. "Yeah, I guess I am."

CHAPTER 18

A gerund is a noun formed by
adding *ing* to a verb.
*Working can be enjoyable when
everyone gets along.*

By Monday, all thoughts of ice cream and Sean
Leeds are gone. The morning brings a steely sky
filled with black, smoky clouds and air so heavy,
I can taste the ozone. The few people on Main
Street scurry along, as though sensing they'll get
caught in a downpour at any moment.

I'm relieved to find a parking space right
across the street from the bike shop, knowing
I'll be able to make a beeline to my car if it's
pouring at the end of the day. I'm standing by the
car, trying to stuff my phone and my spiral
notebook and a bottle of water into my handbag,
when I drop the notebook. It lands, open, on the
street, and when I pick it up, I see handwriting
on one of the pages. But it's not my handwriting;
it's my father's.

It's a poem about seeds—how they blow
around, looking for a place to land and take root,
and whether there are seeds that blow around
forever. It's about a lot more than that, of course,
but that's what sticks with me. I read the poem

several times, trying each time to come up with a different interpretation, but, no matter how I look at it, I know this poem is about Renny. She's the seed the wind blew away, the seed that never took root. He'll always be thinking about Renny. Renny will always come first. I take a deep breath to stop my chin from trembling. Then I slip the notebook into my handbag and cross the street.

When I open the door to the Bike Peddler, Kevin is arranging new cycling helmets on the shelf. He glances at me. A.J. is ringing up a plastic rain jacket for a customer. He gives me a perfunctory nod. There are no friendly hellos or chatty conversations, the way there usually are when I arrive.

As soon as I walk into the workroom, before I even put my handbag in the drawer of the file cabinet, Mitch closes the door, and the room feels as though it's been reduced to a closet. He glares at me.

"Why the hell did you say those things about the store?"

I stand there, frozen, staring at the name Thatcher Academy on his T-shirt, my mouth going dry. "I'm sorry," I say. "Let me explain."

"Why did you say that we're—what was it? We're not competitive, we're old-fashioned and behind the times, and we need to come into the twenty-first century."

"I didn't say that last part."

"You didn't have to. The news guy did." Mitch grabs an old cable from the worktable and throws it into the trash. The muscles in his face are taut. I can hear him breathing.

"I didn't mean to say all of that stuff. The guy was pushing me into it. I tried to explain at the end, but he wouldn't let me."

Mitch slams a drawer in the tool chest, sending its contents clanking. "Looks as if you didn't try hard enough, because it sounds like we're a bunch of idiots here. Why did you do it?"

Thunder rumbles in the distance. I lean against the file cabinet, the limbs in my body heavy and useless. It was all because of Peter. Because I wanted to impress Peter. But I can't tell that to Mitch. He'll think worse of me than he already does.

"I didn't mean to do anything that would hurt the store. The interview just got away from me. I guess I didn't realize what I was saying."

"It got away from you? You didn't realize what you were saying? How could you not realize— *you,* the girl with the Sharpie, who came in here correcting our flyers and talking about the difference between *complimentary* with an *i* and *complementary* with an *e*? The one who goes around correcting menus in restaurants? Isn't that your special talent—understanding language? And now you want me to believe you had no control over your own words?"

My words. My special talent. He's right. I should have been able to control my words. But he's hitting me in my most vulnerable spot, making me feel like a failure at the one thing I know I can do.

I cross my arms. "You know, maybe the store could use a little updating. Did you ever think of that? It's basically been this way for the past thirty years. You've just added more stuff."

"Are you serious?" he says. "You come in here knowing absolutely nothing about bikes and tell me what we need to do?" He looks at me with disgust, takes a wrench off the table, and throws it into one of the drawers.

"Yes, you need updating. Look around. Maybe you'd get more business if you straightened the place out a little. Once every thirty years wouldn't be so bad." I pull the wrench out of the drawer where Mitch tossed it and drop it into the drawer where it belongs. It lands with a clatter.

He takes a step closer. "You think you're so smart. We don't need your advice on how the store should look or how it should be run or on anything. You know, when we were in the apple orchard and at the lighthouse, I thought we knew each other better. I thought maybe I could trust you. But you've turned against me. It's clear you don't belong here. Maybe Hollywood is a better place for you."

I step closer, too, and now I'm right in his face.

"I said I was sorry, and I am. You could accept my apology."

"Well, the damage is done, so being sorry doesn't help."

"Then I don't know what else I can do, Mitch. You just want to be angry, so go ahead. Be angry. See how far that gets you. Good luck with it." I kick a small box lying on the floor. It rips and breaks open, and hundreds of bolts go flying under the worktable, behind the bikes and wheels, around the trash can. And then everything is quiet.

"I can't have you working here anymore," he says, lowering his voice, his gaze fixed on the upended box.

"What do you mean?" Rain begins to tap against the roof.

"This isn't working out, Grace. My dad doesn't know about the TV story. He didn't see the news. Thank God. So I want you to go out there and tell him . . ."

He glances around the room, at the new crates, with their neat labels, at the new pegboard, where I've got the cone wrenches and the spoke wrenches and the headset wrenches neatly displayed.

"Tell him whatever you want, whatever excuse you want to give him for why you have to leave." He picks up the broken box and tosses it into the trash. "And then go."

When I open the workroom door and step into the store, I'm greeted by the sound of rain crashing against the plate-glass windows. Thunder rumbles, sending vibrations like shivers down the walls. For a moment, I can't move. I stand by the counter, biting my lip, trying to calm myself. It's just a job. Just a temporary job. It wasn't meant to be anything more than that.

I peek into the office. Scooter is there, sitting at the desk, thumbing through a catalog. I give a gentle rap on the doorjamb. "May I come in?"

He looks up. "Hey there, Grace. Sure, come on in. Have a seat."

I sit down on the folding chair opposite the desk.

"How was your weekend?" he asks, turning another page.

I'm so relieved he doesn't know what happened. "It had its ups and downs. How was yours?"

"I'm still here," he says with his usual grin.

I don't want to tell him I'm leaving. I don't want him to be disappointed in me. I came in here complaining about how the workroom needed to be cleaned up and reorganized, and he was counting on me to do it. There's so much more I'd planned on accomplishing. I guess that's why I feel so bad, why everything hurts right now, physically hurts. I know I have to tell him, but I don't want to.

"What have you got there, Scooter?"

"Oh, this?" He closes the catalog and holds it up. *Raleigh 1970. The finest bicycles made in England by Raleigh.* There's a photo of a man and woman sitting by a river, a huge wooden ship docked nearby. The woman is wearing a jumper with a long-sleeved blouse, and the man is dressed in brown pants and a brown sweater. In the foreground three different Raleigh bikes are displayed.

"Nineteen seventy," I say as he hands the booklet to me.

"Don't you love those clothes?" He chuckles.

I leaf through a few of the pages, contemplating the simple, odd-looking contraptions bikes were back then. "Where did you get this?"

"I have a little collection up there." Scooter nods toward the shelves above the computer, where dozens of books and catalogs are packed together. "I like to browse through them sometimes. I remember all those bikes. It's kind of like visiting old friends."

I stop at a page showing a dark-green model, the paint sparkling on the fenders, and I read the description aloud: *"The Raleigh Superbe is elegant and unique, the result of ninety years of Raleigh refinement."*

"Those were old classic touring bikes," Scooter says, rocking back in the chair. "Three speeds."

"Equipped with our Sturmey-Archer three-speeds hub," I continue, *"caliper brakes, Brooks B*

seventy-two leather saddle, Dunlop Sprite tires, rear carrier, handy pump, and built-in fork lock to prevent unauthorized use."

"Let me see that," he says. I hand him the catalog. "Dunlop Sprite tires," he mutters, tapping the photo. "I had to buy a couple of those not long ago for an old ten-speed. Found them on eBay. Sixty-nine bucks apiece." His voice rises in pitch as he quotes the price. "And Sturmey-Archer . . ." He flips through a few more pages. "They were a division of Raleigh. Once upon a time they made the greatest products. Top-notch stuff. But after a while they started to let the quality suffer. Same old story. Trying to save a buck. They ended up getting sold to a company in Taiwan." He puts the catalog on the desk, between us. "Their three-speed hubs were always pretty good, though."

"These old bikes are kind of nice," I say. "They're simple. They don't look nearly as sleek as today's bikes, but I like them."

"Oh, they were sleek for their day," Scooter says. "I can promise you that." He looks at the pages lying open, and I wonder if he's recalling a time when he rode those bikes, when they were new.

"Do you think bikes were better then? I mean, made better?"

He runs a hand through the thin strands of his white hair. "What I liked about the old bikes like yours was that they were mostly handmade. There was a lot more craftsmanship to them. And they were made of steel, not aluminum or carbon fiber, like today's bikes. So they're a lot more durable. The older bikes were a lot simpler, too, like you said. Fewer gears, simple shifters. They're sure a lot easier to work on."

"So you like the older ones better."

"No, that's not what I said." He sits up a little straighter and leans toward me. "See, with the newer bikes, they're more mass produced. But ou get a lot more for the money. You get aluminum or carbon fiber, higher technology, and they're usually faster and weigh a lot less."

I think about the Trek I rode with Mitch. He's right about that.

"There's no way a serious racer could compete today with an old bike," he says.

"So the new bikes are better," I say.

Scooter smiles. "Grace, it just depends. You need to know what you want in order to decide whether to go with the old or the new." He closes the catalog and puts it back on the shelf. "I know you love that old Schwinn. But just remember, it's not good to idealize the past too much."

"Well, the old Schwinn is the only bike I have right now," I tell him. And I know I have to say it—that I'm leaving. *Tell him whatever you want, whatever excuse you want to give him.*

"Scooter, while we're on the subject . . ." I steady myself. I don't want to get upset. If he sees I'm upset, he'll start asking questions. "I'm going to be taking the bike home."

"But I don't think much work's been done on it yet."

"I know, but I have to cut my job here short."

He's got *Why?* written all over his face. Those lines that like to travel in their own directions are at it again.

"I'm really sorry," I go on. "But remember the party I told you about? The one my mom is giving my dad?"

"I remember."

"It's this Saturday, and she really needs my help. There's still so much to do, and Mom gets really stressed about this kind of thing. We've got over a hundred people coming, and I think it would be best if I helped her. For the rest of the week."

"Well, sure, Grace," he says. "You should do whatever you need to do."

"I'll come by tomorrow or Thursday, as soon as I can borrow my friend's Jeep, and I'll pick up the bike."

"Ah, there's no rush," he says. "And you know, you can bring it back anytime, and we'll get her done. You've got a lot of credit in the bank here. I really like the changes you've made so far." He stands up and steps around the desk. I stand up, too. Then he comes toward me with open arms, and I fall into his embrace. He smells like Ivory soap and a lemony aftershave my grandfather used to wear. "We'll miss you," he says. "Don't be a stranger."

I nod, because that's all I can do, and I try to keep my eyes from tearing. Then I walk away, out of the office and through the store, where the rain is still pelting the front windows. Outside, it's dark. The street is empty except for a woman running, a red umbrella over her head. I step outside, into an avalanche of rain, and I race across the street to my car. But I don't leave. I sit there, watching the front door of the bike shop, hoping I might see Scooter. Or A.J. or Kevin. Or Mitch. Hoping Mitch might see me out here and tell me he didn't mean to fire me. That I should come back to work. But the door never opens. Nobody comes out. And I tell myself again that it was just a temporary job. It wasn't meant to be anything more than that.

CHAPTER 19

Collective nouns are singular and are
typically paired with singular verbs.
A film <u>crew</u> often <u>works</u> very long hours.

The following afternoon, the sun is out again,
and all signs of yesterday's storm are gone. I
pull into the parking lot of the Dorset Yacht Club,
looking forward to seeing a real movie shoot, with
my favorite director at the helm. The clubhouse,
a white Colonial-style building, looks elegant,
with its dormers on the front and widow's walk
on the roof. It sits on a blanket of grass so green,
I suspect one of the members owns a fertilizer
company.

I try to remember the last time I was here. Four
or five years ago, I think, for a charity luncheon. I
picture the antique nautical prints in their burled
wood frames, hanging in the reception area, and
the main lounge, with its overstuffed sofas and
chairs and tall windows that catch the breeze
from the sound. I imagine members sitting there,
discussing the latest Newport–Bermuda race and
how the stock market is faring.

Toward the left side of the parking lot, a fleet
of trucks and vans is parked, including the red
Panavision truck I saw downtown a week ago.

People are milling around a refreshment tent, drinking Starbucks and Diet Cokes, talking on walkie-talkies and cell phones, texting, and smoking cigarettes. Webs of cable are strewn across the parking lot, running toward the clubhouse.

I pick up my phone to call Peter's assistant, Cassandra, and notice that I've got a voice message. It's the property manager for my building, telling me that my ceiling is already fixed. This is turning into an even better day than I'd expected.

I dial the number for Cassandra, and after two rings she picks up.

"Cassandra Vail." Her voice is quick, snappy, high pitched.

"Hi, Cassandra. This is Grace Hammond, a friend of Peter's. He told me to get in touch with you about coming to the set."

There's noise on the other end, people talking, someone laughing, someone yelling. "Oh, hi, Grace. He told me you were going to call. When are you planning to stop by?"

I glance toward the tent, where a husky man in a gray T-shirt is hitching up his jeans. "Well, actually, I'm here."

"You are?" she says, sounding a little surprised.

Oh, no. Please don't tell me I'm not on the list again. Peter said he would handle it himself. "Peter said it would be a good day to stop by."

"It's fine," she says. "It's crazy, but every day is crazy. Where are you?"

"I'm near the tent," I say, relieved.

"I'll be there in a minute."

I'm touching up my lipstick when I see a girl come around the side of the yacht club, the girl I remember from the party. She's dressed in skinny jeans with wide stitching up the sides, and she's holding a plastic cup with a straw. A walkie-talkie hangs from one side of her belt, a cell phone from the other, and a dozen beaded bracelets wind around her wrist. Her hair, which hangs all the way down her back, bounces as she walks.

"Grace?" She takes a sip of her drink.

"Yes, hi."

"I'm Cassandra. I'll bring you inside."

I look around at all the trucks, at the cables and the tent. "Oh. It's inside?"

She scrunches her eyebrows together. "Yeah. You thought we were filming out here?"

"Um, Peter said something about the parking lot. I guess I misunderstood."

"This shoot's inside," she says. "Follow me." She picks up her walkie-talkie. "Steve? Hey, I've got Peter's friend." I hear a garbled voice. Cassandra looks at me. "They're still turning around. We've got fifteen minutes."

"Turning around?"

"Between scenes."

I nod, and we walk down the path that runs

over the grass and along the side of the club. Sailboat riggings clank softly against masts and booms, and I can smell oysters and mussels in the air. Two crew members in T-shirts and shorts dash past us, heading toward the parking lot, one of them talking nervously into a headset. And then we're at the back of the club.

I have to stop for a moment to take it all in, the place that's been in my memory for so long. The docks stretch in front of me, a long, horizontal line bisected by a few vertical strokes, and the boats loll in their slips, waves lapping at the moorings. A dozen sloops skim the sound farther out, and a fishing boat motors toward the club, its mast and rails gleaming, its engine emitting a pleasant gurgle. I wonder if *Reserved Seating* or *My Girl* is still here. Or *Time Out*, where Peter and I had our kiss. I want to bring Peter back here, to this spot, to relive the magic of that night, to make some new magic. I want him to kiss me here again, in the moonlight, and I want the rest of my life to finally begin.

"This way," Cassandra says, and I look up and realize she's waiting for me. I follow her to a door guarded by a young guy wearing a headset and a baseball cap. We go inside, down a hallway where the carpeting is covered in brown paper and cables run like spaghetti. In a small room to the right, two women are putting makeup on a couple of teenagers. In another room a woman is steaming a gown. People from the crew pass us, men with beards, some with walrus mustaches and stomachs overflowing their belts. Finally we stop in front of a doorway where a guy in camouflage shorts and a walkie-talkie on his belt stands guard.

"Hi, Dan," Cassandra says.

I follow her past him, into a large room. My knees lock, and I take in a quick breath. I'm in the room where the Cinderella Ball took place. Hundreds of silver and white balloons hang in clusters from the ceiling, like bunches of exotic grapes. Yards of gossamer fabric are draped in elegant curves, attached at one end to chandeliers and at the other end to the ceiling. Tables scattered around the room are covered in long, white cloths, and in the center of each table an arrangement of white roses is nestled in a glass slipper. It's as though I've stumbled through a time warp, back to 1998.

At the far wall, there's a little stage where band equipment is set up—drums, microphones on stands, speakers. In front of the stage is a dance floor, and behind the stage, a backdrop, probably twenty feet wide by fifteen feet high. It's a painting of a night sky with blue stars and a bronze crescent moon. In the foreground is a white, horse-drawn Cinderella carriage with a round compartment in a framework of filigree— a carriage that was once a pumpkin.

I can't move. I can't speak. All I can do is gaze at the decorations and feel my heart swell with joy. And then I realize the room is full of people. Crew members in jeans and shorts and T-shirts are standing to the side, some of them talking into headsets. A woman is touching up a boy's makeup, and another woman is spraying a girl's hair. There's a group of teenagers on the dance floor. I spot Peter across the room, in a blue button-down shirt and jeans, talking to a woman with a clipboard.

"Are you okay?" Cassandra asks, and I wonder if I look as hypnotized as I feel.

"How did this happen?" I whisper, gazing at the balloons, the Cinderella carriage backdrop, and a glass-slipper flower arrangement on a nearby table.

"We're filming a dance scene," she says. "A high school dance." She starts to walk across the room, dodging equipment carts and lights on stands, detouring around a camera on a dolly.

I try to keep up with her, but I'm moving in slow motion, unable to absorb this, not quite believing Peter has re-created this night—the best night in my sixteen-year-old life, the night before everything crumbled. Everywhere I look, there's something I remember—the white bows on the backs of the chairs; the silvery crowns decorating the front of the stage; the potted ficus plants around the perimeter of the room, their branches glittering with tiny white lights. I want to put on my emerald-green dress and dance around the room in Peter's arms. I want to go back to that night and never let the next day come. I feel almost dizzy knowing that he cherishes this night as much as I do.

Cassandra waits for me, ten feet away.

"Sorry," I say as I scurry to catch up.

"We had to bring in a lot of background actors for this scene." She arches an eyebrow. "Teenagers. That's always interesting."

"Yes," I say, eyeing the kids on the dance floor. "Well, they *were* sixteen."

She gives me a curious look. "Oh, have you read the script?"

"No," I tell her. "But I think I know the story."

She stops a couple of yards from Peter, who stands by one of the skirted tables, turned away from us, talking to a different woman now. He's got a pair of headphones around his neck, and he's holding something that looks like a long camera lens. And I can't take my eyes off him. I adore this accomplished, brilliant, handsome man who has fashioned this room as a symbol of his deep feelings for me. I'd give up my life in Manhattan in a second to make a new life with him in L.A.

The woman standing next to Peter shuffles some papers. "It happens again in the other scene," she tells him. "Outside the Sugar Bowl."

"Yeah, I thought so," he says. "Well, we're going to have to work it out. Let Marty know."

She scribbles something and walks away.

"Peter?" Cassandra says.

His face lights up when he sees me. "Grace." He pulls me into his arms. "I'm glad you're here." Then he glances at Cassandra. "Thanks, Cassie. Oh, and can you hunt down those new script pages?"

"Will do," she says, and then she's gone.

"This is . . ." I wave my hand across the room while I try to form the words to describe how I feel. "It's incredible. I didn't know you had a scene like this in your movie."

"Yeah, it's one of the nineties flashbacks. Does it look familiar?"

"Completely familiar. I can't believe how you've re-created the dance." I glance at a couple of plastic silver crowns on the table next to us. "Right down to the crowns."

"I'm glad you're here to see it," he says. "Tracy, my set designer, worked like a demon trying to make my vision come true." He picks up one of the crowns, brushes a lock of hair from my face, and places it on my head. "There." Our eyes meet, and I feel a current run through me. I touch the crown and smile.

A woman in a pair of red glasses approaches Peter. "Do you want any of the couples on the dance floor to kiss?" she asks, glancing up under long, black bangs.

"Yes, definitely. Let's get some kissing in there. It's a high school dance, remember? Needs to be authentic." He turns to me and nods, as though he's conferring authenticity on our own kiss seventeen years ago.

"Hey, Peter," a teenage boy says. "Any chance we could go back to the last setup? I don't think that was my best performance. I'd really like to do it over."

Peter puts his hand on the boy's shoulder. "Sorry, Jason, my man. We can't do that. We're pressed for time. And, anyway, I thought you were great."

"Moments away, folks!" a man shouts.

Peter turns to me. "We'll be sitting together in video village."

Oh, good. He's sitting with me. This is even better than I imagined. "Where's video village?"

"It's just a little place in the back of the room with chairs and monitors so we can watch what's being filmed." I look to where he's pointing, across the ballroom, and I see a cluster of director's chairs. "Just be warned. There are a few suits here today."

"Suits?"

"Executives. From the studio. But they probably won't bite."

I laugh. "Oh, okay." I don't care who I'm sitting

with. I'm still pinching myself to make sure I'm really here.

"I'll get Cassie to take you over, and I'll be there in a minute," he says. He picks up a walkie-talkie. "Cassie?"

Two men pass us carrying rolls of white paper and electrical cords. A moment later, Cassie reappears and leads me to the back of the ballroom, where the director's chairs, emblazoned with the name *By Any Chance*, are positioned behind two monitors. Two men in business suits and another in jeans are seated there, along with two women dressed in jeans and T-shirts. One of them is staring at a laptop. The other is thumbing through a binder, a stopwatch on her lap. They're all wearing headphones.

Cassie hands me a set of headphones. "So you can listen to what's going on." She looks at my hair. "Uh, you might have to move your crown, though."

"Oh, right." I adjust the crown, put on the headphones, and sit down.

A man calls, *Quiet on set!* and everyone settles down. Peter takes a seat, too, his arm pressed against mine. I glance at him, and I see the two of us living in Malibu in his beach house, waking up to the sun and the surf, walking on the shore and dodging the waves—well, on the weekends, anyway. I know he has to work during the week. And I'll find a job as a technical writer. There must be some instruction manuals that need to be written out there. Hot tubs for celebrity dressing rooms, maybe?

I'm thinking about all this when I realize there's something happening on the monitor. They've started the scene, and two young actors are on the dance floor, doing a slow dance, while other teens, moving in pairs, orbit them like planets around the sun.

The boy is wearing a navy-blue blazer, and his wavy hair and blue eyes remind me of Peter's. The girl has sandy-brown hair styled in long, loose waves, the way I used to wear mine. I wonder why she's wearing the wrong-color dress, though. It's yellow when it should be green.

There are musicians on the stage, or maybe they're actors pretending to be musicians. I can't tell. Either way, there's music, and a woman is singing a slow, romantic ballad. It's not Shania Twain's voice, but I'd know the song anywhere: "From This Moment On." It's our song. I slide to the edge of my seat. The boy and girl begin to talk, and within the first couple of lines, I know the two of them are meant to be Peter and me. Their words reverberate through me, echoes of what we once said.

"Nice dress, Courtney," the boy says, stepping back to admire her.

"You think so?" Courtney looks down shyly. "Thanks, Tom."

He nods. "You look really cool. I usually don't see you dressed up."

"Yeah, I guess I just never have the chance." Another couple dances closer to Courtney and Tom, and Courtney smiles and waves to them over Tom's shoulder.

I want to lose myself in the moment, and the memory, but I can't stop thinking about the dress. That yellow is so brash. It should be green. And strapless. Peter glances at me and gives my fingers a little squeeze.

Tom and Courtney continue their slow dance to our song, as the singer's words float around me. But her voice seems a bit high, and the beat a little fast.

Courtney gives Tom's tie a tug. "You look nice, too," she says.

"I borrowed this tie from my dad. I couldn't find mine. Maybe it was the weed. I guess I got a little too stoned." He laughs.

Courtney laughs as well.

What is he talking about? I don't remember him being stoned. I wasn't stoned. Is he getting this confused with some other dance? Or have I misunderstood the whole night?

Tom looks at his necktie, and his eyes go dark. "Actually, I just took it. I didn't have a chance to ask him. He and my mom were in the middle of another fight."

"I'm sorry."

"Yeah, well . . ." He looks away. "That's how it's been lately. They can never just talk anymore. It's always yelling and fighting. The other night she threw a glass at him."

"Oh my God."

"Yeah, Mom thinks Dad's cheating on her. I don't know if it's true, but he does act really weird sometimes."

I glance at Peter and wonder what's going on. This isn't the conversation we had. This isn't our night.

On the monitor, two boys are goofing around, doing a head-banging dance. One of them runs into Tom, almost knocking him down.

"Hey, watch it, Greeley!" Tom shouts.

"What's your problem, Baxter?" Greeley says.

"You almost knocked me down, you asshole."

Greeley scrunches up his face. "You're the ass-hole."

The next second they're shoving each other, and then they're on the floor, fists flying. Courtney is screaming, and the other kids, all huddled around the two boys, are screaming as well.

"That's enough, that's it!" A man pushes his way through the crowd and pulls the boys apart.

"And cut!" Peter shouts. The actors stay in their places.

This is crazy. This isn't what happened. He's not telling it the right way. He didn't say anything to me about his father cheating on his mother, and that fight never took place. The whole thing is off. The room feels hot, stuffy. My forehead is throbbing. I pull off the headset, and the silver crown falls to the floor.

I turn to Peter. "I think I need to go. I feel funny." I stand up. "A little nauseous."

He lays his palm against my cheek. "Hmm. You are warm. We've got a medic here. Maybe we should call her."

"No. Thanks. I just need to go home."

He looks worried. "I'll have Cassie walk you out."

"No, no. Please. I'll be fine."

"Grace, come on. You don't look well."

I hold up my hands. "I'll be fine. Just let me go."

I step away from the chairs and the monitors, Peter calling after me, telling me he'll be in touch later to make sure I'm all right. I head toward a set of doors in the back. The balloons hanging from the ceiling look cold and drab, the gauzy fabric limp and lifeless.

Doesn't he remember? We danced and talked and walked outside. We went down to the docks and the boats were in the moorings and the water sparkled as if it were made of a million stars. And he leaned toward me and said, "Hey, you," and then he kissed me. He doesn't even have the kiss in the scene. He has a fight instead. A fight that never happened. He's taken my best night and ruined it, sent it down some dark tributary where it doesn't belong. I need to hang on to that night. Otherwise, what will I have left?

I brush by a bearded man in cargo pants and open the door. I run down the hall and out a side exit that leads to the parking lot. The breeze is damp and briny and cold now, and I shiver as I race toward the VW.

Once I'm in the car, the engine catches, and I press my foot hard on the gas. The VW lurches forward, taking me away from the parking lot and the yacht club and my green dress and our dance and the dock and the stars and the way Peter looked at me that night and everything that was good and true and beautiful, before my world collapsed.

CHAPTER 20

An intransitive verb is a verb that
does not have a direct object.
They grieve.

In my closet, far back on the top shelf, a small plastic bag is tucked away. I open the door and reach for the bag, its green letters still dark against the white background: *Woodside/Your Family Pharmacy.* On my bed, I take out the faded receipt and smooth the wrinkles. Then I remove the bottle from the bag and brush my fingers over the tiny blue flowers that form a border around the name Jardin. Once, a long time ago, it was my favorite shampoo. I twist off the cap and breathe deeply, inhaling the scent of rose, white lily, and violet.

Closing my eyes, all I can see is Renny and me. I want to remember the two of us riding our bikes down Harbor Road, sitting on the dock with our legs in the water. I want to remember lying in the hammock, the tree branches over our heads, the afternoon sun blinking down on us. I want the memories from the days when we're still kids, the days before anything bad has happened. But all I see is the two of us on the evening of the accident.

Renny, I'm sorry, I say. *I'm sorry.* The words come out choked in sobs, tears slipping down my cheeks as I clutch the bottle to my chest. I don't hear my father walking down the hall. He stops at my doorway.

"Grace, are you all right?" He's dressed in his white button-down shirt and gray pants. He must have been teaching today. He looks at me, puzzled.

I turn away and wipe my eyes. "Not really," I say, and then the tears start again.

"What's wrong?" He sits down next to me.

"Doyle? Are you ready?" my mother calls from downstairs.

"I'm up here," he says. "In Grace's room. I think you'd better come up, Leigh."

I hear Mom's footsteps on the stairs. The flash of her smile fades when she sees us. "What's going on?"

I clutch the bottle tighter.

"Grace?" Mom says, quietly drawing out my name. She sits down on the other side of me.

I shake my head. I can't speak.

"Honey?" She brushes her hand across my wet cheek. "What's got you so upset?"

"It was all . . ."

Mom looks at me expectantly. "What? All what?" she asks, her voice soft.

"It was all my fault."

She puts her arm around me. Dad gently pulls

387

the bottle away and looks at it. They know it was in the car the night Renny died. But they don't know she bought it for me that evening, after our fight, as a peace offering. Like the peace offerings Dad leaves. Renny used to do that, too.

Mom puts the shampoo back in the bag. "Grace, it wasn't your fault. How could it have been your fault?"

But it was. And my life is such a mess. How stupid I was to believe Peter could make everything better, to think he could bring back the happiness that died along with Renny. It's as if I'm standing on a shoreline and waves are pulling the sand from under my feet, eroding my foundation. I've lost everything. In a few days I'll be going back to New York, and the only good thing waiting for me there is a new ceiling.

"You didn't have anything to do with the accident," Dad says.

"But I did. I had everything to do with it."

Mom pulls me closer. "Honey, you weren't even in the car."

"No," I say. "But I was here with her . . ." I start to cry again, and she brushes her hand over my hair, and all I can do is wait and catch my breath. "Before it happened," I say. "When you were at that cocktail party. We got into a fight."

I glance at my mother and then my father. Their faces are drawn, still. What have I done? Now I've started this and I have to go on and they're going to hate me. And then I'll lose them, too.

I close my eyes, and there's Renny, lying on her bed in her camo pants and spaghetti-strap tank top, staring at a bottle of fluorescent-yellow nail polish, the *Titanic* poster on the wall behind her, Metallica wailing in the background.

I'd been out all day, and she turned to me. "So, where were you?"

I told her I'd been shopping with Cluny and asked what she'd done with her afternoon. She shrugged. "Nothing. Was out for a while. Now I'm here."

I could tell she'd been drinking. I'd seen her high before, and I'd seen her drunk—eyes glassy, speech thick. "Have you been drinking?" I asked.

"What?" She tried to open the bottle of nail polish, but her fingers fumbled around the cap.

"Have you been drinking? You sound weird."

"Maybe. What do you care?"

"You shouldn't drink so much," I said. "You're going to kill your brain cells."

She flapped a hand at me. "So let 'em die. I've got more where those came from."

"Not really," I said.

"What did you buy?" she asked. "Shopping."

I told her I bought a skirt. "For tomorrow. I'm going out with Peter." It was to be our first real date.

"Peter, Peter, pumpkin eater," she mumbled.

"Had a wife and couldn't keep her." She glanced at me. "Are you going to be Peter's wife, Grace?"

"Leave me alone, Renny. Why don't you go have another beer."

She shrugged. "Maybe I will." She opened the nail polish and started to brush it over one of her toenails, but she missed, and the neon yellow ended up on her foot. "So, Peter's your new boyfriend?" She stared at the yellow splotch. "Guess so, after that *big kiss* and all."

I missed the sister who used to play Barbies with me, and ride bikes, and paste pictures from teen magazines on the wall of our secret space. But now, most of the time, that sister was unreachable.

"You're just jealous because I have a boyfriend," I said.

She dabbed at her toes with the nail polish. "Why should I be jealous? I've had plenty of boyfriends."

"I know, but you don't have one now." It had only been a few days since Elliot Frasier broke up with her.

Renny put the cap on the nail polish and shook the bottle. "You really think a guy like Peter . . ." The bottle slipped out of her hand. She picked it up. "Popular guy like that. Wants to date you?"

"What's that supposed to mean?"

"Peter could date *anybody.*" She stretched the

word as though it were elastic. "Like Missy Faulkner. He dated her, and she's a junior. I mean, *a year older.* I don't think he really wants to *date* you, Grace."

I glanced at the *Titanic* poster. What did she mean, he doesn't really want to date me? "What are you talking about, Renny?"

"I just told you. He could date anybody." She shoved a pillow under her head.

"Do you think he just wants to use me? Is that it? Is that what you're saying?" I looked at her and I wanted to punch her. I didn't care how drunk or stoned or whatever she was. "We've been friends for three years, Renny. I think I know him a lot better than that."

"Well, good for you, Grace." She sat up on the bed. "I'm sure he's totally in love with you, then. You know all about him."

"I do know all about him. Stop being so mean."

"Stop being so mean," she muttered, imitating me. "What are you going to do if Peter wants to have sex? Are you going to tell him you're a virgin?"

"Oh, shut up, Renny!" I started to walk out, and then I turned around. "You know what? I totally get why Elliot broke up with you. He probably couldn't stand being around you anymore. He finally figured out what a total bitch you are!"

"Don't talk about Elliot!" she screamed. She raised her fists, and drops of neon yellow fell to the white bedspread.

"Don't talk about Peter!"

For a moment, she didn't move. Then she got up and walked to the mirror. She straightened one of the straps on her top and muttered, "I'm outta here."

"Where are you going?"

She pushed her hair behind her ears. "To a party."

"Somebody's picking you up?" She couldn't be driving herself there.

She whirled around. "What are you, Mom, now, with all these questions? No, I'm driving."

"You can't. You've been drinking."

"God, you are Mom. I'm fine. Butt out, Grace. Go try on your new skirt. See if you can impress Peter." She glared at me.

"You know, you ought to be happy for me that I have a boyfriend. But it's always about you, Renny. Everything always has to be about you. If you don't have a boyfriend, I can't have one. Well, I do have one. So go to your stupid party. Drink fifty beers or a gallon of vodka. I don't care. I hope you go out and get yourself killed!" I saw the shiny glint of Mom's car keys on Renny's desk, and I picked up the keys and flung them at her.

I turn to my mother. "And she did. She did. I

wished she were dead, and it happened. And I can't get her back."

"Grace, Grace," my mother says, her arms warm around me.

Dad kisses the top of my head. "Sweetheart," he says, "listen to me. You—"

"No, let me say this. I need to say this." I push them away. "I always felt I had to walk in her footsteps." I try to wipe the tears from my face. "Okay, maybe not always, but ever since we were teenagers. I hated the first day of school because when the teachers saw my name, they'd all ask me the same thing: *Are you Renny's sister?* She preceded me in *everything.* I was always second-best. I could never compete with her, never match her abilities, her accomplishments." I take a deep breath. "She was better than me in everything. And I know that's why you loved her more, why you gave her all the attention, all of the encouragement. But it made me feel as though I couldn't do anything right."

Mom puts her hand on my arm. "Oh, Grace. We didn't love Renny more. That's not true."

"There were times," I go on, "—maybe not many, and maybe they were quick, but they were still there—when I wished . . ." I gaze across the room, my chin quivering. "When I wished she didn't exist. I wanted her to be gone." I bury my face in my hands. "And that's what happened. I wasn't careful about what I said. And my words—they set everything in motion, and it couldn't be stopped."

"Grace, come on," my father says. "That's not—"

"It was my fault. You don't understand. I knew about it. I knew about the drinking. I saw her when she'd been drinking. Lots of times. And I should have told you. It was a horrible mistake not to tell you."

I glance at my father. He looks pale.

"You knew she was drinking?" Mom asks. There are fresh lines in her forehead. Her eyes have gone gray.

It's happening just how I imagined it would. Now they know the truth. They hate me. They don't want me around. And I don't blame them.

"I'd give anything," I say. "To change places with Renny. To have her be here, and me be . . . there. I know that would make things better for you. I know how much you miss her and everything she meant to you. I ruined your lives by doing what I did."

"Grace!" Mom says. "Stop right now. That's not true. Don't ever say that or even think it." She turns my face so I'm looking in her eyes. "We love you so much, so very much."

Dad wraps his arms around Mom and me. "None of what happened was your fault, Gracie."

"How do you know?" I ask, my head down.

"How do you really know? Don't you understand? Words have consequences. That's why we have to be so careful with them."

My father lets out a deep breath. "Grace, your sister had some serious problems."

My mother clasps my hand between hers. "We knew about the drinking," she says. "We knew about the pot. We knew about the shoplifting."

I look up. "What? You knew?"

"Parents aren't as unaware as their children might think they are," she says, running her fingers over mine. "We wanted Renny to see a therapist. We tried to get her into a program, but she wouldn't go."

"Did she ever tell you about that?" Dad asks.

I shake my head. "No."

"She got picked up drinking at Captain Henry's one night," Mom says. "At two in the morning. Your father had to go down to the police station. We were lucky they didn't arrest her. The officer was a fan of your dad's. *One free bite at the apple,* I think is what he said. He was very nice. He didn't have to do that."

Captain Henry's. The police station. It all seems crazy. But then I have a distant memory, something so vague, it's more like a shadow of a memory—a Massachusetts driver's license, and on it, the photo of a girl with long, light-brown hair like Renny's and a birth date that made her twenty-one. I discovered it in one of

Renny's bathroom drawers one day when I was rummaging around in her makeup. She told me she'd found it and was going to send it back to the owner. Now I know that was a lie. Looking back, it seems so naive of me not to have realized what was going on, but I think I wanted to fool myself. I didn't want to believe she had changed that much. I wanted to believe she was still the same sister I'd always known and loved and respected.

Dad glances at Mom. "It's hard being a parent," he says. "You never think you'll have to deal with the things you end up dealing with. And half the time you're not happy about the way you've handled them. Maybe more than half. You can't press Pause and Rewind and do it over."

He looks at Mom, whose eyes are misty. "I remember the first time I realized the vodka was being watered down," he says. "And the first time your mom discovered a couple of empty beer cans in Renny's closet. You wonder, is this just teenage experimentation? And you hope it is. But then, over time, you begin to understand the extent of it, and you know it's not. You keep finding the empty beer cans, and then one night, you get a call from the police station telling you they just picked up your daughter with a fake ID at the local bar."

He removes his glasses and rubs the bridge of

his nose. "Do you remember the summer you wanted to visit your cousin Jenny in Boston, and you went up there for a week?"

I have a fleeting memory of the town house on Beacon Hill, Jenny's flaxen hair, my aunt Cordelia and uncle Henry, and their border collie, who slept on the bed with me. That was the summer I turned fourteen. "Yes, why?"

"We never told you this, but while you were away, your sister tried to commit suicide."

I turn and look into my father's eyes, and I feel the world falling away from me. I'm sliding down the side of a mountain, trying to hold on to crags and tree roots, unable to grip anything. "What happened?"

He takes a deep breath. "Mom found her. On the floor of her bathroom, barely conscious. We got her to the hospital, and they pumped her stomach. She'd been drinking vodka, and then she took Percocet. It would have killed her." He closes his eyes, and his chin trembles. Mom puts her hand on his arm.

"Why didn't you tell me about this? Even the police station—you never told me."

"We'd always planned to tell you," my mother says. "After the accident." She looks down and runs her hand over the bedspread. "But then, a year would go by and another year and another, and after a while we didn't really know how to bring it up. I mean, what do you do? Mention it over breakfast one morning? We didn't want you to have to deal with it. You were a kid."

"I wasn't a kid. I was fourteen. And I was her sister." I try to understand their reasoning, but I can't. I feel as though I've been denied something all these years, something I should have had. It's as though I were studying for a final exam and found out right before the test that I'd been given only half the textbook. "She tried to kill herself, and you never told me. I think I had a right to know." I look toward the window again. The light is growing weaker, the sun less intense. The afternoon is waning. What an odd turn of events. Here I assume I'm depositing the ugly truth on my parents' doorstep, bursting the bright bubble in which my sister has floated, and it turns out I'm the one who gets a dose of the truth.

"Renny didn't want you to know," Dad says. "She didn't want anyone to know. For a long time she wouldn't admit it was a suicide attempt."

"What do you mean?"

"She told us it was a mistake," he says. "That she got confused and forgot she'd taken the pills for a headache. And then she had a couple of drinks. But your mother and I . . . we never believed that. And one night Renny finally confessed."

Mom clasps her hands. "She was depressed. And maybe she had an anxiety disorder. I don't know. I'm not a psychiatrist. And, God knows, she wouldn't see one. But you know how she struggled to be perfect at everything." She looks away, tears in her eyes. "I don't know, Grace. I don't know."

"I'm sorry we didn't tell you," Dad says. "But we're telling you now, because you've got to let this go." He looks toward the window, the lace curtains fluttering. "You're right," he says. "We did lavish praise on Renny. We did give her a lot of attention and encouragement. But we had to, with all of her emotional ups and downs. We knew she was heading for trouble, and we thought keeping her focused on sports and things that were good for her would keep her safe. She needed the attention and the encouragement. And it worked. At least for a while."

He places the bottle of shampoo back in the bag. "But you . . ." When he looks at me again, there's a weary smile on his face. "We never had to worry about you. You were the easy one. You did what you needed to do without any fuss or fanfare from us, and you never got into trouble. You just quietly went about your business."

I'd like to believe him, but I know what I saw in the spiral notebook. I know what I saw on the back of the envelope.

"But you're still writing about her," I say. "*She leaves them in her wake.* I saw that line on the back of an envelope. And there's a poem in one of your notebooks, about seeds that get scattered to the wind and blow away. Those things are all about Renny. About Renny leaving us. She'll always be first in your mind, in your heart."

My father's mouth falls open. His eyes widen. "Grace, *She leaves them in her wake* is not about Renny. It has nothing to do with her. It's a line about a sailboat. It's literally about a boat's wake; it's not a metaphor for anything. And the one about the seeds . . ." He pauses, and I see such tenderness in his eyes. "That's actually about you."

Everything is suddenly still. I see dust motes descend in front of the window; I hear the clock in the hallway tick. "It's about me?"

He glances at Mom. "Sometimes your mother and I feel as though . . . well, we think you've pulled away from us. You hardly ever come home."

"And you never stay long when you do," Mom says. "You're in and out in a day." She winces. "I hate to admit this, honey, but we were secretly happy about the problem with your ceiling. At least we knew you'd be staying here for a while."

Dad nods.

Oh my God. I've been that bad?

"Sometimes it's almost as though we've lost you, too," he says.

Lost me?

I'm watching a movie in slow motion, frame by frame. It's a movie I've seen so many times, I thought I knew the beginning, the middle, and the end by heart. But now I realize maybe I didn't. I gaze around the room, at the mirror, framed in seashells; the bookshelves, cluttered with old novels and poetry books; the jar of sea glass on the bureau; and my mother and father, sitting next to me, looking so tired.

"No, you haven't lost me." I stretch my arms toward them, and they lean in. We huddle and hold one another as tightly as we can.

CHAPTER 21

An independent clause is a group of words that
can stand on its own as a sentence.
*A journey of a thousand miles begins
with a single step.*

That night I lie awake for hours, replaying
events from my life, looking at everything
through a new filter, feeling as though the pieces
of the puzzle have come together. When I get up
the next morning, the sun is streaming into the
room. I push aside the lace curtains and stare at
the blue of Long Island Sound. I can see the
place where the float used to be. I could draw a
straight line from the middle of the backyard
into the water and find that spot any day.

I see the float, too. It's bobbing in the water,
the gray paint peeling and flaking, sun glinting
off the metal ladder. And Renny is there. She's in
her pink bikini, standing on the diving board, her
wet hair dripping. She laughs and bounces a
couple of times on the end of the board. Then she
springs off, makes a high arc, and swan dives
into the sound. The water closes around her,
and there's a long moment when she's gone
and all that's left is a line of blue. But then she
comes to the surface, swims a few strokes, and

grabs hold of the ladder. She looks toward my window and sees me. And then she smiles and waves.

Everything is red, white, and blue when Cluny and I drive her Jeep down Main Street on our way to the Dorset Challenge. American flags unfurl in the breeze outside stores, and planters on the sidewalks dazzle with multicolored impatiens.

"Wow, look at that." I point to Bagatelle's window, where two mannequins show off sparkly red cocktail dresses and blue and white streamers dangle from the ceiling.

"Pretty," Cluny says. "Everything looks so festive."

My stomach growls as we pass the Sugar Bowl, giant blue stars on the windows advertising their star-shaped Fourth of July pancakes, served with strawberries, blueberries, and homemade whipped cream.

It's seven thirty, and in just a little over three hours, the Fourth of July parade will be coming down this street, and Cluny and I will be on the side of the road with Greg and the girls, cheering and waving flags as fire trucks and antique cars, town officials, marching bands, and schoolkids go by. But between now and then, we've got a bike ride to conquer.

Cluny parks the Jeep, and we pull the two bikes

from the back—Greg's blue Giant, which she's riding, and Cluny's yellow Cannondale, which I'm riding.

We walk the bikes to the village green. "They've really got a good turnout," I say as I survey the riders gathered on the lawn.

"There must be a hundred and fifty people here," Cluny says.

I scan the crowd, punctuated with riders dressed in red, white, and blue clothing, and I'm glad I decided to wear white shorts and a blue shirt. The gazebo is draped in banners of stars and stripes, and American flags planted around the perimeter of the lawn flap in the breeze.

As we cross the green, I spot Luann, the waitress from the Sugar Bowl. She and a man are walking their bikes to the registration table. We wave to Poppy Norwich, and I wonder if she's working on another book. I still haven't picked up *What You've Been Doing Wrong All Along*, but maybe it's worth a read. I mean, it was a bestseller. She's in cycling gear, and she's got a fancy-looking Cervélo next to her.

A man I don't know keeps staring at me, and I wonder if he recognizes me from the TV interview. God, I hope he doesn't want me to organize his closets. I hurry ahead, Cluny following me. And then I see someone I do know, and I stop.

"Cluny, look to the right," I whisper. "It's

Porcine Thighs!" Cluny follows my gaze toward the woman in black cycling shorts and a bright-orange jersey.

"Oh my God," she says. "Her thighs *are* huge."

I'm about to say *I told you* when I catch Porcine glancing at me. She turns away, and I think I'm home free. But then her head swivels back, our eyes lock, and I can see the wheels turning. Recognition sparks on her face, and my stomach jumps. I could take off—just make a run for it. I'm probably faster than she is. But I don't do that. I can't keep running from everything. I can't tryto escape my demons forever. So I stand there, prepared to meet the enemy, a couple of muscles in my face twitching. But Porcine doesn't come after me. She just raises a hand and flicks me a tepid wave. I flick a wave back, and then I start to breathe again.

Riders are walking around the snack table, picking up coffee and Gatorade, grabbing slices of bagels, bananas, and oranges. Most people are dressed in shorts and T-shirts, like Cluny and me, but a number of riders are in cycling shorts and jerseys and biking shoes that clip onto their pedals. Some are wearing identical jerseys and helmets and even have the name of their team on their shirts.

Cluny and I grab some banana slices, and I spot A.J. working at one of the registration tables. I don't know if he's still angry with me about the interview, but, in the spirit of facing my demons head-on, I tell Cluny I'm going to talk to him, and I walk up and lean the Cannondale against the table.

"Hey, A.J."

His little hoop earring sparkles when he glances up at me. "Grace," he says, a cautious note in his voice.

"It's good to see you," I tell him. "I'm glad you're here, because I'd like to apologize for that TV interview. I didn't mean to say anything bad about the store. I love the place and I'd never want to hurt anyone there . . . or the business. So, I'm sorry, and I hope we can still be friends." I give a tentative smile.

There's a moment of silence. Then he smiles, too. "Yeah, sure."

A feeling of relief washes over me, and I begin to wonder if Mitch is here. Maybe I could straighten things out with him as well. It's too small a town to have enemies. "Is Mitch working here, too? Or is he riding in this?" I ask.

"No, he's at the store today," A.J. says, and he hands a plastic bag to me and one to Cluny, who has pulled her bike up alongside me.

I feel a little disappointed. This seems to be a good place for détente.

Cluny and I open our bags. Inside I find a rider number to pin on my shirt, a wristband to prove

I've paid, coupons from local merchants, a water bottle with Paradise Day Spa's name and phone number on it, and a piece of paper that lists roads and mileage.

"Those are your cue sheets." A.J. points to my paper. "They've got the directions and the distances you'll be traveling on each road. Plus rest and refreshment stops."

Cluny and I glance at the sheets. Twenty-four and seven-tenths miles. It's spelled out right there. I look at the list of roads and turns—3.2 miles, 4.7 miles, 2.9 miles, 7.6 miles, and on and on. And it's got to be eighty degrees out already. "Is it too late to back out?" I whisper to her.

Her eyes widen. "Back out? You can't do that. You're the one who got me into this. And I have a big deadline tomorrow. If I can do this, you can. You're staying."

"Don't forget," A.J. says as he hands a bag to another cyclist, "there's going to be a big breakfast here after the ride. Tulip's is bringing the food."

"I'm not sure I'll make it back alive for breakfast," I tell him.

"Thanks," Cluny says. "We'll be there." She gives me a stern look.

I study the cue sheet again. For the first several miles, we're on the same route as the fifty-mile riders. That can't be good. "Maybe we should just do the five-mile route."

"That one's super easy," A.J. says. "It's for the kids and the old people."

Cluny laughs. "Well, we're definitely not kids."

I look at A.J., who must be a decade younger than us. "And we're not old people." He doesn't say a word. Oh my God. "Are we?"

"I don't *think* so," he says, which fails to make me feel any better. "Anyway, you can always turn around and come back early if you get tired. Or call me, and I'll pick you up. I'll be driving the broom wagon."

"The what?" Cluny asks.

"The van. You know, to help people with flats and things."

"I think we'll be fine," Cluny says, wheeling her bike away from the table. I take down A.J.'s cell number just in case.

"Okay, then," I say as I glance at the toned and muscled riders around us. "I guess we'd better get started."

The crowd is thinning as riders finish their snacks and get on the road. We fill our extra Paradise Day Spa bottles with water, stash our stuff in our saddlebags, and walk the bikes toward the edge of the green. A group of kids pass us, American flag crepe paper threaded through the spokes of their wheels. They're being trailed by a photographer wearing an identification tag on a string around his neck. He's probably with the *Dorset Review.* He looks desperate to get some pictures. I start to run after the kids, to warn them about the dangers of the media, but Cluny pulls me back.

"Are you ready?" she says when we get to the road.

"I'm as ready as I'll ever be."

We take off down Main Street in a pack of colorful bikes and riders, and, although I wish I were riding Renny's bike, the Cannondale is nimble, my legs feel pretty good, and I'm glad to be outside on such a beautiful day.

"Check out Between the Covers," Cluny says as we approach the end of the block. "Looks like Regan's done some holiday decorating, too."

I slow down to look. The window is filled with American flags, patriotic pinwheels, Uncle Sam hats, and a selection of books about the Revolutionary War.

"Do you think . . ." I'm about to ask Cluny if she thinks Regan can actually read those books. But then I catch myself, and I make a resolution not to stoop to that level anymore. You never know what's going on in someone else's life or what battles they might be struggling to fight.

By the time we turn onto Sheffield Avenue, a green, leafy, meandering road, the better riders have sped out of sight, leaving clusters of amateurs like me and Cluny. We ride by an old saltbox house, a field where wild turkeys scratch at the ground for nuts and seeds, and a patch of woods where the air is cooler and the rhythmic tap of a woodpecker echoes.

A mile and a half later, we pass the Everett Library, where my father has given a lifetime of poetry readings and the scent of books is steeped and pressed into every crevice of its two-hundred-year-old structure. I glance at the sign—*Annual Book Sale, August 2–5*—and I picture the opening day, with cars parked a quarter of a mile away and a hundred people lined up, eager to get into the tent.

After another two miles we're at the nature center, with its greenhouse and sand-colored cottage where classes and workshops are held. The parking lot is filled with cars, and a crowd is outside, milling around tables of potted plants.

"It's the annual herb and plant sale," Cluny says, pulling up next to me.

"My mom's probably there," I tell her.

As we pass other riders, I'm thrilled to know there are people slower than me, but farther along, a pack of geared-up cyclists in matching black biking shorts and yellow and black jerseys zooms by us, practically knocking us over with their draft, and I'm brought back to reality. We ride around twists and turns and up and down hills, and I keep pedaling, doing my best to stay in the same gear.

As we cycle past an estuary north of Dorset, the smell of the salt marsh fills my lungs, and patches of tall, yellow-green grass blow in the warm breeze. We catch sight of red barns and stone walls covered with lichen, and deer scampering through the woods. We ride alongside clusters of yellow and pink and purple wild-flowers and a pond where swans glide like fairy-tale creatures. We travel along smooth, paved roads where the only sound is the hum of the tires, and down dirt roads that jostle us in our seats. I'm feeling pretty good. Actually, I'm feeling great.

And then we come to the start of a hill. It's not one of those hills that go straight up, like the one Mitch and I rode over on the way to the lighthouse. At first, this hill doesn't look bad. I downshift a couple of times, thinking that might take care of things. But the road is insidious. It climbs slowly, gradually, and it just keeps going, up and up. And I keep shifting down and down, until I have no gears left. I try to concentrate on the fields and wildflowers going by, telling myself this has to end at some point. But the burn in my legs tells me they might give out before the road does. I'm going slower and slower. I'm panting, and I can hear Cluny behind me, panting as well. My legs are screaming in pain, and the road keeps climbing. I can barely push the pedals.

"Whyyyyy," Cluny groans, "did you get me into this?"

"Sorryyyy," I say, my bike swerving in and out because I can't pedal fast enough to keep it straight.

There's a stretch of near silence—just the sound of two gasping women. Then I hear Cluny's ragged voice. "You said . . . this would be easy. You said . . . we could do this."

"I . . . know. I . . . lied." I'm wheezing, my whole body so weak and wobbly I feel as though I'm going to collapse.

Cluny grunts behind me. "I haaaaate you!"

I'm zigzagging all over the road now, and she's doing the same.

"Are we there yet?" she moans.

All of a sudden, I can't go any farther. I stop, and my feet drop to the road. I straddle the bike. "That's enough," I pant. "I can't do this anymore. I need a break."

"Thank God," she says as we stagger off the bikes and drag them to the side of the road by a field, our legs threatening to buckle under us. We drop to the ground by a fence and tilt back our water bottles.

"How much farther?" I ask after I drain half the bottle.

Cluny wipes her face with a towel and takes out her cue sheet. "Eight more miles."

"Eight? Oh God, that can't be right. Check again." My legs throb, and my bottom is numb. I think about Tulip's breakfast, and I can almost smell the eggs and bacon, the pancakes and maple syrup.

"You're right." She folds up the cue sheet. "It's not eight more miles."

I knew that had to be wrong.

"It's eight and a half."

My heart sinks. "Cluny, I'm at the end of my rope here. I was okay until this hill, but this thing's a killer. And we're not even at the top yet."

"Yeah, this is hard," she says, guzzling more water. "It's a lot harder than I expected."

That's not too comforting, coming from someone who runs and does yoga all the time. I just nod. I'm too tired to talk.

"Even so, I wouldn't mind trying to finish," she says.

I give her a pleading glance.

"But I'll go back with you in the van, if that's what you're saying you want to do."

She gets up and reaches into her saddlebag for her phone. And as she does, I see a rider pedaling up the hill toward us. She's wearing a purple cycling jersey with a black zipper down the middle, a pair of black biking shorts, and purple biking shoes. On her head is a black helmet with a purple stripe in a shade that's the exact color of her shirt. She whizzes by. Yes, whizzes. And she's going *up* the hill.

"That's Regan!" I stand and point at Regan's back as she zips away from us.

Renewed energy courses through me, and suddenly I remember the reason why I committed to this whole endeavor in the first place. "Forget the van!" I tell Cluny. "Come on!"

We get back on the bikes, and I push off, my legs infused with new purpose. I have to finish this ride, no matter what it takes.

The road starts to curve, and the climb becomes steeper, but I keep pedaling, driving myself harder and harder. Sweat streams down my face; my T-shirt is soaked. And then I glimpse Regan's purple and black outfit. She's about seventy-five feet ahead.

"There she is," I tell Cluny. "Come on. Let's try to catch up to her."

Regan is on a high-end road bike, probably handmade in Italy, and she's moving at a pretty good clip, especially considering the slope. But I keep pounding my feet into the pedals, closing the distance between us. I'm about ready to pass out. My legs are falling off, and my ass burns, but I know if Renny were here she'd do it. I know she would. *"This one's for you, Renny!"* I shout, the sound echoing, and I grip the handlebars as though my life depends on it and I force my limbs to go, go, go. And then I'm there. I'm at the top of the hill. The road has finally leveled off, and Regan is standing by a stone wall, taking a water break.

I pull up next to her. She turns, a puzzled

expression on her face. "Grace?" She's breathing hard.

"Hey . . . Regan." I can barely speak.

"Aw, jeez," Cluny says, coming up alongside us, breathless. "Never again, Hammond!"

"Cluny?" Regan says.

"Yeah." She wipes her forehead with the back of her hand. "Hi."

Cluny and I pull out our water bottles, and the three of us drink. Regan dabs her mouth with the back of her riding glove. "Did I pass you two about a half mile back?"

"Yeah," I say, still trying to catch my breath. "You did."

"Wow," she says, nodding in approval. "I've got to hand it to you girls. Not bad."

Cluny and I glance at each other. I don't think I've ever heard Regan Moxley compliment another woman.

"Yeah," I say as I look down the road at a group of riders walking their bikes up the hill. "Not bad at all."

That night, Mom, Dad, and I sit in the Adirondack chairs at the water's edge, watching the evening go from dusk to dark and waiting for the fireworks to begin. Every muscle in my body hurts, even the ones I don't think I used, but I feel great. I take a sip of sauvignon blanc and let out a contented sigh.

"You must be tired, Grace," Mom says. "Twenty-five miles! I can't believe you rode that whole way."

"I can't believe it either," I say. "I feel kind of proud of myself."

"And you should," Dad says, raising his gin-and-tonic glass. "Here's to you, Grace. You did it. That's quite an accomplishment."

Mom lifts her glass as well, and the three of us toast, the chime momentarily interrupting the murmur of crickets and the metallic call of tree frogs. For a split second, while we're still holding our glasses in the air, our three hands silhouetted against the darkening sky, I think about Renny. A couple of days ago, I would have staked my life on the idea that no toast my parents and I could ever make would be complete without her being here. But now I know that's not true. There are still three of us in this family, and we have a lot of love to give one another.

The first boom comes just a minute or two later, a streak of white that zooms straight up into the air and then explodes into a thousand pieces of silver light that fall gracefully like shooting stars.

CHAPTER 22

Abstract nouns are nouns that you cannot
perceive through your five senses.
Memory . . . *is the diary that we all
carry about with us.* (Oscar Wilde)

The roofers are loading their pickup truck when I step outside the following afternoon. "Well, we're done," the bearded man says. "Now you can sleep late again."

Sleep late? "Oh, right," I say, trying to remember the last time I did that. I study the roof, with its crisp, new shingles, and realize I'd almost forgotten the guys were still here, the noise having somehow receded into the background.

The taller man throws a pile of shingles into the bed of the truck. "Okay, that's it." They get in and close the doors.

The bearded man opens the driver's-side window. "See you next time, then."

"Sorry?"

"Next roof." He nods toward the house. "This one should last a good twenty years. Sounds like a long time, but it'll go by faster than you think. So tell the missus to remember us."

Yes, it will go by quickly. "Sure," I say. "I'll tell her."

He raps on the outside of the door and gives me a wave, and the truck rumbles down the driveway.

The shop is busy when I arrive with Cluny's Jeep to pick up the Schwinn. Five women are renting bikes, a man in riding gear is inspecting a new wheel, a mother is looking at tricycles with her daughter, and the phone is ringing. Everybody's out front—Scooter, A.J., Kevin, and Mitch.

Scooter pulls out a rental bike for one of the women, and when he sees me his eyes brighten. "Hey there, Grace. How are you?"

"I'm well," I tell him. "It's good to see you."

"I know you're busy with your mom's party, but, boy, we could sure use your help today. We've been swamped. I'd put you on phone duty right off the bat." He looks toward the counter as Kevin picks up the phone. Then he adjusts the seat of the bike and asks the woman to try it.

Mitch glances my way, and I notice his hair looks a little different. Maybe he got it trimmed. "Yeah," he says. "It's a good thing we're busy. I guess we're not such dinosaurs after all."

Kevin looks at me. I smile and pretend it's a joke. I'll make my apologies to him before I leave.

"I came to pick up the Paramount," I tell Scooter as he wheels another rental bike toward the women. "I have my friend's Jeep outside."

He scratches his head. "I know you said you'd come back for it, but are you sure you want to take

418

it when it's not finished? We were doing a trade, remember?" He turns to one of the women. "Why don't you try this, and we'll adjust the seat if we need to."

"I'll just pick it up now," I say. "I didn't fulfill my end of the bargain anyway."

"Oh, I think you did more than enough. I'll make sure the bike gets done."

I hear Mitch mutter from behind the counter, "Yeah, I'd say she did enough."

I try to push down the hurt I feel as I wave my hand at Scooter. "No, really, it's fine. I think it will just be easier if I take it now. After I get a job, I'll find a bike shop in the city where I can have it restored."

Scooter looks as though he's about to say something else, but then he shrugs. "Okay. Whatever you want, Grace. But remember, if you change your mind, you know where to find us." He pulls another rental bike out of a rack. "As soon as Kevin or A.J. is free, I'll have him get your bike and take it to your car. You can wait in the office if you want. It might be a few minutes."

"Okay, thanks." I walk past the customers, behind the counter, and into the office. Sitting at the desk, I glance at the stacks of papers, the cycling posters on the walls, and the shelves with Scooter's collection of old catalogs. I'll miss this place, but I'm also ready to say good-bye to it. I'm ready to go home and get on with my life.

419

Mitch walks to the counter, rings up the man with the new wheel, and passes him a credit card receipt. Then he turns and steps into the doorway of the office. "I thought we agreed you weren't coming back."

I look up. "We did, but I have to get my bike."

He takes another step inside and closes the pocket door behind him. "If you'd called, we could have had one of the guys drop it off." His tone is more distant than angry. "We do have a van, you know. Or you could have asked your Hollywood boyfriend to pick it up." Now he's got a little sarcasm going.

"He's not my boyfriend."

"I'm sure you're working on it, though."

"No, I'm not working on it. Peter and I . . ." I stop because the full explanation is far too complicated.

Mitch shakes his head. "Yeah, whatever."

"Look, I'm just here to pick up my bike. You'll never have to see me again after this." He turns to go. I can't leave things this way. "Mitch, I really am sorry."

He spins around. "You know, Grace, maybe saying you're sorry always works for you, gets you off the hook with people. But I don't accept apologies that easily."

I only wish he knew how much his words hurt. "Actually, saying I'm sorry hasn't always gotten me off the hook. It's taken a lot more than that."

"Well, there you go," he says, his tone sharp.

I pick up a model of an old-fashioned bicycle from the corner of the desk—the kind with a tiny wheel and a huge wheel. I think about Mitch's mother and the letters she wrote. I put the model down and push it across the desk. "Mitch . . ."

He glances at me.

I'm about to tell him there's no benefit in holding too tightly to the past. That even what we think we know, we're seeing through filters—memory lapses, our own biases, what other people tell us, gaps in information. But I never get to say it because someone in the store starts yelling Mitch's name.

It's A.J., and there's terror in his voice. Mitch slides open the door and runs out, and I follow him into the store. Scooter is on the floor, lying on his side with his knees bent. His eyes are closed, and he's not moving. The skin on his face is pasty and gray, and his cheeks are slack. A.J. and Kevin are crouched next to him while two customers, young guys, look on nervously.

Mitch shakes Scooter's shoulder. "Dad! Dad! Wake up. What's going on?" He shakes him again, but Scooter's head just wobbles. Mitch puts his hand on Scooter's chest, which is perfectly still, and then puts his ear to Scooter's nose and mouth. "Oh God, he's not breathing."

I feel the room closing in around me.

"He was just standing there," A.J. says, his

421

voice trembling. "And then he grabbed those bikes and fell over."

Kevin, his face pale, says, "Yeah, he just collapsed."

Mitch yanks his cell phone from his pocket. "Calling 911."

I look down at Scooter, motionless on the floor. What's wrong with him? Why isn't he breathing? What if he dies? The room is stifling, perspiration edging down my back, prickling along my arms.

"My father just fainted or collapsed or something," Mitch says into the phone, his voice ringed with panic. "No, he's not breathing."

I look at Kevin. "Get those customers out of here and make sure nobody else comes in. Come on, quickly."

"I didn't see it happen," Mitch tells the dispatcher. "But the guys here said he was standing and he fell over, collapsed." He recites the address of the store and his cell number. "It's called the Bike Peddler."

"A.J.," I say. "Get something to put under Scooter's head." I scan the room. "Anything. Biking shorts. Over there!"

"He's seventy-nine," Mitch says.

A.J. grabs three pair of biking shorts, and we fold them and place them under Scooter's head.

"Let's get him on his back," I tell A.J., and we gently move him. I look at Scooter. *Please don't die, please don't die.* I take his hand. It's cool and limp. "Mitch, tell them to hurry."

"Kevin, was he eating anything?" Mitch asks.

"No," Kevin says, and Mitch repeats the information.

He's not breathing. He's going to die. Somebody needs to help him.

"Kevin, go outside," I say. "And flag down the ambulance as soon as you see it so they know where to come. They'll be here any second."

"Okay," he says, and he runs out.

I want the ambulance to come so badly, I'm hearing sirens that aren't there. I look through the windows, hoping for the sight of a blinking strobe light, but outside it's a perfectly quiet summer day—blue sky, dashes of cottony clouds, leaves fluttering in the maple trees.

"CPR?" Mitch says. "No, I don't. What do I do? Yeah? Uh-huh?" He looks at me, his eyes wide.

And then I remember it. The poster in the coffee nook at Jerold Communications, where I used to work. The poster I used to see every day, with its colorful drawings and catchy typeface. *Save a Life! Know CPR!*

"I can do CPR," I tell Mitch, recalling the illustrated steps, each one in its own square. *1. Check the scene for immediate danger. 2. Assess the victim's consciousness. 3. Send for help. 4. Check for breathing.* We've done all of that. There's only one thing left. I place the heel of my left hand on Scooter's plaid shirt, in the middle of his breastbone, with my other hand on top, just the way it looked in step five of the drawing. Then I place my body over my hands, keeping my arms straight.

I look down at Scooter, and I begin pressing up and down and up and down, very fast and very hard on his chest, my hands pushing through skin and muscle to find the heart underneath. I don't know if I'm doing it too slowly or too quickly, but I keep pressing. Mitch is saying something into the phone, but the words are blurred.

Up and down and up and down I'm pushing. I look at Scooter's face. Nothing. *Come on, breathe, open your eyes. Do something. Don't leave me.* I keep pushing, working my arms like bellows. I keep pushing, but I'm starting to think it's too late. He's already gone, and he's not coming back.

"Grace, let me take over," Mitch says. "Have a rest."

"No, I'm fine." My arms ache, but I can't stop. I can't give up. We're attached, Scooter and I, my hands and his heart. I glance at Mitch. He's perfectly still, his eyes on Scooter, his lips moving slightly. He's saying, *Come on, come on.*

And that's when it happens. Scooter blinks, three tiny flutters, and then his eyes open just a little and he starts to wheeze and cough, his chest moving as he struggles to breathe. For a moment he looks straight at the ceiling. Then his eyes dart around, and he finds Mitch, crouched at his side.

"Dad." Mitch beams, lets out a nervous laugh, and clasps Scooter's hand. Scooter's breathing is raspy and ragged as he stares at his son.

"You collapsed," Mitch tells him. "You stopped breathing. The ambulance is coming. You're going to be okay. Just lie still."

Scooter nods, clutching Mitch's hand.

The emergency sirens begin as a faint, high-pitched hum, like bees in a field searching for a good place to land, and then rise to a wail as the trucks race down Main Street. A fire engine and an ambulance pull up in front of the store. Six emergency medical techs burst in, carrying orange boxes and a stretcher.

"Over here," Mitch waves. "It's my dad. He passed out, but he's breathing again."

One of the men introduces himself as Lieutenant Bryce. He asks Mitch questions and talks to Scooter, letting him know what's going on, while the other EMTs move him onto the stretcher and hook him up to monitors and machines. There's a steady *bleep, bleep, bleep* coming from one of the monitors, and I watch the screen, comforted by the rhythm.

"All this fuss?" Scooter whispers, looking at Mitch. He glances at me and gives me a weary smile. "I feel okay."

"I think we should let them do their jobs," Mitch says.

He holds Scooter's hand as they lift the stretcher and carry him through the store. I'm on the opposite side of the stretcher, and when Scooter extends his other hand, I take it, relieved at the warmth I feel in his fingers. He looks at me as though he's going to tell me something, but I can see he doesn't have the strength. And then the emergency techs slide the stretcher into the back of the ambulance, Mitch jumps in after it, and the doors close.

CHAPTER 23

A dependent clause is a group of words
that has a subject and a verb but cannot
stand alone as a sentence.
Preparing to return home after one has been
away often entails tying up loose ends.

"I'm here to see Mr. Dees," I tell the receptionist
at Mercy Hospital the following afternoon.

She removes her yellow headband and slides
it back over her hair. Then she clicks a few
computer keys, rattling the wooden bracelets
on her arms, takes my picture, and hands me a
stick-on visitor's badge. I proceed to a bank of
elevators, where a man in a wheelchair, his leg in
a cast, waits with a white-uniformed aide.

Scooter's room is on the third floor, and when
I get there the door is almost completely closed.
I give a quiet knock, but there's no response, so I
knock again. Then I slowly open the door and
peek inside. It's a double room, but the first bed
is empty. Scooter is lying in the other bed, by the
window, his head raised to a forty-five-degree
angle, his face turned away from me. An
intravenous stand holds two bags of clear fluid, a
tube running from one bag into his arm. Monitors
near the bed emit beeps in various tones and

427

produce small mountain ranges of lines that jag across the screens. The television is on, old black-and-white footage of Frank Sinatra performing somewhere, but the volume is low, and I can't hear what he's singing.

I tiptoe into the room. "Scooter," I whisper, thinking he may be asleep.

He turns. "Hey, if it isn't my hero." He's got a pale-green breathing tube clipped to his nose. There's a book on the bed, a Tom Clancy novel, and a vase of yellow tulips on a set of drawers against the wall.

I lean in and give him a hug. The sheets smell of antiseptics and constantly recirculated air. I kiss his cheek, scratchy with day-old whiskers.

"What a nice surprise," he says. "Here, bring that over." He points to a chair in the corner. I drag it to the bed.

"Well," I say, taking a seat, "after that scare you gave us yesterday, I figured I'd better come over here and see what's going on."

Scooter grimaces. "That was a little dramatic, wasn't it? Sorry I put everybody through that."

"Oh, come on. There's nothing to be sorry for." I pat his shoulder. "Don't be silly."

"I heard you were the one who gave me CPR." He looks out the window, where a tree branch taps the glass, and then turns back to me. "You saved my life, you know."

"No way. It was a team effort. Everybody was

doing something—and it all worked." I think about the poster. *Save a Life! Know CPR!* I think that must have been the most important thing I ever learned from my old job. Maybe that's the real reason I was there. Maybe that's how life works. You don't always know at the time when something powerful is happening to you. It's not until later, when the pieces fit together, that you figure it out.

"Do they know why you collapsed?" I ask.

"The doc said it was my heart—the rhythm. I guess it's off a little."

"Your rhythm."

"Yeah. They're doing some tests to figure out why. I already had an echocardiogram and a stress test. You know, the one where you have to run on a treadmill?"

"It's not anything . . . serious, is it?"

"I hope not. They said they'll know more tomorrow." A nurse comes in, looks at the IV bag, where the glucose is making a silent *drip, drip, drip,* adjusts something on the bag, and leaves.

Scooter glances at the monitors, conversing in their blinks and beeps. "If it were up to me, I'd be out today. I feel fine." He sits up a little straighter and reaches for the cup of water on the table beside him, but it's too far away.

"Just let them do what they need to do," I say, walking to the table. "You'll be out of here soon enough, and you don't want to pass out like that again." I pick up a stainless steel pitcher and pour some water into the cup. "You really had us worried."

"Yeah, yeah. I know," he says with a flick of his hand. "Mitch tells me the same thing—let them do their jobs."

Mitch.

I wish I could forget the look on his face when he walked into the little office, closed the pocket door, and said, *I thought we agreed you weren't coming back.* I hand the cup of water to Scooter.

"Well, Mitch is right." I straighten the blanket on Scooter's bed. "And I'm sure you'll be out of here in no time." Scooter hands me the cup, and I put it back on the table. "You know, there's nothing like having a fresh start, an opportunity to see things differently. It's like getting a second chance . . . at everything." I adjust Scooter's pillow behind his head. "So this could be a fresh start for you, where you make sure you're healthy, and then you'll be ready to take on the world again. Maybe in a whole new way." I walk back to the chair and sit down.

"*The first day of the rest of my life* kind of thing?" Scooter says.

"Sure. There's always another first day. We can always restart and reinvent ourselves, right?"

"Guess so," he says. "Today's as good a day as any." He taps my hand. "Hey, speaking of getting out, they said I ought to be out of here on Sunday.

Maybe you could stop by my house. Celebrate my freedom. I'll even make you a cup of coffee."

"That's very tempting, Scooter, but I'll have to take a rain check. I'll be home by then."

He tilts his head. "What do you mean?"

"I'll be back in Manhattan."

His shoulders droop, as if gravity is just too big a force to be reckoned with. A heavy feeling begins to settle inside me. "Tomorrow's my dad's party. And then I'm leaving first thing Sunday morning." The room is quiet except for the beeps and the faint sound of Sinatra singing "It Was a Very Good Year."

"Oh, sure. I understand. I just didn't realize you were going so soon."

I laugh. "I've been here for more than two weeks. I need to find a job, pay my bills, and get myself back on track." I glance out the window, where a single white cloud is making an appearance. "I'll come see you next time I'm in town, Scooter. I promise. I'm planning to be back soon."

"Okay," he says. "You've got yourself a date. We'll grab some sandwiches at Tulip's again and take them to the green."

"Okay, but it'll be my treat." I glance at the vase of yellow tulips. "Did she give you those?"

"Who?" Scooter asks.

"You know who. Tulip."

He blushes.

"You stud."

431

He laughs.

I refill his water cup and pull the table closer to the bed. "I'll call you on Sunday before I leave," I say, giving him a hug.

I'm halfway across the room when I hear his voice. "Grace, I think my son is in love with you."

I stop. That can't be. Not based on the way Mitch has been acting, that's for sure. "Mitch? In love with me?" I say. "No, Scooter. He's angry with me, and I think he kind of hates me. He's definitely not in love with me."

"Angry with you, hates you. Why would you say that?"

"It's a little complicated. Just take my word for it."

Scooter gives me a skeptical look. "Sometimes we think we know what people are feeling when we really don't. I know my son is in love with you, Grace."

I picture Mitch's face when he said *I can't have you working here anymore.* "I don't think so, Scooter."

But as I walk to the door, I begin to wonder, what if he's right? What if, by some strange chance, Scooter is correct? Before my notorious news segment, Mitch and I were getting along well. We were having fun together. And I'm certain he was making a pass at me at the lighthouse. I know he was. Mitch. The bike guy. The history teacher. Could that be? I feel a bit light-headed thinking about it, as though I've just gulped down a big glass of champagne. He's smart, he's funny, he's good-looking, and he adores his father, all great qualities. But as I think about this some more, I remember the cold way he looked at me the other day in the shop. I remember his tone. And I know it can't be true.

"I'll call you on Sunday," I tell Scooter. As I walk away, a very young Frank Sinatra is singing "Let's Fall in Love."

An hour later I open the door to the Sugar Bowl. Faded lobster buoys hang from one of the walls, and in the corners of the room, fishnets dangle, with buttery-colored slipper shells and knobby periwinkles laced among the strings. I'm not sure how I feel about this decor. The place doesn't look the same. With the shell photos they'd already hung, and now these new nautical additions, it seems like a whole different Sugar Bowl.

But when I glance again at the fishnets, I remember the shells Renny and I used to collect in plastic pails, rinse in Mom's strainer, and set out to dry on the railing of the back porch. And I think maybe it's possible to find something good in anything, even if it's new and different.

Peter waves to me from one of the booths, and I walk over and slide onto the bench across from him. "Hi," I say.

"Hi yourself," he says. "How are you?"

"Better than I was the other day."

"I was worried."

"I know. And I'm sorry I didn't call you back."

"Or text me until last night?"

I grimace. "I know. I needed to think. A lot happened since I saw you."

A young waitress wipes down the table and asks us what we'd like to drink. We both order coffee.

"I'm sorry I ran off," I say, pushing my menu to the side. "I was having a tough time. With the movie. That scene. The dance."

"I knew something was up," he says.

I clasp my hands and put them on the table. "The problem is, I've had that whole event stored in my memory for a long, long time. I know everything that happened, from the second Cluny and I got to the yacht club until the end of the night. At least, I thought I knew." My mind runs to the movie scene where Tom and Courtney danced, and then to the fight that followed. "I don't remember anything about that fight with Pratt Greeley."

"You wouldn't, Grace. That happened the next day, downtown."

Our waitress returns with a carafe and pours coffee into our mugs. "No wonder. At least I know I'm not losing my mind."

"You're not losing your mind," Peter says.

"Do you remember talking to me about your

434

parents? I mean, did we really have that conversation?"

"I thought we did," he says, adding some milk to his coffee. "If I didn't mention it to you, I probably wanted to. That's what was going on at the time with my parents, and it was important to me, so I wrote it into the scene."

Why did I think this was a story only I had the right to tell, as though I owned the copyright to it? Why didn't it ever occur to me that Peter had his own story, that he might have put his own spin on things?

"I'm sorry, Peter. I'm sorry about running off and not calling you back and being so weird about all of it." I look at the paper place mat on the table, not wanting to meet his eye. "When I saw you that first day at the Sugar Bowl, I was convinced I was in love with you all over again. I thought maybe we could pick up our old relationship and get back together." I look up. "But there was really some-thing else going on."

He puts his hands over mine. "I think whatever's going on with you has a lot more to do with enny and the past than it does with me. I wish it didn't. I wish it really was about me, but this isn't a movie, where I can write the story the way I want it to play out."

I stare across the room at a faded yellow and red lobster buoy as servers walk by on their way to the kitchen. Norah Jones's soft voice floats down from the ceiling speakers as she sings "Come Away with Me." I never meant to lead Peter on. That's the last thing I intended to do. I don't know where to start, what to say. I feel as if there's a rock in the pit of my stomach. I look at Peter, and I'm about to cry. And then he saves me.

"So, we've wrapped," he says, with a smile that looks a little forced. "I'm leaving tomorrow."

"Right. You've wrapped. Congratulations on being done."

"Well, we're done here. Now it's on to post-production."

"That's where all the editing and the sound work and everything else gets done, right?"

He nods and takes a sip of coffee. "Ouch, that's bad," he says, looking at the mug and making a face.

I smile. "Some things don't change." I pass him the basket of sugar packets and sweeteners. "Can I ask you something? About the movie?"

He opens three yellow packets and dumps them into his coffee. "Sure."

"I'm curious. What's going on with Regan Moxley?"

He looks amused. "What do you mean, what's going on with her?"

"Well, that picture of you together in the paper, for one thing. You guys looked kind of cozy. And Regan got a part in the movie."

Peter shakes his head and chuckles. "Regan's a piece of work, isn't she?"

"Yeah, she sure is."

"I like to keep her happy. She's an investor in a project Sean and I are going to do."

"Oh. An investor." That's not what I expected at all.

"Yeah. So I gave her a line. No big deal."

"One line? Just a business arrangement, then?"

He sits back in his chair. "Yeah, of course. Why?" There's a brief pause, and then his eyes go wide. "Wait, you didn't think . . ."

I raise my hands. "Oh, no, no. Of course not. I knew it was some kind of, uh, business arrangement. I just wasn't sure . . . about the details."

He gives me a squinty-eyed look, and I feel myself blush.

We pick up our menus, and I grab the blue card that lists the specials. *Tuscan Salad; Apple, Walnut, & Brie Sandwich; Potato Leak Soup.* How can a restaurant misspell the word *leek?* I dig into my handbag and locate my fine-point Sharpie. I pull it out, remove the cap, and hold it over the card for a long time as I stare at the word. And then it suddenly occurs to me that I don't give a damn if the Sugar Bowl spells the word with an *a* or an *e*. In the overall scheme of things, what does it matter? I drop the Sharpie, and it rolls along the table and falls onto the floor, where I leave it.

Peter places a manila envelope on the table.

"What's that?"

"Open it."

I pick it up. My name is on the outside, in my father's scratchy handwriting. I pull out a sheaf of papers. *All She Ever Knew* by Grace Hammond. I flip through the first couple of pages. My screen-play. "Where did you get this?"

"Cluny gave it to me."

"Cluny?" I wonder how Cluny got it, and then I remember her taking it from the chest in the front hall on Founder's Day. I didn't even want *her* to look at it, and now she's passed it on to Peter. "Why did she give this to you?"

"She thought I should read it."

Right. And what does Cluny know about screenplays? Now she's made me look like a fool, and the last thing I need is another reason for Peter to think I'm a fool.

"Look, Peter. I didn't want Cluny to see this. I didn't want anybody to see it. And I certainly would never have given it to you. This is just something I wrote in college. It's not very good, and I didn't even finish it, as I guess you know by now."

"Well, I read it," Peter says. "And—"

"I know, I know." I throw the pages on the table. "I'm sorry you had to waste your time."

He looks confused. "Waste my time? I thought it was pretty good."

438

"Cluny had no right to—wait. What?"

"I really liked it."

I lean in a little closer. "You liked my old screenplay?"

"Yes. Good story line, strong characters, some great dialogue. I do think the father could be developed a little more." He chuckles. "I love that scene where the mother goes to the hardware store and returns all the power tools the father bought. And it needs an ending, of course. You should write one."

"An ending. Oh, of course. Yes." I'm still stuck at *I really liked it.*

Peter takes another sip of coffee and then pushes the mug aside. "You know, you've got talent, Grace. I remember that from high school, and it shows in this script. Cluny told me you're a technical writer. Frankly, I don't know how you juggle both jobs—doing that and being an organizational efficiency . . . What kind of consultant are you again?"

I give him a blank stare, and then I realize what he's talking about, and I want to burst out laughing.

"Anyway, with your talent, you should be doing a lot more than technical writing."

"You really think so?"

He leans toward me, a surprised look on his face. "Sure. Hasn't your father ever told you that?"

CHAPTER 24

Interjections are words or phrases
used to capture short bursts of emotion.
Cheers! Here's to Vondel.

It's three thirty on Saturday, a half hour before
the party is scheduled to start, and there's too
much chaos in the house for me. Mom is fretting
about the hors d'oeuvres, while the caterers keep
trying to escort her from the kitchen. Dad is
holding court in the library with his brother,
Whit, and some other relatives who flew in last
night. They're telling remember-the-time-
when stories that I've heard so often, I've begun
to think they're my own.

I walk into the backyard, where a huge, white
tent sits in the middle of the lawn. The band is
testing the sound system, and two women from
the catering company are making last-minute
adjustments to the tables. The sides of the tent are
open, providing an unobstructed view of Long
Island Sound, where a dozen sailboats puff
along in the breeze. White linen napkins, shiny
flatware, glass hurricane lamps, and vases filled
with blue and white hydrangeas sit atop each
table, arranged with the precision of a drill
sergeant. Around the tent, the grass is clipped and

green, and the flower beds have been treated to a fresh layer of mulch.

I walk to the bar in the new cocktail dress Mom insisted on buying for me at Bagatelle. Full price, no less. The fabric is a silky chiffon of pale greens and blues, and the dress has a fitted waist and a flared skirt that makes me feel as though I'm floating when I move. I head toward the bar, where one of the bartenders is emptying bags of ice into coolers. He watches me as I approach.

"Can I get you something, Miss Hammond?"

"I'd love a sauvignon blanc."

"Sure," he says. And then he adds, "That's a nice dress."

I smile. "Why, thank you."

He pours the wine, and the glass catches a glint of light from the sun. I walk to one of the tables and sit down, and I think about how, at this time tomorrow, I'll be back in my apartment in Manhattan, turning the air conditioner back on, going through the pile of mail I'll find wedged into my box, throwing out the wilted lettuce and the squishy lemons and the other food that's gone bad.

Or maybe I won't. Maybe I'll call a friend and see an off-Broadway play or go to an outdoor concert or take a walk on the High Line. I can wait another day to clean the fridge and toss out the junk mail. I think Katharine Hepburn was right. If you obey all the rules, you *do* miss all the fun. Maybe I've spent too much time worrying about typos and grammar and dotting i's and crossing t's.

Guests begin to make their way across the grass and into the tent, where Mom and Dad greet them, exchanging hugs and handshakes. Buddy and Jan arrive and, not long after, Cluny and Greg.

"I heard you were a hero the other day," Greg says as we stand at the side of the tent near the water. "Cluny told me you did CPR. On Scooter."

"Oh, I'm not a hero. I just knew enough to get by, and it worked."

Cluny leans in and whispers, "He doesn't know we learned that in spy school."

"I was a detective," I correct her, for the millionth time.

"Hey, I came up with a great idea," she says. "And it was all because of that Dorset Challenge. I'm going to do some illustrations of animals on bikes. I've never used bikes before, and I think it could be great. I'm figuring out which breeds I'll put on racing bikes, which ones will get hybrids, mountain bikes, tricycles. My first card is going to be based on the Dorset Challenge. I'll have Main Street in the background."

"Oh my God. I love that idea, Cluny. It's brilliant."

"Yeah, I think it will be a fun addition to the line."

I lean in and whisper, "By the way, they're called *road* bikes, not racing bikes."

"Ah," she says. "Thanks." Then she digs into her clutch bag. "Almost forgot—I have something for you." She whips out a little piece of newsprint—something she's pulled from the paper.

"No way," I say, backing up a step. "No more horoscopes."

"Let me just read this to you. It's an interesting one."

"I've got to go say hi to some people."

She steps closer. "It says, *Breaking the rules can be a good thing, especially if those rules inhibit your creativity.*"

"Okay, thanks." I start to walk away.

"No, wait. There's more. *Today, let any inspiration that comes your way guide you. And don't fall back on old assumptions.* Oh, but here's the really interesting part. *Someone from your past is heading toward your future tonight.* Maybe something will happen right here at this party, Grace. Something romantic."

"How is that possible, Cluny? The only guy from my past is on his way back to the West Coast right this second."

"I don't know the details," she says. "I just know what I read. So be prepared."

One of my parents' neighbors grabs me and pulls me away for a long chat. Lines begin to form at the bar, and the band's singer, a petite woman in a purple dress, starts belting out a jazzy rendition of "It Had to Be You." The guests gather in clusters, talking and laughing and plucking hors d'oeuvres from passing trays, and the dance floor begins to fill.

"How are you doing?" I whisper to Dad as I brush by him on my way to talk to my cousin Allison from Rhode Island. Dad's got Ward Johnson, a partner of Mom's, on his left, and Kiki Ross, who has something to do with Dad's publisher, on his right, and they're all discussing a hotel in Paris where Ward and his wife just stayed. I know some part of Dad would probably prefer to be inside, tinkering with his puzzle or scribbling lines of poetry on the back of an envelope, but he looks happy.

"I'm having fun, Gracie," he says, and when he smiles, the little crinkles around his eyes seem to smile, too. "Although I could use another one of these." He holds up his empty glass, shaking what's left of the ice.

"A G and T?" I ask, although I don't wait for the response, because it's always gin and tonic. "I'll be right back."

Blini and caviar, crab salad canapés, mini ham and Gruyère pastries, tuna Niçoise crostini, truffle risotto balls, and tiny polenta sandwiches with mushroom filling are offered to me on silver trays. I try them all, going back for seconds and thirds on the caviar. I weave my way among the guests, saying hello to the ones I know, smiling politely at the ones I don't, and I get Dad's drink from the bar and deliver it to him.

The cocktail hour goes on for an hour and a half, and then we sit down for dinner. I take my seat across from Mom and Dad and next to a man with a handlebar mustache and a toupee much darker than his sideburns. He leans over and peers at my place card.

"Ah, you're Grace." He thrusts a hand at me. "Paul Duffner here."

Paul Duffner. Where have I heard that name?

"I'm at the university with your father."

Oh my God, now I remember. He's the guy writing the book about that Dutch poet, Joost van der something.

I shake his hand. "Yes, nice to meet you. My dad's, uh, spoken of you. You're writing a book. About Joost . . ." I can't remember his last name, so I leave it at that, as though the dead poet and I are on a first-name basis.

Paul Duffner fiddles with the knot in his tie, wincing for a moment as though he's being choked. "Van den Vondel," he says, completing the name. "Are you familiar with Vondel's work?"

I wouldn't know Vondel's work if a volume of his greatest poems landed on my head. "Of course," I say. "Isn't everyone?"

Duffner's eyes pop open, and he smiles, a huge smile that makes his mustache twitch. "How I wish that were true!" He leans in and lowers his voice. "Most people, outside of literary

445

circles, of course, have never even *heard* of him."

"No!" I say, recoiling. "I find that hard to believe. Aren't they teaching Vonder in school?"

"Vondel."

"Yes, Vondel. Isn't that what I said? Students should be learning about . . ."—I pause to make sure I've got the name right—"Vondel, just as they learn about Shakespeare. Don't you think?"

He tilts his head. "What a refreshing attitude. I happen to agree. He is, after all, the greatest of the Dutch poets and playwrights."

"The greatest. Let me ask you this, Paul—may I call you Paul?"

He smiles and blushes; his eyes gleam. "Of course."

"What do *you* consider to be Vondel's best play?"

A server puts a plate in front of me—lobster, tenderloin, roasted potatoes, baby carrots.

"Well," Duffner says, "I'd have to say *Jephtha*, although I know I'm going against the grain there, most critics choosing *Lucifer.*"

"Of course you're going against the grain. But bravo to you, Paul! How many people would have the courage to do that? It's always *Lucifer, Lucifer, Lucifer.* I have to say, I agree with you about *Jephtha.*"

"You do?" He looks stunned. "Well, a fellow Vondel contrarian. I can hardly believe it."

"Oh, believe it. Definitely believe it." I raise

my glass of wine. "To Vonder," I say. And then I realize my mistake.

But Paul Duffner doesn't notice. He's looking at me as though he would follow me over hot coals. He raises his glass. "Yes, to Vondel!"

Toward the end of the meal, Mom rises from her chair, walks to the stage, and picks up a wireless microphone. I hope she's not going to sing. She's been known to empty a room after even attempting just a few bars of "I Get a Kick out of You." She taps the mic a couple of times as plates of yellow cake with buttercream icing arrive at our table.

"Hello, everyone. Hello." She waits for the chatter to subside. "While we're enjoying our dessert," she says, "I'd like to say a few words. And I do mean a few. I was advised a long time ago that the secret to public speaking is to be brief, be funny, and be seated." There's a roar of laughter and a smattering of applause. Mom smiles, and her cheeks take on a rosy glow.

"We feel so fortunate to have all of you here today," she continues. "And I want to thank you for being here. Some of you have come from far away, and all of you have given up your time to be with us, to celebrate Doyle's birthday." I'm listening to Mom, but I'm also aware of an undercurrent of chatter coming from the opposite side of the tent.

"I look around," Mom says. "And I see family and friends, some of whom we haven't seen in years . . ."

People are whispering and murmuring and turning to look at the entrance to the tent.

"And so," Mom says, "with that, I'd like to ask . . ." She stops and peers across the tent, where a man is standing. He's talking to one of the women from the catering company, and she's pointing at our table. No, more specifically, she's pointing at *me*. The man walks into the tent. It's Sean.

Mom clutches the microphone, looks around as though she needs confirmation that this is really happening, and says, "Sean Leeds?" That's when several women pull out bottles of Catch Me! and begin spraying jasmine into the air and all the guests grab their cell phones and start snapping pictures.

"Come on up here," Mom says, gesturing to Sean. "We want to see if you really are the sexiest man alive."

"Mom!" I yell, mortified. But everybody else laughs, including my father.

Sean walks toward me. "Hello, Grace," he says, in his deepest, smoothest voice. "You look beautiful." Then he adds, "I'll be right back." He walks to the stage, leaving me with my mouth agape.

"It really is you," Mom says as Sean walks over and stands beside her.

"So nice to meet you, Mrs. Hammond," he says, kissing her on the cheek. Her face turns radish pink. "Grace invited me, and I'm sorry to show up unannounced, but I didn't think I'd have a chance to stop by before I flew out."

"Oh, Mr. Leeds, you don't have to apologize," Mom says, fluffing her hair. "Can you stay for dessert? We'll set a place at our table, right over there." She points. "Right next to Grace." She beams at me and mouths, *Sean Leeds!* as if I didn't already know and as if nobody else can see her doing it. Oh my God. Mom, stop!

"I wish I could," Sean says, "but I've only got a few minutes." He touches her arm, and she looks as though she's about to drop. "Grace told me you're a fan, and I knew I had to meet you. I also wanted to wish your husband a happy birthday."

Dad waves to Sean. "Thank you."

Mom blurts out, "Hey, everybody. It's Sean Leeds!" and the whole tent erupts in laughter.

That's when I walk up and rescue him. "Come on." I grab his arm.

"Sean Leeds, everyone," Mom says, clapping like a late-night talk show host whose guest is exiting the stage.

Sean laughs as I lead him out of the tent to the other side of the lawn. We stand under the trees. "I can't believe you came."

"Sorry for the surprise entrance."

"Are you kidding? It was perfect. You've given

my mother something she'll talk about for years. Not to mention my father. And everyone else here."

"It's the least I could do, after the other day." I must look as confused as I feel, because he adds, "When you planned that great escape from the mob at the ice cream store."

"Oh." I laugh. "That was no big deal. It was fun."

Two small boats glide by in the distance, their white triangles of sailcloth catching the wind. We watch them for a moment, and then Sean says, "Well, I'd better run. The other coast calls."

"Have a safe trip," I tell him. "And thanks again for coming. Really."

"You're welcome," he says. "Really." He leans in and kisses my cheek. "See you, Grace." And then he's off.

I return to the tent just in time to hear Mom singing the end of "I Get a Kick out of You." It's painful, especially because it sounds as if the band is trying to drown her out. I take my seat next to Paul Duffner, who looks me up and down.

"I was going to invite you on a date," he says. "But that was before I realized you're already spoken for. I'm not sure I can compete with Sean Leeds."

"Oh, he's quite the beau," I say, silently thanking Sean for his cameo appearance.

"Now I'd like to make a toast," Mom says, raising her glass of champagne. "To Doyle, on this special birthday, and to all of you, for sharing it with us." There's applause and whistling and chants of *Hear, hear* as glasses ring and chime.

I look at my parents and realize maybe this was why I came home to Dorset—to be with my mother and father, to understand the past, and to figure out who I am in this unpredictable world. I can't fix all my mistakes, and I can't plan my life to avoid things I might not want to see happen. But that's okay. The future isn't in my hands. And that means there will be painful things. But there will be good things as well. I think I'm strong enough to handle all of it.

Dad walks to the stage and kisses Mom's cheek. He looks at the crowd, taking it all in, savoring the moment. "As usual," he says, "Leigh has managed to steal my thunder." He pauses and then adds, "Not to mention Sean Leeds." He smiles, and there's a roar of laughter.

"This," Dad says, "is the most extraordinary celebration anyone could ask for." He looks around the tent again. "It really is." He takes off his glasses and dabs his eyes. "I want to thank you all for coming. And I want to thank Leigh for everything she's done to make this perfect, and for everything she does every day.

"I also want to thank our daughter, Grace, for helping with this party. And for being a wonderful daughter." He looks at me and smiles. "She's brilliant and talented and successful at whatever she does, and I'm so very proud of her." He blows me a kiss, and I feel a warm sensation bubble through me. *Brilliant and talented . . . proud of her.* I blow a little kiss back. *Thanks, Dad.*

The guests have gone, the caterers are clearing the tables, and the musicians are packing up their equipment. I walk out of the tent, to the edge of the lawn, and take a seat in one of the Adirondack chairs. The sun is sinking, the light in the sky is soft, and the water is calm. Mom and Dad are in the house with an entourage of family and friends. I can hear Mom's laughter come through the kitchen windows, the sounds drifting across the lawn.

I think about how I'll be leaving tomorrow, and how I'll be packing my things tonight. I think about Renny's bike, which Cluny is going to pick up and store in her air-conditioned garage until I visit again in a few weeks. And I think about Mitch, and I wonder how he's doing. I wonder when he'll stop being angry with me, *if* he'll stop being angry with me.

I think about the day a couple of weeks ago when Cluny and I went into the bike shop and I corrected their flyers. And the day I got sprayed by Porcine Thighs, and how Mitch wanted to report it to the police. I start to laugh when I remember that. And the lighthouse, where I told Mitch about Renny and what happened the day she died. Yes, he was going to kiss me.

Maybe I should have thought of Mitch as more than the bike shop guy or the history teacher, more than the guy who played pool with me at Ernie's or walked with me in the orchard. But what does it matter now? I betrayed him. I went on television and said things that hurt him. And now he won't forgive me.

Twilight settles over the water. I close my eyes and listen to the *clink* of plates and flatware and glassware in the tent. I try to summon Mitch's face—his velvet eyes, the smile that goes up a little more on one side than the other, the lock of hair that sometimes hangs over his forehead. And then I hear a voice behind me, and I'm truly convinced I'm imagining it, because it's his voice.

"Nice view."

When I turn, he's standing there, one hand on the handlebar of a bicycle. "Mitch?"

"I hope I'm not arriving at a bad time," he says. "But your mother told me it was okay to come out here. I wanted to make sure I got the bike to you."

"The bike?" I take a closer look. It's Renny's Schwinn, although it's not the Schwinn I dug out of the garage. The red paint sparkles, and the chrome shines, all of the rust gone. The new seat, lustrous and dark, is a perfect match to the old one, and the bike's cables are glossy and black. The chain and derailleur have been replaced, and the wheels have been rebuilt, every spoke shiny silver. And he's even replaced the bell. It's got a yellow flower in the middle, similar to the old one, but when I move the lever, it chimes.

I run my hand over the new pedals, the freshly wrapped black tape on the handlebars, the pristine leather on the seat. "Wow," I say. "I can't believe this is the same bike."

"So you like it?"

"Like it? I love it." I walk around the Paramount, viewing it from every angle. I bend down and study the gleaming wheels. "I still can't believe it's Renny's bike. It's just the way I remember it."

"Yeah, she came out pretty nice."

"She did, Mitch. She really did."

"I know you want to take it with you tomorrow, when you leave."

I hear Mom and Dad and the group inside the house laugh again. "Yes, right." I try to push aside some bit of reluctance I'm suddenly feeling. "So, you did all this work yourself?"

He nods. "Yes."

I picture him by the repair stand, his hands on the wheels, the tubes, the brakes, the cables, making everything perfect.

Inside the tent, the caterers are folding up chairs and stacking them against the tent poles. "Look, I'm sorry to impose," I say. "Especially after everything you've done, but do you think I could pay half the cost now and half in a couple of weeks? I just need to—"

"Don't worry about that," he says, rubbing a little spot on the down tube with the bottom of his shirt. "My dad was right. You did enough. You did plenty. In fact, I've got Kevin and A.J. working on organizing the rest of the workroom. We're even talking about doing a little redecorating in the store. It could use some fixing up."

"Really? That sounds great." But it also worries me. "Don't do too much. There's something about that place that keeps people coming back year after year. Maybe the clutter is part of it."

He scratches his chin. "I didn't think the word *clutter* was in your vocabulary."

"Ah, well. It's creeping in there."

I gaze at the Schwinn. "Thanks, Mitch. Thank you for the bike. It's beautiful."

He looks into my eyes. My heart starts beating fast. And I remember being a kid, eleven or twelve, bicycling in town one day, when my tires skidded on something slippery—probably oil or sand. I fell and scraped my arm, and it started to bleed. I walked the bike to the Bike Peddler, gritting my teeth so I wouldn't cry. A young guy was working in the shop, a teenager with a nice smile and a lock of hair that fell over his forehead. He took one look at my arm and pulled me into the bathroom, where he gently washed off the blood and dirt, dried the cuts, and applied a bandage. Then he brought me out front and handed me a white baseball cap with the name Shimano on it in blue letters. He told me it was for being so brave.

That guy was Mitch.

I turn to him. "You know, I just remembered something. I fell and scraped my arm one day when I was a kid, and I came into the store. You washed off the blood and put on a bandage and gave me a baseball cap. You said I was brave."

He smiles. "I told you we'd met before."

"You did, but it took me all this time to remember."

"Sometimes things take a while," he says.

He leans the bike against the chair. "I need to say something, Grace. About that interview. The thing on the news."

My heart plummets. I look away, toward the purple horizon. A Boston Whaler with five noisy teenagers in it gurgles past us. "Mitch. I'm sorry. I wish I could turn back time and do it all over again and not—"

He puts a hand on my arm. "Grace, stop. That's not why I'm bringing it up."

I like the feel of his hand on my arm, warm and strong. "It's not?"

"No. That's not why I was angry with you. It wasn't the interview, although I was kind of pissed off about that." He smiles, and there's a long pause. I hear the group on the Whaler and the sound of laughter.

"It was you," he says finally. "I really care about you, Grace. I think I might be falling in love with you. And I couldn't have you around because . . ." He looks away. "Well, because you're in love with Peter. I just wanted to let you know the truth."

I stare into his eyes, and I see honey and caramel and all sorts of colors I never noticed before. He might be falling in love with me. *Me.* Grace Walker Hammond.

"I'm not in love with Peter," I correct him.

He stands up a little straighter. "You're not?"

"No, I'm not. I thought I was, but it was really about something else." I hear a few final hoots and calls from the Whaler, and the boat motors around the bend and drifts out of sight.

"Huh," Mitch says. "Not in love with Peter." He takes a step toward me, and then another step. We're so close, we're almost touching. He reaches out and strokes my face. I look into his eyes, and I can see the future there. It's stretched out before me, and Mitch is part of it. He leans in and kisses me, and I hear the faint sound of a seagull and a splash.

EPILOGUE

"**D**o you think I could take it for a spin?" I glance at the bike.

Mitch laughs. "It's your bike, Grace. You can do whatever you want."

"I'd just like to try it out, ride it down Salt Meadow before it gets dark."

"Then let's do it."

I follow Mitch as he walks the bike across the lawn and over the gravel driveway, down to the road, stopping at the weathered sign that says Private, No Trespass.

"I can't believe you still haven't fixed that," he says.

"That sign will never be fixed," I tell him. "It's kind of a family tradition."

He nods. "Traditions are good."

At the end of the driveway, I glance down the road, where the Percys live, and the Banners and the Rudolphs and the Albans. I can see Mrs. Baylor's white picket fence at the bend, and the pink beach roses that peek through the slats and hang over the top.

I glance at Mitch's hands, still on the handlebars, and I realize I've never taken the time to notice them before. They're nice hands, with long fingers that look strong and dexterous—hands

458

that can fix bikes and write comments on high school essays.

We walk from the driveway to the edge of the road, where the surface is smooth and covered in blacktop. I take the handlebars, but I can see that the seat is too high. I'm wondering how to adjust it when Mitch pulls out a wrench, loosens a bolt, and lowers the seat for me.

"Sorry," he says. "I took it for a test drive."

"I'm glad you did," I say.

He holds the bike as I raise my leg over the top tube and settle into the seat. "It feels pretty good." I place my feet on the ground and run my fingers over the new handlebar tape. I look at the cables that travel from the handbrakes to the brake pads on the wheels. I squeeze the front brake, then the back. Everything is solid. I look up, and Mitch's eyes meet mine. I think about what he said the day in the orchard, when I told him about the first time I ate an apple fresh off a tree. *Those are great moments. When you have this feeling that what's happening is really special and you know you'll always remember exactly what took place. Every detail.* This is one of those moments.

"Are you ready?" he asks.

I take a deep breath. "I'm ready."

He takes his hands off the bike, and I give myself a little push. I pick up my feet, and I'm off, cruising down Salt Meadow. I build up some speed, and then I coast, the freewheel ticking

459

happily, my feet comfortable on the pedals, air rushing past. And Renny is with me, experiencing each bump in the road, each movement of the shifter as I run through the gears. She's with me, listening to the whir of the tires on the asphalt and the bark of the Johnsons' beagle when I round the bend, and I know I'm no longer in sight but that Mitch is still back there, waiting.

ACKNOWLEDGMENTS

A book is a big project and many people have been involved in this one. Kim Witherspoon, my agent, gave me excellent guidance and support. Jamie Cat Callan, my friend, mentor, and earliest reader, once again used her skill and patience to help me navigate the bewildering sea of a first draft. My editor, Judy Clain, provided such insightful suggestions about the manuscript, and so much encouragement, that I was able to improve and strengthen the story in ways I cannot count. Assistant editor Amanda Brower never missed a detail and helped make the prose shine from beginning to end. My copyeditor, Katharine Cooper, saved me on numerous occasions (she's the real stickler for grammar!). And everyone else on my team at Little, Brown did an amazing job, from design to production to sales, in putting the book together and getting it out there. Thank you all.

I would also like to thank Meghan Hibbett, Deborah Krainin, Michael Simses, and Kate Simses for their guidance on how movies are made; Mark Quinn and Philip Elliott of the Palm Beach Bicycle Trail Shop, for their insights into all things bike-related; Lieutenant Michael Marx of the Palm Beach Fire Rescue Department for his emergency medical technician expertise; Joe Norkus for showing me what he can do with a cue stick, and Leanne Distasi for letting us use her pool table; and Pam and Will Braun of ciaobelladesigns.com for their insights about creating beautiful note cards.

I am most grateful to my additional readers, Michael Simses, Kate Simses, Suzanne Ainslie, Rebecca Holliman, Ann Depuy, and Christine Lacerenza, for their observant comments, which led to revisions that improved the story tenfold. To Christine I give another thanks for researching my many inane questions and for conducting the now infamous "water reflection experiment" on the Five Mile River in Rowayton, Connecticut.

Last on the list, but first in my heart, are my husband, Bob, and my daughter, Morgan, who are always there with the emotional support that keeps me going. I love you.

ABOUT THE AUTHOR

Mary Simses grew up in Darien, Connecticut, and lived for many years in New England, where she worked in the magazine publishing industry and later as a corporate attorney. During that time, she wrote fiction on the side, and several of her short stories have appeared in literary magazines. Simses now lives with her husband–law partner and their daughter in South Florida. She enjoys photography and listening to old jazz standards. She does *not* go around with a Sharpie correcting other people's grammar. Mary Simses is the author of *The Irresistible Blueberry Bakeshop & Café*.

marysimses.com

Center Point Large Print
600 Brooks Road / PO Box 1
Thorndike, ME 04986-0001 USA

(207) 568-3717

US & Canada:
1 800 929-9108
www.centerpointlargeprint.com